中級美語　上

序

這本書是《英語從頭學》系列叢書的第四本。

《英語從頭學》系列叢書共分六本,分別是:

《會話入門》:內容全為基礎會話,教您如何用簡易而實用的字開口說英語。

《初級美語》:分上、下冊,內容有會話及簡易閱讀文章,培養您會話及閱讀的基礎。

《中級美語》:亦分上、下冊,是初級美語的延讀。

《高級閱讀》:培養看懂 *Time* 及 *Newsweek* 的閱讀能力。

這六本書均由本人及外籍編輯按國人英語學習的環境構思情境會話及閱讀文章,內容由淺入深。特別值得一提的是,所有課文均附完全解析,舉凡單字、片語、句型及文法均有實用的例句解說,每課後面均附練習及解答。這也就是為何每本書均厚達 300 頁以上的原因。

讀者拿到本書時,千萬不要嫌它厚重。紮實的內容正是本書的特色。若按部就班,一定可學好英語。

其實,這六本書同時也在大陸中央人民廣播電台及地方台播出,由本人親自在空中講解,數年來在整個大陸地區培養了萬千的英語愛好者。其中令我印象最深刻的就是大連市的王馨穎小妹妹,她七歲之前沒學過英語,只會唸 ABC 廿六個字母,

在爸爸的鼓勵下，以七個半月的時間，學完會話入門及初級美語上、下冊，竟然在二○○二年就**勇奪全中國青少年英語演講比賽冠軍**。如今她九歲了，已成了當地電台及電視台的小小英文老師，爸爸也因此開了一家英語補習班。學習英語改變了他們一家的命運！

　　吉林省長春市的初中二年級鄭陽同學，也唸這套系列叢書學了兩年英文，於二○○三年**勇奪吉林省青少年英文演講大賽冠軍。上海一位高中輟學的空調裝配員**則使用本系列業書配合我在中央台的廣播教學學了五年英文，竟然也唸完了**《高級閱讀》**，練就一口流利的美語及精湛的閱讀能力，**如今已是某外商公司的副總經理。**

　　這些大陸學子的成功全靠著讀本系列叢書。他們能如此，難道您也不能如此嗎？！但願這套《英語從頭學》系列叢書為所有想從頭學好英語的讀者重拾學習英語的信心、開拓光明的前程！

目錄
CONTENTS

Lesson 1

Rome Wasn't Built in a Day

羅馬不是一天造成的

Reading

閱　讀

English is an international language. Therefore, it is necessary for us to learn it. It can be rewarding or just a waste of time. It's up to you. It depends on how you study it. Here are some tips about learning English.

First, don't be afraid to make mistakes. You will learn from them. Second, you must not be shy. Be thick-skinned and speak up! Finally, you must be patient. Remember, "Rome wasn't built in a day."

> 　　英語是國際語言。所以，我們必須學英文。學英文可以使我們獲益，也可能是白白浪費時間。那得看你了。那要看你如何去學習。以下是一些關於學習英語的訣竅。
>
> 　　首先，別怕犯錯。你可以從錯誤中學習。其次，千萬不要害羞。厚臉皮一點大聲說出來！最後，一定要有耐心。記住：『羅馬不是一天造成的。』

Vocabulary & Idioms
單字 & 片語註解

1. **Rome wasn't built in a day.**　　羅馬不是一天造成的。(諺語)

   Rome [rom] n. 羅馬 (義大利首都)

   例: A: My new restaurant isn't doing very well.

   　B: Don't worry. Rome wasn't built in a day.

   (甲：我剛開的餐廳生意不怎麼好。)

   (乙：別擔心，羅馬不是一天造成的。)

2. **international** [͵ɪntɚˋnæʃənḷ] a. 國際的

3. **language** [ˋlæŋgwɪdʒ] n. 語言 (可數); 言詞 (不可數)

   foul language　　下流話, 粗話, 髒話

   * foul [faʊl] a. 粗俗的, 猥褻的

   例: You must have patience and determination to learn a second language.

   (學習第二種語言一定要具備耐心和決心。)

   People who use foul language show their poor upbringing.

   (口出穢言的人表示他缺乏教養。)

   　* upbringing [ˋʌp͵brɪŋɪŋ] n. 教養

4. **rewarding** [rɪˋwɔrdɪŋ] a. 有 (獲) 益的; 值得做的,划算的

例: Teaching is a very rewarding profession.
(教書是一種很有價值的職業。)

5. **It's up to you.**　　由你決定。

例: A: Should I get a part-time job?
B: It's up to you.
(甲：我應不應該去兼差？)
(乙：你自己決定。)

6. **depend on...**　　視……而定

例: My future depends on my exam results.
(我的未來取決於我考試的成績。)

7. **tip** [tɪp] n. 建議; 小費

give＋人＋tips on/about＋事　　給某人關於某事的一些建議

例: Can you give me some tips on how to study English?
(你可不可以告訴我一些學習英文的訣竅？)

We gave the waitress a big tip because the service was excellent.
(因為那名女服務生的服務非常好，所以我們給了她一大筆小費。)

8. **be afraid to** ＋ 原形動詞　　害怕去做……

afraid [əˈfred] a. 害怕的, 恐懼的

例: Mr. Wang was afraid to ask his boss for a raise.
(王先生不敢向老闆要求加薪。)

9. **shy** [ʃaɪ] a. 羞怯的

例: The shy boy didn't dare to ask the girl to dance.
(那個害羞的男孩不敢邀請那女孩跳舞。)

10. **thick-skinned** [ˌθɪkˈskɪnd] a. 厚顏的

例: If you want to be a good salesman, you must be thick-skinned.
(如果你想要成為一個好的業務員，一定要厚臉皮。)

11. **speak up**　　大聲說話; 開口說出來

例: Please speak up; I can't hear you.
(請說大聲一點,我聽不到。)

If you have something to say, speak up.
(如果你有話要說,儘管開口說出來。)

12. **patient** ['peʃənt] a. 有耐心的 (常與介系詞 with 並用)

be patient with... 對……有耐心

例: A good teacher is always patient with his students.
(好老師對學生總是很有耐心。)

Grammar Notes
文法重點

本課介紹由疑問詞引導的名詞子句之形成及其用法, 以及表示『第一點』、
『第二點』等序數詞的用法。

1. **It depends on <u>how you study it.</u>** 那要看你如何去學習。

上列句中, how you study it 是疑問詞引導的名詞子句。此類名詞子句均
由疑問詞 (what, when, who, how, why, where 等) 引導的問句轉變而成,
茲就其形成及用法分述如下:

a. 疑問句如何轉變為名詞子句:

1) 問句有 be 動詞時:
主詞與 be 動詞還原, 前面保留疑問詞。

例: Where <u>is she</u>?
(她在哪裡?)

→ where <u>she is</u>
(她在哪裡)

2) 問句有一般助動詞 (如 will、can、may 等) 時:
主詞與助動詞還原, 前面保留疑問詞。

例: When <u>will you</u> leave?
(你何時離開？)

→ when <u>you will</u> leave
(你何時離開)

3) 問句有 do、does、did 等助動詞時:

此類疑問句變成名詞子句時, 先保留句首的疑問詞, 再將 do、does 或 did 去掉, 其後的原形動詞則按主詞人稱及時態作變化。

例: Where <u>does he live</u>?
(他住在哪裡？)

→ where <u>he lives</u>
(他住在哪裡)

What <u>did you buy</u>?
(你買了什麼？)

→ what <u>you bought</u>
(你買了什麼)

注意:

在疑問句中, 若疑問代名詞 who, what, which 作主詞, 則疑問句變成名詞子句時, 句子結構不變。

例: <u>Who</u> will go?
(誰會去？)

→ <u>who</u> will go
(誰會去)

<u>What</u> happened?
(發生了什麼事？)

→ <u>what</u> happened
(發生了什麼事)

<u>Which</u> was bought?
(哪個被買走？)

→ <u>which</u> was bought
(哪個被買走)

由上述得知,本文中的"how you study it"乃由問句"How do you study it?"變化而成。

b. 名詞子句的功能:

名詞子句應被視為名詞, 故與名詞一樣, 在句中可作主詞、受詞、或置於 be 動詞後作主詞補語。

1) 作主詞

例: Where he lives remains a mystery.
　　　　主詞
　　(他住在哪裡仍是個謎。)

注意:

名詞子句作主詞時, 往往會形成主詞過大的現象, 因此可用虛主詞 it 代替, 置於句首, 而被代替的名詞子句則置於句尾。故上列例句亦可寫為:

It remains a mystery where he lives.

2) 作受詞

例: I don't know why she is crying.
　　　　及物動詞　　　　受詞
　　(我不知道她為什麼哭。)

I didn't pay attention to what you were saying.
　　　　　　　　　　介詞　　　　受詞
　　(我沒留意你在說什麼。)

3) 置於 be 動詞後作主詞補語

例: The problem is how we can get there.
　　　　　　　　　　主詞補語
　　(問題是我們要怎麼到那裡去。)

2. **...First, don't be afraid to make mistakes....Second, you must not be shy.**

……首先, 別怕犯錯。……其次, 千萬不要害羞。

上列句中, First 及 Second 為序數詞, 分別表示『第一點、首先』及『第二點、其次』的意思, 用於陳列重點, 或陳述概念、想法時。

例: When you are at the beach, play safe. <u>First</u>, don't swim too far out. <u>Second</u>, don't swim immediately after eating.
(當你在海灘的時候，要以安全為上。首先，不要游得太遠。其次，吃完東西後不要馬上游泳。)

注意:

a. First、Second、Third...亦可改用 Firstly、Secondly、Thirdly...替代。

另外, First 亦可等於 First of all, 但無 Second/Third...of all 的用法，故上列例句亦可改寫為:

When you are at the beach, play safe. <u>Firstly</u>, don't swim too far. <u>Secondly</u>, don't swim immediatly after eating.

b. 常常有些人會將 at first 與 first 混為一談, 但這是錯誤的。at first 使用於一般過去式中, 用以敘述過去的狀態, 表『起初』之意, 而 first 則用以強調次序的概念, 故兩者用法不同。in the end 則表『最後』, 常與 at first 搭配使用。

例: <u>At first</u>, the new student felt out of place. <u>In the end</u>, he became one of us.
(起初，那個新來的學生覺得格格不入。最後，他和我們打成一片。)

Substitution
代　　換

1. **It depends on** | how you study it.
　　　　　　　　　| when you do it.
　　　　　　　　　| where you go.

那要看你如何去學習。
那要看你何時去做。
那要看你去哪裏。

2. **Don't be afraid to** | make mistakes.
　　　　　　　　　　　| ask questions.
　　　　　　　　　　　| speak up.

別怕犯錯。
別怕問問題。
別怕大聲說出來。

Lesson 2

How to Improve Your English

如何加強你的英文

Dialogue

實用會話

Mack is talking to his friend Don.

(M=Mack, D=Don)

M: Hi, Don! How are you doing in your English class?

D: Not so well, I'm afraid.

M: What's the problem?

D: I'm not improving. Tell me, how come your English is so good?

M: Well, uh...I have an American girlfriend.

D: Aha! That's it. Now I know what to do. (He runs off.)

M: Hey, come back! I was just kidding!

麥克正在和他的朋友唐聊天。

麥克：嗨，阿唐！你英文課上得怎麼樣？

　唐：恐怕不怎麼理想。

麥克：出了什麼問題？

　唐：我一直沒進步。告訴我，為什麼你的英文那麼棒？

麥克：呃，這個嗎……我交了個美國妞。

　唐：啊哈！就是這樣。現在我知道該怎麼做了！(他跑走了。)

麥克：嘿，回來啊！我只是在開玩笑！

Key Points
重點提示

1. **improve** [ɪmˈpruv] vi. & vt. (使) 進步; 改善
   improvement [ɪmˈpruvmənt] n. 進步
   make (a lot of/little) improvement in... 在……上有 (很大/些許的) 進步
   例: If you don't listen to your tennis coach, how can you improve?
   (如果你不聽網球教練的話,又怎麼能進步呢?)

   Listening to English teaching radio programs can help you improve your English.
   (聽英語教學廣播節目能夠幫助你加強英文。)

   I hear that your son is making a lot of improvement in his studies.
   (我聽說令郎的學業進步很多。)

2. **How are you doing in...?** 你在……做得怎麼樣?
   例: How are you doing in your new job?
   (你的新工作做得怎麼樣?)

3. 本文:
   Not so well, I'm afraid. 恐怕我英文課表現得不怎麼理想。
   = I'm afraid (that) I'm not doing so well in my English class.
   注意:
   此處的 I'm afraid 並不表示『害怕』,而是一種客氣的用法,即等於"I think + (that) 子句"的用法。
   唯使用"I'm afraid + (that) 子句"比使用"I think + (that) 子句"在語氣上較為婉轉客氣。
   例: I'm afraid (that) I can't help you this time.
   (恐怕這次我沒辦法幫你了。)

4. **How come + 主詞 + 動詞……?** 為什麼……?
   = Why + 倒裝句?

注意:

使用"How come...?"時, 其後不採倒裝句構, 用直述句即可; 而使用"Why...?"時, 則其後的句子要倒裝。

例: How come <u>didn't you</u> show up at the party? (✕)

→ How come <u>you didn't</u> show up at the party? (○)

= Why <u>didn't you</u> show up at the party?
(你為什麼沒去那場派對？)

How come <u>do you eat</u> so much? (✕)

→ How come <u>you eat</u> so much? (○)

= Why <u>do you eat</u> so much?
(你為什麼吃那麼多？)

5. kid [kɪd] vi. & vt. (口語) (與……) 開玩笑 & n. 小孩

例: A: I'm going to quit my job today.
B: Are you kidding?
(甲：我今天要辭職。)
(乙：你在開玩笑吧？)

John was only kidding you when he said he's gay.
(約翰跟你說他是同性戀只是在開你玩笑。)

＊ gay [ge] a. (男) 同性戀的

That kid over there looks just like my son.
(那邊那個小孩和我兒子長得好像。)

 請選出下列各句中正確的一項

A: Hi, Jack. How are you _(1)_ in your job?

B: Not so well, I'm _(2)_.

A: What's the _(3)_?

B: The boss says business is not _(4)_.

A: So?

B: So, he's not happy.

A: Tell him Rome wasn't _(5)_ in a day.

1. (A) making   (B) doing   (C) working   (D) kidding

2. (A) sorry   (B) scared   (C) afraid   (D) bad

3. (A) question   (B) problem   (C) cost   (D) mistake

4. (A) progress   (B) improving   (C) fun   (D) patient

5. (A) built   (B) build   (C) made   (D) done

解答:

| 1. (B) | 2. (C) | 3. (B) | 4. (B) | 5. (A) |

Lesson 3
The City of Song
音樂之都

Reading
閱　讀

    Listening to music is the favorite pastime of many people all over the world. This is especially true for people living in Vienna, the city of song. Being the home of Mozart, this city is the birthplace of classical music and the waltz.

    Music fills the air in Vienna. Going to public concerts is often free of charge. And don't forget, Vienna is also home to the world famous Vienna Boys' Choir. No wonder people say Austria is always alive with the sound of music.

聽音樂是全世界許多人最喜愛的消遣。這個對生活在音樂之都的維也納人民來說更是貼切。這個城市不但是莫札特的故鄉，也是古典音樂和華爾茲舞曲的發源地。

音樂繚繞於整個維也納。欣賞公開的演奏會通常都是免費的。別忘了，維也納也是世界著名維也納少年合唱團的所在地。難怪有人說奧地利永遠充滿著音樂的聲音。

Vocabulary & Idioms
單字 & 片語註解

1. **favorite** [ˈfevərɪt] a. & n. 最喜愛的 (人或物)

   例: Going to the movies is my favorite pastime.
   (看電影是我最喜歡的消遣。)

   This old CD is a favorite of mine.
   (這張舊的雷射唱片是我的最愛。)

2. **pastime** [ˈpæsˌtaɪm] n. 消遣, 娛樂

   例: Dad plays golf as a pastime.
   (老爸打高爾夫球作消遣。)

3. **all over the world**　　全世界

= across the world

= the world over

   注意:

   使用 the world over 時, 其前不可加任何介詞。

   例: The rich man has traveled the world over many times.
   (那個富翁已經環遊過全世界好幾次。)

4. **especially** [əˈspɛʃəlɪ] adv. 格外地, 尤其

   例: Brad is especially nice to pretty girls.
   (布萊德對漂亮女孩子特別好。)

5. **Vienna** [vɪˈɛnə] n. 維也納 (奧地利首都)

6. **Mozart** [ˈmozɑrt] n. 莫札特 (奧地利作曲家, 1756-1791)

7. **birthplace** [ˈbɝˌθˌples] n. 誕生地; 發源地

8. **classical** [ˈklæsɪkḷ] a. 古典的

   classical music　　古典音樂

   例: Classical Chinese literature is difficult to understand.
   (中國古典文學很難懂。)
   ＊ literature [ˈlɪtərətʃɚ] n. 文學

9. **waltz** [wɔlts] n. 華爾茲舞 (曲), 圓舞曲

10. 事物 **+ fill the air**　　充滿著某物的氣氛

    例: Romantic love songs fill the air in that cozy Italian restaurant.
    (那家溫馨的義大利餐館充滿著羅曼蒂克的情歌。)
    ＊ romantic [roˈmæntɪk] a. 浪漫的
    　 cozy [ˈkozɪ] a. 溫暖而舒適的

11. **concert** [ˈkɑnsɚt] n. 演奏會, 音樂會

    例: The concert was attended by thousands of fans.
    (那場音樂會有數以千計的樂迷參加。)

12. **charge** [tʃɑrdʒ] n. 費用 & vt. (向人) 索價

    be free of charge　　免費

    例: These pamphlets are free of charge.
    (這些小冊子是免費的。)
    ＊ pamphlet [ˈpæmflɪt] n. 小冊子

    My coach charges me US$50 an hour for teaching me how to play tennis.
    (我教練教我打網球一小時收我五十塊美金。)

13. **famous** [ˈfeməs] a. 有名的, 著名的

例: I'm sure this singer will be famous one day.
(我確信這名歌手有一天會走紅。)

14. **Vienna Boys' Choir**　　維也納少年合唱團

choir [kwaɪr] n. 合唱團

15. **Austria** [ˈɔstrɪə] n. 奧地利

16. **be alive with...**　　充滿……

alive [əˈlaɪv] a. 活的; 充滿的

例: The room is alive with children's laughter.
(房間裡面充滿了小朋友的笑聲。)

Grammar Notes
文法重點

本課主要介紹動名詞片語作主詞的用法, 以及分詞句構化簡法, 和"地方名詞 + be the home of..."及"地方名詞 + be home to..."的分別, 另介紹"no wonder"作副詞的用法。

1. **Listening to music is the favorite pastime of many people all over the world.**

   聽音樂是全世界許多人最喜愛的消遣。

   Going to public concerts is often free of charge.

   欣賞公開的演奏會通常都是免費的。

   上列兩句皆使用動名詞片語作主詞。

   初學寫作者, 極易用動詞作主詞, 這是不對的; 動詞不能直接作主詞, 一定要變成動名詞或不定詞(片語)方可作主詞。

   a. 動名詞(片語)作主詞:

   　用動名詞 (片語) 作主詞時, 通常用以表示已知的事實或經驗。

例: <u>Play basketball</u> is fun. (✗)

→ <u>Playing basketball</u> is fun. (○)

(打籃球很有趣。)

由上列句中, 可知『打籃球』是一種經驗, 故將 Play basketball 改為動名詞片語 Playing basketball。

b. 不定詞 (片語) 作主詞:

用不定詞 (片語) 作主詞時, 通常表示一種未完成或想要完成的願望、企圖或目的。

例: <u>Study abroad</u> is my greatest desire. (✗)

→ <u>To study abroad</u> is my greatest desire. (○)

(留學是我最大的願望。)

上列句中, 由 desire (願望) 得知此處的『留學』乃是一種想要完成的事, 故將 Study abroad 改為不定詞片語 To study abroad。

根據上述, 可知本文的『聽音樂』及『欣賞公開的演奏會』均是一種已知的事實或經驗, 故用動名詞片語 Listening to music 及 Going to public concerts 來表示。

2. **Being the home of Mozart, this city is the birthplace of classical music and the waltz.**

這個城市不但是莫札特的故鄉, 也是古典音樂和華爾茲舞曲的發源地。

上列句中的"Being the home of..."是現在分詞片語, 作形容詞用, 修飾其後的主詞 this city。

本句原為: "This city was the home of..., this city is the birthplace of...", 但如此一來造成兩句在一起無連接詞連接的錯誤句構, 故將第一個句子化簡, 變成分詞片語, 其法則如下:

a. 被化簡的子句中主詞與主要子句的主詞相同時, 該主詞要刪除; 若主詞不同時, 則予以保留;

b. 之後的動詞要變成現在分詞;

c. 若該動詞為 be 動詞 (如 is, was, are...等) 時, 則變成現在分詞 being 之後可予以省略, 但亦可不省略, 以強調『因為』之意。

故本句因主詞相同,因此將相同主詞 this city 刪除,其後動詞 was 變成現在分詞 being,即成本句。

This city was the home of..., this city is the birthplace of... (✗)
   Being

→ Being the home of..., this city is the birthplace of... (○)

 例: I stand on the top of the mountain, I can see the whole city. (✗)
   Standing

 → Standing on the top of the mountain, I can see the whole city. (○)

  (站在山頂上,我可以看到整座城市。)

3. "地方名詞 + be the home of..."及"地方名詞 + be home to..."的分別:

 a. 地方名詞 + be the home of... 某地是……的故鄉/家

  例: This beautiful house is the home of the former city mayor.
   (這棟漂亮的屋子是前任市長的家。)

 b. 地方名詞 + be home to... 某地是…的所在地/出產地/聚集地

  例: This deserted old building is home to mice and cockroaches.
   (這棟廢棄的古老建築物是老鼠和蟑螂的聚集地。)

4. **No wonder people say Austria is always alive with the sound of music.**

難怪人們說奧地利永遠充滿著音樂的聲音。

No wonder + 主詞 + 動詞 難怪……

注意:

no wonder 雖是名詞片語,卻視為副詞,使用時置於句首,修飾全句; 乃由"It is no wonder + that 子句"化簡而來。

例: No wonder you're so thin; you eat so little.
 (難怪你會這麼瘦,你吃得好少啊。)

Substitution 代　換

1. | **Listening to music** | is the favorite pastime of many people.
   | Reading
   | Biking

   聽音樂是許多人最喜愛的消遣。
   閱讀是許多人最喜愛的消遣。
   騎單車是許多人最喜愛的消遣。

2. | **Going to public concerts** | is often free of charge.
   | Using public toilets
   | Making local calls

   欣賞公開的演奏會通常都是免費的。
   使用公廁通常都是免費的。
   打當地電話通常都是免費的。

Lesson 4
He Who Hesitates Is Lost
遲疑者將喪失良機

Dialogue
實用會話

Mike is in Vienna with his girlfriend Daisy.

(M = Mike; D = Daisy)

M: Are you having a good time, Daisy?

D: Are you kidding? I'm having the time of my life. I loved the concerts.

M: Concert going is fantastic, but what else can we do?

D: Biking along the banks of the river Danube could be fun.

M: It sounds like a great idea!

D: Let's do it then.

M: You're right. As they say, "He who hesitates is lost."

邁可和他的女朋友黛西現在正在維也納。

邁可：妳玩得愉快嗎，黛西？

黛西：開玩笑！我正在享受我一生最快樂的時光。我愛死那些演奏會了。

邁可：去聽演奏會固然很棒，但是我們還可以做些什麼呢？

黛西：沿著多瑙河河岸騎單車應該蠻好玩的。

邁可：這個主意聽起來非常不錯！

黛西：那我們快去吧。

邁可：妳說得對。就像人們說的：『遲疑者將喪失良機。』

Key Points
重點提示

1. **hesitate** [ˈhɛzəˌtet] vi. 猶豫, 遲疑

   hesitate to + 原形動詞　　做……猶豫不決

   例: Do not hesitate to give me a call if you need help.
   (如果你需要幫助就打電話給我，不要猶豫。)

2. 句型分析:

   <u>He</u> <u>who hesitates</u> <u>is</u> <u>lost</u>.　　遲疑者將喪失良機。
   　(1)　　　　(2)　　　　(3) (4)

   (1) 主詞

   (2) 關係代名詞 who 引導的形容詞子句, 修飾 (1)。

   (3) 不完全不及物 be 動詞

   (4) lose 的過去分詞作形容詞用, 表『輸的』,為主詞補語。

   注意:

   He who...+ 單數動詞　　凡是……的人……

   = One who...+ 單數動詞

   = Those who...+ 複數動詞

   　例: <u>He</u> who <u>lives</u> by the sword <u>dies</u> by the sword.
   　　= <u>One</u> who <u>lives</u> by the sword <u>dies</u> by the sword.
   　　= <u>Those</u> who <u>live</u> by the sword <u>die</u> by the sword.
   　　　(刀口舔血者必死刀下／玩火自焚。——諺語)

3. **have the time of one's life**　　度過某人一生最愉快的時光

   例: My family and I had the time of our lives in Hawaii last summer.
   (我和家人去年夏天在夏威夷度過了我們一生中最愉快的時光。)

4. **fantastic** [fænˈtæstɪk] a. (口語) 極好的, 美妙的

   例: Mark played a fantastic game and beat John at tennis.
   (馬克打了一場漂亮的網球賽，打敗了約翰。)

5. **bike** [baɪk] vi. 騎腳踏車

例: Although your place is not very near, let's bike there.
(雖然你住的地方離這兒有一段路，我們還是騎腳踏車去吧。)

6. **bank** [bæŋk] n. 河岸; 銀行

例: Dad went fishing on the bank of the river.
(老爸到那條河的河岸釣魚。)

The bank is the safest place to keep your money, I guess.
(我想銀行是放錢最安全的地方。)

7. **As they say, "..."** 　　諺語有云/俗話說的好:『......。』

= As people say, "..."

= As an old saying goes, "..."

= As the saying goes, "..."

= As the saying puts it, "..."

例: As the saying goes, "Live and learn."
(諺語有云：『活到老，學到老。』)

 請選出下列各句中正確的一項

1. The newlyweds had the time _____ their lives during their honeymoon.
   (A) for 　　　(B) with 　　　(C) of 　　　(D) from

2. Are you _____ about getting married next week?
   (A) playing 　(B) kidding 　(C) hoping 　(D) saying

3. The boss pays and treats you well; what _____ do you want?
   (A) too 　　　(B) also 　　　(C) other 　　　(D) else

4. My brother _____ like Michael Jackson when he's singing in the bath.

(A) looks　　(B) sounds　　(C) moves　　(D) dances

5. The tennis player _____ for a second and lost the point.

(A) moved　　(B) played　　(C) hesitated　　(D) excited

解答:

> 1. (C)　　2. (B)　　3. (D)　　4. (B)　　5. (C)

L esson 5

Bungee Jumping
高空彈跳

Reading
閱　　讀

Bungee jumping looks like fun. It makes me nervous just to watch someone do it. It certainly takes a lot of guts to jump one thousand feet above the water with only a rope tied to your legs. It scares me just to think about it. However, it is something I really want to do one day.

Some people think I'm crazy. They say to jump is foolish enough, but to have to pay for it is madness. I don't agree. For me, to live a short and exciting life is far better than to live a long and boring one. What do you think?

　　高空彈跳看起來蠻好玩的。光是看別人做這件事就會讓我緊張。雙腿只用一條繩索綁著，從水面上一千呎的高度跳下的確需要很大的膽量。光是想到這點就夠讓我害怕的了。可是，這是我總有一天真的想做的事。

　　有些人認為我瘋了。他們說去跳就已經夠蠢了，而還要付錢則不啻為瘋狂的行為。我並不同意。對我來說，過個短暫而刺激的生活比過漫長卻無聊的日子好得多。你認為呢？

Vocabulary & Idioms
單字 & 片語註解

1. **bungee jumping** [ˈbʌndʒi ˌdʒʌmpɪŋ] n. 高空彈跳
   例: Bungee jumping looks exciting but I won't dare try it.
   (高空彈跳看起來雖然很刺激，可是我不願嘗試。)

2. **nervous** [ˈnɝvəs] a. 緊張的

3. **guts** [gʌts] n. 勇氣 (恆用複數)
   have the guts to + 原形動詞　　有做……的勇氣/膽量
   = have the courage to + 原形動詞
   例: Do you have the guts to ask the boss's secretary out to dinner?
   (你有膽子約老闆的秘書出去吃晚餐嗎？)

4. **rope** [rop] n. 繩索

5. **tie** [taɪ] vt. 綁, 繫
   tie A to B　　把 A 綁/繫在 B 上
   例: The cowboy tied his horse to a tree.
   (那位牛仔把馬栓在樹上。)

6. **scare** [skɛr] vt. 驚嚇
   scare + 人 + to death　　把某人嚇得要死

例: The lion's roar scared the kids to death.
(那隻獅子大吼一聲把孩子們嚇得要死。)

7. **crazy** [ˈkrezɪ] a. 瘋狂的; 狂熱的

be crazy about...　　對……瘋狂/著迷

例: Tony is crazy about your sister.
(湯尼為你妹妹瘋狂。)

8. **foolish** [ˈfulɪʃ] a. 愚蠢的

9. **pay for...**　　支付……

例: Ron chose the tie and his wife paid for it.
(朗恩選了那條領帶,而由他太太出錢。)

10. **madness** [ˈmædnɪs] n. 瘋狂似的行為 (不可數)

mad [mæd] a. 瘋的

例: The doctors don't know how to cure his madness.
(醫生們對他的瘋病束手無策。)

The mad woman ran around naked in the streets.
(那個瘋女人光著身子在街上到處亂跑。)

11. **agree** [əˈgri] vi. 同意

agree with + 人　　同意某人 (的看法)

例: You don't have to agree with the boss on everything, do you?
(你不必事事都同意老闆的看法,不是嗎?)

Grammar Notes
文 法 重 點

本課主要介紹用虛主詞 it 代替不定詞片語作主詞, 及不定詞片語直接作主詞的用法, 另介紹"It takes + 表條件的名詞 + to + 原形動詞"及知覺動詞的用法。

1. **It makes me nervous just to watch someone do it.**
   光是看別人做這件事就會讓我緊張。

   It certainly takes a lot of guts to jump one thousand feet above the water...
   ……從水面上一千呎的高度跳下的確需要很大的膽量。

   It scares me just to think about it.　　光是想到這點就夠讓我害怕的了。

   上列句中使用虛主詞 It 代替不定詞片語作主詞的用法,因不定詞片語作主詞時,往往會形成主詞過長的現象,故通常用代名詞 it 作虛主詞,置於句首,而將真主詞 (即不定詞片語) 移至句尾。由此可知,上列例句原為:

   Just to watch someone do it makes me nervous.

   To jump one thousand feet above the water... certainly takes a lot of guts.

   Just to think about it scares me.

   試以虛主詞 it 代替不定詞片語作主詞譯出下列句子:

   中文: 準時是有必要的。

   英文: It is necessary to be on time.

   中文: 看到我生病的母親受苦真是令我傷心。

   英文: It hurts me to see my sick mother suffer.

   中文: 努力工作是值得的。

   英文: It pays to work hard.

2. **It makes me nervous just to watch someone do it.**
   光是看別人做這件事就會讓我緊張。

   注意:

   本句中,及物動詞 watch (看) 接受詞 someone 後,另接原形動詞 do 作受詞補語。英文中,表『看』、『聽』、『感覺』等三類及物動詞稱為知覺動詞,接了受詞後,可用原形動詞作受詞補語,表已發生的事實; 或用現在分詞作受詞補語,表進行的狀態; 亦可用過去分詞作受詞補語,表被動的概念。常見知覺動詞如下:

看: see、watch、look at (注視)。

聽: heare、listen to。

感覺: feel。

a. 以原形動詞作受詞補語:
　　旨在強調確有事情發生。

　　例: I <u>saw</u> her <u>leave</u>.
　　　　(我看到她離開了。)

　　　　I <u>heard</u> him <u>cry</u>.
　　　　(我聽到他哭了。)

　　本文中"...just to <u>watch</u> someone <u>do</u> it."即屬此用法。

b. 以現在分詞作受詞補語:
　　旨在強調事情正在發生。

　　例: I <u>saw</u> her <u>leaving</u>.
　　　　(我看到她正要離開。)

　　　　I <u>heard</u> him <u>crying</u>.
　　　　(我聽到他正在哭。)

　　　　When the teacher came in, I <u>felt</u> my legs <u>trembling</u>.
　　　　(當老師進來時,我感覺自己的雙腿在發抖。)

c. 以過去分詞作受詞補語:
　　旨在強調被動的狀態。

　　例: I <u>saw</u> him <u>robbed</u>.
　　　　(我看到他被搶了。)

　　　　I <u>heard</u> the door <u>shut</u>.
　　　　(我聽見門被關起來了。)

　　　　I <u>felt</u> myself <u>lifted</u>.
　　　　(我感覺自己被舉了起來。)

3. <u>**It**</u> certainly <u>**takes**</u> **a lot of guts** <u>**to jump**</u> **one thousand feet above the water...**
　　……從水面上一千呎的高度跳下的確需要很大的膽量。

上列句中, 使用了"It takes + 表條件的名詞 + to + 原形動詞"的句型, 表『從事……需要……的條件』。其中 it 是虛主詞,代替其後的不定詞片語 "to + 原形動詞", 此不定詞片語才是真主詞。

It takes + 表條件的名詞 + to + 原形動詞　　從事……需要……的條件

例: It takes patience to be a good mother.
(要做個好母親需要有耐心。)

It took courage for him to admit that he was wrong.
(對他來說,要承認自己是錯的需要勇氣。)

4. **...with only a rope <u>tied to your legs</u>.**

= ...with only a rope <u>which is</u> tied to your legs.
雙腿只用一根繩索綁著……。

注意:

本句中的 tied to your legs 是過去分詞片語, 作形容詞用, 修飾前面的名詞 a rope, 而 tied 之前則省略了 which is。

5. **They say <u>to jump</u> is foolish enough, but <u>to have to pay for it</u> is madness.**

= They say <u>it</u> is foolish enough <u>to jump</u>, but it is madness <u>to have to pay for it</u>.
他們說去跳就已經夠蠢了, 而還要付錢卻是瘋狂的行為。

For me, <u>to live a short and exciting life</u> is far better than to live a long and boring one.

= For me, <u>it</u> is far better <u>to live a short and exciting life</u> than to live a long and boring one.
對我來說, 過個短暫而刺激的生活比過漫長卻無聊的日子好得多。

a. 上述兩句均可用虛主詞 it 代替不定詞片語, 置於句首, 而將不定詞片語置於句尾。

b. live a/an + 形容詞 + life　　過著……的生活

= lead a/an + 形容詞 + life

例: The famous singer <u>lives</u> a simple <u>life</u>.
= The famous singer <u>leads</u> a simple <u>life</u>.
(那位名歌手過著簡樸的生活。)

Substitution 代　換

1. **It makes me nervous just to watch someone do it.**

   It makes Mary go wild to hear Michael Jackson sing.

   It surprised me to hear my mom scream.

   光是看別人做這件事就會讓我緊張。

   聽到邁可・傑克森唱歌會讓瑪麗瘋狂。

   聽到我媽媽尖叫令我驚訝。

2. **It scares me just to think about it.**

   It is good for you to exercise regularly.

   It is essential to have a physical checkup once a year.

   光是想到這點就夠讓我害怕的了。

   時常運動對你有益。

   一年一次全身健康檢查是必要的。

Lesson 6
Nothing Ventured, Nothing Gained
不入虎穴，焉得虎子

Dialogue
實用會話

Lisa and Bill are talking about their future.

(L = Lisa; B = Bill)

L: What's your goal in life, Bill?

B: To fly in the sky and feel as free as a bird.

L: That's easy.

B: What do you mean?

L: Go bungee jumping.

B: You must be kidding. It's too dangerous.

L: Well, nothing ventured, nothing gained.

莉莎和比爾聊到他們的未來。
莉莎：比爾，你人生的目標是什麼？
比爾：像鳥兒般自由地在空中遨翔。
莉莎：那簡單。
比爾：怎麼說呢？
莉莎：去高空彈跳。
比爾：妳一定在說笑。那太危險了。
莉莎：可是，不入虎穴，焉得虎子呀。

Key Points
重點提示

1. **Nothing ventured, nothing gained.** 不入虎穴, 焉得虎子。(諺語)

= If nothing is ventured, nothing will be gained.

* venture [ˈvɛntʃɚ] vt. 冒險; 賭注

* gain [gen] vt. 獲得

例: I don't know the answer to the question, but I can venture a guess.
(我不知道這個問題的答案, 不過我可以試著猜一猜。)

I gained a lot of experience working abroad.
(我在國外工作時獲得很多經驗。)

2. **future** [ˈfjutʃɚ] n. 前途; 未來

carve out a bright future 開創光明的前途

* carve [kɑrv] vt. 開創 (命運、事業等)

in the future 在未來

in the near future 在最近的未來, 不久

例: By graduating top of the class, Jim has carved out a bright future for himself.
(吉姆在班上以優異的成績畢業, 為自己刻劃出美好的前程。)

Ben intends to start a restaurant in the near future.
(班打算在不久的將來開一家餐廳。)

3. **goal** [gol] n. 目標

例: Everybody should have a goal in life.
(每個人都應該有人生目標。)

4. **feel as free as a bird** 感覺像鳥般自由, 感覺非常自由

例: Ever since Sam lived on his own, he has felt as free as a bird.
(山姆自從獨立生活以來覺得自由極了。)

5. 本文:

To fly in the sky and feel as free as a bird.

= My goal is to fly in the sky and feel as free as a bird.
像馬兒般自由地在空中遨翔。

請選出下列各句中正確的一項

1. My _____ is to become a successful businessman one day.
   (A) gift   (B) game   (C) goal   (D) want

2. _____ successful, you must work hard.
   (A) For being   (B) To be   (C) You are   (D) Having been

3. My friend was _____ when he said he had two wives.
   (A) speaking   (B) talking   (C) gaining   (D) kidding

4. The rich man _____ a lot of money buying and selling houses.
   (A) took   (B) gave   (C) ventured   (D) gained

5. An honest man always _____ what he says.
   (A) mean   (B) means   (C) meaning   (D) to mean

解答:

1. (C)	2. (B)	3. (D)	4. (D)	5. (B)

Lesson 7
Doctor Death
死亡醫生

> No, don't do it !

Reading
閱　讀

Whether very sick people should be helped to end their own lives is a question many people cannot answer. However, Dr. Kevorkian is an exception. That he has done this more than twenty times is known to everyone. Some say what he is doing is immoral. They call him Doctor Death. Others say what he is doing is merciful. They call it mercy killing.

Whether Dr. Kevorkian should be allowed to continue doing this is a real problem for the government. There seem to be two sides to the argument. Which side are you on?

　　是否應該幫助病入膏肓的人結束他們的生命是一個令許多人難以回答的問題。然而，凱渥肯醫生是個例外。大家都知道他幫人這麼做已經有二十多次了。有些人說他所做的是不道德的。他們稱他為死亡醫生。有些人則說他所做的事很仁慈。他們稱之為安樂死。

　　對於政府來說，是否應該繼續讓凱渥肯醫生結束病人的生命真的是個問題。這項爭議似乎正反兩面都有人支持。你站在哪一邊呢？

Vocabulary & Idioms
單字 & 片語註解

1. **end one's life**　　結束某人的生命

   life [laɪf] n. 生命 (複數形為 lives [laɪvz])

   例: The man tried to end his life by taking poison.
   (那個人試圖服毒自殺。)

2. **exception** [ɪk'sɛpʃən] n. 例外

   except [ɪk'sɛpt] prep. 除……之外

   with the exception of...　　除……之外

= except...

   例: With the exception of Molly, everyone's going to the party.
   (除了莫莉之外，每個人都會去參加那個派對。)

3. **be known to + 人**　　為某人所熟知

   be known for + 事物　　以某事物而聞名/為人所知

   be known as + 身分　　以某身分聞名/為人所知

   known [non] a. 聞名的

   例: It is known to everyone that Sue lied about her age.
   (蘇謊報年齡是人盡皆知的事。)

   The old man is known for his generosity.
   (那個老人以慷慨聞名。)

Mr. Chen is known as a smart politician.
(眾所周知陳先生是位精明的政治人物。)

4. **immoral** [ɪˈmɔrəl] a. 不道德的

moral [ˈmɔrəl] a. 道德的

例: It's immoral to be unfaithful to your girlfriend.
(對女友不忠實是不道德的。)

Different countries have different moral standards.
(不同的國家有不同的道德標準。)

5. **merciful** [ˈmɝ·sɪfəl] a. 仁慈的

例: The merciful judge was very lenient with the accused.
(那位仁慈的法官對被告非常寬大。)
   * lenient [ˈlinɪənt] a. 寬大的

6. **mercy killing**　　安樂死(一般口語)

= euthanasia [ˌjuθəˈneʒə] n. (醫學術語)

mercy [ˈmɝ·sɪ] n. 仁慈

7. **argument** [ˈɑrgjəmənt] n. 爭論

argue [ˈɑrgjʊ] vi. 爭論

argue over...　　為……爭論

例: Their argument turned into a fight.
(他們的爭辯演變成打鬥。)

The old couple argued over trivial matters all day long.
(那對老夫婦成天為一些芝麻蒜皮的小事爭吵。)

8. 本文:

There seem to be two sides to the argument.

= It seems that there are two sides to the argument.
這項爭議似乎正反兩面都有人支持。

9. **Which side are you on?**　　你站在哪一邊呢？

= Which side do you support?

Grammar Notes
文 法 重 點

本課介紹三種名詞子句的形成及其用法。

Whether very sick people should be helped to end their own lives is a question (which) many people cannot answer.
是否應該幫助病入膏肓的人結束他們的生命是一個令許多人難以回答的問題。

That he has done this more than twenty times is known to everyone.
大家都知道他幫人這麼做已經有二十多次了。

Some say (that) what he is doing is immoral.
有些人說他所做的是不道德的。

Others say (that) what he is doing is merciful.
有些人則說他所做的事很仁慈。

Whether Dr. Kevorkian should be allowed to continue doing this is a real problem for the government.
對於政府來說,是否應該繼續讓凱渥肯醫生結束病人的生命真的是個問題。

上列句中, "whether very sick people should... lives"、"that he has done this more than twenty times"、"(that) what he is doing is immoral"、"(that) what he is doing is merciful"及"whether Dr. Kevorkian should... this"均為名詞子句, 其中"(that) what he is doing is immoral"和"(that) what he is doing is merciful"因作及物動詞 say 的受詞, 故 that 可省略。以下為名詞子句的種類及其功能。

1. 名詞子句的形成

   名詞子句一共有三種: that 引導的名詞子句、whether 引導的名詞子句、疑問詞 (what、when、why、how、where...等) 引導的名詞子句。

   a. that 引導的名詞子句:

      此種子句乃由陳述句變化而成; 我們在陳述句之前冠以 that 即成名詞子句。

例: He doesn't like music.
(他不喜歡音樂。)

→ that he doesn't like music
(他不喜歡音樂)

b. whether (是否) 引導的名詞子句:

此種子句乃由一般疑問句 (即可用 Yes 或 No 回答的問句) 變化而成。
在一般疑問句前冠以 whether, 原倒裝的句子結構還原成不倒裝的型態即成名詞子句。

1) 問句有 be 動詞時:

主詞與 be 動詞還原, 前面冠以 whether。

例: Is she beautiful?
(她漂亮嗎?)

→ whether she is beautiful
(她是否漂亮)

2) 問句有一般助動詞 (can、will、may、should、must、have 等) 時, 主詞與助動詞還原, 前面冠以 whether。

例: Should I tell the truth?
(我應該說出真相嗎?)

→ whether I should tell the truth
(我是否應該說出真相)

Have you been to Thailand?
(你去過泰國嗎?)

→ whether you have been to Thailand
(你是否去過泰國)

3) 問句有 do、does、did 等助動詞時:

此種助動詞引導的疑問句變成名詞子句時, 前面先冠以 whether, 次將 do、does 或 did 去除, 句中的原形動詞再按主詞人稱和時態作變化。

例: Do you like it?
(你喜歡它嗎?)

→ whether you like it
(你是否喜歡它)

Does she like it?
(她喜歡它嗎?)

→ whether she likes it
(她是否喜歡它)

Did he go there?
(他去了那裡嗎?)

→ whether he went there
(他是否去了那裡)

c. 疑問詞引導的名詞子句:

此種子句乃由疑問詞 (what、where、when、why、how、who、whom、which、whose 等) 引導的特殊疑問句 (即不能用 Yes 或 No 回答的問句) 變化而成。我們保留原疑問詞, 原來倒裝的句子結構還原成不倒裝的型態即成名詞子句。

1) 問句有 be 動詞時:

主詞與 be 動詞還原, 前面保留疑問詞。

例: What is he doing?
(他在做什麼?)

→ what he is doing
(他在做什麼)

2) 問句有一般助動詞時:

主詞與助動詞還原, 前面保留疑問詞。

例: Where can I find it?
(我在哪裡能找到它?)

→ where I can find it
(我在哪裡能找到它)

3) 問句有 do、does、did 等助動詞時:

此種疑問句變成名詞子句時, 先保留句首的疑問詞, 再將 do、does 或 did 去掉, 其後的原形動詞則按主詞人稱及時態作變化。

例: Why <u>do you say</u> that?
(你為何那樣說?)

→ why <u>you say</u> that
(你為何那樣說)

When <u>did she leave</u>?
(她什麼時候離開的?)

→ when <u>she left</u>
(她什麼時候離開的)

注意:

在特殊疑問句中, 疑問代名詞 who、what、which 作主詞, 則變成名詞子句時, 句子結構不變。

例: <u>Who</u> did it?
　　主詞
(誰做了這件事?)

→ <u>who</u> did it
(誰做了這件事)

<u>What</u> happened yesterday?
　主詞
(昨天發生了什麼事?)

→ <u>what</u> happened yesterday
(昨天發生了什麼事)

<u>Which</u> was chosen?
　主詞
(哪一個被選到?)

→ <u>which</u> was chosen
(哪一個被選到)

2. 名詞子句的功能

名詞子句與名詞一樣,在句中可作主詞、受詞,或置於 be 動詞後作主詞補語。

a. 作主詞

例: <u>That honesty is the best policy</u> is a proverb (which) we should
           主詞

always keep in mind.

(『誠實為上策』是一句我們應時時謹記在心的箴言。)

<u>Whether he can do it</u> remains to be seen.
        主詞

(他能否勝任仍有待觀察。)

<u>Where he lives</u> is still in doubt.
     主詞

(他住哪裡仍不確定。)

注意:

名詞子句作主詞時,往往會形成主詞過大的現象,因此可用虛主詞 it 代替,置於句首,而被代替的名詞子句則置於句尾。故上列例句亦可寫成:

<u>It</u> is a proverb we should always keep in mind <u>that honesty is the best policy</u>.

<u>It</u> remains to be seen <u>whether he can do it</u>.

<u>It</u> is still in doubt <u>where he lives</u>.

b. 作受詞

名詞子句作動詞的受詞:

例: I <u>know</u> <u>that he will go abroad in the near future</u>.
   及物動詞   受詞

(我知道他最近即將出國。)

I <u>wonder</u> <u>whether he has finished the work yet</u>.
  及物動詞   受詞

(我懷疑他是否已做完工作了。)

I don't <u>know</u> <u>how he'll handle it</u>.

  及物動詞   受詞

(我不知道他將如何處理這件事。)

注意:

1) that 引導的名詞子句作及物動詞的受詞時, that 可予以省略。

 故: I know <u>that he will go abroad in the near future</u>.

  = I know <u>he will go abroad in the near future</u>.

2) whether 引導的名詞子句作及物動詞的受詞時, whether 可用 if 取代, if 仍譯為『是否』, 而非『如果』。

 故: I wonder <u>whether</u> he has finished the work yet.

  = I wonder <u>if</u> he has finished the work yet.

名詞子句作介詞的受詞:

1) 此時僅能用 whether 或疑問詞引導的名詞子句作受詞。that 引導的名詞子句不可直接作介詞的受詞。

 例: I am worried <u>about</u> <u>whether he can do it</u>.

    介詞   受詞

  (我很擔心他是否能做這件事。)

 I am unsure <u>of</u> <u>how he'll cope with the problem</u>.

    介詞   受詞

  (我不確定他將如何應付這問題。)

2) 遇有介詞, 且非要使用 that 子句作受詞時, 其補救方法如下:

 a) 介詞 + the fact + that 子句

  如此一來, 就可用 the fact 作介詞的受詞, 而 that 子句就成了 the fact 的同位語。

  例: I am worried <u>about</u> <u>that he doesn't study</u>. (✗)

      介詞   受詞

  → I am worried <u>about</u> <u>the fact</u> <u>that he doesn't study</u>. (○)

      介詞 受詞   同位語

  (他不唸書令我操心。)

b) be 動詞 + 形容詞 + that 子句

也就是去掉介詞, 將 that 子句置於形容詞後面, 使 that 子句成為副詞子句, 修飾該形容詞。

例: I am sure of that the team won the game. (✕)

→ I am <u>sure</u> <u>that the team won the game.</u> (○)
　　　　形容詞　　　　　副詞子句
(我確定那一隊贏了比賽。)

I am worried about <u>that he plays around all day</u>. (✕)

→ I am <u>worried</u> <u>that he plays around all day</u>. (○)
　　　　形容詞　　　　　副詞子句
(我為他整天游手好閒擔心。)

c. 置於 be 動詞後作主詞補語

例: The truth <u>is</u> <u>that nobody really cares what you do</u>.
　　　　　　　　　　　主詞補語
(事實上沒有人真的在乎你做什麼。)

The question <u>is</u> <u>whether the project is worth doing</u>.
　　　　　　　　　　　主詞補詞
(問題是這個企劃案是否值得進行。)

The problem <u>is</u> <u>how it should be done</u>.
　　　　　　　　　主詞補詞
(問題是該怎麼做這件事。)

Substitution

代　換

1. **Whether very sick people should be helped to end their own lives is a question many people cannot answer.**

   Whether the company should hire him is something the boss has to decide.

   Whether the man killed his wife is something we'll never know.

   是否應該幫助病入膏肓的人結束他們的生命是一個令許多人難以回答的問題。

   那家公司該不該雇用他要由老闆來決定。

   我們永遠無法得知那名男子是否殺了他的太太。

2. **That he has done this more than twenty times is known to everyone.**

   That he divorced his nagging wife is not surprising.

   That the prisoners escaped was an embarrassment to the guards.

   大家都知道他幫人這麼做已經有二十多次了。

   他和嘮叨不休的妻子離婚一點也不令人驚訝。

   那些囚犯的脫逃令獄卒非常難堪。

Lesson 8

No Hearts or No Brains?

鐵石心腸還是沒腦筋？

Dialogue
實用會話

Helen and Dick are talking about the previous article.

(H=Helen; D=Dick)

H: I don't understand how people can think Dr. Kevorkian is doing the right thing.

D: Well, helping people die with dignity is not that bad, is it?

H: Don't you know? Where there is life, there is hope.

D: Come on. Be realistic. Those people who want to die are suffering. It's better that they go quickly and painlessly.

H: All you men have no hearts.

D: And all you women have no brains.

海倫和狄克正在討論前面那篇文章。

海倫：我真搞不懂人們怎麼會認為凱渥肯醫生所做的事情是正當的。

狄克：可是，幫助人死得有尊嚴不是件壞事，是不是？

海倫：你難道不知道嗎？留得青山在，不怕沒柴燒。

狄克：算了吧。想法要實際點。那些尋死的人飽受折磨。還是讓他們不要受到痛苦快快地死去比較好。

海倫：你們這些男人都是鐵石心腸。

狄克：而妳們這些女人都沒腦筋。

Key Points
重點提示

1. **brain** [bren] n. 腦

   have no brains　　沒有大腦/腦筋

   rack one's brains　　絞盡腦汁

   rack [ræk] vt. 折磨; 榨取

   * 上述片語中, brain 恆用複數形 brains。

   例: How could you believe that crook? You have no brains.
   (你怎麼會相信那個騙子呢？你真是沒有大腦。)

   You don't have to rack your brains to get the answer to that simple question.
   (你用不著絞盡腦汁就可以想出那個簡單問題的答案。)

2. **talk about...**　　討論……

= discuss [dɪˈskʌs] vt.

   例: There's one thing I want to <u>talk about</u> with you.
   = There's one thing I want to <u>discuss</u> with you.
   (有件事我要跟你討論。)

3. **help** + 人 + **(to)** + 原形動詞　　幫助某人……

   例: Can you help me (to) move this table to the living room?
   (你可否幫我把這張桌子搬到客廳？)

4. **dignity** [ˈdɪɡnətɪ] n. 尊嚴

   例: You can lose everything you own but never lose your dignity.
   (人可以失去所擁有的一切，但不可以失去尊嚴。)

5. 本文:

   Well, helping people die with dignity is not that bad, is it?
   可以, 幫助人死得有尊嚴不是件壞事, 是不是？

注意:

本句使用反問句, helping people die with dignity 是主詞, 反問部份用代名詞 it 取代, 形成"is it?"的反問句。

反問句句構如下:

敘述句為肯定句時, 接否定反問句; 敘述句為否定時, 接肯定反問句。此外, 反問句的主詞一定要用代名詞。

a. 敘述句有 be 動詞時, 反問句沿用 be 動詞 (如本句)。

　　例: Jim <u>is</u> having his summer vacation in Japan, <u>is Jim</u>? (✗)

　→ Jim <u>is</u> having his summer vacation in Japan, <u>isn't he</u>? (◯)
　　　(吉姆正在日本過著假, 不是嗎?)

b. 敘述句有一般動詞時, 反問句則依人稱時態使用 do、does 或 did。

　　例: Carlos <u>rides</u> a bike to work, <u>doesn't</u> he?
　　　(卡洛士騎腳踏車上班, 不是嗎?)

c. 敘述句有助動詞時, 反問句沿用助動詞。

　　例: You <u>cannot</u> sing, <u>can</u> you?
　　　(你不會唱歌, 是嗎?)

d. 與命令句使用時, 反問句一律用 will you。

　　例: Shut up, will you?
　　　(閉嘴, 好嗎?)

e. 與"Let's..."句型使用時, 反問句一律用 shall we。

　　例: Let's go dancing, shall we?
　　　(咱們去跳舞, 好不好?)

6. **Where there is life, there is hope.**　得青山在, 不怕沒柴燒。(諺語)

= If there is life, there is hope.

此處的 Where 可視為副詞連接詞, 相當 If (如果) 之意, 引導副詞子句, 修飾之後的主要子句。

類似用法的諺語尚有:

Where there's a will, there's a way.　　有志者事竟成。

Where there's smoke, there's fire.　　無風不起浪。

7. **realistic** [ˌriəˈlɪstɪk] a. 實際的

例: Be realistic! That pretty girl will never go out with you.
(實際點！那個漂亮女孩絕不會和你約會的。)

8. **suffer** [ˈsʌfɚ] vi. 受苦; 罹患 & vt. 遭遇到

suffer from + 疾病　　(長期) 患……(疾病)

注意:

suffer 作及物動詞時, 表遭受短期的痛苦, 而 "suffer from..." 則表遭受長期的痛苦 (尤指慢性病所造成的痛苦)。

例: My mother suffers from migraine headaches.
(我媽媽患有偏頭痛。)

＊ migraine [ˈmaɪgren] n. 偏頭痛

The lion trainer suffered wounds all over his body.
(那個馴獅師全身是傷。)

9. **painlessly** [ˈpenlɪslɪ] adv. 無痛苦地

painless [ˈpenlɪs] a. 無痛苦的

painful [ˈpenfəl] a. 痛苦的

例: They say that acupuncture is painless.
(據說針灸不會痛。)

＊ acupuncture [ˈækjʊpʌŋktʃɚ] n. 針灸

It was a painful experience to watch my pet dog pass away.
(看著我的愛狗死去是一種痛苦的經驗。)

10. **have no heart**　　鐵石心腸, 沒有同情心

例: A: I made my husband sleep on the floor when he came home drunk last night.
　　B: You have no heart.
(甲：昨晚我老公喝醉酒回家，我叫他睡地板。)
(乙：妳真是鐵石心腸。)

請選出下列各句中正確的一項

1. _____ there is a will, there is a way.
   (A) How   (B) Why   (C)Where   (D) What

2. _____ you like it or not, I'm going to the party.
   (A) When   (B) Whether   (C) As   (D) How

3. _____ he asked me to marry him is too good to be true.
   (A) Why   (B) What   (C) Whether   (D) That

4. _____ better to be safe than sorry.
   (A) I am   (B) You are   (C) He is   (D) It is

5. The cruel man has no _____.
   (A) heart   (B) brain   (C) head   (D) mind

解答:

1. (C)	2. (B)	3. (D)	4. (D)	5. (A)

Lesson 9
Be Thoughtful
為別人著想

Reading
閱　讀

Being thoughtful simply means thinking of others before yourself. What you say or do will have an effect on others. So it is important that you think before you say or do anything. In this way, you can avoid hurting others' feelings. Moreover, a thoughtless act or remark can spoil a perfect relationship.

Remember these rules. If you don't have anything nice to say, don't say anything. Likewise, if you think what you do will hurt others, don't do it. After all, what goes around comes around.

　　為別人設想的意思就是在想到自己之前先替別人著想。你所說或所做的每一件事都會對別人產生影響。因此，在你說或做任何事情之前先想一下是很重要的。這樣的話，你可以避免傷害到別人的感情。此外，欠缺考慮的行動或言論也可能破壞完美的關係。

　　記住這些規則：如果你沒有好話要說就什麼也不要說；同樣地，如果你認為你所做的事會傷人的話，那麼就別做它。畢竟，種什麼因，得什麼果。

Vocabulary & Idioms
單字 & 片語註解

1. **thoughtful** [ˈθɔtfəl] a. 體貼的; 設想周到的

   It's thoughtful of + 人 + to + 原形動詞　　某人……真是體貼/設想周到

   例: It is thoughtful of you to remember my birthday.
   (你真是體貼還記得我的生日。)

2. **have an effect on...**　　對……有影響

   = have an impact on...

   = have an influence on...

   effect [ɪˈfɛkt] n. 影響

   例: Whatever a teacher does in the classroom will have an effect on the students.
   (老師在教室裡的一言一行都會影響學生們。)

3. **in this/that way**　　這樣的話, 如此一來

   例: Don finishes all his work at the office. In this way, he has time for his family when he is at home.
   (唐在辦公室裏做完所有的工作。這樣一來，他在家時就有空陪家人。)

4. **avoid** [əˈvɔɪd] vt. 避免

注意:

avoid 須用動名詞或名詞作受詞, 而不可接不定詞作受詞。

例: You can avoid a lot of trouble by being honest.
(誠實可以使你避免許多麻煩。)

Always avoid <u>to swim</u> alone. (✗)

→ Always avoid swimming alone. (○)
(始終要避免獨自一個人游泳。)

5. **feeling** [ˈfilɪŋ] n. 感情 (複數); 感覺

have feelings for + 人　　對某人有感情

have a feeling + that 子句　　有……的預感/感覺

例: John has special feelings for his cousin, Jane.
(約翰對他堂妹珍有特殊的感情。)

I have a feeling that Bob's going to quit his job soon.
(我有預感鮑伯很快就會辭職。)

6. **thoughtless** [ˈθɔtlɪs] a. 欠考慮的; 粗心的

例: The thoughtless remark cost him his job.
(欠思慮的言論使他失去了工作。)

7. **remark** [rɪˈmɑrk] n. 言論 (常與動詞 make 並用)

例: The secretary made a favorable remark about her boss.
(那位秘書說她老闆的好話。)

8. **spoil** [spɔɪl] vt. 破壞 & vi. 變餿, 變壞

例: The plane crash reported on TV spoiled my appetite.
(電視報導的空難事件破壞了我的食慾。)

Without proper preservation, food spoils easily.
(食物沒有適當保存就容易變壞。)

＊ preservation [ˌprɛzəˈveʃən] n. 保存, 保藏

9. **perfect** [ˈpɝˈfɪkt] a. 完美的

例: Practice makes perfect.
(熟能生巧。──諺語)

10. **relationship** [rɪˈleʃənˌʃɪp] n. 關係

    例: What is your relationship with that girl?
    (你和那女孩的關係為何?)

11. **Likewise, S + V**　　同樣地,……
 = By the same token, S + V
    token [ˈtokən] n. 標記

    例: When it rains, Mom stays indoors. Likewise, when it's too sunny, she never goes out.
    (下雨時,老媽就待在室內。同樣地,當太陽太大時,她也從來不出門。)

12. **What goes around comes around.**　　種什麼因, 得什麼果。(諺語)
 = What you do to others may one day be done to you.

Grammar Notes
文　法　重　點

　　本課介紹"it is + 表『有必要的』形容詞 + that 子句"的用法。

　　So it is important that you think before you say or do anything.
 = So it is important that you should think before you say or do anything.
　　因此, 在你說或做任何事之前先想一下是很重要的。
　　上列句中的 important 為形容詞, 表『有必要的』, 此類表『有必要的』形容詞用於"It is + 此類形容詞 + that 子句"之句構中時, that 子句中須使用助動詞 should, 但 should 常予以省略, 而直接接原形動詞。常見的此類形容詞計有下列數個:
　　其句型如下:

It is	important (重要的)	+ that + 主詞 + (should) + 原形動詞
	imperative (有必要的)	
	necessary (有必要的)	
	essential (有必要的)	
	urgent (極重要的)	
	desirable (合乎理想的)	
	advisable (適當的)	

例: It is imperative that Carlos (should) get married before his girlfriend changes her mind.
(卡洛士應該趕緊在女友改變心意前娶她。)

It is essential that the nurses (should) learn to be patient.
(做護士的有必要學會有耐心。)

Substitution
代　　換

1. **What you say or do will have an effect on others.**
   What you ordered is not available.
   What the child needs is love.
   你所說或所做的每一件事都會對別人產生影響。
   你所點的食物賣光了。
   這孩子所需要的是愛。

2. **It is important that you think before you say or do anything.**
   It is essential that you abide by these rules.
   It is necessary that he see a doctor immediately.
   在你說或做任何事之前先想一下是很重要的。
   遵守這些規則是必要的。
   他立刻看醫生是必要的。

Lesson 10
What Are Friends for?
要不然要朋友幹嘛？

Dialogue
實用會話

Jane meets her old friend, Fred.

(J = Jane; F = Fred)

J: Hi, Fred! How's everything?

F: Not so good, I'm afraid. Supporting a family is becoming more and more difficult these days.

J: What you say can't be more true. Everything is so expensive. I can hardly make ends meet myself.

F: Oh, really? Do you need any money? What I have is not much, but I can loan you some.

J: I'm OK. Thanks for being so thoughtful anyway.

F: What are friends for?

珍和她的老朋友弗瑞德碰面。

　　珍：嗨，弗瑞德！一切都好嗎？

弗瑞德：恐怕並不太好。這年頭要扶養一個家庭越來越不容易了。

　　珍：你說的對極了。現在東西都好貴。我幾乎是入不敷出。

弗瑞德：哦，真的嗎？妳需不需要錢？我這裏的錢不多，但是我可以
　　　　借給妳一點。

　　珍：我還過得去。無論如何還是要謝謝你這麼體貼。

弗瑞德：要不然要朋友幹嘛？

Key Points
重點提示

1. **How's everything?**　　一切都好嗎/你好嗎?
   相同意思的問候語尚有:
   How's everything going?
   How's it going?
   How are you getting along?
   How have you been?
   How are you?
   例: A: How's everything?
   　　B: Same as usual.
   　　(甲:一切都好嗎?)
   　　(乙:老樣子。)

2. **support** [səˋport] vt. 供養; 支持 & n. 支持
   例: Will you support me if I ask the boss for a raise?
   　　(如果我向老闆要求加薪的話,你會支持我嗎?)
   　　The politician asked us for our support.
   　　(那位政治人物要我們支持他。)

3. **What you say can't be more true.**　　你說的對極了。
   主詞 + cannot be + 比較級形容詞　　再……也沒有了; ……到極點了
   例: The answer you gave cannot be more wrong.
   　　(你的答案大錯特錯。)

4. **hardly** [ˋhɑrdlɪ] adv. 幾乎不
   例: I can hardly hear what you are saying.
   　　(我幾乎聽不到你在說什麼。)

5. **make ends meet**　　使收支平衡

例: To make ends meet, Tom has to do a part-time job in the evening.
(為使收支平衡，湯姆得在晚上兼差。)

6. **loan** [lon] vt. 提供貸款, 借給 & n.貸款

    loan ＋ 人 ＋ 金錢   借給某人金錢

= lend ＋ 人 ＋ 金錢

例: If you loan me US$1,000, I'll repay you US$1,100 next month.
(如果你借我一千塊美金的話，下個月我會還你一千一百塊美金。)

The young couple asked the bank for a loan to buy a house.
(那對年輕夫婦向銀行貸款買房子。)

請選出下列各句中正確的一項

1. After I get a job, I will not need my parents to _____ me.
(A) advise   (B) provide   (C) loan   (D) support

2. Speak louder! I can _____ hear you.
(A) almost   (B) seldom   (C) hardly   (D) really

3. If you can make _____ meet, you won't be worried about money.
(A) one end   (B) ends   (C) the end   (D) endings

4. Since getting a job, Mark has _____ himself.
(A) helped   (B) afforded   (C) survived   (D) supported

5. It's _____ of you to remember my birthday.
(A) careful   (B) painful   (C) playful   (D) thoughtful

解答:

1. (D)   2. (C)   3. (B)   4. (D)   5. (D)

Lesson 11
Power without Pollution
只要能源，不要污染

Reading
閱　讀

Pollution is a big problem in almost all the big cities of the world. City people are, therefore, becoming more and more worried about how they can get rid of pollution. They are also concerned about whether the government is doing enough to protect the environment.

However, people in Ireland don't have these worries. They are sure that they have found the answer to the problem. They use windmills. These windmills can create power without creating pollution. This method is so successful that other countries are thinking of doing the same. Why not? What works for Ireland can work for any other country.

污染幾乎是全世界各大城市的一大問題。因此，居住在城市的人對他們如何能消除污染也愈來愈擔心。他們也很關心政府對環境是否盡心保護。

然而，住在愛爾蘭的人就沒有這些憂慮。他們確信他們已經找到了問題的解決之道：他們使用風車。這些風車能夠產生能源而不製造污染。這個方法那麼成功，因此其他國家紛紛想要效法。這有何不可呢？在愛爾蘭行得通，那麼在其他國家也可以行得通。

Vocabulary & Idioms
單字 & 片語註解

1. **power** [ˈpauɚ] n. 能源
   a power failure　停電
   例: Make sure you have some candles at home in case of a power failure.
   (務必在家裏擺些蠟燭以備停電時使用。)

2. **pollution** [pəˈluʃən] n. 污染
   pollute [pəˈlut] vt. 污染
   water pollution　水污染
   noise pollution　噪音污染
   air pollution　空氣污染
   例: The campers polluted the river with their garbage.
   (那些露營者留下的垃圾污染了該河流。)

3. **worried** [ˈwɝɪd] a. 擔心的, 憂慮的
   worry [ˈwɝɪ] vt. & n. 擔心, 擔憂

be worried about...　　擔心/擔憂……

例: If you're worried about money, why go on vacation?
(如果你擔心錢的問題，幹嘛還去度假呢？)

The happy couple don't seem to have a worry in the world.
(那對快樂的夫妻似乎一點憂愁都沒有。)

4. **get rid of...**　　除去/戒除……

例: The boss should get rid of that lazy worker.
(老闆應該把那個懶惰的員工開除。)

5. **be concerned about...**　　關心……

concerned [kənˈsɝnd] a. 關切的

例: Mary is too concerned about her looks.
(瑪麗太過在意她的外表。)

6. **protect** [prəˈtɛkt] vt. 保護

例: It is your duty to protect your children.
(你有責任保護自己的小孩。)

7. **environment** [ɪnˈvaɪrənmənt] n. 環境

例: The writer needs a quiet environment to do his work.
(該作家需要安靜的環境來從事寫作。)

8. **Ireland** [ˈaɪrlənd] n. 愛爾蘭

9. **windmill** [ˈwɪndˌmɪl] n. 風車

10. **create** [krɪˈet] vt. 產生; 創造, 製造

例: When you go for a job interview, it is important to create a good first impression.
(去面試時，製造良好的第一印象是很重要的。)

11. **method** [ˈmɛθəd] n. 方法

例: My father's method of bringing children up is really old-fashioned.
(我父親教育孩子的方法真的很落伍。)

12. **think of...**　　考慮……

例: I'm thinking of starting my own business next year.
(我在考慮明年自己創業。)

Grammar Notes
文法重點

本課介紹副詞 almost 的用法,以及介紹名詞 answer 與介詞 to 並用,和"so...
that..." (如此……以致於……) 的用法。

1. **Pollution is a big problem in <u>almost all</u> the big cities of the world.**

   污染幾乎是全世界各大城市的一大問題。

   almost(幾乎)用來修飾形容詞或副詞時,這些形容詞或副詞必須是具有完全性概念的詞類, 故形容詞如 all (全部)、every (每一個)、any (任一)、no (沒有) 等字均可與 almost 並用,但無 almost many (幾乎許多)、almost most (幾乎大部分)的用法,因 many 與 most 所表示的並非完全性的概念,故不可造出下列的句子:

   例: Almost <u>many</u> sailors are good swimmers. (✗)

   → Almost all sailors are good swimmers. (○)
   (幾乎所有的水手都很會游泳。)

   Almost <u>every</u> school has a basketball court.
   (幾乎每一所學校都有籃球場。)

2. **They are sure that they have found the answer <u>to</u> the problem.**

   他們確信他們已經找到了問題的解決之道。

   在英文中, 有些名詞後面固定要與介詞 to 並用, 主要是因為此類名詞通常表示『針對』後者具有開啟的作用, 故介詞要用 to。常見此類名詞有 key、road、answer、solution 等。

the key of the room (✕)

→ the key to the room 　　房間的鑰匙

the key of success (✕)

→ the key to success 　　成功之鑰, 成功的祕訣

the road of victory (✕)

→ the road to victory 　　勝利之路

the answer of the question (✕)

→ the answer to the question 　　問題的答案

the answer/solution of the problem (✕)

→ the answer/solution to the problem 　　問題的解決方法

例: Hard work is the key <u>of</u> success. (✕)

→ Hard work is the key <u>to</u> success. (○)
(努力是成功之鑰。)

Only one student knew the answer <u>of</u> the question. (✕)

→ Only one student knew the answer <u>to</u> the question. (○)
(只有一個學生知道那個問題的答案。)

3. **This method is <u>so</u> successful <u>that</u> other countries are thinking of doing the same.**

本句使用了"so...that..."(如此……以致於……) 的句構, 在此句構中, so 是副詞, 譯成『如此』, 故其後須置形容詞或副詞以供修飾; 而 that 則為副詞連接詞, 譯成『以致』, 其所引導的副詞子句修飾其前的 so。相同用法的句構尚有"such...that...", 但由於 such 是形容詞, 故其後只能接名詞。

so + adj./adv. + that 子句 　　如此……以致於……

such + 單/複數名詞 + that 子句 　　如此……以致於……

例: It's so hot in summer that we can't do without an air conditioner.
(夏天的天氣熱得我們少不了冷氣機。)

＊ air conditioner [ˈɛr kənˌdɪʃənɚ] n. 空氣調節機, 冷氣機

The teacher spoke so fast that I couldn't understand what he was saying.

(老師講得太快以致我聽不懂他在說什麼。)

He is such a genius that he doesn't have to study much for exams.
(他是個天才，所以他考試都不用怎麼唸書。)

They are such good basketball players that everybody wants to watch their games.
(他們個個都是很棒的籃球員，所以每個人都想去看他們打球。)

Substitution
代　　換

They are sure that they have found the answer to the problem.
The coach said that the road to victory is through practice.
他們確信他們已經找到了問題的解決之道。
麥克認為他擁有成功之鑰。
教練說勝利之路是經由練習。

Lesson 12
Stop the Noise
別吵了

Dialogue
實用會話

Mr. Chen is talking to his neighbor Mrs. Wang.

(C = Mr. Chen; W = Mrs. Wang)

C: May I have a word with you?

W: Sure. What's the problem?

C: It's about your son. I'm tired of his making so much noise at all hours of the day.

W: I'm sorry. I'm sure he's not doing it on purpose.

C: I'm sure he's not. But we can do without the noise pollution, you know?

W: You're absolutely right. By the way, how was your party last night? It sure sounded like you had a great time.

C: Uh...

陳先生正在和他的鄰居王太太談話。

陳先生：我可以和妳講句話嗎？

王太太：當然。有什麼問題嗎？

陳先生：是關於貴公子的。我對他一天到晚製造噪音已經感到很厭煩了。

王太太：對不起。我確信他不是故意那麼做的。

陳先生：我確信他不是。但我們實在不該有噪音污染，妳知道嗎？

王太太：你完全正確。哦，對了，你們昨晚的派對怎麼樣呢？聽起來你們好像玩得很開心嘛。

陳先生：呃……

Key Points
重點提示

1. **have a word with**＋人　　和某人談談

   例: I wonder why my teacher wants to have a word with my parents.
   (我想知道為什麼我的老師要找我父母親談談。)

2. **be tired of...**　　厭煩……, 受夠了……

   例: I'm tired of taking so many tests in school.
   (我受夠了在學校要考那麼多試。)

3. **on purpose**　　故意地, 有意地

   例: I didn't step on that old lady's foot on purpose.
   (我不是故意要踩那位老婆婆的腳。)

4. **can do without...**　　無……亦可以

   cannot do without...　　無……則不行

   本片語中的 do 是不及物動詞, 表『過得去』之意。

   例: In fact, we can do without your help.
   (其實, 我們沒有你的幫助也行。)

Fish cannot do without water.
(魚沒有水是不能活的。)

5. **absolutely** [ˌæbsəˈlutlɪ] adv. 完全地, 絕對地

例: There's absolutely no truth in what he said.
(他的話完全不對。)

6. **By the way,** 主詞＋動詞　　哦, 對了,……

例: By the way, when is your son coming home from abroad?
(哦，對了，你兒子什麼時候要從國外回來？)

請選出下列各句中正確的一項

1. The teacher had a _____ with the naughty student.
(A) argument　(B) speech　　(C) word　　(D) report

2. Jack's sister is sick of his _____ on the phone for hours.
(A) word　　(B) saying　　(C) talked　　(D) talking

3. Everyone knows the answer _____ the question except me.
(A) of　　(B) about　　(C) to　　(D) for

4. Mom taught me _____ to make apple pies.
(A) what　　(B) how　　(C) why　　(D) which

5. Mary is a really good singer. She _____ like Madonna.
(A) feels　　(B) thinks　　(C) sounds　　(D) smells

解答:

> 1. (C)　　2. (D)　　3. (C)　　4. (B)　　5. (C)

Lesson 13
Health Comes First
健康至上

Reading
閱　讀

　　Smoking is bad in that it is harmful to one's health. In spite of the fact that doctors have even warned that it causes cancer, people still keep on smoking.

　　In some Western countries, however, people are beginning to kick the bad habit. They realize that health should come first. To help them quit smoking, there are laws against cigarette advertising and smoking in public places. This is praiseworthy except that Western countries are now selling cigarettes in the East in greater numbers than ever. That they are doing this is immoral, don't you think?

　　抽煙不好，因為它有害健康。儘管醫師甚至已經警告說抽煙會致癌，但人們還是照抽不誤。

　　然而，在一些西方國家中，人們開始戒除這個壞習慣。他們了解健康應該重於一切。為了幫助他們戒煙，法律明文規定在公共場所禁止做香煙廣告與吸煙。此舉值得讚許，但美中不足的是西方國家現在賣往東方的香煙達到空前的數量。他們這麼做是不道德的，您不覺得嗎？

Vocabulary & Idioms
單字 & 片語註解

1. **health** [hɛlθ] n. 健康

   be in good health 　　健康良好

   be in poor health 　　健康不佳

   例: My grandpa is old but in good health.
   (我祖父年紀雖大，但是身體仍然很健康。)

2. **be harmful to...** 　　對……有害

   harmful [ˈhɑrmfəl] a. 有害的

   例: Working at a computer all day is harmful to the eyes.
   (整天使用電腦對眼睛有害。)

3. **warn** [wɔrn] vt. 警告, 告誡

   warn + that 子句　　警告說……

   warn + 人 + against + 名詞/動名詞　　警告某人不要……

   warn + 人 + of + 事　　警告某人某事

   例: The weather bureau warned that a fierce typhoon is approaching.
   (氣象局提出警告說強烈颱風即將來襲。)

   ＊fierce [fɪrs] a. (風雨等) 強勁的

The teacher warned the new student against cutting class.
(老師警告那個新來的學生不要曉課。)

This sign warns people of the dangers of swimming too far out.
(這個標示牌警告人們游得太遠會有危險。)

4. **cause** [kɔz] vt. 導致, 造成

例: The driver's carelessness caused the terrible accident.
(那個駕駛的粗心大意造成了這場可怕的車禍。)

5. **cancer** [ˈkænsɚ] n. 癌

lung cancer　　肺癌

6. **keep on Ving**　　繼續……

= keep Ving

例: The woman kept on nagging her husband till he eventually left her.
(那個女人一直對老公嘮叨個沒完，直到他最後離開了她。)
　＊nag [næg] vt. 嘮叨, 絮聒不休

7. **kick the bad habit**　　戒除這個壞習慣

= get rid of the bad habit

例: I wish I could kick the bad habit of going to bed late every night.
(我希望自己可以戒掉每晚晚睡的壞習慣。)

8. **quit smoking**　　戒煙

= give up smoking

quit [kwɪt] vt. 停止; 放棄

動詞三態均為 quit。

注意:

quit 之後接名詞或動名詞作受詞, 而不可接不定詞作受詞。

例: The doctor warned the alcoholic to quit drinking once and for all.
(醫生警告那個酒徒要他徹底戒酒。)
　＊alcoholic [ˌælkəˈhɔlɪk] n. 酗酒者

9. **cigarette** [ˈsɪɡəˌrɛt] n. 香煙

10. **advertising** [ˈædvəˌtaɪzɪŋ] n. 廣告

    advertise [ˈædvəˌtaɪz] vt. 為…做廣告 & vi. 登廣告

    例: I advertised my old car for sale.
    (我登廣告賣舊車。)

    Mr. Wang advertised for a maid.
    (王先生登廣告徵求女傭。)

11. **praiseworthy** [ˈprezˌwɝðɪ] a. 值得讚許的

    例: Mr. Chen's teaching skills are praiseworthy.
    (陳先生的教學技巧很值得稱許。)

12. **in great numbers**   大量地

    * 本文 greater 為 great 的比較級。

    例: The doves gather in the park in great numbers.
    (公園裏經常有大群鴿子聚集。)

13. 含有比較級形容詞或副詞的子句 **+ than ever**   比以往更……

    例: Pete played better than ever and won the tennis game easily.
    (彼得網球打得比以往都來得更好，而輕而易舉地贏得比賽。)

Grammar Notes
文法重點

本課介紹"in that" (因為) 作副詞連接詞的用法, 以及『介系詞 + the fact + that 子句』的用法, 並複習 that 引導的名詞子句作主詞的用法。

1. **Smoking is bad in that it is harmful to one's health.**
   抽煙不好, 因為它有害健康。
   上列句中的 in that (因為) 是副詞連接詞, 而非『介詞 in + that 子句』, 即等於 because 之意, 但不同於 because 的是, in that 使用時, 通常置於主要子句之後, 而不置於句首。而 because 引導的副詞子句則可置於主要子句之前, 兩子句間用逗點相隔, 或置於主要子句之後, 中間不置逗點。

例: Jogging is good for you <u>in that</u> it helps you keep fit.
（慢跑對人體很好，因為它有助你保持身體健康。）

Because he is so shy, he seldom goes out with girls.
= He seldom goes out with girls because he is so shy.
（因為他很害羞，所以他很少和女孩子出去。）

2. <u>**In spite of the fact that** doctors have even warned that it causes cancer, people still keep on smoking.</u>
儘管醫師甚至已經警告說抽煙會致癌, 但人們還是照抽不誤。

in spite of...　　儘管/雖然……
= despite...
* despite [dɪˈspaɪt] prep. 儘管

注意:
上述句構中的 in spite of 是片語介詞 (即數個字形成的介詞), despite 是介詞, 其後可接名詞或動名詞作受詞, 但不可接 that 子句作受詞, 因為 that 引導的名詞子句不可作介詞的受詞。使用時, 須先在 in spite of 或 despite 之後加 the fact 作其受詞, 然後再接 that 子句, 此時的 that 子句乃其前 the fact 之同位語。

In spite of the fact + that 子句, 主要子句　　儘管/雖然……, ……
= Despite the fact + that 子句, 主要子句

例: In spite of working two jobs, Mr. Chen can hardly make ends meet.
= Despite working two jobs, Mr. Chen can hardly make ends meet.
（儘管兼了兩份工作，陳先生幾乎還是入不敷出。）

<u>In spite of that</u> I lent my friend US$1 million, his company went bankrupt. (✗)
→ <u>In spite of the fact that</u> I lent my friend US$1 million, his company went bankrupt. (○)

= Despite the fact that I lent my friend US$1 million, his company went bankrupt.
(儘管我借給朋友一百萬美金，他的公司還是破產了。)

3. <u>That they are doing this</u> is immoral, don't you think?
= It is immoral <u>that they are doing this</u>, don't you think?
他們這麼做是不道德的, 您不覺得嗎？

Substitution
代　換

1. **Smoking is bad in that it is harmful to one's health.**
Swimming is healthful in that almost every muscle in the body is being exercised.
Reading is a good hobby in that you can learn and enjoy at the same time.
抽煙不好, 因為它有害健康。
游泳有益健康, 因為全身的肌肉幾乎都有運動到。
閱讀是很好的嗜好, 因為你可以同時學習和享受。

2. **In spite of the fact that doctors have even warned that it causes cancer, people still keep on smoking.**
In spite of the fact that Carl Lewis is getting old, he can still run very fast.
In spite of the fact that Tom's rich, he's not proud.
儘管醫生甚至已經警告說抽煙會致癌, 但人們還是照抽不誤。
儘管卡爾・路易士年紀漸長, 但他還是跑得很快。
儘管湯姆很有錢, 但他並不驕傲。

Lesson 14
Quit Cold Turkey
斷然戒煙

Dialogue
實用會話

Jane is talking to her boyfriend.

(J = Jane; B = boyfriend)

J: You promised me that you were going to give up smoking. What's that in your hand?

B: I'm sorry. I really want to except that every time I get nervous, I can't help smoking.

J: That's just an excuse.

B: No. It's true. I've tried everything: chewing gum, biting my fingernails and even meditation, but nothing works.

J: Well, if you want to be with me, you'll just have to quit cold turkey.

B: That will work!

珍正在和她的男朋友交談。

珍：你答應過我要戒煙的。你手上拿的是什麼？

男友：對不起。我真的想要戒煙，但我每次緊張時就忍不住要抽煙。

珍：那只是藉口。

男友：不是，是真的。我試過各種方法：嚼口香糖、咬手指甲、甚至打坐，可是都沒效。

珍：呃，你如果想和我在一起，就得斷然戒煙。

男友：那會有效哦！

Key Points
重點提示

1. **quit cold turkey**　　斷然戒煙/毒

注意:

在上述片語中, quit 為不及物動詞, 表『戒除』之意; "cold turkey"原為名詞, 指『冷火雞』, 在此則作副詞用, 表示『斷然地』或『一次徹底地』, 因此本片語乃表示『一次徹底戒除煙毒, 而不採漸進方式』, 此種戒毒方式極其痛苦, 身體常會打寒顫並起雞皮疙瘩, 故稱之為"quit cold turkey"。

例: Trying to quit smoking slowly doesn't work. You've got to quit cold turkey.
(慢慢戒煙是行不通的。你必須斷然戒除。)

2. **promise** [ˈprɑmɪs] vt. 允諾 & n. 諾言

promise (+ 人) + that 子句　　答應 (某人) 做…

= promise (+ 人) + to + 原形動詞

make a promise to + 原形動詞　　答應做……

例: Andy promised his teacher that he wouldn't cut class again.
(安迪答應老師不再蹺課。)

Bob made a promise to be on time for work in the future.
(鮑勃允諾以後會準時上班。)

3. 本文:

I really want to except that... 我真的想要戒煙, 但……

= I really want <u>to give up smoking</u> except that...

＊此處 except [ɪk'sɛpt] 是介詞, 與 that 並用形成 except that 時, 可視為連接詞, 表『只不過是、只可惜』之意。

4. **nervous** ['nɝvəs] a. 緊張的

例: The nervous tennis player eventually lost the game.
(那個緊張的網球選手最後輸了那場比賽。)

5. **can't help** ＋ 動名詞 禁不住/忍不住……

= can't resist ＋ 動名詞

= can't help but ＋ 原形動詞

＊resist [rɪ'zɪst] vt. 抗拒

例: My sister <u>can't help biting</u> her fingernails when she gets nervous.

= My sister <u>can't resist biting</u> her fingernails when she gets nervous.

= My sister <u>can't help but bite</u> her fingernails when she gets nervous.
(我妹妹緊張時就忍不住會咬手指甲。)

6. **excuse** [ɪk'skjus] n. 藉口

例: Sam had no excuse for failing the exam.
(山姆這次考試不及格一點藉口都沒有。)

7. **chewing gum** ['tʃuɪŋ ˌɡʌm] n. 口香糖 (不可數)

a piece/stick of chewing gum 一片口香糖

a pack of chewing gum 一包口香糖

8. **bite** [baɪt] vt. 咬

動詞三態: bite、bit [bɪt]、bitten ['bɪtn̩]。

例: A snake bit the camper's foot.
(有一條蛇咬了那個露營者的腳。)

9. **fingernail** [ˈfɪŋgɚ‚nel] n. 指甲

10. **meditation** [‚mɛdəˈteʃən] n. 打坐; 冥想

　　meditate [ˈmɛdə‚tet] vi. 打坐; 冥想

　　例: Meditation can help ease one's mind.
　　（打坐有助於放鬆心情。）

　　John meditates for twenty minutes before he goes to bed every day.
　　（約翰每天上床睡覺前會先打坐二十分鐘。）

 請選出下列各句中正確的一項

1. If you _____ to be a good boy, I'll buy you a bicycle.
　 (A) admit　　　(B) happen　　　(C) promise　　　(D) quit

2. Tom would have gone to the party _____ he was sick.
　 (A) in spite of the fact that　　　(B) in that
　 (C) for　　　　　　　　　　　　(D) except that

3. Bill made an _____ for being late for work.
　 (A) answer　　(B) excuse　　　(C) accuse　　　(D) example

4. The students tried to play a trick on the teacher but it didn't _____.
　 (A) happen　　(B) joke　　　(C) bite　　　(D) work

5. All the students were very _____ before the exam.
　 (A) happy　　(B) nervous　　　(C) late　　　(D) sorry

解答:

1. (C)	2. (D)	3. (B)	4. (D)	5. (B)

Lesson 15

Don't Rely on Luck!
勿心存僥倖！

Reading
閱　讀

Passing exams is every student's dream. Failing them is their nightmare. So, to realize their dreams, many students try anything. They even go to fortunetellers, buy lucky charms and follow old customs.

In Korea, many students bury something personal in the university they want to enter. They believe that these things will act as magnets and "pull" them into the university. Whether it works or not, nobody really knows. At least it does ease the students' minds about passing exams. Remember, though, you can't always rely on luck. There is no substitute for hard work.

考試考及格是每個學生的夢想；考不及格則是他們的夢魘。因此，許多學生為了實現他們的夢想，會去嘗試各種方法。他們甚至會去找算命師、買幸運符並遵循古老的風俗。

在韓國，有很多學生會把自己的一些私人物品埋在想要就讀的那所大學的地下。他們相信這些東西會像磁鐵一樣，把他們『吸』進那所大學。它是不是真的有效，沒有人真正知道。至少可以使學生想到通過考試時，心情能夠舒緩下來。不過要記住，你不能永遠靠運氣過日子。努力可是無法取代的。

Vocabulary & Idioms
單字 & 片語註解

1. **rely on...** 　　依靠/依賴/指望……

   例: Don't rely on me to help you every time you get into trouble.
   (別指望我在你每次闖禍時幫你。)

2. **fail** [fel] vt. (使) 不及格 & vi. 失敗

   例: The old lady failed the driving test for the tenth time.
   (那位老太太是第十次考駕照失敗。)

   If you keep fooling around, you're bound to fail.
   (如果你繼續鬼混的話，一定會失敗。)

3. **nightmare** [ˈnaɪtˌmɛr] n. 惡夢, 夢魘

4. **realize** [ˈrɪəˌlaɪz] vt. 實現; 了解

   例: He realized his ambition when he became president of the company.
   (他實現了他的抱負成為該公司的董事長。)

   I didn't realize how smart Bill is until I spoke with him.
   (我直到和比爾談話之後才瞭解他有多麼聰明。)

5. **fortuneteller** [ˈfɔrtʃənˌtɛlɚ] n. 算命者

例: Some gamblers go to fortunetellers to ask for lucky numbers.
(有些賭徒會到算命先生那兒求取幸運號碼。)

6. **lucky charm**　幸運符

lucky [ˈlʌkɪ] a. 幸運的

例: If we're lucky, we'll be able to get good seats for the show.
(如果運氣好的話，我們將可以弄到那場表演的好座位。)

7. **custom** [ˈkʌstəm] n. 風俗, 習慣

例: It is an Eskimo custom to rub noses as a greeting.
(相互摩擦鼻子以示問候是愛斯基摩人的習俗。)

8. **bury** [ˈbɛrɪ] vt. 埋藏

bury + 反身代名詞 + in...　　埋首於/專心……

例: The man tried to forget his sadness by burying himself in his work.
(那個人試圖以埋首工作來忘掉悲傷。)

9. **personal** [ˈpɝsənḷ] a. 私人的

例: Be sure to take your personal belongings before getting off the train.
(下火車前務必要帶好個人的物品。)

10. **enter** [ˈɛntɚ] vt. 進入

例: The teacher entered the classroom with an angry look on his face.
(那位老師面有慍色地走進教室。)

11. **magnet** [ˈmægnɪt] n. 磁鐵

12. **pull** [pʊl] vt. 拉

push [pʊʃ] vt. 推

例: The little boy pulled his sister's hair till she cried.
(那個小男孩拉姊姊的頭髮直到她哭出來為止。)

The rude young man pushed his way through the crowd.
(那個粗魯的年輕男子在人群中推擠而過。)

13. **at least** 　　至少

例: You could have at least telephoned me.
(你那時至少應該打電話給我。)

14. **ease** [iz] vt. 舒緩, 減輕 (痛苦、壓力等)

例: The medicine eased the patient's pain.
(這個藥減輕了那個病人的疼痛。)

15. **substitute** ['sʌbstəˌtjut] n. & vt. 代替

substitute A for B 　　用 A 代替 B

例: If you don't have sugar, you can use honey as a substitute.
(如果你沒有糖的話,可以用蜂蜜來代替。)

Let's substitute this new dictionary for the old one.
(咱們用這本新字典來代替那本舊的吧。)

Grammar Notes
文法重點

本課主要介紹不定詞片語 (to + 原形動詞) 作副詞,用以表示『目的』的用法,
以及 though 作副詞的用法。

1. **So, <u>to realize their dreams,</u> many students try anything.**
因此,許多學生為了實現他們的夢想,會去嘗試各種方法。

上列句中的 to realize their dreams 為不定詞片語 (即『to + 原形動詞』),
作副詞用,修飾全句。不定詞片語作副詞時,可置於句首或句尾,用以表示
『目的』,譯成『為了 (要)……』; 置於句首時, 其後通常置逗點, 再接主
要子句; 置於句尾時, 則其前不得置逗點。
置於句首:

例: To succeed in life, you must be determined.
(要在人生的旅途上成功,你必須意志堅定。)

置於句尾:

例: Peter left home early, to avoid the heavy traffic. (✗)

→ Peter left home early to avoid the heavy traffic. (○)
(彼得提早出門以避開壅塞的交通。)

注意:

表示『目的』的不定詞片語亦可用下列片語取代:

to + 原形動詞　　為了 (要)……

= in order to + 原形動詞

= so as to + 原形動詞

= with a view to + 動名詞

= with an eye to + 動名詞

* 上述片語除了"so as to + 原形動詞"須置於句尾使用外, 其餘均可置於句首或句尾。而在 with a view to 及 with an eye to 中的 to 是介詞, 故其後接動名詞作其受詞, 而不是原形動詞。

例: Ron is saving money | to / in order to / so as to | buy a house.

= Ron is saving money | with a view to / with an eye to | buying a house.

= | To / In order to | buy a house, Ron is saving money.

= | With a view to / With an eye to | buying a house, Ron is saving money.

(朗恩正在存錢以便能買棟房子。)

2. **Remember, <u>though</u>, you can't always rely on luck.**

= Remember, <u>however</u>, you can't always rely on luck.

不過要記住, 你不能永遠靠運氣過日子。

上列句中的 **though** 為副詞, 置於句中, 作插入語用, 表『不過』、『但是』, 即等於 however 之意, 但兩者用法不同。**though** 使用時可置於句中, 作插入語用, 兩旁置逗點, 亦可置於句尾, 其前置逗點; 而 **however** 使用時, 則可置於句首, 其後加逗點, 或置於句中作插入語, 兩旁以逗點相隔, 但很少置於句尾使用。

例: Bruce is an American. He, <u>though,</u> acts very Chinese.
  = Bruce is an American. He acts very Chinese, <u>though</u>.
  = Bruce is an American. <u>However,</u> he acts very Chinese.
  = Bruce is an American. He, <u>however,</u> acts very Chinese.
    (布魯斯是個美國人, 但是他的行為表現卻非常中國化。)

    Bruce is an American. He acts very Chinese, <u>however</u>. (少用)

注意:

though 置於句首使用時, 則為副詞連接詞, 表『雖然』之意, 即等於 **although**, 其所引導的副詞子句修飾句中的主要子句, 兩子句中以逗點相隔, 但此副詞子句亦可置於主要子句之後, 此時兩子句間則不須用逗點。

例: | Though | he is smart, he's not well liked by his classmates.
     | Although |
  = He's not well liked by his classmates (al)though he is smart.
    (雖然他很聰明, 卻不怎麼受同學的喜愛。)

Substitution 代 換

So, to realize their dreams, many students try anything.

To help the poor, Ron donates five percent of his salary every month.

To improve his English, Sam tries to make friends with foreigners.

因此, 許多學生為了實現他們的夢想, 會去嘗試各種方法。

朗恩為了幫助窮人, 他每個月把百分之五的薪資捐給他們。

山姆為了增進英文能力, 努力結交外國朋友。

Lesson 16
Study or Flunk
讀書或被當

Dialogue
實用會話

Kim bumps into her classmate, Pak.

(K = Kim; P = Pak)

K: What's the matter, Pak? You look depressed. Did someone just die or what?

P: Well, someone is going to soon.

K: Oh, my God! Really? Who is it?

P: Me. I flunked the exam and my dad's going to kill me.

K: How come you flunked? I thought you did everything the fortuneteller told you to do.

P: I thought so, too. I was sure of passing. That's why I went to see him this morning.

K: Well, what did he say?

P: He said I flunked because I did everything very well except that I forgot one thing.

K: What's that?

P: I didn't study!

金偶然遇見她的同學派克。

金：派克，怎麼回事？你看起來很沮喪。是不是有人剛死了還是什麼？

派克：呃，有人就快死了。

金：哦，我的天啊！真的嗎？是誰？

派克：是我。這次考試我被當了，我老爸會宰了我。

金：你怎麼會被當呢？我以為你都照算命先生叫你做的去做了。

派克：我也是這麼想。我有把握會通過考試的。這就是為什麼我今天早上去找他的原因。

金：那他說什麼呢？

派克：他說我被當掉是因為我每件事都做得很好，只除了忘記一件事。

金：什麼事？

派克：我沒唸書。

Key Points
重點提示

1. **flunk** [flʌŋk] vi. 考試不及格 & vt. 使不及格

* 本字是 fail 的俚語用法。

例: If you don't work harder, you're sure to flunk.
(如果你不用功一點的話，你一定會被當掉。)

If I flunk my English exam, my American girlfriend will kill me.
= If I <u>fail</u> my English exam, my American girlfriend will kill me.
(如果我英文考試被當的話，我的美國女友會殺了我。)

2. **bump into...**   偶遇……, 和……不期而遇

= run into...

= come across...

例: Winnie bumped into her ex-boyfriend in London.
(溫妮在倫敦偶遇她的前任男友。)

3. **depressed** [dɪ'prɛst] a. 沮喪的

depressing [dɪ'prɛsɪŋ] a. 令人沮喪的

depress [dɪ'prɛs] vt. 使沮喪, 使消沈

depression [dɪ'prɛʃən] n. 沮喪

例: I hate movies that make me feel depressed.
(我討厭令我心情沮喪的電影。)

The boy's exam results were depressing.
(那個男孩的考試成績令人失望。)

It depresses me to be broke.
(身無分文令我感到很沮喪。)

Many old people suffer from depression.
(許多老人飽受沮喪之苦。)

4. **...or what?** ……還是什麼的?

例: Do you think I'm crazy or what?
(你認為我瘋了還是什麼的?)

5. **How come + 主詞 + 動詞?** 為何……?
= Why is it + that 子句?
= Why + 倒裝句?

例: How come your father looks so young?
= Why is it that your father looks so young?
= Why does your father look so young?
(你父親怎麼會看起來那麼年輕?)

6. **be sure of...** 確信/有把握……

例: The team was sure of winning the game.
(那支隊伍有把握會贏得這場比賽。)

請選出下列各句中正確的一項

1. Tom's depressed because he just _____ the driver's test.
   (A) passed   (B) flunked
   (C) succeeded to pass   (D) failed in passing

2. Mr. Wang was _____ getting the job.
   (A) sure   (B) surely   (C) sure to   (D) sure of

3. Mike is a nice person _____ that sometimes he talks too much.
   (A) accept   (B) expect   (C) except   (D) exact

4. I don't understand _____ he could be so rude.
   (A) what   (B) when   (C) where   (D) how

5. Mother went to see a _____ about our moving to a new house.
   (A) doctor   (B) dentist
   (C) teacher   (D) fortuneteller

解答:

| 1. (B) | 2. (D) | 3. (C) | 4. (D) | 5. (D) |

Lesson 17
A Computer Car
電腦車

Where are we?

Reading
閱　讀

　　You are in a strange city. It's late at night and you're tired. But you can't find your hotel. You sigh a deep sigh. It seems like you are dreaming a terrible dream. What is happening?

　　This situation often happens to people who travel by car. But it may become a thing of the past. New auto computers are being designed to tell you how to reach your destination. A small screen in your car displays a map of the city and shows you where you are. Just give the computer the name of your hotel. You'll see it on the map. To top it off, a voice will give you

directions while you drive. With a car like this, what else would you expect?

你身在一個陌生的城市裏。天色已晚而且你也累了，但是你卻找不到你訂的旅館。你深深地嘆了一口氣，彷彿你是在作惡夢一般。這到底是怎麼一回事？

這種情況經常發生在開車旅行的人身上，但這種事可能會成為過去。新的汽車電腦就是設計來告訴你如何抵達你的目的地。你車上的小螢幕會顯示出該城市的地圖並且指出你所在的位置。只要將你要去的旅館名稱輸入電腦，你就能在地圖上看到。最棒的是，你開車時會有聲音為你指路。有一輛像這樣的車子，你還奢望什麼？

Vocabulary & Idioms
單字 & 片語註解

1. **strange** [strendʒ] a. 陌生的; 奇怪的
   例: We've had very strange weather here all week.
   (我們這裏一整個星期的天氣都很怪。)

2. **situation** [ˌsɪtʃʊˈeʃən] n. 情況 (常與介詞 in 並用)
   例: The host was in an embarrassing situation when he ran out of food for the guests.
   (那位主人請客時菜不夠吃而處境尷尬。)

3. **a thing of the past**　一件過去的事
   例: My naughty youth is a thing of the past.
   (我那調皮搗蛋的年輕時代已經過去了。)
   *naughty [ˈnɔtɪ] a. 調皮的

4. **auto computer** 汽車電腦

   auto ['ɔto] n. (美) 汽車

= automobile ['ɔtəməˌbil]

   例: Many car owners in America belong to the American Automobile Association.
   (美國有許多車主是美國汽車協會的會員。)

5. **be designed to + 原形動詞** 被設計來……

   design [dɪ'zaɪn] vt. 設計

   例: This car is designed to help the handicapped drive.
   (這部車的設計是為了方便殘障者駕駛。)
   * the handicapped = handicapped people 殘障人士
     handicapped ['hændɪˌkæpt] a. 殘障的

6. **destination** [ˌdɛstə'neʃən] n. 目的地

   例: Because of the bad weather, we arrived at our destination an hour late.
   (由於天候不佳，我們晚了一小時才到目的地。)

7. **screen** [skrin] n. 螢幕

8. **display** [dɪ'sple] vt. 顯示; 展示 & n.展覽

   on display 展覽

= on exhibition

   exhibition [ˌɛksə'bɪʃən] n. 展示, 展覽 (會)

   例: The street vendor displayed a variety of cheap watches from Switzerland.
   (那個街頭小販展示各式各樣來自瑞士的便宜手錶。)
   * vendor ['vɛndɚ] n. 小販

   High quality bicycle parts are on display at the exhibition.
   (那個展覽會場正展出高品質的腳踏車零件。)

9. **map** [mæp] n. 地圖

   例: It's easy to get lost if you drive without a road map in America.
   (如果你在美國開車不帶地圖的話，就很容易迷路。)

10. **to top it off**　更棒/糟的是; 此外

= in addition

   top [tɑp] vt. 勝過, 優於

   例: Germany beat every soccer team in Europe. To top it off, their forward won the best player award.
   (德國打敗歐洲所有的足球隊；更棒的是，他們的前鋒還贏得最佳球員獎。)

   ＊forward [ˈfɔrwɚd] n. (足球隊中的) 前鋒

   We went camping but didn't bring enough food. To top it off, nobody remembered to bring the tent.
   (我們去露營卻沒有帶足夠的食物。更糟的是，也沒有人記得帶帳篷。)

11. **direction** [dəˈrɛkʃən] n. 方向

   例: They were late because they had been traveling in the wrong direction for a while.
   (他們因為走錯路耽擱了一會兒，所以遲到了。)

Grammar Notes
文 法 重 點

本課旨在介紹少數動詞接同系名詞作受詞的用法。

You <u>sigh</u> a deep <u>sigh</u>.　　你深深地嘆了一口氣。

It seems like you are <u>dreaming</u> a terrible <u>dream</u>.
彷彿你是在作惡夢一般。

有些不及物動詞可變成及物動詞, 此時其後以其同系名詞作受詞; 所謂同系名詞乃指其詞源和意義與動詞相同的名詞, 其形態與動詞一樣, 但有時稍有改變。此類用法常見如下:

die (死)	→	death (死)
dream (作夢)	→	dream (夢)
laugh (笑)	→	laugh (笑)
live (過活)	→	life (生活)
sigh (嘆氣)	→	sigh (嘆氣)
sleep (睡覺)	→	sleep (睡眠)
smile (微笑)	→	smile (微笑)

＊ dream 作不及物動詞時, 與介詞 of 並用。

例: The victims of the plane crash <u>died</u> a terrible <u>death</u>.
(那次空難的罹難者死得很慘。)

I <u>dreamed of</u> my deceased grandfather last night.
(我昨晚夢到我已過世的祖父。)

＊ deceased [dɪˋsist] a. 死 (亡) 的, 已故的

After going out with my girlfriend, I always <u>dream</u> a sweet <u>dream</u> of her at night.
(和女友外出後，我晚上總會夢到有關她的美夢。)

The fat man <u>laughed</u> a hearty <u>laugh</u> when his friend called him Mr. Slim.
(當那個胖子的朋友叫他瘦先生時，他開懷大笑了起來。)

＊ slim [slɪm] a. 瘦的, 苗條的

I <u>live in</u> Hong Kong but work in Kowloon.
(我住在香港，但在九龍上班。)

Though I am not rich, I <u>live</u> a comfortable and happy <u>life</u>.
(雖然我並不富有，卻過得很舒適很快樂。)

After the picnic, the child <u>slept</u> a really sound <u>sleep</u>.
(野餐後，那個小孩睡得很熟。)

Substitution
代　　換

1. **You sigh a deep sigh.**

   Jane lives a happy life.

   The old man smiled a sad smile.

   你深深地嘆了一口氣。

   珍過著快樂的生活。

   那個老人悲傷地笑了笑。

2. **You'll see it on the map. To top it off, a voice will give you directions.**

   On Chinese New Year we get a bonus. To top it off, we get ten days off.

   Mike won the race. To top it off, he broke the world record.

   你在地圖上可看到它。最棒的是, 還會有聲音為你指路。

   過年時我們會拿到一筆獎金。更棒的是, 我們還會放十天假。

   麥克贏得賽跑。更棒的是, 他還打破世界紀錄。

Lesson 18
Nothing Is Perfect
天下無『完』事

Dialogue
實用會話

The computer in Dan's car is helping him reach his hotel.

(D = Dan; C = Computer)

D: OK, computer, how do we get there?

C: Go one block and take a left.

D: That looks easy. (He turns right.)

C: Left! I said "left," you idiot!

D: Sorry! Wow, you don't have to get so angry.

C: I'm sorry. I guess I'm just having a bad day.

D: A bad day? You're a computer! How can you have a bad day?

C: Well, I think I've got a virus.

D: Ha! And I thought computers could never be wrong.

丹汽車裏的電腦正導引他前往旅館。

　　丹：好吧，電腦先生，我們怎麼去呢？

電腦：往前走過一個街區，然後左轉。

　　丹：好像很簡單。(他往右轉。)

電腦：左轉！我說『左轉』，你這個白痴！

　　丹：對不起嘛！哇，你也用不著這麼生氣啊。

電腦：抱歉。我想大概是我今天過得不順利吧。

　　丹：不順利？你是部電腦，怎麼會過得不順利呢？

電腦：呃，我想我被病毒感染了。
　丹：哈！我還以為電腦永遠不會出錯呢。

Key Points
重點提示

1. 本文:

   Go one block and...

= Go for one block and...

   注意:

   go 為不及物動詞, 其後可接表示距離的名詞作副詞用, 因理論上 go 之後應有一介詞 for,但實際使用時, for 一律省略。類似用法的動詞尚有 walk、run 等。

   例: Walk ten steps forward and look right.
   （往前走十步然後向右看。）

2. **block** [blɑk] n. 街區

   例: The post office is two blocks from here.
   （郵局離這裏有兩條街。）

3. **take a left**　　左轉

= take/make a left turn

   left [lɛft] n. 左邊 & a. 左邊的 & adv. 左邊

4. **idiot** [ˈɪdɪət] n. 白痴

   注意:

   idiot 雖常出現在美式口語中, 但有粗俗的意味, 因此我們應該避免使用此字。

   例: That's not the way to do it, you idiot!
   （不是那樣做, 你這個白痴！）

5. **have a bad day**　一天過得很不順利

have a good/wonderful day　一天過得很愉快

例: My classmates and I had a wonderful day at the beach.
(我和同學在海灘上度過愉快的一天。)

6. **virus** [ˈvaɪrəs] n. 病毒

例: While traveling in South Africa, the man caught a virus and died.
(那個人在南非旅遊時感染到病毒死了。)

請選出下列各句中正確的一項

1. I was a champion boxer when I was young but that's a thing _____.
   (A) of the future　　　　　　(B) of the past
   (C) of the present　　　　　　(D) of now

2. The movie theater is designed _____ two thousand people.
   (A) for seat　　(B) seating　　(C) to seat　　(D) to sit

3. The monks really _____ a simple life.
   (A) make　　(B) live　　(C) do　　(D) pass

4. Go down two blocks and _____ a left turn.
   (A) drive　　(B) turn　　(C) make　　(D) have

5. The shop has at least a hundred different kinds of watches _____ display.
   (A) in　　(B) by　　(C) on　　(D) under

解答:

> 1. (B)　　2. (C)　　3. (B)　　4. (C)　　5. (C)

Lesson 19

Blame It on Men
都怪男人

Reading
閱　　讀

What's the real reason women get fat? It's not chocolate or ice cream. According to a recent report which was published in London, it's men! A magazine suggested men have a special warning written on their foreheads: "I can make you fat!" What do you think of that idea?

The report claims that when women fall in love, they tend to eat more. When they get married, they cook more. And when they get pregnant, of course, they gain weight. They blame it on men. So, girls, if you want to lose weight, you don't have to go on a diet; just dump your boyfriends!

　　女性發胖的真正原因是什麼？並不是巧克力或冰淇淋。根據一份最近在倫敦出版的報告指出——是男人！有一本雜誌建議男人應該在額頭寫上一則特別的警語：『我可以使妳發胖！』你認為那個主意如何？

　　該報告中說女人一旦墜入情網就往往會吃得比較多，她們結婚後煮菜會煮得比較多，而她們懷孕後體重當然會增加。她們把這怪到男人頭上。因此，各位小姐，如果妳們要減肥，不必節食；只要把男友甩掉就行了！

Vocabulary & Idioms
單字 & 片語註解

1. **blame** [blem] vt. 責備; 歸咎
   blame + 事 + on + 人　　因某事責備某人; 將某事歸咎於某人
   = blame + 人 + for + 事
   例: The student blamed the teacher for failing the exam.
   (那個學生把考試不及格歸咎於老師。)

2. **fat** [fæt] a. 肥胖的 & n. 脂肪 (不可數)
   fatty [ˈfætɪ] a. 油膩的, 脂肪過多的
   fattening [ˈfætənɪŋ] a. 令人發胖的
   例: If you want to be slim, don't eat too much fat.
   (如果你想要身材苗條的話，別吃得太油膩。)

   Eating fatty foods makes you fat.
   (吃油膩的食物會令你發胖。)

   French fries are fattening.
   (薯條會令人發胖。)

3. **chocolate** ['tʃɔkəlɪt] n. 巧克力 (不可數)

例: The boy got sick from eating too much chocolate.
(那個男孩因為吃了太多巧克力而生病。)

4. **ice cream** ['aɪs ˌkrim] n. 冰淇淋 (不可數)

a scoop of ice cream 　一杓冰淇淋

a gallon of ice cream 　一加侖冰淇淋

＊ scoop [skup] n. 杓子

＊ gallon ['gælən] n. 加侖 (容量單位)

注意:

在美國購買冰淇淋時, 常用的單位是 gallon。

5. **according to...** 　根據……

例: According to this map, we are far from our destination.
(根據這張地圖，我們離目的地還很遠。)

6. **publish** ['pʌblɪʃ] vt. 出版

例: It took us six months to publish our first book.
(我們花六個月的時間出版第一本書。)

7. **magazine** [ˌmægəˈzin] n. 雜誌

8. **warning** ['wɔrnɪŋ] n. 警語; 警告

例: The policeman gave us a warning not to drive too fast.
(那個警察警告我們車不要開得太快。)

9. **forehead** ['fɔrˌhɛd] n. 前額

例: The pebble hit the boy on the forehead.
(那顆小石子打中那個男孩的額頭。)

　＊pebble ['pɛbḷ] n. 小 (圓) 石

10. 本文:

A magazine suggested men have a special warning written on their foreheads:"..."

有一本雜誌建議男人應該在額頭寫上一則特別的警語……

注意:

此處的 suggest 表『建議』, 之後的 that 子句句構為 "(that) men <u>should</u> <u>have</u> a special warning <u>written</u> on their foreheads:"...", should 可省略, have 是使役動詞, 譯成『把』, 句型為 "have + 受詞 + 過去分詞" (把…… 被……), 故此處 written 是過去分詞。

例: I'll have my car washed.
(我會把車送洗。)

11. **claim** [klem] vt. 宣稱, 聲言

claim + that 子句　　宣稱……

例: Kenny claims that he can run as fast as Carl Lewis.
(肯尼宣稱他可以跑得跟卡爾‧路易士一樣快。)

12. **fall in love**　　墜入情網

例: Tom met a beautiful girl and fell in love for the first time.
(湯姆遇到了一位漂亮的女孩而生平第一次墜入愛河。)

13. **tend to** + 原形動詞　　有……的傾向; 易於……; 往往……

例: The woman tends to exaggerate how bad her husband is.
(那個女人往往誇大其辭地說她先生有多壞。)

＊exaggerate [ɪgˋzædʒəˌret] vt. 誇大, 誇張

14. **pregnant** [ˋprɛgnənt] a. 懷孕的

例: The pregnant woman threw up on the bus.
(那位孕婦在公車上嘔吐。)

15. **weight** [wet] n. 體重

gain weight　　發胖; 體重增加

＝ put on weight

lose weight　　變瘦; 體重減輕

例: Mr. Wang has gained a lot of weight since he got married.
(王先生自從結婚之後胖了很多。)

You don't have to go on a diet to lose weight.
(你不需要靠節食來減肥。)

16. **go on a diet** 節食

diet [ˈdaɪət] n. (規定的) 飲食

例: Sally decided to go on a diet when her beautiful dresses didn't fit her anymore.
(莎莉美麗的洋裝不再合她身時，便決定節食。)

17. **dump** [dʌmp] vt. 傾倒 (垃圾等); 甩掉

注意:

dump 本為把垃圾倒掉之意,而今在俚語中常被用來表示『甩掉/拋棄』異性朋友。

例: We dump our garbage at the collection site every evening.
(我們每天傍晚把垃圾倒在收集場。)

John dumped his girlfriend because she was dishonest.
(約翰把女友給甩了，因為她不誠實。)

Grammar Notes
文 法 重 點

本課介紹關係副詞的用法, 以及動詞 suggest 的用法。

1. **What's the real reason women get fat?**

= What's the real reason why women get fat?
女性發胖的真正原因是什麼？

上列句中的 the real reason 之後省略了關係副詞 why,此處 why 引導的形容詞子句修飾其前的名詞 the real reason。有關關係副詞的用法茲說明如下:

關係副詞共有四個: when、where、why、how。

a. where 用以修飾表地方的名詞。

例: That's the town where I was born.
(那就是我出生的小鎮。)

b. when 用以修飾表時間的名詞。

例: Next Saturday is the day when I am scheduled to leave for America.
(下星期六是我預定前往美國的日子。)

c. why 只用以修飾 the reason (理由)。

例: James was always late for work. That's the reason why he was fired.
(詹姆士上班老是遲到。那就是他被開除的原因。)

d. how 只用以修飾 the way (方式、方法), 但使用時, the way 之後的 how 一定要省略, 如不省略反而會成為贅述。

例: I work two jobs. That's the way I make ends meet.
= I work two jobs. That's how I make ends meet.
(我兼了兩份工作。那就是我使收支平衡的方法。)

然而實際運用關係副詞時, 在限定修飾 (即形容詞子句之前無逗點) 的句構中, when、why 均可省略; 而 how 則非省略不可; where 則不可省略。

例: That's the place where he grew up.
(那就是他成長的地方。)

I shall never forget the day when I first met her.
= I shall never forget the day I first met her.
(我永遠也不會忘記我初次遇見她的那一天。)

Nobody knows the reason why she quit her job.
= Nobody knows the reason she quit her job.
(沒有人知道她辭去工作的原因。)

That's the way how he treats his friends. (✗)
→ That's the way he treats his friends. (○)
(那就是他的待友之道。)

不過 where、when、why 及 how 所修飾的名詞若置於 be 動詞之後作主詞補語時, 我們亦可省略該名詞, 而保留關係副詞。

例: That's <u>the place</u> <u>where</u> we first met each other.

= That's <u>where</u> we first met each other.
(那就是我倆初次見面的地方。)

That's <u>the day</u> <u>when</u> my son graduated from college.

= That's <u>when</u> my son graduated from college.
(那就是我兒子大學畢業的那天。)

That's <u>the reason</u> <u>why</u> I am angry.

= That's <u>why</u> I am angry.
(那就是我生氣的原因。)

That's <u>the way</u> Carl makes tea.

= That's <u>how</u> Carl makes tea.
(那就是卡爾泡茶的方法。)

2. **A magazine suggested men have a special warning written on their foreheads: "I can make you fat!"**

= A magazine suggested <u>that</u> men <u>should</u> have a special warning written on their foreheads: "I can make you fat!"
有一本雜誌建議男人應該在額頭寫上一則特別的警語:『我可以使妳發胖！』

suggest [səgˋdʒɛst] vt. 建議; 暗示, 示意

suggest + (that) 子句　　建議……; 暗示/示意……

注意:

suggest 後接 that 引導的名詞子句(that 可省略)作受詞時, 有下列兩種情況:

a. suggest 作『建議』時, 為一意志動詞, 故其後 that 子句中須使用助動詞 should, 但 should 往往予以省略, 而直接接原形動詞。意志動詞計有下列:

建議: suggest, recommend, advise, urge, propose, move。

要求: ask, desire, demand, require, request。

命令: order, command。

規定: rule, regulate, stipulate, prescribe。

主張: insist, advocate, maintain。

例: I propose that we (should) continue this meeting tomorrow.
(我建議我們明天再繼續開會。)

I demand that you (should) get the manager of this restaurant here right now.
(我要你馬上將餐廳經理找來。)

The law rules that youngsters under the age of 18 (should) not be allowed to drive a car.
(法律規定未滿十八歲的年輕人不可開車。)

b. suggest 若作『暗示、示意』時, 則其後 that 子句中的動詞用一般時態。

例: Bob's attitude suggested (that) he was fed up with his job.
(鮑勃的態度暗示著他對工作厭煩了。)

Substitution
代　　換

What's the real reason women get fat?

This is the place where they first met.

Midnight is the time everyone wishes each other "Happy New Year."

女性變胖的真正原因是什麼？

這是他們初次見面的地方。

午夜是大家互祝『新年快樂』的時刻。

Lesson 20
A Weighty Problem
『沈重』的負擔

Dialogue
實用會話

Eve and Adam are talking.

(E = Eve; A = Adam)

E: Do you know I've put on 5 kilos since going out with you?

A: Why's that?

E: You're always taking me to fancy restaurants.

A: Well, you don't have to eat so much when we eat out, you know.

E: But I can't resist all the delicious food.

A: Besides, it's not cheap.

E: I guess you're right. Maybe I should start cooking again. (Adam turns pale.)

A: Uh...Let's just forget about your weight problem, OK? I don't care how fat you are.

E: Really?

夏娃和亞當在交談。

夏娃：你知道我開始和你約會以後增加了五公斤嗎？

亞當：怎麼會這樣呢？

夏娃：你每次都帶我上豪華的餐館。

亞當：呃，妳知道的嘛，我們出去吃的時候妳可以不必吃那麼多啊。

夏娃：但是我抗拒不了那些美食的誘惑。

亞當：況且那樣吃一次也不便宜。

夏娃：我想你說得對。也許我應該再開始煮飯。(亞當的臉色變得蒼白。)

亞當：呃……我們把妳過重的問題忘掉好不好？我才不在乎妳有多胖。

夏娃：真的嗎？

Key Points
重點提示

1. **weighty** [ˈwetɪ] a. 沈重的; 重大的

   例: Eddie looks like he has a weighty problem on his mind.
   (艾迪看起來心事重重。)

2. **put on + 重量**　　增加……(重量)

= gain + 重量

   例: After giving up smoking, Greg put on 5 kilos in one month.
   (葛雷格在戒煙之後，一個月內重了五公斤。)

3. **kilo** [ˈkɪlo] n. 公斤

= kilogram [ˈkɪləˌgræm]

4. **fancy** [ˈfænsɪ] a. 高級的; 花俏的, 別緻或奇特的

   例: I don't trust people who wear fancy clothes.
   (我不信任穿著花俏的人。)

5. **eat out**　在外頭用餐

　例: We can only afford to eat out once a week.
　　(我們只負擔得起一星期在外面用餐一次。)

6. **resist** [rɪ'zɪst] vt. 抗拒

　例: The little boy can't resist hamburgers.
　　(那個小男孩抗拒不了漢堡的誘惑。)

7. **delicious** [dɪ'lɪʃəs] a. 好吃的, 美味的

　例: My mother makes the most delicious apple pies.
　　(我母親做的蘋果派最好吃。)

8. **cheap** [tʃip] a. 便宜的

　inexpensive [ˌɪnɪk'spɛnsɪv] a. 不貴的

　expensive [ɪk'spɛnsɪv] a. 昂貴的

　注意:

　a. cheap 通常指物品價格低廉, 且品質低劣; 而 inexpensive 則指東西不貴, 但品質未必很差。

　b. 上述三字用來修飾物品, 而不可修飾價錢; 價錢的昂貴或便宜要用 high 或 low 來修飾。

　　例: This car is cheap.
　　　(這輛車子很便宜。──亦指品質低劣)

　　　This dress is inexpensive.
　　　(這件洋裝不貴。──未指出品質之優劣)

　　　The price of the apartment is expensive. (✗)

　　→ The price of the apartment is high. (○)
　　　(這間公寓價格昂貴。)

9. **turn + 表情緒或顏色的形容詞**　變成……

　例: When he saw his ex-wife, he turned pale.
　　(當他看到前妻時，臉色變得很蒼白。)

　　Father's hair is turning gray.

(爸爸的頭髮逐漸變白了。)

10. **pale** [pel] a. 蒼白的

例: The sick man looks pale.
(那個病人臉色看起來很蒼白。)

11. **care** [kɛr] vt. 在乎

care + 疑問詞 (how、what、where...)引導的名詞子句　　在乎……

例: Lisa doesn't care where her husband goes or what he does.
(莉莎並不在乎丈夫去哪裏或做什麼。)

 請選出下列各句中正確的一項

1. Since working in the restaurant, Peter has _____ a lot of weight.
   (A) put in　　(B) put off　　(C) put on　　(D) put away

2. On Mother's Day we usually _____ instead of having dinner at home.
   (A) cook　　(B) stay in　　(C) eat in　　(D) eat out

3. Tina _____ pale when she thought she saw a ghost.
   (A) changed　(B) turned　　(C) got　　(D) became

4. Ron doesn't _____ what people say about him.
   (A) dare　　(B) matter　　(C) care　　(D) resist

5. Do you know _____ hard it is to make money nowadays?
   (A) what　　(B) why　　(C) how　　(D) which

解答:

1. (C)　　2. (D)　　3. (B)　　4. (C)　　5. (C)

Lesson 21
Coffee Bathing
咖啡浴

Reading
閱　讀

　　When the Japanese ask you, "Would you like some coffee?" think twice before you answer. In Japan, it is quite popular to have a "coffee bath." For about US$20, you can get a ground coffee bath; that is, they "boil" you in coffee. The coffee smells good, but you'll probably feel the heat. It sounds like fun, doesn't it?

　　Well, the Japanese don't do it for fun. They believe it helps cure diseases. Who knows? Maybe it's true. But in spite of what they say, I'll just take my coffee in a cup, thank you.

　　當日本人問你：『要來點咖啡嗎？』你要三思之後再回答。在日本洗『咖啡浴』是很風行的。大約美金二十塊，你就可以洗一個研磨咖啡澡；也就是說，他們會把你放在咖啡裡『煮』。 咖啡聞起來很香，但是你大概會感覺到它的熱度。聽起來好像很好玩，不是嗎？

　　而日本人不是為了好玩去洗的。他們相信洗咖啡浴有助於治療疾病。誰曉得呢？或許是真的。但拜託，不管他們怎麼說，我只要喝裝在杯子裏的咖啡就行了。

Vocabulary & Idioms
單字 & 片語註解

1. **coffee** [ˈkɔfɪ] n. 咖啡

   fix/make/prepare coffee for + 人　　為某人沖泡咖啡

   例: Mom fixes a cup of coffee for Dad every morning before he goes to work.
   (老媽每天早上在老爸上班前都會為他沖泡一杯咖啡。)

2. **bathe** [beð] vi. 洗澡; 浸洗

   bath [bæθ] n. 沐浴, 洗澡

   have/take a bath　　泡澡; 浸浴

   take a shower　　淋浴

   例: I bathe at least twice a day in summer.
   (我夏天一天至少洗兩次澡。)

   The poor beggar can't remember the last time he had a bath.
   (那個可憐的乞丐記不得上次洗澡是什麼時候。)

   Dad sings every time he takes a shower.
   (老爸每次淋浴時都會唱歌。)

3. **think twice**　　三思, 再三考慮

   例: Think twice before you go bungee jumping.
   (你要去高空彈跳前請三思。)

4. **popular** [ˈpɑpjələ] a. 受歡迎的; 流行的

be popular with...　　受……歡迎

be popular among...　　在……之間受歡迎

例: Cute Ben is very popular with the girls.
(可愛的班很受那些女孩的歡迎。)

Our magazine is very popular among students.
(我們的雜誌很受學生歡迎。)

5. **that is, ...**　　換言之／也就是說, ……

= that is to say, ...

= in other words, ...

例: John's coming to pick you up at 6 p.m.; in other words, be ready by then.
(約翰下午六點會來接你; 換句話說, 到時候要準備好。)

6. **ground coffee**　　研磨咖啡

ground [graʊnd] a. 被研磨的 & n. 地面

grind [graɪnd] vt. 磨碎

動詞三態: grind、 ground、ground。

＊ 本文 ground 為過去分詞作形容詞用。

例: Some people grind their teeth while sleeping.
(有些人睡覺時會磨牙。)

The boy fell from his bike and knocked his head on the ground.
(那個男孩從腳踏車上摔下來頭撞到地上。)

7. **boil** [bɔɪl] vt. 使沸騰, 煮沸

boiled [bɔɪld] a. 煮 (沸) 過的

boiling [ˈbɔɪlɪŋ] a. 沸騰的

boiled water　　開水

boiling water　　正在沸騰的水

注意:

表『開水』時, 英文應譯為"boiled water", 不可譯為"boiling water"。
boiling water 表『正在沸騰的水』, 喝下去後整個食道會變豬大腸, 故切記『喝開水』絕不可說成"drink boiling water"。

例: He's so stupid that he can't even boil an egg right.
(他笨得連煮個蛋都煮不好。)

I prefer boiled water to bottled mineral water.
(我比較喜歡喝白開水而不喜歡喝瓶裝礦泉水。)

We always have boiling water at home in case someone wants some hot coffee.
(我們家裏總是有熱水以備萬一有人想喝熱咖啡。)

8. **cure** [kjʊr] vt. 治療; 使痊癒

cure + 疾病　　治療/癒某疾病

cure + 人 + of + 疾病　　治癒某人的疾病

例: This herb is said to cure cancer.
(據說這種草藥可以治好癌症。)

The doctors cured her of asthma.
(那些醫生治好了她的氣喘。)
* asthma [ˈæsmə] n. 氣喘

9. **in spite of...**　　不管/儘管……

= despite...

例: In spite of his objection, we bought Tom a TV for his birthday.
(儘管湯姆反對，我們還是買了一台電視送給他當生日禮物。)

Grammar Notes
文法重點

本課介紹介詞 for 表『當作』的用法, 及動詞 help 的用法。

1. <u>For</u> about US$20, you can get a ground coffee bath; that is, they "boil" you in coffee.

   大約美金二十塊，你就可以洗一個研磨咖啡澡；也就是說，他們會把你放在咖啡裡『煮』。

   上列句中的介詞 for 表示『當作……的價值』之意，有『等價值交換』的概念，之後接表金錢的名詞，用來表示『價格』。

   例: I bought this book <u>with</u> fifty dollars. (✗)

   → I bought this book <u>for</u> fifty dollars. (○)
      (這本書我是用五十塊錢買的。／我買了這本書當作五十塊錢的價值。)

      <u>With</u> only fifty dollars, you can take in two movies in that theater.
      (✗, 此處會誤解為『你跟五十元可一塊兒在那家戲院一次看兩部電影。』)

   → <u>For</u> only fifty dollars, you can take in two movies in that theater. (○)
      (只要五十塊錢，你就可以在那家戲院一次看兩部電影。)

   注意:

   表『吃……當作早/午/晚餐』的介詞亦用 for 來表示。

   例: What would you like to eat <u>for</u> dinner?
      (你晚餐想吃什麼？／你想吃什麼當作晚餐？)

      Peter had a big steak <u>for</u> lunch.
      (彼得午餐吃了一塊很大的牛排。)

   比較:

be <u>at</u>	breakfast	在吃	早	餐
	lunch		午	
	dinner		晚	

   例: We <u>were at breakfast</u> when the telephone rang.

   = We <u>were having breakfast</u> when the telephone rang.
      (我們正在吃早餐這時電話鈴響了。)

2. **They believe it <u>helps cure</u> diseases.**
他們相信洗咖啡浴有助於治療疾病。

有關動詞 help 的重要用法如下:

a. help + (to) + 原形動詞　　幫助/忙……

＊上列句中的 help 即屬此用法。

例: Mother wants me to <u>help (to) do</u> the dishes.
(媽媽要我幫忙洗碗盤。)

　Could you <u>help (to) correct</u> this composition?
(你可以幫忙改這篇作文嗎?)

故: They believe it <u>helps cure</u> diseases.
= They believe (that) it <u>helps to cure</u> diseases.

b. help + 人 + (to) + 原形動詞　　幫某人……

例: Little Johnny <u>helped his father (to) wash</u> the car.
(小強尼幫爸爸洗車子。)

　My friends <u>helped me (to) paint</u> my new house.
(我朋友幫忙我油漆新房子。)

c. help with + 名詞　　幫助/忙……

例: Tom agreed to <u>help with our plan</u>.
(湯姆同意幫助我們的計畫。)

　Father never <u>helps with the housework</u>.
(老爸從來不幫忙做家事。)

d. help + 人 + with + 名詞　　幫某人……

例: My older brother always helps me with my homework.
(我哥哥總是幫我做家庭作業。)

　In the beginning, the manager had to help the new worker with his job.
(剛開始的時候,經理得幫助那位新進員工做他的工作。)

Substitution
代　　換

1. **For about US$20, you can get a ground coffee bath.**

   For a small sum of money, you can be a shareholder of this company.

   You can get this painting for next to nothing.

   大約美金二十塊, 你就可以洗一個研磨咖啡澡。

   花一小筆錢, 你就可以成為這家公司的股東。

   你幾乎不用花錢就可以得到這幅畫。

   * 此處的 next to 等於 almost (幾乎)。

2. **They believe it helps cure diseases.**

   A piece of ice can help lessen the pain.

   This cream will help stop the bleeding.

   他們相信洗咖啡浴有助於治療疾病。

   一塊冰塊有助於減輕疼痛。

   這藥膏將有助於止血。

Lesson 22
Whiskey or Coffee?
威士忌還是咖啡？

Dialogue
實用會話

Jack and his Japanese friend, Norie, are on their way home from school.

(N = Norie; J = Jack)

N: What a hard day I had at school! I feel like having a coffee or something.

J: Me, too.

N: Let's go to Rick's Coffee Shop.

J: That sounds good. (They are at the coffee shop.)

N: What kind of coffee do you like?

J: I feel like having an Irish coffee.

N: OK. I'll have the same. (After two cups Norie is drunk.) Why am I feeling tipsy?

J: There's whiskey in Irish coffee, you know.

N: Why didn't you tell me? Boy, it can be dangerous to have a simple cup of coffee with an American.

傑克和他的日本朋友則惠正在從學校返家的途中。

則惠：今天在學校過得好辛苦！我想要喝杯咖啡或什麼的。

傑克：我也是。

則惠：那我們去瑞克咖啡館吧。

傑克：聽起來不錯。(他們在咖啡館裏面。)

則惠：你喜歡喝哪種咖啡？

傑克：我想來杯愛爾蘭咖啡。

則惠：好吧。我也要一樣的。（喝完兩杯後則惠就醉了。）為什麼我覺得有點醉？

傑克：妳知道的，愛爾蘭咖啡裏有加威士忌。

則惠：你為什麼沒跟我講呢？天啊，連和美國人喝杯咖啡都可能會有危險。

Key Points
重點提示

1. **whiskey** [ˈhwɪskɪ] n. 威士忌酒 (不可數)

2. **coffee** [ˈkɔfɪ] n. 咖啡

   注意:

   coffee本為不可數名詞,『一杯咖啡』應譯為"a cup of coffee", 但在現代美語中, coffee 常被視為可數名詞, 因此『一杯咖啡』、『兩杯咖啡』便可譯為"a coffee"、"two coffees"。類似用法的名詞尚有 beer (啤酒)、milk (牛奶)、coke (可樂)等。

   例: How about going for a coffee after work?
   (下班後去喝杯咖啡怎麼樣？)

   Dad likes to have a beer while reading.
   (老爸喜歡看書邊喝啤酒。)

3. **on one's way** + 地方副詞　　某人往某地途中

   on one's way to + 地方名詞　　某人往某地途中

   in one's way　　擋了某人的路

注意:

地方副詞指的是 home、downtown、here、there 等; 地方名詞則為 school、train station 等。

例: On my way downtown I saw a terrible car accident.
(我往市區途中目睹了一場可怕的車禍。)

On my way to the movie theater, I ran into my boss.
(我去電影院的途中遇到老闆。)

I missed my stop because there were too many people in my way on the bus.
(因為公車上有太多人擋住我的路,因此我錯過了站。)

4. **feel like** + 動名詞　　想要……

例: Mary feels like taking a trip to Paris.
(瑪麗想去巴黎旅遊。)

5. **Irish** ['aɪrɪʃ] a. 愛爾蘭 (人) 的;愛爾蘭語的

6. **drunk** [drʌŋk] a. 喝醉的

例: The man was fined for drunk driving.
(那個人因為酒醉駕車而被罰鍰。)

7. **tipsy** ['tɪpsɪ] a. 微醉的

例: Jenny felt tipsy after only one beer.
(珍妮只喝了一罐啤酒就覺得有點醉意。)

請選出下列各句中正確的一項

1. John is so tired that he doesn't feel like _____ anything but sleep.
   (A) to do   (B) having to do (C) doing   (D) to have done

2. Larry felt _____ after a glass of whiskey.
   (A) like drunk (B) like to drink (C) tipsy   (D) happily

3. Mr. Chen sold his car _____ $10,000.
   (A) with   (B) to   (C) for   (D) about

4. Could you please help me _____ this heavy luggage?
   (A) carry   (B) with carry   (C) carrying   (D) with carrying

解答:

> 1. (C)   2. (C)   3. (C)   4. (A)

Lesson 23

Earthquake Survival Tips
地震時如何自保

Reading
閱　讀

　　Would you know what to do during a really big earthquake? Experts have looked into the matter carefully. It may be worth your while to look over the following tips they have for us.

　　If the ground begins shaking while you are driving, pull over and stay in your car. If you are in a building, try to get near a strong wall. The corner of a room or the space under a doorway is the safest. As soon as the quake is over, check the gas pipe in the building. Gas fires often result from earthquakes. These tips may prove to be lifesavers. We should, therefore, keep them

in mind. Remember to always hope for the best but prepare for the worst.

你知道在巨大的地震發生時該怎麼辦嗎？專家對此作了深入的研究。以下他們所提供給我們的小建議或許值得您看一看。

如果您在開車時，地面開始搖晃，把車開到路邊並待在車裡面。如果您在建築物裡面，設法到堅固的牆壁邊。房間的角落或門框的正下方是最安全的。地震一旦停止，立刻檢查建築物內的瓦斯管。瓦斯造成的火災通常是由地震引起的。這些小建議或許能救您一命。因此，我們應該將它們謹記在心。記住要永遠抱最大的希望但作最壞的打算。

Vocabulary & Idioms
單字 & 片語註解

1. **earthquake** [ˈɝθˌkwek] n. 地震 (亦可簡寫成 quake [kwek])

2. **survival** [səˈvaɪvl̩] n. 生存

   survive [səˈvaɪv] vi. 生存 & vt. 熬過, 從……生還

   例: For many people, survival is their only goal in life.
   (對許多人來說，生存是他們一生唯一的目標。)

   Though many people were killed in the disaster, a few people survived.
   (雖然有許多人在那次災難中喪生，仍有一些人存活。)

   John survived the auto accident.
   (約翰從那次車禍中生還。)

3. **tip** [tɪp] n. 提示, 建議 (可數); 小費

   give + 人 + a tip + on + 事　　在某事上給某人建議

   = give + 人 + advice + on + 事

＊ advice [əd'vaɪs] n. 忠告, 建議 (不可數)

a piece of advice 　　一則忠告, 一項建議

例: Linda gave Carlos some | tips | on how to quit smoking.
　　　　　　　　　　　　　　| advice |

(琳達就如何戒煙給了卡洛士一些建議。)

I gave the taxi driver US$1.00 as a tip.
(我給了那名計程車司機一塊美金作為小費。)

4. expert ['ɛkspɝt] n. 專家 & a. 熟練的, 專門的

be expert in... 　　對……熟練/專門

= be skilled in...

例: Mr. Brown is an underline{expert} in operating a computer.
　　　　　　　　　　　　名詞

(布朗先生在操作電腦方面是個專家。)

Mr. Brown is underline{expert} in operating a computer.
　　　　　　　　　形容詞

(布朗先生對操作電腦很在行。)

5. look into... 　　研究/調查……

例: The mayor promised to look into the scandal.
(市長答應要調查那椿醜聞。)

＊ scandal ['skændḷ] n. 醜聞

6. It is worth one's while to + 原形動詞 　　值得某人……

It is worthwhile | to + 原形動詞 | ……很值得/有用
　　　　　　　　　| + 動名詞 |

worth [wɝθ] prep. 值得

worthwhile [ˌwɝθ'hwaɪl] a. 值得做的, 有用的

例: It's worth your while to see a play like this.
(像這樣的一齣戲值得你觀賞。)

Jim's stamp collection is worth US$5,000.
(吉姆的郵票收藏價值五千美金。)

Your proposal is worth considering.
(你的提議值得考慮。)

   * proposal [prə'pozl] n. 提議, 建議

It's worthwhile | to take | his advice.
            | taking |

(聽從他的勸告是值得的。)

7. **look over...**   過目/大略看一看……

  例: Can you help me look over my homework before I hand it in?
    (在我繳交家庭作業前,你能幫我看一下嗎?)

8. **shake** [ʃek] vi & vt. 震動; 搖動

動詞三態: shake、shook [ʃuk]、shaken ['ʃekən]。

  例: Shake the bottle before you drink the milk.
    (喝牛奶前先把瓶子搖一搖。)

9. **pull over**   (把車) 開到路邊 (口語用法)

  例: When you hear an ambulance behind you, you should pull over.
    (當你聽到車子後面有救護車的聲音時,應該把車開到路邊。)
    * ambulance ['æmbjələns] n. 救護車

10. **corner** ['kɔrnɚ] n. 角落

in the corner   在 (空間內的) 角落

on/at the corner   在轉角處

around/round the corner   在轉角附近

  例: The teacher told the naughty student to stand in the corner.
    (老師叫那名頑皮的學生到角落裡站著。)

There's a convenience store at the corner of these two streets.
(在這兩條街道的轉角處有家便利商店。)

There's a bank just around the corner.
(有一家銀行就在轉角附近。)

11. **doorway** ['dɔr,we] n. 門口

12. **gas pipe** [ˈgæs ˌpaɪp] n. 瓦斯管線

13. **result from...**　　起因於……
   例: Success results from hard work.
   (成功出自於努力。)

14. **prove to be...**　　被發現是/結果是……
 = turn out to be...
   例: The weakest player on the team proved to be the hero.
   (隊中最弱的選手結果成為英雄。)

15. **lifesaver** [ˈlaɪfˌsevɚ] n. 救命者

16. **keep/bear...in mind**　　將……牢記在心
   keep/bear in mind + that 子句　　將…牢記在心
   例: I always keep my father's advice in mind.
   (我始終牢記父親的忠告。)

   You must keep in mind that not everyone is as honest as you.
   (你必須牢記並非每個人都像你一樣誠實。)

17. **hope for the best but prepare for the worst**
   抱最大希望但作最壞的打算
   例: A: Do you think there are any survivors of the plane crash?
   B: Let's hope for the best but prepare for the worst.
   (甲：你認為這次空難有任何生還者嗎？)
   (乙：咱們就抱最大希望但作最壞打算吧。)
   ＊ survivor [səˈvaɪvɚ] n. 生還者

Grammar Notes
文 法 重 點

本課介紹名詞片語的用法, 及副詞連接詞 as soon as 的用法。

1. **Would you know <u>what to do</u> during a really big earthquake?**
   你知道在巨大的地震發生時該怎麼辦嗎？

   上列句中的 what to do 稱作名詞片語。所謂名詞片語乃由『疑問詞＋不定詞片語』形成, 如:

when to leave	什麼時候離開
where to go	要去哪裡
how to get there	如何到那裡去
what to do	做什麼
which to take	要拿哪一個
whom to believe	要相信誰
whom to talk to	要跟誰談

   注意:

   a. 上述這些名詞片語中, when、where 及 how 為疑問副詞, 用來修飾其後不定詞片語中的動詞。而 what、which 及 whom 則為疑問代名詞, 故要作其後不定詞片語中及物動詞或介詞的受詞, 因此 what、which、whom 在上列名詞片語中分別作及物動詞 do、take、believe 及介詞 to 的受詞。

   b. 名詞片語因具名詞的功能, 故在句中可作主詞、受詞或置於 be 動詞後作主詞補語。本文中的 what to do 即作及物動詞 know 的受詞。

   例: <u>Where to go on vacation</u> is not decided yet.
   　　　　主詞
   　　(到哪裡度假尚未決定。)

   　　Do you <u>know</u> <u>how to make a cake</u>?
   　　　　及物動詞　　受詞
   　　(你知道怎麼做蛋糕嗎？)

The question <u>is</u> <u>whom to believe</u>.
                主詞補語
(問題是要相信誰才好。)

2. **As soon as the quake is over, check the gas pipe in the building.**
地震一旦停止,立刻檢查建築物內的瓦斯管。

上列句中的 as soon as 是副詞連接詞, 表『一……就……』之意, 其所引導的副詞子句修飾句中的主要子句。as soon as 亦可用 the instant/ moment 來取代, 其句型如下:

As soon as + 主詞 + 動詞, 主要子句   一……就……
= The instant + 主詞 + 動詞, 主要子句
= The moment + 主詞 + 動詞, 主要子句

   例: <u>As soon as</u> I arrived home, it started to pour.
    = <u>The instant</u> I arrived home, it started to pour.
    = <u>The moment</u> I arrived home, it started to pour.
    (我一回到家便下起傾盆大雨。)

   注意:
本句構亦可用下列句型取代:
no sooner...than...
hardly...when (或 before)...
scarcely...before (或 when)...
以上句構均譯為『一……就……』。
造句法:
中文: 海倫一看到蟑螂就尖叫了起來。
第一步:
先造一個過去完成式的句子, 表示先發生的動作。
Helen had seen the cockroach.
第二步:
再造一個過去式的句子, 表示後發生的動作。
She screamed.

第三步:

兩句放在一起。

Helen had seen the cockroach. She screamed.

第四步:

將 no sooner、hardly、scarcely 插入第一句中過去完成式助動詞 had 之後, 再將 than、when、before 置於第二個句子之前, 即:

Helen had <u>no sooner</u> seen the cockroach <u>than</u> she screamed.

海倫先看到蟑螂, 沒有比她後來尖叫快多少。(直譯)

→ 海倫一看到蟑螂就尖叫了起來。(實際翻譯)

Helen had <u>hardly/scarcely</u> seen the cockroach <u>when</u> she screamed.

當海倫尖叫時, 幾乎沒看到蟑螂。(直譯)

→ 海倫一看到蟑螂就尖叫了起來。(實際翻譯)

Helen had <u>hardly/scarcely</u> seen the cockroach <u>before</u> she screamed.

在海倫尖叫之前, 幾乎沒看到蟑螂。(直譯)

→ 海倫一看到蟑螂就尖叫了起來。(實際翻譯)

注意:

由於 no sooner、hardly 及 scarcely 均為否定副詞, 故置於句首時, 其後過去完成式助動詞 had 須與主詞倒裝。故上列例句亦可寫成:

No sooner <u>had Helen</u> seen the cockcroach than she screamed.

= Hardly <u>had Helen</u> seen the cockroach when/before she screamed.

= Scarcely <u>had Helen</u> seen the cockroach when/before she screamed.

Substitution

代　　換

1. Would you know <u>what to do</u> during a really big earthquake?

   Would you know <u>where to go</u> to buy fishing equipment?

   Helen told us <u>when to leave</u> for the party.

   你知道在大地震發生時該怎麼辦嗎？

   你知道在哪兒可以買到魚具嗎？

   海倫告訴我們何時動身參加派對。

2. As soon as the quake is over, check the gas pipe in the building.

   As soon as Dad got home, we had dinner.

   As soon as Ben got a job, he moved out.

   地震一旦停止，立刻檢查建築物內的瓦斯管。

   老爸一到家，我們就吃晚飯。

   阿班一找到工作就搬出去了。

Lesson 24

Just Like a Woman
像個女人一樣

Dialogue
實用會話

Jenny and Andy are having a cup of coffee at a café.

(J = Jenny; A = Andy)

J: Hey, Andy. Did you feel that earthquake yesterday?

A: Sure. I was at work. Some of the women in the office felt dizzy and screamed.

J: You know, the ground shook so violently that I was terrified.

A: That sounds just like how a woman would feel.

J: I guess we women should be brave like you, huh?

A: Of course! (Jenny shakes the table with her leg.) Aaagh! Earthquake! Help! (He gets under the table.)

J: Look at you—I was just playing. You're worse than a woman. You even sounded worse than the women at the office.

A: Uh...I knew it was just a joke. I was only trying to scare you.

J: Ha! I bet!

珍妮和安迪正在一家咖啡館裡喝咖啡。

珍妮：嘿，安迪。你昨天有沒有感覺到那個地震？

安迪：當然有。當時我正在上班。辦公室裡的一些女同事覺得頭昏而尖叫。

珍妮：你也知道嘛，地面晃得那麼厲害把我給嚇壞了。

安迪：聽起來好像女人都會有這種感受。

珍妮：我想我們女人應該像你一樣勇敢囉？

安迪：當然！（珍妮用她的腿搖桌子。）

啊！地震！救命啊！（他鑽到桌子底下。）

珍妮：看看你我只是在開玩笑。你比女人還不如。你叫得比辦公室的女同事還悽慘。

安迪：呃……我知道妳在開玩笑。我只是要嚇嚇妳。

珍妮：哈！是哦！

Key Points
重點提示

1. **café** [kəˈfe] n. 咖啡館; 小吃店

   注意:

   café 通常不僅供應飲料, 也供應些簡單的食物。

2. **at work**　　工作中

   at play　　玩樂中

   例: Tom got fired because he fell asleep at work.
   （湯姆因為工作時睡覺而被解雇。）

   When the children are at play, they can't help being noisy.
   （小孩子在玩耍時，不可能不吵鬧。）

3. **dizzy** [ˈdɪzɪ] a. 昏眩的

   例: The man felt dizzy after jogging for ten minutes.
   （那個男子在慢跑十分鐘後便覺得頭昏。）

4. **scream** [skrim] vi. 尖聲叫喊 & vt. 高聲說出

例: When girls are frightened, they scream.
(女孩受驚時會尖叫。)

Little Billy screamed himself sick.
(小比利大聲尖叫說他生病了。)

5. **terrified** [ˈtɛrəˌfaɪd] a. 感到恐懼的 (修飾人)

terrifying [ˈtɛrəˌfaɪɪŋ] a. 可怕的; 令人恐懼的 (修飾事物)

terrify [ˈtɛrəˌfaɪ] vt. 使恐懼; 嚇壞

be terrified of...　　害怕……

= be afraid of...

= be frightened of...

例: My mother is terrified of rats.
(我媽媽怕老鼠。)

Riding on a roller coaster is terrifying.
(坐雲霄飛車令人心驚膽戰。)

　＊ roller coaster [ˈrolɚ ˌkostɚ] n. 雲霄飛車

The kidnappers terrified the poor boy.
(綁匪嚇壞了那個可憐的男孩。)

　＊ kidnapper [ˈkɪdnæpɚ] n. 綁匪

6. **brave** [brev] a. 勇敢的

例: The brave boy jumped into the lake to save the old man.
(那個勇敢的男孩跳到湖裡去救那名老翁。)

7. **scare** [skɛr] vt. 驚嚇

scare ＋ 人 ＋ to death　　把某人嚇得要死

例: Your shadow scared me to death.
(你的影子把我嚇得半死。)

8. **I bet!**　　我確信!

＊ bet [bɛt] vi. 原指『打賭』, 此表『確信』

注意:

"I bet!"本為『我確信!』之意, 但在本句中為反諷的說法; 用以表達對於對方所發表的言論表示懷疑, 譯成『怎麼會/不可能/才怪』或『鬼才相信!』。

例: A: I can eat ten bowls of noodles in a minute.

B: I bet!

(甲:我一分鐘可以吃十碗麵。)

(乙:才怪!)

請選出下列各句中正確的一項

1. The police are _____ the murder.

   (A) looking for   (B) looking up

   (C) looking into   (D) looking on

2. The policeman in the police car next to us told us to _____.

   (A) stop over   (B) put up   (C) pull over   (D) push up

3. Let me give you some _____ on studying English.

   (A) tips   (B) advices

   (C) piece of tips   (D) piece of advices

4. If you can _____ in mind all these rules, you'll have no problem.

   (A) stay   (B) keep   (C) put   (D) remember

解答:

> 1. (C)   2. (C)   3. (A)   4. (B)

Lesson 25
Restaurant Do's and Don'ts
餐廳禮節

Reading
閱　讀

When you want to eat at a Western restaurant, you should first consider making a reservation. If not, you risk having to wait for a long time for a table.

When eating, the Japanese and some Chinese are in the habit of slurping their food. By doing so, they show their host how much they like the food. Westerners find eating soup this way most unpleasant. They also consider picking one's teeth and putting on makeup at the table no-nos. And when it comes to tipping, they just leave some money on the table. The amount is up to you, but it's usually 15 to 20 percent of the check.

　　當你想到西餐廳用餐時，應該考慮先訂位。否則你就要冒上枯等桌位的風險。

　　用餐時，日本人和一些中國人有吃東西出聲的習慣。這麼做是向主人表示他們有多麼喜歡那些菜餚。西方人覺得這種喝湯法會令人非常不愉快。他們還認為在餐桌上剔牙和上妝很要不得。而說到給小費，他們就把一點錢留在餐桌上，給多少由你自己決定，但通常都是帳單的百分之十五到二十。

Vocabulary & Idioms
單字 & 片語註解

1. **do's and don'ts**　　該做和不該做的事; 注意事項

   例: First, you have to learn the do's and don'ts of scuba diving.
   (首先，你得學習深海潛水的守則。)

2. **Western restaurant**　　西餐廳

   western ['wɛstən] a. 西方的

   注意:

   western 若指『西邊方向的』則無須大寫, 但若特指『西洋的』、『歐美的』或『美國西部的』, W 須用大寫, 即 Western, 如: Western civilization (西洋文明)、Western nation (西方國家)。

   例: Your way of doing business is not acceptable in Western nations.
   (你做生意的方式在西方國家是行不通的。)

   Vancouver is a city in western Canada.
   (溫哥華是位於加拿大西部的一個城市。)

3. **make a reservation (for...)**　　預約/訂 (座位、房間等)

   = make a booking (for...)

   reservation [ˌrɛzəˈveʃən] n. 保留; 預約, 預訂

   reserve [rɪˈzɜv] vt. 保留; 預約, 預訂

= book [bʊk] vt.

例: If you want to eat at that restaurant, you'll have to make a reservation for a table.
(如果你想在那家餐廳用餐，就得先訂桌位。)

I'll be late for the dinner party tonight. Can you reserve a seat next to you for me?
(今晚的晚宴我會晚點到。你可不可以幫我在你旁邊留個位子給我？)

4. **be in the habit of...**　有……的習慣

habit [ˈhæbɪt] n. 習慣

例: The boy is in the habit of drinking a glass of milk before he goes to bed.
(那個男孩習慣在上床睡覺前喝一杯牛奶。)

5. **slurp** [slɝp] vt. 飲食出聲

slurp one's food　吃/喝食物發出聲音

例: Can you imagine how noisy it would be if everyone slurped his food at dinner?
(你能想像如果每個人晚餐時都吃出聲音的話，那會有多吵嗎？)

6. **By doing so,...**　(藉由) 這麼做，……

例: You should stay persevering in learning English. By doing so, you'll master this language someday.
(你學英文應執著。這麼做的話，總有一天你會把英文學得很精。)
＊ persevering [ˌpɝsəˈvɪrɪŋ] a. 執著的

7. **host** [host] n. (男) 主人 & vt. 主辦

hostess [ˈhostɪs] n. 女主人

例: Our host entertained us with slides of his trip to Hawaii.
(招待我們的主人把他在夏威夷旅行所拍的幻燈片放給我們欣賞。)
＊ slide [slaɪd] n. 幻燈片

My dad hosted a dinner for his overseas customers.
(我老爸招待他的外國客戶吃晚餐。)

8. **Westerner** [ˈwɛstɚnɚ] n. 西方人士

9. **soup** [sup] n. 湯 (不可數)

    eat soup   喝湯

    a bowl of soup   一碗湯

* **bowl** [bol] n. 碗

    注意:

    表『喝湯』須用 "eat soup" 來表示, 也許是因為外國人的湯中固體食物較多之故, 因此『喝湯』的動詞須用 eat, 而非 drink。

10. **unpleasant** [ʌnˈplɛznt] a. 令人不愉快的

    pleasant [ˈplɛznt] a. 令人愉快的

    例: What's that unpleasant smell coming from the toilet?
    (廁所傳來的是什麼怪味？)

    I had a pleasant time at my parents-in-law's house in the mountains.
    (我在岳父母山區的家裡玩得很愉快。)

11. **pick one's teeth**   剔牙

    pick one's nose   挖鼻孔

    例: The man picked his teeth with a toothpick.
    (那個人用牙籤剔牙。)

    * toothpick [ˈtuθˌpɪk] n. 牙籤

    Picking your nose in front of others is a bad habit.
    (在別人面前挖鼻孔是個壞習慣。)

12. **put on...**   塗抹……

    例: Dad asked Mom not to put on too much face powder.
    (爸爸叫媽媽不要在臉上撲太多粉。)

13. **makeup** [ˈmekˌʌp] n. 化妝

    cosmetics [kɑzˈmɛtɪks] n. 化妝品(恆用複數)

例: Putting on too much makeup is not good for the skin.
(化粧化得太濃對皮膚不好。)

14. **no-no** [ˈnoˌno] n. 禁止的事物

例: Smoking in a movie theater nowadays is a no-no.
(現今在電影院抽煙是不可以的。)

15. **When it comes to + 名詞/動名詞,...** 　　說到/提到……, ……

例: When it comes to saving money, no one can compare with Peter.
(說到存錢，沒有人比得上彼得。)

16. **be up to + 人** 　　由某人決定

例: A: Where should we go for dinner?
　　B: It's up to you.
(甲：我們該去哪兒吃晚餐？)
(乙：你來決定。)

17. **percent** [pɚˈsɛnt] n. 百分比

例: One percent of <u>the students</u> <u>have passed</u> the exam.
　　　　　　　　可數名詞　　複數動詞
(有百分之一的學生已經通過了考試。)

Ten percent of <u>the gold</u> <u>has been stolen</u>.
　　　　　　　不可數名詞　　單數動詞
(有百分之十的金子被偷走。)

Grammar Notes
文 法 重 點

本課介紹少數及物動詞之後須接動名詞作受詞的用法, 以及 **find** 作不完全及物動詞的用法。

1. **When you want to eat at a Western restaurant, you should first consider making a reservation.**
當你想到西餐廳用餐時, 應該考慮先訂位。

If not, you <u>risk</u> <u>having</u> to wait for a long time for a table.
否則你就要冒上枯等桌位的風險。

They also <u>consider</u> <u>picking</u> one's teeth and <u>putting</u> on makeup at the table no-nos.
他們也認為在餐桌上剔牙和上妝簡直要不得。

以上三句中的 making a reservation、having to wait...、picking one's teeth and putting on makeup 分別作及物動詞 consider 及 risk 的受詞。

注意:

有些及物動詞之後只可接動名詞作受詞, 而不可接不定詞片語作受詞, 常見的如下:

enjoy (喜歡)、deny (否認)、admit (承認)、avoid (避免)、consider (考慮)、practice (練習)、escape (逃避)、risk (冒險)、quit (禁止)、resent (討厭)、suggest (建/提議)、recommend (建議)、mind (在乎) 等。

例: Bill enjoys <u>to read.</u> (✗)
→ Bill enjoys <u>reading.</u> (○)
(比爾喜歡閱讀。)

Little Billy denies <u>to break</u> the vase. (✗)
→ Little Billy denies <u>breaking</u> the vase. (○)
(小比利否認打破了花瓶。)

Little Henry admitted <u>to steal</u> my watch. (✗)
→ Little Henry admitted <u>stealing</u> my watch. (○)
(小亨利承認偷了我的錶。)

We should avoid <u>to judge</u> a person by his appearance. (✗)
→ We should avoid <u>judging</u> a person by his appearance. (○)
(我們應該避免以貌取人。)

Sarah practices <u>to play</u> the guitar two hours a day. (✕)

→ Sarah practices <u>playing</u> the guitar two hours a day. (◯)
(莎拉每天都練習彈吉他兩個小時。)

The brave young man risked <u>to lose</u> his own life to save the drowning girl. (✕)

→ The brave young man risked <u>losing</u> his own life to save the drowning girl. (◯)
(那個勇敢的年輕人冒著生命危險去救那溺水的女孩。)

Peter quit <u>to smoke</u> two years ago. (✕)

→ Peter quit <u>smoking</u> two years ago. (◯)
(彼得兩年前戒煙了。)

Would you mind <u>to open</u> the door for me? (✕)

→ Would you mind <u>opening</u> the door for me? (◯)
(你介意幫我開個門嗎?)

2. **Westerners <u>find</u> <u>eating soup this way</u> <u>most unpleasant.</u>**
   西方人覺得這麼喝湯令人非常不愉快。

   在上列句中, find 是不完全及物動詞, eating soup 是受詞, (in) this way 是副詞片語, 修飾 eating, 而 most unpleasant 則是形容詞, 作受詞補語。所謂不完全及物動詞就是此類動詞加了受詞後, 意思並不完整, 而須在受詞之後另置形容詞或名詞以補充其意思的不足。此時該形容詞或名詞就稱為受詞補語。

   a. find 可作完全及物動詞, 亦可作不完全及物動詞。

   find 作完全及物動詞時, 其後只須加受詞便可使句意完整, 此時 find 譯成『發現、找到』, 之後可接名詞、代名詞或名詞子句作受詞。

   例: The police <u>found</u> <u>the lost child</u>.
   　　　　　　　　　名詞
   (警方找到了那名失蹤的小孩。)

   I <u>found</u> <u>that Tom was a hypocrite</u>.
   　　　　　　名詞子句
   (我發現湯姆是個偽君子。)

＊ hypocrite [ˈhɪpəˌkrɪt] n. 偽善者, 偽君子

find 作不完全及物動詞時, 其後可用名詞、代名詞或動名詞作受詞, 再接形容詞或名詞作受詞補語, 此時 find 譯成『發現/覺得……是……』。

例: I ___found___ ___the businessman___ ___dishonest___.
　　不完全及物動詞　　受詞　　受詞補語
　　(我發現那個商人不誠實。)

　　I ___find___ ___him___ a good salesman.
　　不完全及物動詞　受詞　　受詞補語
　　(我發現他是個很不錯的推銷員。)

　　Tony ___finds___ ___mountain hiking___ ___interesting___.
　　　　不完全及物動詞　　　受詞　　　受詞補語
　　(東尼發現爬山很好玩。)

注意:

find 作不完全及物動詞時, 可直接以名詞或動名詞作受詞, 再接補語; 但不可直接用不定詞片語 (to + 原形動詞) 作受詞, 而要先用虛受詞 it 取代, 加了補語後, 再接不定詞片語, 此不定詞片語才是真受詞。句型如下:

find it + 受詞補語 (形容詞/名詞) + 不定詞片語 (to + 原形動詞)

例: I found ___to work at a record company___ ___exciting___. (✗)
　　　　　　不定詞片語作受詞　　　　受詞補語

→ I found ___it___ exciting ___to work at a record company.___ (○)
　　　　　　虛受詞　　　　　　真受詞
　　(我覺得在唱片公司工作很令人興奮。)

　　Billy found ___to baby-sit his sister all day___ ___a bore___. (✗)
　　　　　　　　不定詞片語作受詞　　　　受詞補語

→ Billy found ___it___ a bore ___to baby-sit his sister___ all day. (○)
　　　　　　　虛受詞　　　　真受詞
　　(比利覺得整天看顧他妹妹很無聊。)

由於 find 可作完全及物動詞, 其後接 that (可省略) 引導的名詞子句作受詞, 故上列兩句亦可寫成:

I found (that) <u>it was</u> exciting to work at a record company.

Billy found (that) <u>it was</u> a bore to baby-sit his sister all day.

b. think、consider、believe 等亦可作不完全及物動詞，think、consider 譯成『認為……是……』，believe 譯成『相信/認為……是……』。

例: I <u>think</u> her a good teacher.
(我認為她是個好老師。)

I <u>consider</u> him generous.
(我認為他很慷慨。)

We believe him trustworthy.
(我們相信他值得信賴。)

如同 find 一樣，think、consider、believe 作不完全及物動詞時，其後不得直接以不定詞片語作受詞，而要先用虛受詞 it 取代，加了受詞補語後，再接此不定詞片語。

例: Nancy thinks <u>it</u> strange <u>to ask a boy out on a date.</u>
　　　　　虛受詞　　　　　真受詞
(南西認為開口邀男孩子約會很奇怪。)

I don't consider <u>it</u> polite <u>to burp in front of others.</u>
　　　　　　虛受詞　　　　真受詞
(我認為在別人面前打嗝是件不禮貌的事。)

* burp [bɝp] vi. (口語) 打嗝

I believe <u>it</u> healthful <u>to go swimming.</u>
　　　虛受詞　　　　真受詞
(我相信游泳有益健康。)

由於 think、consider、believe 亦可作完全及物動詞，其後以 that (可省略) 引導的名詞子句作受詞，故上列例句亦可寫成:

Nancy thinks (that) it is strange to ask a boy out on a date.

I don't consider (that) it is polite to burp in front of others.

I believe (that) it is healthful to go swimming.

1. **You should first consider making a reservation.**

    The accused admitted robbing the bank.

    Nancy wants to avoid bumping into her ex-boyfriend.

    你應該考慮先訂位。

    被告承認搶了銀行。

    南西想避免碰見前任男友。

2. **Westerners find eating soup this way most unpleasant.**

    John finds his job very interesting.

    Jack finds Jane very attractive.

    西方人覺得這麼喝湯令人非常不愉快。

    約翰覺得他的工作非常有趣。

    傑克覺得珍非常吸引人。

Lesson 26
The Missing Tip
失蹤的小費

Dialogue
實用會話

Chen is in America. His American friend, Daisy, suggested having lunch with him at a restaurant.

(C=Chen; D=Daisy)

C: Why's that waiter so angry?

D: Those people who just left didn't seem to give him any tip, which made him angry.

C: Is that absolutely necessary here?

D: Kind of. It's the custom. You can't really avoid leaving at least a small tip.

C: But suppose the service is bad?

D: In that case, of course, we don't leave one.

C: And does the waiter know that's why you didn't give him a tip?

D: Exactly. It's just like telling him off.

C: No wonder he's so angry.

D: Well, in fact, the people did leave him a tip, but that kid over there took it.

小陳在美國。他的美國朋友黛西提議和他到餐廳吃午飯。

小陳：那個服務生為什麼那麼生氣？

黛西：那些剛走的人似乎沒給他小費，這令他不悅。

小陳：在這兒給小費有絕對的必要嗎？

黛西：多多少少。給小費是個習慣，你免不了至少要留一點小費。

小陳：但是假如服務不好呢？

黛西：那樣子的話，我們就當然不留。

小陳：而服務生知道那就是為什麼你們沒給他小費的原因嗎？

黛西：正是，那就像是在責備他。

小陳：難怪他那麼生氣。

黛西：嗯，其實那些人確實有留小費給他，但是那邊那個小鬼把它拿走了。

Key Points
重點提示

1. **missing** [ˈmɪsɪŋ] a. 失蹤的; 行蹤不明的

   miss [mɪs] vt. 錯過; 想念

   例: I will give $1,000 to anyone who can find my missing dog.
   (我會付一千元給任何能夠找到我失蹤狗兒的人。)

   He arrived at the airport too late and missed the flight.
   (他太晚抵達機場而錯過班機。)

   Diana studies in America; she misses her family in England a lot.
   (黛安娜在美國唸書；她非常想念她在英國的家人。)

2. **kind of**　　多多少少; 有點

= sort of

   a kind of + 名詞　一種……

= a sort of + 名詞

   注意:

kind of、sort of 為副詞片語, 其後可接動詞、形容詞或副詞。本文中的"Kind of."等於"It is kind of necessary here."。kind of、sort of 在口語中, 速度變快後即成 kinda [ˈkaɪndə]、sorta [ˈsɔrtə]。

例: I <u>kind of</u> like taking exams.
(我有點喜歡考試。)

He's <u>kind of</u> lazy.
(他有點懶。)

This is <u>a kind of</u> local vegetable, but I don't know what it's called.
(這是一種本地的蔬菜，但我不知道它叫什麼。)

3. **custom** [ˈkʌstəm] n. 習俗

例: The aborigines have some really strange customs.
(這些原住民有些非常奇怪的習俗。)
　* aborigine [ˌæbəˈrɪdʒəni] n. 原始居民, 土著

4. **service** [ˈsɝvɪs] n. 服務

be at your service　　隨時為你服務/效勞; 請隨時吩咐

例: Mr. Chen: Can you help me move tomorrow?
Neighbor: Sure. I'm at your service.
(陳先生：你明天能幫我搬家嗎？)
(鄰　居：當然。隨時為你效勞。)

5. **In that case,...**　　如此一來/那樣 (的話), ……
In some cases,...　　在有些情形下/有時, ……
In most cases,...　　在大部分情形下/往往, ……
In many cases,...　　在許多情形下, ……

例: Son: The weather report says it'll probably rain tomorrow.
Dad: In that case, let's postpone our picnic.
(兒子：氣象報告說明天可能會下雨。)
(爸爸：那樣的話，咱們野餐就延期吧。)
　* postpone [postˈpon] vt. 延期

In most cases, people who play the stock market lose money.

(玩股票的人大都會賠錢。)

6. **exactly** [ɪɡ'zæktlɪ] adv. 正是, 確實地

例: What exactly do you intend to do after you graduate?
(你畢業後究竟打算做什麼？)

7. **tell + 人 + off** 責備某人

例: The principal told the teacher off for hitting the student.
(校長責備那位老師打學生。)

請選出下列各句中正確的一項

1. My co-worker suggested _____ to the movies after work.
   (A) to go   (B) to have gone
   (C) going   (D) having gone

2. Lisa enjoys _____ the piano every morning.
   (A) play   (B) plays   (C) to play   (D) playing

3. It is the _____ of the Chinese to give money in a red envelope to their children on Chinese New Year Day.
   (A) method   (B) custom   (C) thing   (D) hobby

4. I find _____ every day very boring.
   (A) study   (B) studies   (C) to study   (D) studying

5. Some people believe it dangerous _____ motorcycles.
   (A) for riding   (B) to ride   (C) to riding   (D) ride

解答:

> 1. (C)   2. (D)   3. (B)   4. (D)   5. (B)

Lesson 27
Thank Your Lucky Stars
福星高照

Reading
閱　讀

I remember when I was a young boy, life was tough. My parents made me do many things for them. For example, they had me do the laundry, the dishes and the house cleaning. They even got me to work part-time to help with the family expenses. If I was naughty, they would spank me. They would not let me go outside the house for days.

Nowadays, life is quite different for kids. Parents can't force them to do anything. On the contrary, it seems as if children can get their parents to do anything for them. Parents and teachers are even afraid to spank children for fear of being sued. It amazes me, therefore, whenever I hear youngsters complain. Instead, they should be thanking their lucky stars.

> 我記得我小的時候，日子過得很苦。我父母叫我幫他們做很多事情。例如，他們會叫我洗衣服、洗碗盤和打掃家裡。他們甚至叫我去打工來貼補家用。我如果調皮搗蛋的話，他們就會打我屁股，而且好幾天都不讓我出門。
>
> 　　現在小孩的生活卻大不相同。做父母的不能強迫他們做任何事。相反地，做孩子的似乎有辦法叫父母為他們做任何事。父母和老師甚至因怕被控告而不敢打小孩。因此，每當我聽到青少年抱怨時，就感到很驚訝。他們應該慶幸才是。

Vocabulary & Idioms
單字 & 片語註解

1. **thank one's lucky stars**　　自慶幸運, 感謝自己的好運氣
   lucky [ˈlʌkɪ] a. 幸運的
   例: You should thank your lucky stars you missed your plane. It crashed soon after taking off.
   (你應該慶幸沒搭上那班飛機。它起飛後不久就墜機了。)

2. **tough** [tʌf] a. 艱苦的; 困難的 (= difficult)
   例: The English test was pretty tough.
   (這次的英文考試很難。)

3. **laundry** [ˈlɔndrɪ] n. 待洗的衣服 (不可數)
   do the laundry　　洗衣服
   例: With the new washing machine, doing the laundry is <u>a piece of cake</u>.

(有了這台新洗衣機，洗衣服是輕而易舉的事。)
　　＊ be a piece of cake　　很容易
　　＝ be quite easy

4. **dish** [ˈdɪʃ] n. 碗盤; 餐具
　 do the dishes　　洗碗盤
＝ wash the dishes
　 例: Mom cooks and Dad does the dishes.
　　　(媽媽煮飯而爸爸洗碗盤。)

5. **part-time** [ˌpɑrtˈtaɪm] adv. & a. 兼職/任地 (的)
　 full-time [ˌfʊlˈtaɪm] adv. & a. 全職地 (的)
　 work part-time　　兼差
　 a part-time teacher　　兼職老師
　 a full-time job　　全職工作
　 例: Emma likes to work part-time, not full-time.
　　　(愛瑪喜歡兼差的工作而非全職的。)

　　　Dr. Wang was once a part-time professor at Harvard University.
　　　(王博士曾經是哈佛大學的兼任教授。)

6. **expense** [ɪkˈspɛns] n. 支出, 花費; 犧牲

7. **spank** [spæŋk] vt. 拍擊 (尤指打在屁股上)
　 例: Believe it or not, my parents never spanked us.
　　　(信不信由你，我爸媽從沒打過我們屁股。)

8. **force** [fɔrs] vt. 強迫
　 force + 人 + to + 原形動詞　　強迫某人……
　 例: The nurse forced the patient to take the medicine.
　　　(那個護士強迫該病人吃藥。)

9. **On the contrary,** 主詞 + 動詞　　相反地, ……
＝ Instead, 主詞 + 動詞

contrary ['kɑntrɛrɪ] n. 反面, 相反

instead [ɪn'stɛd] adv. (反) 而

例: Sally is not stingy at all. On the contrary, she's quite generous.
(莎莉一點也不吝嗇；相反地，她相當慷慨。)
　　* stingy ['stɪndʒɪ] a. 吝嗇的, 小氣的

10. **for fear of + 動名詞**　　以免/唯恐……
= for fear + that + 主詞 + may/might + 動詞
= lest + 主詞 + (should) + 動詞

注意:

lest (以免/唯恐) 為副詞連接詞, 引導副詞子句, 修飾主要子句; 且在該副詞子句中, 須與助動詞 should 並用, 但 should 亦可予以省略, 而直接接原形動詞。

例: We took a cab for fear of being late.
= We took a cab for fear that we might be late.
= We took a cab lest we (should) be late.
(我們搭計程車以免遲到。)

11. **sue** [su] vt. 控告

sue + 人 + for + 事　　控告某人某事

例: The customer sued the company for late delivery of the goods.
(那個顧客控告該公司延遲送貨。)

12. 本文:

Parents and teachers are even afraid to spank children <u>for fear of being sued</u>.

= ...to spank children <u>for fear that they may be</u> sued.
= ...to spank children <u>lest they (should) be sued</u>.
……父母和老師甚至因怕被控告而不敢打小孩。

13. **amaze** [ə'mez] vt. 使驚訝

amazed [ə'mezd] a. 感到驚訝的

be amazed at...　　對……感到驚訝
= be surprised at...

例: Modern technology never ceases to amaze me.
(現代科技總是令我驚訝不已。)

I was amazed at how young my girlfriend's mother is.
(我非常驚訝女友的媽媽這麼年輕。)

14. **youngster** [ˈjʌŋstɚ] n. 青少年; 年輕人

15. **complain** [kəmˈplen] vi. 抱怨, 不滿; 控訴 & vt. 抱怨 (以 that 引導的子句作受詞)

complain of/about + 名詞/動名詞　　　抱怨/不滿……; 控訴……
complain + that 子句　　抱怨……

注意:

complain 是不及物動詞, 故其後不可直接加受詞, 而須先置介詞 of 或 about 後, 再接受詞; 但 complain 亦可作及物動詞, 此時其後僅能接 that 引導的名詞子句作受詞。

例: Have you met anyone who doesn't complain about his boss?
(你曾經見過任何不抱怨老闆的人嗎?)

The manager complained that the boss does not appreciate his hard work.
(經理埋怨老闆不知感激他辛勞的工作。)

Grammar Notes
文法重點

本課旨在介紹使役動詞的用法。

My parents <u>made</u> me <u>do</u> many things for them.
我父母叫我幫他們做很多事情。

For example, they <u>had</u> me <u>do</u> the laundry, the dishes and the house cleaning.
例如, 他們會叫我洗衣服, 洗碗盤和打掃家裡。

They even <u>got</u> me <u>to work</u> part-time to help with the family expenses.
他們甚至叫我去打工來貼補家用。

They would not <u>let</u> me <u>go</u> outside the house for days.
他們好幾天都不讓我出門。

Parents can't <u>force</u> them <u>to do</u> anything.
做父母的不能強迫他們做任何事。

On the contrary, it seems as if children can <u>get</u> their parents <u>to do</u> anything for them.
相反地, 做孩子的似乎有辦法叫父母為他們做任何事。

注意:

上列句中的 made、had、got、let、force 稱為使役動詞。所謂使役動詞就是一種命令某人從事某件事的動詞, 加了受詞後, 可用原形動詞或不定詞片語 (to + 原形動詞) 作受詞補語。茲分類敘述如下:

a. 叫/令/使……

    make/have + 人 + 原形動詞　　叫某人做……

    get + 人 + to + 原形動詞　　叫某人做……

    例: Paul's father <u>made</u> him <u>paint</u> the house.
    (保羅的父親叫他漆房子。)

    The boss <u>had</u> the secretary <u>type</u> the letter for him.
    (老闆叫祕書幫他打那封信。)

    Dad <u>got</u> me <u>to wash</u> the car for him.
    (老爸叫我幫他洗車。)

注意:

1) make 可使用於被動語態中, 但 have 及 get 則無被動語態。句型如下:

    be made to + 原形動詞　　被要求/命令做……

    例: 主動語態:

Mom <u>made</u> me <u>do</u> the laundry.
(老媽叫我洗衣服。)

被動語態:

I <u>was made to do</u> the laundry.
(我被命令洗衣服。)

I <u>was had to do</u> the laundry. (✗)
I <u>was got to do</u> the laundry. (✗)

2) have 及 get 加受詞後, 其後亦可接過去分詞作受詞補語, 此時的 have 及 get 譯成『把……』。句型如下:

have/get + 受詞 + 過去分詞　　把……(被)……

例: I <u>had</u> my computer <u>fixed</u>.
(我把我的電腦修理好了。)

When did you <u>get</u> your hair <u>cut</u>?
(你什麼時候理的髮?)

上列兩句的 fixed 及 cut 均為過去分詞, 分別表示『被修理』、『(頭髮) 被理』, 暗示這些動作均是委託別人所做, 而非自己所為。

b. 讓……

表『讓……』的動詞只有 let 一字, 其後亦用原形動詞作受詞補語, 並可使用被動語態 (唯較少使用), 句型如下:

let + 人 + 原形動詞　　讓某人……
be let to + 原形動詞　　被允許……(少用)

例: 主動語態:

They won't <u>let</u> me <u>play</u> with them.
(他們不讓我和他們一起玩耍。)

被動語態:

I <u>am not let to play</u> with them. (罕)
主動語態:

We <u>let</u> Mary <u>join</u> our club.
(我們讓瑪麗加入我們的俱樂部。)

被動語態:

Mary <u>was let to join</u> our club. (罕)

c. 強迫/要求/慫恿/催促……

此類動詞 + 人 + to + 原形動詞

例: I <u>forced</u> him <u>to recite</u> the lesson.
(我強迫他背這課給我聽。)

I <u>asked</u> him <u>to write</u> the letter.
(我要求他寫這封信。)

I <u>urged</u> him <u>to work</u> harder.
(找督促他工作努力些。)

He <u>compelled</u> me <u>to do</u> it against my will.
(他強迫我做那件我不願做的事。)

He <u>told</u> me <u>to finish</u> the work by ten.
(他叫我十點鐘以前做完這件工作。)

注意:

此類動詞變被動語態時,仍用不定詞片語作補語。

例: I <u>asked</u> him <u>to write</u> the letter.
(我要求他寫這封信。)

→ He <u>was asked to write</u> the letter.
(他被要求寫這封信。)

Substitution
代　　換

1. **My parents made me do many things for them.**
   My wife had me mow the lawn.
   Mr. Lin let me paint the room for him.
   我父母叫我幫他們做很多事情。
   我太太叫我除草。
   林先生讓我為他油漆房間。

2. **Parents and teachers are even afraid to spank children for fear of being sued.**
   We left the house early for fear of missing our plane.
   Mr. Wang got home early for fear of getting his wife angry.
   父母和老師甚至因怕被控告而不敢打小孩。
   我們提早出門以免錯過飛機。
   王先生早早回家唯恐太太生氣。

Lesson 28
Going on a Diet
節食

Dialogue
實用會話

Little Johnny is talking to his mother.
(J=Little Johnny; M=Mother)

J: How come you always make me do things I don't want to?

M: What do you mean?

J: Well, for instance, you always force me to eat steaks, pork chops and chicken, day in and day out.

M: OK. What do you want?

J: All I want is vegetables and fruit from now on.

M: What's wrong with you? Are you sick?

J: No, but I want to go on a diet.

M: Why?

J: Everyone's calling me Fatty at school.

M: Oh...I get it now.

小強尼正和他媽媽說話。

小強尼：為什麼妳總是要我做我不想做的事？

媽　媽：你這話怎麼說？

小強尼：嗯，舉個例子，妳每天都強迫我吃牛排、豬排和雞肉。

媽　媽：好吧。那你想吃什麼？

小強尼：從現在起我只要吃蔬菜和水果。

媽　媽：你怎麼了？你生病了嗎？

小強尼：沒有，可是我想要節食。

媽　媽：為什麼？

小強尼：學校裡每個人都叫我『小胖』。

媽　媽：哦……現在我懂了。

Key Points
重點提示

1. **pork chop** [ˈpɔrk ˌtʃɑp] n. 豬排

2. **day in (and) day out**　　日復一日; 天天

   例: The housewife is bored with the same routine day in day out.
   (那個家庭主婦厭倦日復一日相同的例行工作。)

3. **vegetable** [ˈvɛdʒətəbl̩] n. 蔬菜(可數)

   例: The prices of vegetables go up at the approach of a typhoon.
   (颱風來臨時菜價都會上揚。)

4. **from now on**　　從現在起

   例: From now on I'll try to concentrate on my studies more.
   (從現在起，我會設法多專注於課業上。)

5. **I get it now.**　　我懂了。

* **get** [gɛt] vt. 了解, 聽懂

   例: Do you get what the stranger was trying to tell us?
   (你聽懂了那個陌生人想要告訴我們什麼嗎？)

請選出下列各句中正確的一項

1. The teacher made me _____ behind after class because I didn't do
   my homework.
   (A) to stay   (B) staying   (C) stayed   (D) stay

2. You can bring a horse to a lake but you can't force it _____ the water.
   (A) drink   (B) drinking   (C) to drink   (D) drank

3. My boss asked me to _____ a letter for him.
   (A) types   (B) type   (C) typed   (D) typing

4. I didn't _____ what he said. Did you?
   (A) have   (B) get   (C) make   (D) listen

解答:

1. (D)	2. (C)	3. (B)	4. (B)

L esson 29

Just a Dream

惡夢一場

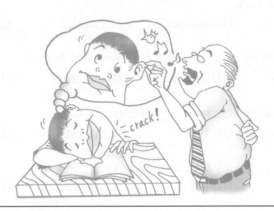

crack!

Reading
閱　讀

One day I was at home listening to music when suddenly I felt a pain in my neck. As I tried to turn my head, I heard my neck crack. I got the fright of my life. I was so scared that I could feel my legs trembling. "What's the matter with me?" I thought to myself.

Just then, I felt myself slapped by someone. I opened my eyes and saw my teacher standing over me with an angry look in his face. I realized then that I had been dreaming. I didn't mind getting caught dozing off in class. I was happy what happened was just a dream.

　　有一天我在家裡聽音樂的時侯，脖子突然感到疼痛。當我想要轉頭時，便聽到自己的脖子發出啪啪的聲音。我嚇得魂都沒了。我怕得可以感覺到自己的腿在抖。我心裡想：『我到底怎麼了？』

　　就在那時，我感覺到自己被人拍了一下。我睜開眼睛看到老師面有慍色地站在我身邊。當時我恍然大悟原來我是在作夢。我倒不在乎上課打瞌睡被逮到；我很高興那只是一場夢。

Vocabulary & Idioms
單字 & 片語註解

1. **crack** [kræk] vi. 發出啪啪的聲音
   例: The old man's bones crack every time he stands up.
   (那個老人每次站起來骨頭都會啪啪作響。)

2. **get the fright of one's life**　　某人受到一生中最大的驚嚇; 嚇破膽
   fright [fraɪt] n. 驚駭, 驚嚇
   例: Mom got the fright of her life when she thought she lost her diamond wedding ring.
   (老媽以為她丟了結婚鑽戒時嚇死了。)

3. **scared** [skɛrd] a. 害怕的
   be scared of...　　害怕……
   = be afraid of...
   例: My grandma is scared of thunder and lightning.
   (我奶奶害怕打雷和閃電。)

4. **tremble** [ˈtrɛmb!̩] vi. 顫抖
   例: Little Bill trembled as soon as the monster appeared on the TV screen.
   (那隻怪物在電視螢光幕上一出現，小比爾就發抖。)

5. **slap** [slæp] vt. 用手掌拍擊

   例: Mrs. Green slapped her son for lying to her.
   (格林太太因兒子對她說謊而打了他。)

6. **doze off** 打瞌睡, 打盹

   doze [doz] vi. 打瞌睡

   例: The old man dozed off while getting his haircut.
   (那個老先生在理髮時打瞌睡。)

Grammar Notes
文 法 重 點

本課主要複習表『看』、『聽』、『感覺』三類知覺動詞的用法。

As I tried to turn my head, I heard my neck crack.
當我想要轉頭時, 便聽到自己的脖子發出啪啪的聲音。

I was so scared that I could feel my legs trembling.
我怕得可以感覺到自己的腿在抖。

Just then, I felt myself slapped by someone.
就在那時, 我感覺到自己被人拍了一下。

I opened my eyes and saw my teacher standing over me with an angry
look in his face.
我睜開眼睛看到老師面有慍色地站在我身邊。

注意:

上列各句中, 及物動詞 heard (聽)、feel (感覺)、felt (感覺) 及 saw (看) 接了
受詞後, 分別用原形動詞 crack、現在分詞 trembling、過去分詞 slapped 及
現在分詞 standing 作受詞補語。

表『看』、『聽』、『感覺』三類知覺動詞接了受詞後, 可用原形動詞作受
詞補語, 表已發生的事實; 或用現在分詞作受詞補語, 表進行的狀態; 亦可用過
去分詞作受詞補語, 表被動的概念。常見的知覺動詞如下:

看: see、watch、look at (注視)。

聽: hear、listen to。

感覺: feel。

a. 以原形動詞作受詞補語:

旨在強調確有事情發生。

例: I cannot bear to <u>see</u> women <u>cry</u>.
(我受不了看到女人哭。)

We <u>heard</u> the guests <u>arrive</u>.
(我們聽到客人到了。)

The pregnant woman <u>felt</u> the baby <u>move</u>.
(那名孕婦感到寶寶動了。)

b. 以現在分詞作受詞補語:

旨在強調事情正在發生。

例: Mary <u>watched</u> her boyfriend <u>leaving</u>.
(瑪麗看著她男友正在離去。)

I think I <u>heard</u> someone <u>crying</u> for help.
(我想我聽到有人在喊救命。)

I <u>felt</u> my heart <u>beating</u> very fast.
(我感覺自己的心正跳得好快。)

c. 以過去分詞作受詞補語:

旨在強調被動的狀態。

例: I <u>saw</u> a man <u>hit</u> by a car on my way to school this morning.
(今早我在上學途中看到一名男子被車子撞了。)

I <u>heard</u> the child <u>scolded</u> by his father.
(我聽到那個小孩被爸爸責罵。)

I <u>felt</u> my hair <u>pulled</u> by someone from behind.
(我感到頭髮被人從後面扯了一下。)

Substitution
代　　換

1. **As I tried to turn my head, I heard my neck crack.**

   Soon after I heard the explosion, I saw the building collapse.

   As soon as I bent down, I felt my back ache.

   當我想要轉頭時, 便聽到自己的脖子發出啪啪的聲音。

   我聽到爆炸聲後不久, 便看到那棟建築物倒塌。

   我一彎下腰, 就感到背痛了起來。

2. **I was so scared that I could feel my legs trembling.**

   Dan is so rich that money means nothing to him.

   He is so dishonest that nobody trusts him.

   我怕得可以感覺到自己的腿在抖。

   丹非常有錢, 所以錢對他來說一點也不重要。

   他非常不誠實, 所以沒有人信任他。

Lesson 30

Yes, Sir

是的，老師

Dialogue

實用會話

The teacher wakes me up from my dream.

(T=Teacher; M=me)

T: Get up, you lazybones!

M: Oh...sorry, sir. I must have fallen asleep.

T: You bet. And we could see you shaking like a leaf.

M: Really? Wow! Thank goodness I was dreaming.

T: What? You were dreaming in class and you are happy about it?

M: Uh...yes, sir.

T: What? Do you take me for a fool?

M: Yes, sir...I mean no, sir.

T: As punishment you are to write "I must not sleep in class" 100 times.

M: No, sir.

T: Wrong. You should say, "Yes, sir."

M: Whatever, sir.

T: Oh, I give up.

M: Good, sir.

老師把我從夢中叫醒。

老師：起床了，你這懶骨頭！

　我：哦……對不起，老師。我一定是睡著了。

老師：當然。我們還看到你抖得好厲害。

　我：真的嗎？哇！感謝老天爺我是在作夢。

老師：什麼？你上課作夢還自鳴得意？

　我：嗯……是的，老師。

老師：什麼？你把我當傻瓜嗎？

　我：是的，老師……我是說不是，老師。

老師：我要罰你寫『我上課時絕不可以打瞌睡』一百遍。

　我：不要，老師。

老師：錯了。你應該說：『是的，老師。』

　我：隨便，老師。

老師：哦，我放棄了。

　我：太好了，老師。

Key Points
重點提示

1. **wake + 人 + up**　　叫醒某人

   wake up　　醒來

   wake [wek] vt. 喚醒 & vi. 醒

   動詞三態: wake、woke [wok]/waked、woken ['wokən]/waked。

   例: I asked the hotel clerk to wake me up at 6 a.m.
   (我叫旅館櫃檯早上六點鐘叫醒我。)

   If I drink wine, I find it difficult to wake up early the next day.
   (我發現我如果喝酒的話，隔天便很難早起。)

2. **lazybones** ['lezɪ,bonz] n. 懶骨頭, 懶人 (單複數同形, 即 a lazybone**s**、
   two lazybone**s**...)

例: The teacher punished the lazybones by making him stand in the corner.
(老師罰那個懶鬼站在牆角。)

The lazybones promised to work harder in the future.
(那個懶人答應以後要努力點。)

3. **fall asleep**　　入睡, 睡著

　　fall ill　　生病

　　fall [fɔl] vi. 變為

　　動詞三態: fall、fell [fɛl]、fallen ['fɔlən]。

　　例: They couldn't fall asleep last night because of all the mosquitoes.
　　(他們昨晚因蚊子太多而無法入睡。)

　　＊ mosquito [məˈskito] n. 蚊子

　　Anita fell ill the day before her wedding.
　　(安妮塔在婚禮前一天病了。)

4. **shake like a leaf**　　抖得很厲害

　　shake [ʃek] vi. 搖動; 發抖

　　leaf [lif] n. 樹葉

　　動詞三態: shake、shook、shaken。

　　例: The little boy was so cold that he was shaking like a leaf.
　　(那個小男孩非常冷，所以他抖得很厲害。)

5. **Thank goodness** (+ 主詞 + 動詞)　　感謝老天(……)
= Thank God (+ 主詞 + 動詞)

　　注意:

　　有宗教信仰的人不太提及 God 一字, 因此『我的天啊！』, 許多人會說"My goodness!"而非"My God!"。

　　例:　　Man: The murderer was finally caught.
　　Woman: Thank goodness!
　　(男子：那個殺人犯終於被抓到了。)
　　(女子：感謝老天爺！)

6. **take A for B**　　誤把 A 當作 B

例: The hunter mistakenly took the dog for a fox and shot it.
(那個獵人誤把這隻狗當成狐狸而射殺了牠。)

7. **fool** [ful] n. 傻瓜 & vt. 欺騙 & vi. 鬼混, 游手好閒

fool around　　鬼混, 游手好閒

例: Bob is a fool for shouting at the manager.
(鮑勃對著經理大叫真是不智。)

I can never fool my mother; she's too smart.
(我從無法欺騙我媽媽；她太精明了。)

Stop fooling around and get back to work.
(不要混了，回去工作吧。)

8. **punishment** ['pʌnɪʃmənt] n. 處罰

例: Most people thought the punishment was very light for the crime
the man committed.
(大多數的人認為那男子犯了那種罪行的處罰太輕了。)

＊ commit [kə'mɪt] vt. 犯 (罪)

9. 本文:

Whatever, sir.

= Whatever you say, sir.
隨便, 老師。

＊ whatever [hwɑt'ɛvɚ] n. 任何東西

例:　　Father: We have to go visit aunt Mary tomorrow.
Daughter: Whatever.
(父親：我們明天得去看瑪麗姑媽。)
(女兒：隨便。)

10. **give up**　　放棄 (不及物)

give up ＋ 名詞/動名詞　　放棄……(及物)

例: Although Mike lost the game, he never gave up.
(雖然麥克輸了那場比賽，但他從不放棄。)

Gary gave up playing the piano and took up ballet.
(蓋瑞放棄彈鋼琴而學跳芭蕾舞。)

請選出下列各句中正確的一項

1. Mr. Wang _____ asleep during the boss's speech.
   (A) feel   (B) fall   (C) fell   (D) felt

2. The children could hear their mother _____ in her room.
   (A) to cry   (B) cries   (C) cried   (D) crying

3. I _____ that long-haired boy for a girl.
   (A) gave   (B) wanted   (C) took   (D) had

4. I saw a man _____ by a dog.
   (A) bite   (B) bit   (C) beaten   (D) bitten

5. The tennis player is not very good but he never _____.
   (A) wakes up   (B) gets up   (C) gives up   (D) sits down

解答:

| 1. (C) | 2. (D) | 3. (C) | 4. (D) | 5. (C) |

Lesson 31

Good Feng Shui in New York

紐約好風水

Reading

閱　讀

Feng shui, or geomancy in English, is becoming more and more popular in America. The Chinese consider feng shui old news, but to Americans, it's something brand-new. Store and home owners are consulting feng shui masters for advice.

How did this ancient Chinese tradition make its way across the seas? The answer is quite simple. Chinese businessmen have been building high rises in America. They deem it necessary to rely on feng shui experts, just as they would at home. More and more wealthy Americans are beginning to

believe in geomancy. They say that geomancers in New York make US$250 an hour! In view of this, we can foresee a bright future for geomancy in America.

> 　　風水，英文稱作geomancy，在美國越來越受到歡迎。風水對中國人來說已稀鬆平常，但對美國人來說卻頗為新鮮。時下店主和屋主紛紛向風水師求教。
> 　　這個中國古老的傳統是如何遠渡重洋的呢？答案很簡單。中國商人不斷地在美國興建高樓大廈，而他們認為有必要照風水專家的話去做，就像他們在國內那樣。有越來越多有錢的美國人開始相信風水。據說紐約的風水師一小時可以賺進兩百五十塊美金！有鑑於此，我們可以預見風水在美國將大有可為。

Vocabulary & Idioms
單字 & 片語註解

1. **geomancy** [ˈdʒiəˌmænsɪ] n. 土占, 地卜, 風水
   例: We moved to the next street because of bad geomancy.
   (由於風水不好，我們遷移到隔壁一條街。)

2. **brand-new** [ˌbrændˈnu] a. 嶄新的
   例: The rich man's son was seen driving a brand-new sports car.
   (有人看到那個富家子弟開著一輛嶄新的跑車。)

3. **owner** [ˈonɚ] n. 主人
   例: The owner of the pub treated me to a drink.
   (那家酒館的主人請我喝了一杯。)

4. **consult** [kənˈsʌlt] vt. 請教 & vi. 商量, 磋商
   consult with...　　和……討論/商量

例: Before any business agreement is signed, it's best to consult a lawyer.
(簽定任何生意合約之前最好先請教律師。)

You should consult with your parents about your future plans.
(你應該和父母親商量你未來的計畫。)

5. **master** [ˈmæstɚ] n. 大師 & vt. 精通

例: Bruce Lee was a great kung fu master.
(李小龍是一名偉大的功夫大師。)

Linda said that she had never mastered the art of public speaking.
(琳達說她一直無法精通演講的藝術。)

6. **ancient** [ˈenʃənt] a. 古老的

例: The national library has some really ancient books.
(那間國立圖書館有一些非常古老的書籍。)

7. **tradition** [trəˈdɪʃən] n. 傳統

例: It has long been the Chinese tradition to have a reunion dinner on Chinese New Year's Eve.
(除夕夜吃團圓飯是中國人長久以來的一項傳統。)

8. 本文:

How did this ancient Chinese tradition make its way across the seas?

= How did this very old Chinese tradition get to be known abroad?
這個中國古老的傳統是如何遠渡重洋的呢?

9. **high rise** [ˈhaɪ ˌraɪz] n. 高樓大廈

例: Taiwan claims to have the tallest high rise in the world.
(台灣聲稱擁有全世界最高的大樓。)

10. **deem** [dim] vt. 認為 (= consider)

例: I deem it a great honor to be invited to your party.
(我認為受邀到你的派對是極大的榮幸。)

11. **rely on...** 依賴/信賴……

例: Joe always relies on his parents to get him out of trouble.
(喬總是靠父母幫他解圍。)

12. 本文:

They deem it necessary to rely on feng shui experts, just as they <u>would</u> at home.

= They deem it necessary to rely on feng shui experts <u>in America</u>, just as they <u>would rely on feng shui experts</u> at home.
他們認為有必要照風水專家的話去做, 就像他們在國內那樣。

* 助動詞 would 之後省略了與前句相同之述詞部分。

13. **wealthy** [ˈwɛlθɪ] a. 富有的

例: A wealthy person is not necessarily a happy person.
(有錢人不一定快樂。)

14. **believe in...** 相信/篤信……為真

例: I believe in hard work.
(我認為人應該努力工作。)

15. **geomancer** [ˈdʒiəˌmænsɚ] n. 風水地理師

例: The geomancer told us to move our furniture around.
(那個風水師告訴我們要移動家具的位置。)
* furniture [ˈfɜˌnɪtʃɚ] n. 家具 (不可數)

16. **in view of...** 有鑒於……

例: In view of what the boss just said, the manager intends to quit his job.
(有鑒於老闆剛說的話, 經理有意辭職。)

17. **foresee** [fɔrˈsi] vt. 預見

動詞三態: foresee、foresaw、foreseen。

例: Nobody could foresee the plane crash.
(沒有人能夠預料那次墜機。)

18. **bright** [braɪt] a. 光明的

例: A bright future lies ahead for that smart student.
(那個聰明的學生前途光明。)

Grammar Notes
文法重點

本課介紹"They say..."表『據說……』的用法。

They say that geomancers in New York make US$250 an hour!
據說紐約的風水師一小時可以賺進兩百五十塊美金!

上列句中的"They say..."表『據說……』,They用來泛指一般人。表『據說……』可用下列句型表示:

They say that...
= It is said that...
= People say that...

例: They say that the Chinese are very frugal.
 = It is said that the Chinese are very frugal.
 = People say that the Chinese are very frugal.
(聽說中國人很節儉。)
 * frugal [ˈfrugl] a. 節儉的

They say that Al was once a member of the Mafia.
= It is said that Al was once a member of the Mafia.
= People say that Al was once a member of the Mafia.
(據說艾爾曾參加過黑手黨。)
 * the Mafia [ˈmɑfɪɑ] n. 黑手黨

注意:

表『謠傳……』時, 可用下列句型表示:

Word has it that...

= Rumor has it that...

= It is rumored that...

注意:

上列用法中的 rumor 及 word 兩字前不可使用任何冠詞。

例: <u>The</u> word/rumor has it that the bank is about to close down. (✕)

→ Word has it that the bank is about to close down. (○)

= Rumor has it that the bank is about to close down.

= It is rumored that the bank is about to close down.
  (謠傳該銀行即將歇業。)

Substitution
代　　換

They say that geomancers in New York make US$250 an hour!

They say that New Yorkers aren't very polite.

Rumor has it that a big earthquake will hit California soon.

據說紐約的風水師一小時可以賺進兩百五十塊美金！

聽說紐約人並不怎麼有禮貌。

謠傳加州不久將發生大地震。

Lesson 32
Goldfish, Souls and Coffee Tables
金魚、靈魂和茶几

Dialogue
實用會話

Ms. Smith, an American, is talking to Mr. Ting, an expert on feng shui. (S=Ms. Smith; T=Mr. Ting)

S: What changes would you suggest for my house?

T: I think that you should get an aquarium with goldfish.

S: Why?

T: Goldfish bring good luck.

S: OK. Anything else?

T: You should also get rid of that mirror in front of your bed.

S: Why?

T: Your soul travels at night. It must find its way back to the body. The soul might see your body in the mirror and get confused.

S: Hmm...really? What else?

T: Um...(He bumps into a coffee table.) ouch! And get rid of this table.

S: Why? It's just a coffee table.

T: It's dangerous. It will bring you bad luck.

S: Uh...are you sure?

美國籍的史密斯小姐正和風水專家丁先生交談。

史小姐：你建議我房子應該做些什麼改變？

丁先生：我認為妳應該買個水族箱，裡面養些金魚。

史小姐：為什麼？

丁先生：金魚會帶來好運。

史小姐：好啊。還有什麼？

丁先生：妳還應該把妳床前的那面鏡子拿走。

史小姐：為什麼？

丁先生：妳的靈魂晚上會出來遊蕩。它必須找到回軀殼的路。妳的靈魂可能會看到妳鏡子裡的軀殼而搞糊塗。

史小姐：呣……真的嗎？還有呢？

丁先生：嗯……(他撞到茶几。)哎哦！把這張茶几也拿走。

史小姐：為什麼？只是張茶几嘛。

丁先生：那東西很危險，會給妳帶來厄運的。

史小姐：呃……你確定嗎？

Key Points
重點提示

1. **goldfish** [ˈgoldˌfɪʃ] n. 金魚 (單複數同形)

   例: I have a fishbowl with only two goldfish in it.

   (我有一個只有兩隻金魚的魚缸。)

   * fishbowl [ˈfɪʃˌbol] n. (玻璃作形狀像碗或甕的) 金魚缸

2. **soul** [sol] n. 靈魂

   例: Some people believe that the body dies but the soul lives on forever.

   (有些人相信肉體會死但靈魂永生。)

3. **aquarium** [əˈkwɛrɪəm] n. (四方形) 魚缸; 水族箱

4. **get rid of...** 除去……; 擺脫……

例: Mary finally got rid of all her dirty old shoes.
(瑪麗終於把她那些又髒又舊的鞋子處理掉了。)

5. **mirror** [ˈmɪrɚ] n. 鏡子

例: The prisoner got a shock when he looked at himself in the mirror.
(那個犯人照鏡子時大吃了一驚。)

6. **in front of...** 在……之前/前面

front [frʌnt] n. 前面

例: Nancy is not afraid to say what she feels in front of her elders.
(南西不怕在長輩面前說出她心裡的感受。)

7. **bump into...** 撞到……; 偶遇……(= run into...)

例: The poor blind man bumped into the lamppost.
(那名可憐的盲胞撞上了路燈柱。)

＊ lamppost [ˈlæmpˌpost] n. 路燈柱

I bumped into my teacher at the disco.
(我在迪斯可舞廳和老師不期而遇。)

請選出下列各句中正確的一項

1. Can you give me some advice _____ how to improve my English?
   (A) to   (B) on   (C) for   (D) with

2. In _____ of his injury, the player decided not to play in the tennis tournament.
   (A) spite   (B) despite   (C) view   (D) because

3. I think _____ important to exercise.
   (A) that   (B) it   (C) its   (D) that's

4. The gentleman accidentally ＿＿＿＿ into the girl and apologized.
   (A) hit　　　　(B) run　　　　(C) bumped　　　(D) came

解答：

> 1. (B)　　2. (C)　　3. (B)　　4. (C)

Lesson 33
A Deadly Current
死亡暗流

Reading
閱　　讀

It is a pity that every summer a few people drown at the beach. In some cases, these people were good swimmers. So how did it happen? Riptide!

Riptide is a strong underwater current. It moves quickly away from shore and out to sea. It appears suddenly and pulls its victim under and far off shore. Therefore, people should make it a rule never to swim too far out from the beach.

If you find yourself in a riptide, don't panic. And by no means should you try to go against the tide and swim back to shore.

You'll tire yourself out and probably drown. Instead, swim parallel to the beach. A riptide is very narrow. So just a few strokes in the right direction and you'll be out of danger.

很遺憾，每年夏天總有一些人在海邊溺斃，而這些溺水的人中有些是很會游泳的。那麼這究竟是怎麼發生的呢？是激潮在作祟！

激潮是海面下一種強大的暗流，從海岸迅速地流向大海。它出現的時候毫無預警，會將受害者拉下水面並拖離岸邊。因此，人們應該養成不要游得離海灘邊太遠的習慣。

假如你發現自己被捲入激潮時，別驚慌。而且千萬別試圖逆著潮水往岸上游，那會使你筋疲力竭而可能遭到滅頂。你游的方向應該和海灘保持平行。激潮的範圍很窄，所以只要朝正確方向游幾下，那麼你就能脫離險境了。

Vocabulary & Idioms
單字 & 片語註解

1. **deadly** ['dɛdlɪ] a. 致命的, 致死的
   例: AIDS is a deadly disease.
   (愛滋病是種致命的疾病。)

2. **current** ['kɝənt] n. 海流, 潮流
   例: The lifeguard closed the beach because the currents were too strong.
   (那名救生員關閉了海灘，因為海浪太大了。)

3. **pity** ['pɪtɪ] n. 不幸的事; 遺憾
   It's a pity + that 子句　　很遺憾/可惜……
   例: It's a pity that you couldn't come to the party; we had a great time.
   (很遺憾你沒能來參加派對，我們玩得很愉快。)

4. **drown** [draʊn] vi. 溺斃

   例: The boy didn't drown; he was eaten by a shark!
   (那個男孩不是溺斃，他是被鯊魚吃了！)

5. **beach** [bitʃ] n. 海灘, 海濱

6. **riptide** [ˈrɪpˌtaɪd] n. (兩個海流衝撞而成的) 激潮

   例: The sailboat was caught in a riptide and soon sank.
   (那艘帆船被困在激流裡不久便沈沒了。)
   * sailboat [ˈselˌbot] n. (比賽、休閒用的) 帆船

7. **underwater** [ˈʌndɚˌwɔtɚ] a. 水面下的, 水中的 & adv. 在水面下

   例: With an underwater flashlight we could see many amazing fish.
   (帶著水中手電筒我們可以看到許多令人驚奇的魚類。)

8. **shore** [ʃor] n. 海岸

   on shore　　在岸邊

   off shore　　離開岸邊

   例: The fishermen went on shore as soon as they unloaded the boat.
   (漁民把船卸完貨後便上岸了。)
   * unload [ʌnˈlod] vt. 卸貨

   The raft is about 50 yards off shore.
   (那艘木筏大約離岸五十碼遠。)
   * raft [ræft] n. 木筏

9. **victim** [ˈvɪktɪm] n. 受害者

   例: The victims of the typhoon were mainly farmers.
   (這次颱風的受害者主要是農人。)

10. **panic** [ˈpænɪk] vi. & n. 慌張, 恐慌

    in panic　　在驚慌中

    動詞三態: panic、panicked、panicked。

    注意:

panic 作動詞時, 其動詞之過去式和過去分詞須加-k 後, 再加-ed, 現在分詞和動名詞則為 panicking。

例: People panicked and jumped from the third floor of the burning building.
(人們慌張地從那棟起火的大樓三樓跳下來。)

People were panicking when war threatened their country.
(當戰爭威脅到他們國家時, 人民都很恐慌。)

People ran in panic when the bomb exploded.
(炸彈爆炸時, 人們都驚惶奔跑。)

11. **by no means**　　絕對不

注意:

by no means 可放在句首或句中, 且因 by no means 為一否定副詞片語, 故置於句首時, 其後須採倒裝句構。

例: By no means will I cheat on an exam.
(我考試絕對不會作弊。)

Jack is by no means the worst student in the class.
(傑克絕不是班上最糟的學生。)

12. **tide** [taɪd] n. 潮水

例: This tiny bottle was washed ashore by the tide.
(這個小瓶子被潮水沖上岸。)

13. **tire** [taɪr] vt. (使) 累; 令人疲倦

tired [taɪrd] a. 疲倦的

tire oneself out　　(某人) 筋疲力竭/累得要死

= get tired

= get exhausted

* exhausted [ɪɡˈzɔstɪd] a. 疲憊的, 筋疲力竭的

例: Mark tired himself out playing pool all day.
(馬克因打了一整天的撞球而累得要死。)

14. **parallel** [ˈpærəˌlɛl] adv. 平行地 & a. 平行的(皆與介詞 to 並用)

A is parallel to B　　A 與 B 平行

例: These two bars must be parallel to each other.
(這兩根桿子必須相互平行。)

15. **narrow** [ˈnæro] a. 狹窄的

例: The roads are very narrow in Hong Kong.
(香港的街道非常狹窄。)

16. **stroke** [strok] n. (游泳的) 划

例: That swimmer has a strong stroke but a weak kick.
(那位泳者的手划得很有力,但腳踢得軟弱。)

17. **be out of danger**　　脫離危險

danger [ˈdendʒɚ] n. 危險

例: After the operation, the patient is out of danger for the moment.
(手術後,病人暫時脫離險境了。)

Grammar Notes
文法重點

本課介紹"make it a rule to + 原形動詞" (養成……的習慣; 習慣於……)的用法, 並介紹"數量詞 + 名詞 + and + 主詞 + 助動詞 + 原形動詞"的用法。

1. **Therefore, people should <u>make it a rule</u> never <u>to</u> swim too far out from the beach.**
   因此, 人們應該養成不要游得離海灘邊太遠的習慣。
   上列句中, 使用了"make it a rule to + 原形動詞"的句型, 字面意思為『將……的情形變成一種規則』, 亦即『習慣於……』之意。在此句型中, make 是不完全及物動詞, 表『使……成為……』; it 是虛受詞, 代替真受詞, 即其後的不定詞片語 (to + 原形動詞); 而 a rule 則是受詞補語。

make it a rule to + 原形動詞　　習慣於……

= be in the habit of + 動名詞

例: Peter <u>makes it a rule to take</u> a walk after dinner.

　= Peter <u>is in the habit of taking</u> a walk after dinner.
　(彼得習慣晚飯後去散個步。)

2. **So just <u>a few strokes</u> in the right direction <u>and you'll be</u> out of danger.**

所以只要朝正確方向游幾下,那麼你就能脫離險境了。

本句使用了"數量詞 + 名詞 + and + 主詞 + 助動詞 + 原形動詞"的句型, 在此句型中, and 譯成『那麼』,但亦可不必譯出。

數量詞 + 名詞 (,) and + 主詞 + 助動詞 (will、can...) + 原形動詞

……, (那麼)……

類似用法:

以原形動詞為首的命令句 (,) │ and │ + 主詞 + 助動詞 (will、can...) +
　　　　　　　　　　　　　　│ or │

原形動詞

……, │ 那麼 │ ……
　　　│ 否則 │

例: One more step <u>and</u> I'll shoot.
　(再走一步,我就開槍了。)

Two more hours <u>and</u> I'll be leaving for America.
(再過兩個小時,我就要動身前往美國了。)

Scratch my back <u>and</u> I will scratch yours.
(你幫我抓背,我就幫你抓背/喻:你對我好,我也就對你好。──諺語)

＊ scratch [skrætʃ] vt. 抓; 搔 (癢)

Shut up <u>or</u> you'll be in trouble.
(住嘴,否則你就會有麻煩。)

Substitution
代　　換

1. **People should make it a rule never to swim too far out from the beach.**

   Ian makes it a rule to speak only when (he is) spoken to.

   Mr. Richey makes it a rule to make a big donation to charity once a year.

   人們應該養成不要游得離海灘邊太遠的習慣。

   伊安有別人跟他講話時才講話的習慣。

   里奇先生固定每一年捐一大筆錢給慈善機構。

2. **So just a few strokes in the right direction and you'll be out of danger.**

   Just one more point, and we will win the game.

   Take this medicine every day or you won't get well.

   所以只要朝正確方向游幾下, 那麼你就能脫離險境了。

   只要再得一分, 我們就贏得比賽了。

   每天服這種藥, 否則你不會復原。

Lesson 34
A Lifesaving Kiss
救命的一吻

Dialogue
實用會話

Tonya is a beautiful lifeguard. She has just saved Marvin from drowning in the ocean.

(M=Marvin; T=Tonya)

M: I feel a little groggy.

T: That's natural. You nearly drowned a minute ago.

M: You saved my life! You're my savior!

T: Don't get too excited. A minute ago you weren't breathing, and I had to give you CPR.

M: Oh, I wish I could remember that mouth-to-mouth resuscitation with such a beautiful woman as you.

T: Take it easy, OK?

M: Oh, wait...I feel faint again.

T: Nice try, buddy, but don't even dream about it.

譚雅是位美麗的救生員,她剛剛從海中把險些溺水的馬文救起來。

馬文:我覺得有點四肢無力。

譚雅:那當然。你剛才差點淹死。

馬文:妳救了我一命!妳是我的救命恩人!

譚雅:別太激動!剛才你的呼吸停了,因此我非得給你做心肺復甦術不可。

馬文:哦,我希望我能記得像妳這樣的美女曾給我做的口對口人工呼吸。

譚雅:你冷靜點,好嗎?

馬文:哦,等等……我覺得我又快昏倒了。

譚雅:掰得好,老兄,但是你想都別想。

Key Points
重點提示

1. **lifesaving** [ˈlaɪfˌsevɪŋ] a. 救生的

2. **lifeguard** [ˈlaɪfˌgɑrd] n. 救生員

3. **save** [sev] vt. 解救

   save + 人 + from...　　解救某人免於……

   例: The bank loan saved Mr. Smith from bankruptcy.
   (那筆銀行貨款解救史密斯先生免於破產。)

4. **groggy** [ˈgrɑgɪ] a. (因疲勞、生病、喝酒而) 軟弱無力的

   例: Denis felt groggy after a few beers.
   (丹尼斯喝了幾瓶啤酒後便全身無力。)

5. **savior** [ˈsevjɚ] n. 拯救者

   例: The savings I put away for a rainy day turned out to be my savior.
   (這筆我為了以防萬一而存的積蓄結果成了我的救星。)

6. **breathe** [brið] vi. 呼吸

breath [brɛθ] n. 呼吸; 氣息

hold one's breath　　屏息靜氣

catch one's breath　　喘過氣來

take a deep breath　　深呼吸

例: The bus was so packed that I could hardly breathe.
(這輛公車擠得我幾乎不能呼吸。)

＊ packed [pækt] a. 擁擠的, 擠滿人的

The lifeguard can hold his breath under water for five minutes.
(那個救生員可以在水中憋氣五分鐘。)

I need a minute to catch my breath before I tell you what happened.
(我得需要一分鐘喘口氣才能告訴你發生什麼事。)

Ben took a deep breath before he dived into the pool.
(班在跳水進入游泳池前深深地吸了口氣。)

7. **CPR**　　心肺復甦術

= cardiopulmonary resuscitation

give + 人 + CPR　　替某人做心肺復甦術

cardiopulmonary [ˌkɑrdɪoˈpʌlməˌnɛrɪ] a. 心肺的

resuscitation [rɪˌsʌsəˈteʃən] n. 復甦

例: Because of AIDS, some doctors are reluctant to give people CPR.
(由於愛滋病的緣故,有些醫生不願意替人做心肺復甦術。)

8. **mouth-to-mouth resuscitation**　　口對口人工呼吸

例: I once saved a girl by giving her mouth-to-mouth resuscitation.
(我曾經用口對口人工呼吸救了一個女孩子。)

9. **Take it easy.**　　冷靜點。

例: Doris: I'm going to kill Don for standing me up.
Edith: Take it easy.
(桃樂絲:唐放我鴿子,我要殺了他。)
(伊蒂絲:冷靜點。)

10. **faint** [fent] a. 暈眩的, 即將昏倒的 & vi. 昏倒

feel faint　　覺得快要昏倒

例: The old lady felt faint under the scorching heat.
(在這種酷熱的天氣下，那個老婦人覺得快要昏倒了。)

 ＊ scorching [ˋskɔrtʃɪŋ] a. 灼熱的

Please open the windows and let some fresh air into the room before I faint.
(麻煩打開窗戶讓些新鮮的空氣進到室內來，免得我會昏倒。)

11. **buddy** [ˋbʌdɪ] n. 老兄, 好友 (常用於口語中)

例: My buddies were willing to lend me some money but I refused to be a borrower.
(我的好朋友都很願意借錢給我，但我不想當個借貸者。)

12. **dream about...**　　夢想……; (作夢) 夢到……

= dream of...

例: I dreamt about winning the lottery last night.
(我昨晚夢到中了彩券。)

13. 本文:

Nice try, buddy, but don't even dream about it.

= You made a good attempt, pal, but don't even dream about it.
老兄, 你的企圖倒是不錯, 但 (想吻我) 門都沒有。

＊ pal [pæl] n. 朋友; 夥伴

請選出下列各句中正確的一項

1. The wine made Mr. Wang a little _____.
   (A) cloudy　　(B) groggy　　　(C) misty　　　(D) greedy

2. My brother tired _____ out preparing for the exam.
   (A) he　　　　(B) his　　　　(C) him　　　　(D) himself

3. John makes it a rule _____ to bed early every night.
   (A) and go　　(B) to go　　　(C) going　　　(D) to going

4. It was so crowded in the room I couldn't _____.
   (A) breathe　　(B) breath　　(C) breadth　　(D) breathing

5. The old man _____ when he heard his son had died in the war.
   (A) afraid　　(B) fainted　　(C) frightened　　(D) fought

解答:

1. (B)	2. (D)	3. (B)	4. (A)	5. (B)

Lesson 35

A Sense of Security

安全感

Reading
閱　讀

Some people take the view that sometimes in life we have to take chances in order to make progress. I admire such people. It certainly takes courage to take risks. Maybe it's due to my upbringing, but I am the type who likes to play it safe.

People like me believe in the saying, "A bird in the hand is worth two in the bush." Conservative as it may be, it keeps me out of trouble. I must confess, however, that such a lifestyle may, at times, be boring. Admittedly, my life is not half as colorful or exciting as other people's, but at least it gives me a sense of security.

　　有些人認為我們一生中有時候必須冒險以求得進步。我很欽佩這種人。冒險的確需要勇氣。或許是因為我所受的教養，我卻是那種行事謹慎以策安全的人。

　　像我這種人相信俗話說的：『一鳥在手勝於兩鳥在林。』雖然這種想法也許很保守，但卻使我避免惹上麻煩。然而，我必須承認這種生活方式有時候可能很無聊。不可否認地，我的生活雖不及別人生活一半的多采多姿或刺激，但至少它能帶給我安全感。

Vocabulary & Idioms
單字 & 片語註解

1. **sense** [sɛns] n. 感覺

   a sense of duty　　責任感

   a sense of humor　　幽默感

   例: I find people without a sense of humor rather boring.
   (我發覺缺乏幽默感的人很乏味。)

2. **security** [sɪˈkjʊrətɪ] n. 安全; 防護

   secure [sɪˈkjʊr] a. 安全的

   例: There was tight security at the news conference.
   (記者招待會的安全措施非常嚴密。)

   The poor orphan doesn't feel secure about his future.
   (那個可憐的孤兒對他的未來感到很不安。)
   ＊ orphan [ˈɔrfən] n. 孤兒

3. **take the view + that** 子句　　認為……

   例: Emily takes the view that all men are bad.
   (艾蜜莉認為全天下的男人都不是好東西。)

4. **take chances**　　冒險

例: If you don't take chances in life, you'll never get anywhere.
(如果你在生活中不冒險的話，就不會有成就。)

5. **progress** [ˈprɑɡrɛs] n. 進步 (常與動詞 make 並用)

make progress　　進步

例: The lazy student is making no progress at all.
(那個懶惰的學生一點進步也沒有。)

6. **admire** [ədˈmaɪr] vt. 敬佩, 敬仰; 讚賞

例: I admire Michael Jackson's talent, but I don't admire his lifestyle.
(我敬仰麥可‧傑克遜的才幹，但不欣賞他的生活方式。)

7. **courage** [ˈkɝ·ɪdʒ] n. 勇氣

courageous [kəˈredʒəs] a. 勇敢的

例: Do you have the courage to ask Jane out on a date?
(你有勇氣約珍外出約會嗎？)

The courageous boy jumped in front of a bus to save a stray dog.
(那個勇敢的男孩跳到公車前救了一隻野狗。)

＊ stray [stre] a. 走失的, 迷路的

8. **risk** [rɪsk] n. 危險; 風險

take risks　　冒險
= take chances

at the risk of...　　冒……之險

例: Tightrope walkers take risks every time they perform.
(走鋼索藝人每次表演都冒著很大的危險。)

In fact, tightrope walkers make a living at the risk of their lives.
(事實上，走鋼索藝人冒生命的危險謀生。)

9. **upbringing** [ˈʌpˌbrɪŋɪŋ] n. 教養

例: You can tell from that boy's behavior that he's had good upbringing.
(從那男孩的行為舉止你可以知道他很有教養。)

10. **play it safe**　　謹慎行事以策安全

例: I'm going to play it safe and set two alarm clocks to make sure I get up early tomorrow morning.
(為確保明天早上早起，我設定了兩個鬧鐘。)

11. **A bird in the hand is worth two in the bush.**
一鳥在手勝於兩鳥在林。(諺語)

＊ bush [bʊʃ] n. 矮樹林, 叢林

12. **conservative** [kənˈsɝ·vətɪv] a. 保守的

例: The younger generation of Chinese girls are becoming less and less conservative.
(中國年輕一代的女孩子變得越來越不保守了。)

13. **confess** [kənˈfɛs] vt. 承認

例: Robert confessed that he had stolen the money.
(羅伯特承認錢是他偷的。)

14. **lifestyle** [ˈlaɪfˌstaɪl] n. 生活方式

例: The old Chinese couple couldn't get used to the American lifestyle and returned to their homeland.
(那對年老的中國夫婦無法適應美國的生活方式而返回故鄉去了。)
　＊ homeland [ˈhomˌlænd] n. 家園; 祖國

15. **at times**　　偶爾, 有時 (= sometimes)

例: At times I wonder what my purpose in life is.
(有時我會納悶我生活的目的何在。)

16. **admittedly** [ədˈmɪtɪdlɪ] adv. 公認 (明白) 地; 不可否認地

例: Mr. Bailey is admittedly the fastest runner in the world.
(百利先生被公認為是世界上最快的跑者。)

Grammar Notes
文法重點

本課複習"It takes＋表條件的名詞＋to＋原形動詞" (從事……需要……條件) 的用法, 並介紹 as 取代 though 的用法, 以及"倍數詞＋as...as..." (是……的 幾倍) 的用法。

1. **It** certainly **takes courage to take** risks.

    冒險的確需要勇氣。

    本句使用了"It takes＋表條件的名詞＋to＋原形動詞"的句型, It 是虛主詞, 代替其後的不定詞片語 (to＋原形動詞), 此不定詞片語才是真主詞。

    It takes＋表條件的名詞＋to＋原形動詞
    從事……需要……(條件)

    例: It takes a lot of imagination to be a science fiction writer.
    (要做個科幻小說家需要有很豐富的想像力。)
    ＊ science fiction [ˈsaɪəns ˌfɪkʃən] n. 科幻小說

    It takes patience and energy to teach in a kindergarten.
    (在幼稚園任教需要有耐心和精力。)

2. **Conservative as it may be, it keeps me out of trouble.**

= Conservative <u>though</u> it may be, it keeps me out of trouble.

= <u>Though</u> it may be conservative, it keeps me out of trouble.

    雖然這種想法也許很保守, 但卻使我避免惹上麻煩。

    注意:

    though (雖然) 引導的副詞子句, 若有下列句構出現時, though 可用 as 取代:

    a. Though＋主詞＋be 動詞/連綴動詞 (seem、appear、look...)＋形容詞, 主要子句

    ＝形容詞＋<u>though</u>＋主詞＋be 動詞/連綴動詞, 主要子句

    ＝形容詞＋<u>as</u>＋主詞＋be 動詞/連綴動詞, 主要子句

例: Though he is rich, he is very stingy.

= Rich <u>though</u> he is, he is very stingy.

= Rich <u>as</u> he is, he is very stingy.
(雖然他很有錢，但卻很吝嗇。)

Though she looked calm, she was nervous inside.

= Calm <u>though</u> she looked, she was nervous inside.

= Calm <u>as</u> she looked, she was nervous inside.
(雖然她看起來平靜，但內心卻很緊張。)

b. Though + 主詞 + 動詞 + 副詞, 主要子句

= 副詞 + <u>though</u> + 主詞 + 動詞, 主要子句

= 副詞 + <u>as</u> + 主詞 + 動詞, 主要子句

例: Though he ran fast, he didn't win the race.

= Fast <u>though</u> he ran, he didn't win the race.

= Fast <u>as</u> he ran, he didn't win the race.
(雖然他跑得很快，但還是沒贏得賽跑。)

3. **Admittedly, my life is not <u>half as</u> colorful or exciting <u>as</u> other people's, but at least it gives me a sense of security.**

= <u>I must admit that</u> my life is not half as colorful or exciting as other people's <u>lives,</u> but at least it gives me a sense of security.
不可否認地, 我的生活雖不及別人生活一半的多采多姿及刺激, 但至少它能帶給我安全感。

注意:

本句使用了"倍數詞 + as...as..." (是……的幾倍) 的句型, 在此句型中, 第一個 as 是副詞, 譯成『一樣地』, 其後須接形容詞或副詞以供修飾; 而第二個 as 則為副詞連接詞, 譯成『和……』, 其所引導的副詞子句修飾其前第一個 as。其造句步驟如下:

譯: 她的年紀是我的兩倍。

第一步: 先譯『她的年紀和我一樣。』

She is <u>as</u> old <u>as</u> I.

第二步: 再將倍數詞『兩倍』(twice) 置於第一個 as 之前。

　　　　She is <u>twice as</u> old <u>as</u> I.

注意:

倍數詞除了 half (一半), twice (兩倍), three/four/five...times (三/四/五……倍) 外, 下列詞類亦可視為倍數詞:

one-third	三分之一
two-third<u>s</u>	三分之二
⋮	⋮
three-fourth<u>s</u>	四分之三
one-fifth	五分之一
two-fifth<u>s</u>	五分之二
⋮	⋮

例: This bridge is <u>three times as</u> long <u>as</u> that one.
　　(這座橋是那座橋的三倍長。)

She eats only <u>half as</u> much <u>as</u> he.
(她的食量只有他的一半。)

This car is only <u>one-third as</u> expensive <u>as</u> that one.
(這部車的價格只有那部的三分之一。)

Substitution
代　　換

1. **It certainly takes courage to take risks.**

   It takes patience to learn a language well.

   It takes a lot of strength to lift that heavy box up.

   冒險的確需要勇氣。

   學好一種語言需要有耐心。

   舉起那個笨重的箱子需要很大的力氣。

2. **My life is not half as colorful or exciting as other people's.**

I'm not half as rich as you think I am.

Sam is twice as strong as his brother.

我的生活不及別人生活一半的多采多姿及刺激。

我沒有你想的一半有錢。

山姆有他弟弟的兩倍壯。

Lesson 36
The Sex Maniac
大色狼

Dialogue
實用會話

Randy is consoling his friend Steve, whose girlfriend has just left him.

(R=Randy; S=Steve)

R: Come on, Steve. No point in crying over spilt milk.

S: I shouldn't have let her go.

R: Forget her. There're plenty of fish in the sea.

S: But there's only one that I like.

R: How do you know if you haven't tried others?

S: You know me. I'm a one-woman man.

R: You're a fool!

S: And you're a sex maniac!

朗迪正在安慰他的朋友史帝夫，史帝夫的女友離開他了。

朗　迪：好了啦，史帝夫。覆水難收啊。

史帝夫：我不應該讓她走的。

朗　迪：忘了她吧。天涯何處無芳草。

史帝夫：可是我愛的只有一個。

朗　迪：你還沒試過別人怎麼會知道呢？

史帝夫：你了解我這個人。我是個感情專一的男人。

朗　迪：你是個大傻瓜！

史帝夫：而你是個大色狼！

Key Points
重點提示

1. **maniac** [ˈmenɪˌæk] n. 熱中者; 瘋子

   例: That maniac is driving much too fast.
   (那個瘋子車開得太快。)

2. **console** [kənˈsol] vt. 安慰

   例: People tried to console the widow at the funeral.
   (人們在葬禮上試著安慰那名寡婦。)

3. **No point in ＋ 動名詞.**　　做……是沒有意義的/沒有用的。

= There is no point in ＋ 動名詞.

= There is no sense in ＋ 動名詞.

= It is no use ＋ 動名詞.

   例: There's no point in repeating the question; it's obvious no one knows the answer.
   (重覆問那個問題是沒有意義的；很顯然沒有人知道答案。)

   It's no use trying to convince the stubborn old man to give up drinking.
   (要勸服那個頑固的老人戒酒是沒有用的。)

4. **cry over...**　　為……而哭

例: You're wasting your tears crying over that lousy guy.
（為那個差勁的男人哭泣妳是在浪費妳的眼淚。）

5. **spilt milk**　　灑出的牛奶

spilt [spɪlt] a. 灑/溢出的

* spilt 為 spill 的過去分詞作形容詞用。

spill [spɪl] vt. 灑; 使溢出

動詞三態: spill、spilt/spilled、spilt/spilled。

例: The spilt Coke attracted cockroaches.
（溢出的可樂引來蟑螂。）

The child spilt the milk all over herself.
（那個小孩灑得她全身都是牛奶。）

6. **plenty of + 複數可數名詞/不可數名詞**　　許多……

plenty [ˈplɛntɪ] n. 許多, 豐富

例: Mom has plenty of coins in her purse.
（老媽的皮包內有許多硬幣。）

I get plenty of fresh air living in the mountains.
（住在山上我呼吸到很多新鮮的空氣。）

7. **a one-woman man**　　感情專一的男人; 從一而終的男人

例: My dad has been a one-woman man all his life.
（我爸爸終其一生是個感情專一的男人。）

請選出下列各句中正確的一項

1. The race car driver took too many _____ and eventually got killed in the race.
   (A) opportunities　　　　　　(B) methods
   (C) cases　　　　　　　　　　(D) chances

2. It'll take _____ two years to build my dream house.
   (A) at first　　(B) at last　　(C) at least　　(D) at once

3. My classmates _____ the view that all politicians are sly.
   (A) take　　(B) choose　　(C) try　　(D) give

4. A good friend will _____ you when you are depressed.
   (A) cancel　　(B) console　　(C) control　　(D) cheat

5. There's no point _____ someone to do something if he doesn't want to do it.
   (A) to force　　(B) force　　(C) in forcing　　(D) forcing

解答:

> 1. (D)　　2. (C)　　3. (A)　　4. (B)　　5. (C)

Lesson 37
Garbage Could Mean Money
垃圾即黃金

Reading
閱　　讀

Fashion never ceases to surprise me. Recently, a fashion designer came up with another strange creation. His idea comes straight from the garbage dump, so to speak. He makes sweaters from used plastic bottles. What a weird sweater that's going to be!

This new kind of sweater will protect you from the rain and cold. They will, therefore, be especially attractive to outdoor people such as fishermen, hunters and mountain climbers. However, they're not cheap. They sell at prices ranging from US

$100 to US$150. What a great idea for making money! Don't you think?

> 流行服飾總是不斷地令我驚奇。最近，一名時裝設計師想出另一種奇異的時裝。他的這個點子可以說是直接來自垃圾堆。他利用使用過的塑膠瓶罐來製造毛衣。那將是一件多麼怪異的毛衣啊！
> 這種新款式的毛衣能夠為你擋雨禦寒。因此，這些毛衣對戶外活動的人士像是漁夫、獵人和登山者特別具有吸引力。然而，這些毛衣並不便宜。它們的售價在一百到一百五十塊美金之間。這真是個賺錢的妙點子，不是嗎？

Vocabulary & Idioms
單字 & 片語註解

1. **garbage** [ˈɡɑrbɪdʒ] n. 垃圾

   注意:

   garbage、rubbish [ˈrʌbɪʃ]、trash [træʃ] 皆表垃圾, 且均為不可數名詞, 故表『一件垃圾』, 須與 a piece of 並用。

   例: Mother asked me to take out the garbage after dinner.
   (老媽叫我晚餐後把垃圾拿出去。)

2. **fashion** [ˈfæʃən] n. 流行服飾; 時尚

   be in fashion　　流行

   be out of fashion　　不再流行

   例: Miniskirts are in fashion again.
   (迷你裙又再度流行了。)

   Having a beard is out of fashion nowadays.
   (現在不流行留鬍子。)

3. **cease** [sis] vt. 停止

例: As soon as we called off the outing, it ceased to rain.
(我們一取消郊遊，雨就停了。)

4. **recently** [ˈrisəntlɪ] adv. 最近, 近來
例: The old man had a stroke only recently.
(那個老人就在最近中風過一次。)
＊ stroke [strok] n. 中風

5. **designer** [dɪˈzaɪnɚ] n. 設計師
例: You must have imagination to be a good designer.
(要成為一個好的設計師，你必須要有想像力。)

6. **come up with...** 想出……
例: Frank came up with the best solution to the problem.
(法蘭克想出了這個問題最好的解決辦法。)

7. **creation** [krɪˈeʃən] n. (時裝款式等的) 新製作 (可數); 創作 (不可數)
例: These clothes are the latest creations from Paris.
(這些衣服是來自巴黎的最新款式。)

The poor economic situation was responsible for the creation of social unrest.
(經濟蕭條導致社會動盪不安。)
＊ unrest [ʌnˈrɛst] n. (社會上的) 不安, 不穩

8. **straight** [stret] adv. 直接地; 筆直地
例: The drunk couldn't walk straight.
(那個醉漢走路東倒西歪的。)

9. **dump** [dʌmp] n. 堆 & vt. 傾倒 (垃圾等)
a garbage dump 垃圾場; 垃圾堆
例: The awful smell is coming from the garbage dump.
(這可怕的氣味是來自那垃圾場。)

The woman dumped her garbage on the corner of the street.
(那個婦人把垃圾丟在街角。)

10. **so to speak** 可以說, 可謂

本片語通常作插入語, 可置於句中或句尾。

例: All men are animals, so to speak.

= All men are, so to speak, animals.

(所有的人可以說都是動物。)

11. **sweater** [ˈswɛtɚ] n. 毛衣

12. **plastic** [ˈplæstɪk] a. 塑膠的

13. **bottle** [ˈbɑtḷ] n. 瓶子

14. **weird** [wɪrd] a. 怪異的

例: The girl over there gave me a weird look.

(那邊那個女孩用怪異的表情看了我一眼。)

15. **protect** [prəˈtɛkt] vt. 保護, 防禦

protect...from... 保護/防禦……免於……

例: Animals will protect their young from danger.

(動物會保護其子女不受到危險。)

＊ young [jʌŋ] n. (動物、鳥類的) 幼獸; 雛 (集合名詞不可數, 使用時之前置 the 或所有格 their, your, his 等)

16. **attractive** [əˈtræktɪv] a. 吸引人的, 迷人的

例: All the men couldn't help looking at that attractive woman.

(所有的男人忍不住盯著那個誘人的女人瞧。)

17. **outdoor** [ˈaʊtˌdor] a. 戶外的, 室外的

indoor [ˈɪnˌdor] a. 戶內的, 室內的

outdoors [ˌaʊtˈdorz] adv. 戶外地

indoors [ɪnˈdorz] adv. 戶內地

例: I prefer outdoor sports.

(我比較喜歡戶外運動項目。)

You'd better stay indoors during the typhoon.
(颱風期間，你最好待在室內。)

18. **fishermen** [ˈfɪʃəmən] n. 漁夫

＊ 單數形為 fisherman [ˈfɪʃəmən]。

19. **hunter** [ˈhʌntɚ] n. 獵人

20. **mountain climber** [ˈmaʊntn̩ ˌklaɪmɚ] n. 登山者

21. **range** [rendʒ] vi. (範圍) 涉及, 擴展

range from A to B　　(範圍) 從 A 到 B

例: We have shoes ranging from size 10 to size 30.
(從十號鞋到三十號鞋我們都有。)

Grammar Notes
文法重點

本課介紹及物動詞 cease 的用法, 以及 so to speak 和"ranging from...to..."
的用法。

1. **Fashion never <u>ceases to surprise</u> me.**

= Fashion never <u>ceases surprising</u> me.

= Fashion never <u>stops surprising</u> me.
流行服飾總是不斷地令我驚奇。

及物動詞 cease [sis] (停止) 後可接不定詞片語 (to + 原形動詞) 或動名詞
作受詞, 兩者意思相同, 均表『停止做……』、『不做……』之意, 即等於
stop 接動名詞的用法。

cease to + 原形動詞　　停止做……, 不做……

= cease + 動名詞

= stop + 動名詞

例: If I <u>cease to work</u>, my family will starve.
 = If I <u>cease working</u>, my family will starve.
 = If I <u>stop working</u>, my family will starve.
 (我若不工作的話，家人就要挨餓了。)

注意:

stop 後除可接動名詞作受詞, 表『停止做……』的意思外, 亦可接不定詞片語作受詞, 但意思不同於前, 而是表『停下某事, 而改做另一件事』的意思。

stop + 動名詞　　停止做……

stop to + 原形動詞　　停卜某事去做……

例: Mr. Chen <u>stopped working</u> as a fireman when he was sixty years old.
 (陳先生六十歲時就不再當救火員了。)

 <u>I stopped to buy</u> some groceries on my way home.
 (我在回家的路上停下來買了些雜貨。)

2. **His idea comes straight from the garbage dump, <u>so to speak</u>.**
 他的這個點子可以說是直接來自垃圾堆。

 上列句中使用了 so to speak (可以這麼說) 置於句尾的用法, 但 so to speak 亦常作插入語使用, 尤其置於句中 be 動詞之後。

 so to speak　　可以這麼說

 例: Ted's so stupid that he can't tell the difference between black and white, so to speak.
 (泰德可以說是笨到分不清黑與白。)

 The brilliant doctor is, so to speak, a magician.
 (那位才氣縱橫的醫師可說是個魔術師。)

3. **They sell at prices <u>ranging from</u> US$100 <u>to</u> US$150.**
= They sell at prices <u>which range from</u> US$100 <u>to</u> US$150.
 它們的售價在一百到一百五十塊美金之間。

上列句中的"ranging from US$100 to US$150"是現在分詞片語,作形容
詞用,修飾其前的名詞 prices,乃由形容詞子句 which range from US$100
to US$150 化簡而來。

range from...to...　　(範圍) 從……到……

例: The ages of the students in my class range from eight to twelve.
(我班上學生的年齡從八歲到十二歲都有。)

Substitution
代　　換

1. **Fashion never ceases to surprise me.**
   Bars must cease selling alcoholic drinks to minors.
   Ann says she'll never stop loving her boyfriend.
   流行服飾總是不斷地令我驚奇。
   酒吧必須停止販賣含有酒精的飲料給未成年者。
   安說她將不會中止她對男友的愛。

2. **They sell at prices ranging from US$100 to US$150.**
   The singer can sing songs ranging from popsongs to rock.
   People from all walks of life, ranging from waiters to bank managers,
   were at the party.
   它們的售價在一百到一百五十塊美金之間。
   那名歌手從流行歌曲到搖滾樂都會唱。
   宴會上各行各業的人,從侍者到銀行經理都有。

Lesson 38
That's Fashion
那才叫做時髦

Dialogue
實用會話

Andy and Jess are at a fashion designer's party.

(A=Andy; J=Jess)

A: My God, Jess. What's that on Betty's head?

J: Beats me. How weird! I think it's a new kind of hat.

A: Oh, really? If you ask me, it's more like a bird's nest. How stupid it looks!

J: You think so? Hey, wait a minute. You might be right. There's something moving in the nest...I mean, hat.

A: Gee whiz! It's a bird.

J: Holy cow! How does she keep it from flying away?

A: Don't you see? She's got it fastened to a gold chain around her neck.

J: If the bird were strong enough, it could fly her to the moon, so to speak.

A: That would really be funny.

J: Well, that's fashion!

安迪和潔絲在一場由時裝設計師開的派對上。

安迪：我的天啊，潔絲，貝蒂頭上那什麼玩意兒啊？

潔絲：問倒我了。真是很怪異！我想那是一種新款式的帽子吧。

安迪：哦，是嗎？如果妳問我的話，我倒覺得那比較像個鳥巢。那東西看起來好愚蠢喔！

潔絲：你真這麼想嗎？嘿，等一下。你可能說得對。那鳥巢裡……我是指帽子裡有東西在動。

安迪：哇！是一隻鳥喔。

潔絲：天啊！她是怎麼不讓那隻鳥飛走的？

安迪：妳看不出來嗎？她用一條繞在脖子上的金項鍊把牠栓住。

潔絲：如果那隻鳥力氣夠大的話，牠甚至可以帶她飛到月球。

安迪：那一定很有趣。

潔絲：呃，那就是時髦嘛！

Key Points
重點提示

1. **Beats me.** 問倒我了。

   本句為"It beats me."的化簡。

   * beat [bit] vt. 打擊

   動詞三態: beat、beat、beaten。

   例: Secretary: How old do you think the boss is?
   　　　Clerk: Beats me.
   （秘書：你認為老闆幾歲？）
   （職員：問倒我了。）

2. **nest** [nɛst] n. 鳥巢

   例: Birds often build nests from twigs.
   （鳥類通常用小樹枝築巢。）
   　　* twig [twɪg] n. 小細枝

3. **Gee whiz!** [ˈdʒi ˌhwɪz] int. 哇！

---

4. **keep...from...** 保持……免於……

例: How can I keep my dog from biting up the furniture?
(我怎麼才能不讓我的狗咬壞傢俱呢？)

5. **fasten** [′fæsn̩] vt. 使牢固

fasten A to B 把 A 繫/綁在 B 上

例: Joe fastened his bicycle to a lamppost but it got stolen just the same.
(喬把腳踏車綁在路燈柱上但照樣被偷。)

* just the same = still 仍然

6. **gold chain** 金鍊

chain [tʃen] n. 鍊子

請選出下列各句中正確的一項

1. Paris is sometimes called the _____ capital of the world.
   (A) French (B) fashion (C) garbage (D) designer

2. The frightened birds flew _____ as soon as they heard the noise.
   (A) by (B) along (C) away (D) to

3. Todd never ceased _____ to get a date with Sharon.
   (A) try (B) tries (C) trying (D) to trying

4. I didn't know _____ smart he was until his teacher told me.
   (A) why (B) what (C) where (D) how

解答:

1. (B)   2. (C)   3. (C)   4. (D)

Lesson 39
At the Foreign Exchange
出國結匯

Reading
閱　讀

When you go abroad, what's the thing you need most? Money, of course! You'll need to go to the bank to buy some traveler's checks. Then when you arrive at your destination, you'll have to go to a bank to cash the checks. Every bank has a foreign exchange department. However, you'll have to speak with the teller in English because he or she will probably not understand Chinese.

You should, therefore, brush up on some of the words and phrases that are commonly used when changing money at a bank. For example, you might want to know what the day's exchange rate is, or if there are any handling charges, etc. Worried? Don't be. Our next lesson will give you a good idea of what you need to say and how to say it.

你出國的時候最需要的東西是什麼？當然是錢！你得先去銀行買好旅行支票。等你到達目的地，再到當地的銀行將支票換成現金。每家銀行都有外匯部門，但是行員可能不懂中文，所以你必須跟他們說英文。

因此你該把銀行兌換外幣常用的字詞片語溫習一下。比方說，你可能想知道當日的匯率或者銀行是否收取任何手續費等等。擔心嗎？用不著。我們下一課會教你該說什麼和怎麼說。

Vocabulary & Idioms
單字 & 片語註解

1. **foreign exchange** [ˏfɔrɪn ɪksˈtʃendʒ] n. 外匯
   exchange [ɪksˈtʃendʒ] n. & vt. 交換
   exchange A for B　　用 A 交換 B
   例: The girl working at the foreign exchange probably speaks English.
   (在外匯部工作的那個女孩可能會講英文。)

   I'll exchange my pen for your book if you like.
   (如果你喜歡的話，我可以拿我的筆換你的書。)

2. **traveler's check** [ˈtrævlɚz ˏtʃɛk] n. 旅行支票
   例: Isn't it more convenient to have credit cards than traveler's checks?
   (持有信用卡不是比旅行支票方便嗎？)

3. **arrive** [əˋraɪv] vi. 到達

arrive at + 小地方 (如: 郵局、學校、車站……等建築物)

arrive in + 大地方 (如: 城市、國家……等大區域)

例: We arrived at the airport just in time to see Bob off.
(我們及時抵達機場為鮑勃送行。)

The plane arrived in Atlanta on schedule.
(那班飛機按時抵達亞特蘭大。)

4. **destination** [ˌdɛstəˋneʃən] n. 目的地

例: If you spend so much here, we'll run out of money before we get to our next destination.
(如果你在這裡花這麼多錢的話，在我們到下一個目的地前錢就花光了。)

5. **cash** [kæʃ] vt. 兌換現金

例: It's better to have some identification when you go cash a check.
(你將支票兌換成現金時，最好帶著身分證件。)

＊identification [aɪˌdɛntəfəˋkeʃən] n. 能證明身分之物 (如身分證等, 是不可數名詞)

ID card　　身分證 (可數名詞; ID 是 identity [aɪˋdɛntətɪ] 的縮寫, 表『身分』)

6. **department** [dɪˋpɑrtmənt] n. 部門

例: Which department of the bank do you work for?
(你在銀行的哪一個部門工作？)

7. **teller** [ˋtɛlɚ] n. (銀行) 櫃員, 出納員

8. **brush up on...**　　複習……

例: If you're going to Paris, you'd better brush up on your French.
(如果你要去巴黎，最好複習一下你的法文。)

9. **phrase** [frez] n. 片語

例: Some students recite useful phrases to include in their compositions.
(有些學生會背有用的片語以便用在作文中。)

10. **commonly** [ˈkɑmənlɪ] adv. 普遍地; 常用地

例: Idioms are commonly used in conversation.
(習慣語常用於會話中。)

11. **exchange rate** [ɪksˈtʃendʒ ˌret] n. 匯率
注意:

在表示一種貨幣對另一種貨幣的匯率時應使用介詞against, 譯作『對』。

例: What's today's exchange rate for US dollars against Japanese yen?
(今天美元對日圓的匯率是多少？)

12. **handling charge**　手續費

handle [ˈhændl̩] vt. 處理

例: The bank deducts US$10 as a handling charge every time I send some money abroad.
(每次我匯錢到國外，銀行都扣除十塊錢美金作為手續費。)

The manager handles every office problem very diplomatically.
(經理非常圓滑地處理每個辦公室問題。)

　＊ diplomatically [ˌdɪpləˈmætɪklɪ] adv. 圓滑地; 以外交方式

13. 本文:

Worried? Don't be.　擔心嗎？用不著。

= Are you worried? Don't be worried.

＊ worried [ˈwɝɪd] a. 擔心的
be worried about...　擔心……

例: Ted is worried about tomorrow's English test because he hasn't studied.
(泰德很擔心明天的英文考試，因為他沒唸書。)

Grammar Notes
文 法 重 點

本課介紹"need to + 原形動詞"的用法, 以及 if 取代 whether 引導名詞子句作及物動詞受詞的用法。

1. **You'll <u>need to go</u> to the bank to buy some traveler's checks.**
   你得先去銀行買好旅行支票。

   Our next lesson will give you a good idea of what you <u>need to say</u> and how to say it.
   我們下一課會教你該說什麼和怎麼說。

   上列句中, 使用了"need to + 原形動詞" (必須……)的句型。

   在肯定句中, need 為一般動詞, 有人稱和時態的變化, 其後可接名詞或不定詞片語 (to + 原形動詞)作受詞。

   need + 名詞　　需要……

   need to + 原形動詞　　必須……

   例: She <u>needs</u> <u>our help</u>.
   (她需要我們的幫助。)

   I <u>need</u> <u>to go</u> now.
   (我現在必須走了。)

   若某物『需要』某種方法處理時, need 之後可接不定詞片語, 但一定為被動語態; 或接動名詞, 但一定為主動語態。

   例: The door needs <u>being fixed</u>. (✕)
   → The door needs <u>to be fixed</u>. (○)
   　　　　　　不定詞片語

   = The door needs <u>fixing</u>.
   　　　　　　動名詞
   (這扇門需要修理。)

My car needs <u>being checked</u>. (✕)

→ My car needs <u>to be checked</u>. (○)
　　　　　　　　 不定詞片語

= My car needs <u>checking</u>.
　　　　　　　　 動名詞
(我的車子需要檢查一下。)

注意:

a. need 與 not 並用時, need not 視為助動詞, 無人稱和時態的變化, 其後直接置原形動詞。

need not + 原形動詞　　不必……

例: He <u>needs</u> not go. (✕)
　　　He need not <u>to</u> go. (✕)
→ He <u>need not go</u>. (○)
= He <u>doesn't need to go</u>.
　　　(他不必去。)

　　　You <u>need not pay</u> this bill immediately.
= You <u>don't need to pay</u> this bill immediately.
　　　(你不必馬上付這筆帳。)

b. 表過去狀況時:

didn't need to + 原形動詞　　當時不必……(而且亦未……)

need not have + 過去分詞　　當時不必……(但卻做了)

此兩種句法完全不同。第一種句法表示『過去的事實』,而第二種句法則為『與過去事實相反』的假設語氣。

例: He <u>didn't need to attend</u> the meeting, so he stayed home.
　　　(當時他不必去開會,所以就留在家裡。)

　　　You <u>need not have given</u> me so much money.
　　　(你當時並不必給我這麼多錢。——但卻給了)

2. For example, you might want to know what the day's exchange rate is, or <u>if</u> there are any handling charges, etc.

比方說, 你可能想知道當日的匯率或者銀行是否收取任何手續費等等。

上列句中, what 引導的名詞子句與 if 引導的名詞子句為對等連接詞 or 所連接, 共同作其前及物動詞 know 的受詞。此處的 if 即等於 whether, 因 whether 引導的名詞子句在句中若作及物動詞的受詞時, 則 whether 可用 if 取代, 此時 if 譯成『是否』, 而非『如果』。

例: We don't know <u>whether</u> John and Mary will come to our party.

= We don't know <u>if</u> John and Mary will come to our party.

(我們不知道約翰和瑪麗是否會來參加我們的派對。)

if 若作『如果』解時, 是副詞連接詞, 引導副詞子句, 修飾主要子句。

例: <u>If</u> I have time, I will certainly help you.

(我若有時間, 就一定會幫你忙。)

Substitution 代　換

1. **You'll need to go to the bank to buy some traveler's checks.**

   My air conditioner needs to be fixed.

   My motorcycle needs oiling once a month.

   你得先去銀行買好旅行支票。

   我的冷氣機需要修理。

   我的摩托車一個月需要加一次潤滑油。

2. **You might want to know what the day's exchange rate is, or if there are any handling charges, etc.**

   It's hard to say whether he really wants to marry her.

   Please check to see if I have any mail.

   你可能想知道當日的匯率或者銀行是否收取任何手續費等等。

   他是不是想娶她很難說。

   請查看看有沒有我的郵件。

Lesson 40
Changing Money
兌換外幣

Dialogue
實用會話

Richie Li is at a bank in Australia. He tries not to show how nervous he is about speaking English.

(R=Richie; T=Teller)

R: Excuse me, miss. I would like to change 500 US dollars into Australian dollars, please.

T: Are you changing cash or traveler's checks?

R: Traveler's checks.

T: Can I have a look at your passport?

R: Sure. Here you are. By the way, do you charge any commission?

T: Not at this bank. Please sign here on your checks. How do you want your money?

R: Four one-hundred-dollar bills and the rest in smaller bills, please.

T: Here you are, sir.

R: Thanks. You've been very helpful.

T: Thank you. Have a nice day.

R: You too. Goodbye. (Richie says to himself.) Whew! That wasn't so difficult after all.

李瑞奇在澳洲的一家銀行裡。他想要隱藏他講英文的緊張心情。

瑞奇：抱歉，小姐。我想要把五百美元換成澳幣。

行員：您是要用現金還是旅行支票來換？

瑞奇：旅行支票。

行員：我可以看一下您的護照嗎？

瑞奇：當然。拿去吧。對了，你們要收手續費嗎？

行員：我們這家不收。請在支票上這邊簽個名。您的錢要哪些面額的？

瑞奇：麻煩妳給我四張百元大鈔，餘額就給我小面額的鈔票。

行員：先生，好了。

瑞奇：謝謝。妳幫了我一個大忙。

行員：謝謝您。祝您今天愉快。

瑞奇：妳也一樣。再見。(瑞奇對自己說。)唔！沒那麼難嘛。

Key Points
重點提示

1. **Australia** [ɔ'streljə] n. 澳大利亞, 澳洲

   Australian [ɔ'streljən] a. 澳洲 (人) 的 & n. 澳洲人

2. **nervous** ['nɝ·vəs] a. 緊張的

   例: My hands were all wet with sweat. That's how nervous I was.
   (我的手流滿了汗，可見我多緊張。)

3. **change** [tʃendʒ] vt. 交換

   change...into...　　把……換成……

   例: The magician changed the flower into a rabbit.
   (魔術師把那朵花變成了一隻兔子。)

4. **have a look at...**　　看一下……

   例: Can I have a look at your new watch?
   (我可否看一下你的新錶？)

5. **passport** [ˈpæsˌpɔrt] n. 護照

    例: You don't need a passport to travel on a domestic flight.
    (搭乘國內班機不需要護照。)

6. **Here you are.**　　拿去吧/在這裡。

= Here you go.

    例: A: Can I borrow your pen for a second?

    B: Sure. Here you are.
    (甲：能不能借一下你的筆？)
    (乙：當然可以，拿去吧。)

7. **By the way,...**　　對了/順便一提, ……

    例: By the way, do you know that there's a typhoon coming?
    (對了，你知道有一個颱風要來了嗎？)
    ＊ typhoon [taɪˈfun] n. 颱風

8. **charge** [tʃɑrdʒ] vt. 收費; 索價

    例: The doctor charged me ten thousand dollars for the operation.
    (做這個手術醫生收了我一萬元。)

9. **commission** [kəˈmɪʃən] n. 佣金

    例: The salesman's commission is much more than his basic salary.
    (那個業務員賺的佣金比他的基本薪資多很多。)

10. **sign** [saɪn] vi. & vt. 簽名

    例: Please sign (your name) on the form, please.
    (請在這份表格上簽名。)

11. **bill** [bɪl] n. 紙鈔

12. **helpful** [ˈhɛlpfəl] a. 有幫助的; 有用的

    例: This electronic dictionary is really helpful.
    (這部電子字典真的很有用。)

 請選出下列各句中正確的一項

1. As soon as you _____ New York, give me a call.
   (A) arrive   (B) arrive in   (C) arrive to   (D) arrive at

2. If you want to meet that Italian guy, you'd better _____ your Italian.
   (A) brush up on (B) brush away   (C) brush on   (D) brush up to

3. We stopped to _____ a look at some books on our way home.
   (A) have   (B) make   (C) give   (D) look

4. Without this _____ road map, we would have gotten lost.
   (A) help   (B) use   (C) helpful   (D) playful

5. _____ the way, when did you say you are leaving for Canada?
   (A) In   (B) By   (C) At   (D) To

解答:

| 1. (B) | 2. (A) | 3. (A) | 4. (C) | 5. (B) |

Lesson 41
Getting a Tan
曬黑

Reading
閱　讀

Both my brother and I are outgoing people. He as well as I likes being in the sun. It goes without saying, therefore, that we spend a lot of our free time at the beach. We go there to relax as well as to keep fit. To be frank, though, he no less than I enjoys looking at the beautiful "scenery" around the beach.

However, if you are anything like us, we have a piece of advice for you. Don't forget to rub a good amount of sunscreen lotion all over your body. Not only does it protect you from getting skin cancer, but it also helps to keep you nicely tanned. Both my

brother and I forgot to do that and now we look like Afro-Americans rather than Chinese.

> 　　我弟弟和我都是外向的人。他和我都喜歡曬太陽。所以不用說你也知道我們在海灘上消磨掉許多閒暇。我們去那兒讓自己放鬆心情以及保持健康。不過坦白說,他和我都喜歡欣賞海灘那兒的美『景』。
> 　　然而,如果你和我們志同道合的話,我們有一項建議要給你。別忘了全身上下要抹上大量的防曬乳液。防曬乳液不只是可以防止你得到皮膚癌,還可以讓你曬得一身古銅色。我弟弟和我都忘了要那麼做,而我們現在看起來像美國黑人而不像中國人。

Vocabulary & Idioms
單字 & 片語註解

1. **tan** [tæn] n. (皮膚因日曬而成的) 黃褐色 & vt.使曬成黃褐色
   動詞三態: tan、tanned [tænd]、tanned。
   ＊ tanned 於本文為過去分詞作形容詞用。
   例: The girl lay in the sun to tan her body.
   (那個女孩子躺在陽光下將她的身體曬成古銅色。)

2. **outgoing** [ˈaʊtˌɡoɪŋ] a. 外向的
   例: The outgoing boy spends too much time with his friends.
   (那個外向的男孩花了太多時間和他朋友在一起。)

3. **relax** [rɪˈlæks] vi. & vt. (使) 放鬆, (使) 鬆弛
   例: What do you do to relax on weekends?
   (你週末都做什麼來放鬆自己?)

   The old man relaxed his legs on a stool.
   (那個老人把腿放在凳子上輕鬆一下。)

4. **keep fit**　　保持身體健康
= remain fit
> 例: Jogging is a good way to keep fit.
> (慢跑是一個保持身體健康的好方法。)

5. **frank** [fræŋk] a. 坦白的
> 例: John hurt Sally's feelings by being too frank.
> (約翰太坦白而傷了莎莉的心。)

6. **scenery** [ˈsinərɪ] n. 風景 (不可數)
scene [sin] n. 風景 (可數)
> 例: Many people visit Guilin for its unique scenery.
> (許多人到桂林旅遊是為了欣賞那裡獨特的山水。)
>
> The scenes from the top of the mountain were breathtaking.
> (從山頂向下瞭望的風景令人嘆為觀止。)
> * breathtaking [ˈbrɛθˌtekɪŋ] a. 驚人的, 扣人心弦的

7. **advice** [ədˈvaɪs] n. 建議 (不可數)
a piece of advice　　一項建議
take one's advice　　接受某人的建議
> 例: The boy took his teacher's advice and studied harder.
> (那男孩接受了老師的建議而更加用功。)

8. **rub** [rʌb] vt. 塗抹
> 例: Henry rubbed some oil on his wife's back.
> (亨利在他太太背上抹了些油。)

9. **a good amount of** + 不可數名詞　　大量的……
= a large amount of + 不可數名詞
> 例: A good amount of money is needed to rebuild the library.
> (重建那座圖書館需要一大筆錢。)

10. **sunscreen lotion** ['sʌn‚skrin ‚loʃən] n. 防曬乳液

例: Sunscreen lotion can help prevent skin cancer.
(防曬乳液可以防止皮膚癌。)

11. **skin cancer**　　皮膚癌

cancer ['kænsɚ] n. 癌

例: Smoking causes cancer.
(抽煙會致癌。)

12. **Afro-American** [‚æfroˈmɛrɪkən] n. 非洲裔美國人

Grammar Notes
文法重點

本課旨在介紹對等片語連接詞的用法, 另介紹 **to be frank** 作獨立不定詞片語的用法。

1. 對等片語連接詞可用以連接對等的單字、片語或子句, 常見的有下列:

a. both...and...　　……和……
...as well as...　　……以及……
連接單字:

例: The professor's speech was both <u>interesting</u> and <u>instructive</u>.
　　　　　　　　　　　　　　　形容詞　　　　　形容詞
= The professor's speech was <u>interesting</u> as well as <u>instructive</u>.
(該教授的演說既有趣又有益。)

連接片語:

例: She is interested both <u>in music</u> and <u>in writing</u>.
　　　　　　　　　　　　　介詞片語　　　　介詞片語
= She is interested <u>in music</u> as well as <u>in writing</u>.
(她對音樂和寫作都有興趣。)

連接子句:

例: He succeeded both <u>because he was intelligent</u> and
副詞子句

<u>because he was diligent</u>.
副詞子句

= He succeeded <u>because he was intelligent</u> as well as <u>because he
was diligent</u>.
(他成功是因為他既聰明又勤奮。)

注意:

1) "both...and..."若連接主詞時, 主詞視為複數, 故其後要用複數動詞。

例: Both Carl and I <u>are</u> interested in playing baseball.
(卡爾和我都對打棒球很有興趣。)

2) "...as well as..."若連接主詞時, 其後動詞要隨第一個主詞作變化。

例: Peter as well as I <u>am</u> satisfied with the result. (✗)

→ Peter <u>as well as I</u> is satisfied with the result. (○)

= Peter <u>no less than I</u> is satisfied with the result.

= Peter <u>along with me</u> is satisfied with the result.

= Peter <u>together with me</u> is satisfied with the result.
(彼得和我都滿意這樣的結果。)

＊上列句中, 由於 as well as 和 no less than 是對等連接詞, 故
其後接主格形態 I; 而 along with 及 together with 則視為介
詞, 故之後接受格形態 me, 以作為介詞 with 的受詞。

本文:

To be frank, <u>he</u> <u>no less than</u> I enjoys...

= To be frank, <u>he</u> <u>as well as</u> I enjoys...
坦白說, 他和我都喜歡……

＊ no lss than 及 as well as 均表『以及』, 連接主詞時, 由於第一個主
詞是 he, 故動詞 enjoys 應為第三人稱單數。

b. not only...but (also)...　　不僅……而且……

= not only...but...as well

not...but...　　並非……而是……

either...or...　　要不……就是……

neither...nor...　　既非……也非……

連接單字:

例: He is not only <u>a doctor</u> but (also) <u>a writer</u>.
　　　　　　　　名詞　　　　　　　名詞

= He is <u>not only</u> a doctor <u>but</u> a writer <u>as well</u>.
(他不僅是位醫生,而且還是位作家。)

He is not <u>stingy</u> but <u>generous</u>.
　　　　　形容詞　　　形容詞

(他不是吝嗇而是慷慨。)

Can you speak either <u>English</u> or <u>Japanese</u>?
　　　　　　　　　　　名詞　　　　名詞

(你會說英語或日語嗎?)

It is neither <u>cold</u> nor <u>hot</u> in fall.
　　　　　　形容詞　　形容詞

(秋天的天氣既不冷也不熱。)

連接片語:

例: He is known not only <u>as a businessman</u> but (also)
　　　　　　　　　　　　　　　　介詞片語

<u>as a statesman</u>.
　　介詞片語

= He is known <u>not only</u> as a businessman <u>but</u> as a statesman <u>as</u>
<u>well</u>.
(他不僅是知名的實業家,而且也是知名的政治家。)

She was not <u>in Paris</u> but <u>in London</u>.
　　　　　　介詞片語　　　介詞片語

(她當時人不在巴黎,而是在倫敦。)

He is either <u>at home</u> or <u>at school</u>.
　　　　　　介詞片語　　介詞片語

(他要不是在家，就是在學校。)

He is neither <u>at home</u> nor <u>at work</u>.
　　　　　　介詞片語　　　介詞片語
(他既不在家，也沒上班。)

連接子句:

例: He is famous not only <u>because he is rich</u> but (also)
　　　　　　　　　　　　副詞子句

<u>because he is generous</u>.
　　　副詞子句

= He is famous <u>not only</u> because he is rich but because he is generous <u>as well</u>.
(他出名不僅是因為他有錢，也是因為他很慷慨。)

I want to buy this not <u>because it is cheap</u>, but <u>because it is useful</u>.
　　　　　　　　　　　　副詞子句　　　　　　　副詞子句
(我想買這樣東西不是因為便宜，而是因為實用。)

Either <u>you are wrong</u>, or <u>I am</u>.
　　　　主要子句　　　　主要子句
(不是你錯，就是我錯了。)

Helen wants to marry Tom neither <u>because he is rich</u> nor
　　　　　　　　　　　　　　　　副詞子句

<u>because he is good-looking</u>.
　　　副詞子句
(海倫想嫁給湯姆既不是因為他有錢，也不是因為他長得帥。)

注意:

1) 上述四個對等連接詞連接對等的主詞時,其後動詞要隨最近的主詞作變化。

例: Not only you but <u>I am</u> wrong.
(不僅你，連我也錯了。)

Not I but <u>she is</u> responsible for it.
(不是我，而是她該負責任。)

　　　　Either you or <u>he has</u> made the mistake.
　　　　(不是你就是他犯了這個錯。)

　　　　Neither she nor <u>I am</u> free.
　　　　(她和我都沒空。)

2) not only...but also...連接對等的主要子句時, not only 之後的主要子句要採倒裝句構; 且 but also 在連接的主要子句中, also 要省略, 或置於句中, 而不可在 but also 後直接接主要子句。

　　例: Not only <u>he is</u> clever, <u>but also</u> he is humorous. (✗)
　→　Not only <u>is he</u> clever, <u>but</u> he is (also) humorous. (○)
　＝　Not only <u>is he</u> clever, <u>but</u> he is humorous <u>as well</u>.
　　　(他不僅聰明而且還很幽默。)

c. ...rather than...　　……而非……
連接單字:
　例: She is <u>sad</u> rather than <u>happy</u>.
　　　　　　形容詞　　　　　　　形容詞
　　　(她是悲傷而非快樂。)

連接片語:
　例: He is interested <u>in painting</u> rather than <u>in music</u>.
　　　　　　　　　　介詞片語　　　　　　　　　介詞片語
　　　(他對繪畫有興趣，而非對音樂有興趣。)

連接子句:
　例: He failed <u>because he was lazy</u> rather than <u>because he was</u>
　　　　　　　　　　副詞子句　　　　　　　　　　　　副詞子句
<u>stupid</u>.
　　　(他失敗是因為懶，而非因為他笨。)

注意:
rather than 連接對等的主詞時, 其後動詞始終要隨第一個主詞作變化。

　例: <u>He</u> rather than <u>I</u> <u>is</u> in charge of the office.
　　　(辦公室是由他負責，而不是我。)

2. **To be frank, though, he no less than I enjoys...**
   不過坦白說, 他和我都喜歡……

   上列句中的 **To be frank** (坦白說) 是獨立不定詞片語, 用以修飾其後整個主要子句。

   所謂獨立不定詞片語就是用以修飾句中整個主要子句, 而不修飾句中的主詞或動詞。這種不定詞片語使用時通常置於句首, 之後加逗點, 再接主要子句。常見的此類不定詞片語有:

to be frank	坦白 (跟你) 說
= to be frank with you	
= frankly speaking	
to tell (you) the truth	老實 (跟你) 說
to make matters worse	更糟的是
to put it differently	換言之
to put it simply	簡言之
to sum up	總而言之
to begin with	首先
to do + 人 + justice	為某人說句公道話

   例: To be frank with you, I don't care much for material comforts.
   (坦白說，我並不太在乎物質享受。)

   Mr. Wang got fired. To make matters worse, his wife fell ill.
   (王先生被開除了。更糟的是，他太太生病了。)

   To do Tom justice, he occasionally arrives on time.
   (為湯姆說句公道話，他偶爾也是會準時到的。)

Substitution
代　　換

1. **Both my brother and I are outgoing people.**
   Jim as well as James is coming.
   Not only Chris but also Tom is a good singer.
   我弟弟和我都是外向的人。
   吉姆和詹姆士都要來。
   不僅克里斯是好歌手, 湯姆也是。

2. **To be frank, though, he no less than I enjoys looking at the beautiful "scenery" around the beach.**
   To tell you the truth, I don't care too much about money.
   To sum up, the speech was more entertaining than educational.
   不過坦白說, 他和我都喜歡欣賞海灘那兒的美『景』。
   老實跟你說, 我不太在乎錢。
   總而言之, 那場演講的娛樂性超過教育性。

Lesson 42

Roast Beef

烤牛肉

Dialogue
實用會話

My brother, Luke, goes to see his girlfriend, Daisy.

(D=Daisy; L=Luke)

D: What on earth happened to you?

L: Oh, I just had a lazy day at the beach.

D: My goodness! You're really burnt. Are you alright?

L: Well, yes, but I feel like I've been roasted.

D: In that case, let's eat in rather than go out for dinner.

L: Up to you.

D: What would you like to eat?

L: Uh...

D: How about your favorite: roast beef?

L: Uh...Not today, please.

D: OK. I understand.

我的弟弟路克去見他的女朋友黛西。

黛西：你到底怎麼了？

路克：哦，我剛在海灘渡過慵懶的一天。

黛西：我的天啊！你真的曬傷了。你還好吧？

路克：嗯，還好，但是我覺得自己好像被烤過一樣。

黛西：那樣子的話，我們晚餐就在家裡吃，不要出去吃了。

路克：妳決定就行了。

黛西：你要吃什麼呢？

路克：呃……

黛西：你最喜歡的烤牛肉怎麼樣？

路克：呃……今天不要，拜託。

黛西：好吧。我能諒解。

Key Points
重點提示

1. **roast beef** [ˋrost ˏbif] n. 烤牛肉

   roast [rost] vt. 烤

   例: Mom roasted a duck for dinner.
   (老媽晚餐烤了一隻鴨。)

2. 本文：

   What <u>on earth</u> happened to you?　　你到底怎麼了？

   = What <u>in the world</u> happened to you?

   注意：

   此處 on earth 通常置於疑問詞之後, 表強調之意, 相當於 in the world, 中文譯為『到底/究竟』。

   例: Where on earth are you going?

   = Where in the world are you going?
   (你到底要上哪兒去？)

Who on earth is the screaming girl?

= Who in the world is the screaming girl?

(那個在尖叫的女孩究竟是誰呢？)

3. 本文:

...feel like I've been roasted.　　……覺得自己好像被烤過一樣。

= ...feel as if I've been roasted.

注意:

feel like 在嚴謹文法中, like (像) 為介詞, 其後照理說應接名詞作受詞, 但在現代美式口語中 (甚至在書寫英文中) 有以 like 來取代 as if 的趨勢, 即" feel like + 主詞 + 動詞" (= feel + as if 子句), 如本文的例子。

例: Peter feels like he has been cheated.

(彼得覺得自己被騙了。)

4. **eat in**　　在家裡用餐

eat out　　在外面用餐; 吃館子

例: We always eat in on weekdays.

(我們平日總是在家吃飯。)

＊ weekday [ˈwikˌde] n. 平常日, 普通日 (星期天以外或星期天與星期六以外的日子)

5. **Up to you.**　　由你決定。

＊ 本片語係"It's up to you."化簡而成。

例: James: Let's go see this movie, shall we?

Alice: Up to you.

(詹姆士：我們去看這部電影，好不好？)

(愛麗絲：由你決定。)

6. **favorite** [ˈfevərɪt] a. & n. 最喜愛的 (人或事物)

例: This game is a favorite of mine.

(這是一種我最喜愛的遊戲。)

Mrs. White spoils her favorite son.
(懷特太太慣壞了她的寶貝兒子。)

* spoil [spɔɪl] vt. 寵壞 (孩子等)

請選出下列各句中正確的一項

1. I don't know _____ on earth happened to my ex-girlfriend.
   (A) how   (B) why   (C) what   (D) who

2. Both my girlfriend and I _____ Chinese.
   (A) is   (B) am   (C) as   (D) are

3. Because of the typhoon, we had to _____.
   (A) eat out   (B) eat in   (C) eat   (D) eaten

4. I prefer to read a good book _____ listen to music.
   (A) instead of   (B) rather than   (C) other than   (D) in order to

解答:

> 1. (C)   2. (D)   3. (B)   4. (B)

Lesson 43
Hi-tech Romance
高科技戀情

Reading
閱　讀

　　Both Charlene and Robert are librarians. Charlene is from America and Robert is from Australia. Four days after they met face to face for the first time, they got married. "That was quick," you might think. Actually, they had known each other for nine months before they met. Thanks to e-mail (electronic mail), they had been corresponding with each other through their computers.

　　It all started when Charlene came across Robert's note in her computer. She replied to it. From then on, they would not

only get in touch but flirt with each other. That was how this "hi-tech" romance began. Sound interesting? Well, if you're looking for a spouse, why not give it a try? Who knows? You might be just as lucky as Charlene and Robert.

> 夏琳和羅伯特兩人都是圖書館員。夏琳是美國人，而羅伯特是澳洲人。他們頭一次碰面的四天後就結婚了。你可能會認為：『那真快啊。』其實，他們在見面之前就已經互相認識九個月了。因為電子郵件的關係，他們一直透過電腦互通信息。
>
> 　這段姻緣是夏琳無意中在她的電腦裡看到羅伯特的留言時結下的。她回信了。從那時起，他們不只是互相聯絡，還互訴情衷。這段『高科技』戀情就是這樣展開的。聽起來很有趣嗎？如果你正在尋找終身伴侶，何妨試一試呢？誰知道呢？你可能會跟夏琳還有羅伯特一樣走運呢。

Vocabulary & Idioms
單字 & 片語註解

1. **hi-tech** [ˌhaɪˈtɛk] a. 高科技的 (high-technology 的縮寫)
   technology [tɛkˈnɑlədʒɪ] n. 科技
   例: Movies are more enjoyable now because of the hi-tech sound system.
   (拜高科技音響系統之賜，現在觀賞電影更是一種享受。)

2. **romance** [ˈromæns] n. 羅曼史, 愛情故事
   romantic [roˈmæntɪk] a. 浪漫的
   例: Mr. Lee was not happy to hear of his daughter's romance.
   (李先生聽到有關她女兒的羅曼史頗為不悅。)

We had a romantic evening on Valentine's Day.
(情人節那天我們共度了一個浪漫的夜晚。)

3. **librarian** [laɪˈbrɛrɪən] n. 圖書館管理員

例: The introvert wants to be a librarian one day.
(那個內向的人想要有一天成為圖書館員。)
* introvert [ˈɪntrəˌvɝt] n. 個性內向的人
extrovert [ˈɛkstroˌvɝt] n. 個性外向的人

4. **face to face**　　面對面地, 當面地
注意:
本片語作副詞用, 通常置於動詞之後。
例: I once saw the president face to face.
(我有一次當面看到總統。)

5. **for the first time**　　第一次
例: I had raw oysters for the first time last night.
(我昨晚生平第一次吃生蠔。)
* raw [rɔ] a. 生的
oyster [ˈɔɪstɚ] n. 牡蠣, 蠔

6. **thanks to...**　　由於……; 幸虧……
= because of...
例: Thanks to my parents, I had a wonderful childhood.
(多虧我的父母, 我才能擁有一個美好的童年。)
* childhood [ˈtʃaɪldˌhʊd] n. 童年時代

7. **e-mail** [ˈiˈmel] n. 電子郵件
= electronic mail
例: Many people get acquainted with each other through e-mail.
(許多人透過電子郵件而彼此認識。)

8. **correspond** [ˌkɔrəˈspɑnd] vi. 通信
correspond with...　　和……通信

例: Do you ever correspond with your overseas friends?
(你有和國外的朋友通信嗎？)

9. **come across...**   偶然發現/遇見……
= happen on...
= find/meet...by chance
   例: I came across an old friend at the restaurant.
   (我在那家餐廳與一位老友不期而遇。)

10. **note** [not] n. 留言, 便條
    例: Lisa wrote Jeff a note thanking him for his help.
    (莉莎寫了一張便條給傑夫感謝他的協助。)

11. **reply** [rɪˋplaɪ] vi. & n. 答覆, 回答
    reply to...   答覆……
    例: The boss told the secretary to reply to the customer at once.
    (老闆叫祕書立刻答覆那位客戶。)

    Brad sent out many applications for a job but hasn't got any replies yet.
    (布萊德寄出許多求職信，但是至今仍未收到任何回信。)
    * application [͵æpləˋkeʃən] n. 申請書

12. **from then on**   從那時候起
    例: Alex graduated last year. From then on, he stopped living with his parents.
    (艾里克斯去年畢業。從那時起他就不再和父母一塊住了。)

13. **get in touch with...**   與……聯絡
    例: I'll get in touch with you as soon as I arrive in California.
    (我一到達加州就會馬上與你聯絡。)

14. **flirt** [flɝt] vi. 調情
    flirt with...   和……調情

例: The secretary appears to be flirting with the boss.
(那位秘書顯然在和老闆調情。)

15. 本文:

Sound interesting? 聽起來很有趣嗎？

= Does it (=the story) sound interesting?

16. **look for...** 尋找……

例: I'm looking for a blue tie to match my suit.
(我在找一條藍色的領帶來配西裝。)

＊ suit [sut] n. 西裝

17. **spouse** [spauz] n. 配偶

例: The office trip to England was free for all staff members and their spouses.
(公司到英國的旅遊對所有的員工和其配偶都是免費的。)

18. **give...a try** 嘗試……

= give...a shot

例: I would love to give golfing a try one day.
(我很想有一天去嘗試打高爾夫球。)

Grammar Notes
文法重點

本課介紹"thanks to..." (因為/由於……) 的用法。

<u>**Thanks to**</u> **e-mail (electronic mail), they had been corresponding with each other through their computers.**
因為電子郵件的關係, 他們透過電腦互相通信。
上列句中, 使用了片語介詞 (由兩個以上的字形成的介詞) "thanks to...", 表
『由於/因為……』之意。

thanks to...　　由於/因為……
= due to...
= owing to...
= because of...
= on account of...
= as a result of...

注意:

上述片語介詞接受詞後形成介詞片語, 作副詞用, 使用時通常置於句首或句尾,用以修飾句中動詞或主要子句; 但其中由於 due 是形容詞, 故 due to 亦可置於 be 動詞後作主詞補語, 其餘則不可。

例: Thanks to the pilot's experience, a terrible accident was avoided.
(多虧飛行員的經驗才免掉一場可怕的意外。)

Tim eventually got fired as a result of his complaints about his job.
(由於對工作抱怨,提姆最後被開除了。)

The car accident <u>was</u> <u>owing to</u> the driver's carelessness. (✗)

→ The car accident <u>was</u> <u>due to</u> the driver's carelessness. (○)
(那場車禍是由於該駕駛粗心大意造成的。)

Substitution
代　　換

Thanks to e-mail (electronic mail), they had been corresponding with each other through their computers.

Owing to the firemen's bravery, many people were rescued.

As a result of the bomb scare, security has been tightened.

因為電子郵件的關係, 他們透過電腦互相通信。

由於消防隊員的英勇, 許多人得以獲救。

由於炸彈的恐嚇, 使得安全措施加強。

Lesson 44
Better Off with E-mail?
電子郵件會更好？

Dialogue
實用會話

Steve is chatting with his sister, Diana.

(S=Steve; D=Diana)

S: Gee, Diana, you're always at home. Don't you have any friends to go out with?

D: Sure, I do. But all my friends are either out shopping or they're boring. And you know I hate shopping.

S: Get a boyfriend. I'm sure you won't be bored then.

D: Actually, I want to meet some interesting guys but I don't know how to.

S: Why don't you try e-mail? You might get lucky.

D: I don't think so. Besides, dating through e-mail is neither personal nor romantic. Why don't you introduce me to some of your friends?

S: Why didn't I think of that? How about my best friend, Fred?

D: Uh...maybe I'll be better off with e-mail.

史帝夫正在和他妹妹戴安娜聊天。

史帝夫：咦，戴安娜，妳老是待在家裏。妳沒有朋友可以一起出去的嗎？

戴安娜：我當然有。但是我的朋友不是出去購物了就是很無聊，而且你知道我很討厭去購物。

史帝夫：找個男朋友嘛。我相信那樣妳就不會覺得無聊了。

戴安娜：其實我想認識些有趣的男生，但是我不知道該怎麼做。

史帝夫：妳何不試試電子郵件？妳可能會走運。

戴安娜：我才不這麼認為呢。何況透過電子郵件約會既沒有親切感又不浪漫。你為什麼不介紹一些你的朋友給我認識呢？

史帝夫：我為什麼沒想到呢？我最要好的朋友弗瑞德怎麼樣？

戴安娜：呃……我用電子郵件可能會比較好些。

Key Points
重點提示

1. **be better off** (+ 介詞片語/現在分詞)　　(……) 處境更佳/境遇更好

* be better off 是 be well off (處境好) 的比較級。

例: Many Americans don't work because they think they are better off getting welfare.

(許多美國人不工作因為他們認為領社會救濟金更好。)

　　* welfare [ˈwɛlˌfɛr] n. 社會福利; 此處指 (美國的)『社會救濟金』

2. **chat** [tʃæt] vi. & n. 閒談

chat with...　　和……聊天

例: Ruth chatted with her boyfriend on the phone for hours.

(露絲和男友講電話講了好幾個鐘頭。)

I had a pleasant chat with my teacher at the party.

(我和老師在派對中聊得很愉快。)

3. **gee** [dʒi] int. 感歎語, 相當於口語的『咦、哇』等等

4. 本文:

Don't you have any friends to go out with?

= Don't you have any friends whom you can go out with?
你沒有朋友可以一起出去的嗎？

5. **boring** [ˈbɔrɪŋ] a. 無聊的

bored [bɔrd] a. 感到無聊的; 厭煩的

be bored with...　　厭煩做……

= be tired of...

例: I spent a boring afternoon cleaning my room.
(我花了一個無聊的下午清理我的房間。)

The housewife is bored with doing the housework day in and day out.
(那個家庭主婦厭煩日復一日地操勞家事。)

6. 本文:

...I hate shopping.　　……我討厭去購物。

= ...I hate to shop.

＊ hate [het] vt. 討厭; 恨

注意:

hate、start (開始)、begin (開始)、like (喜歡)、love (愛)、continue (繼續) 等及物動詞其後可接動名詞或不定詞作受詞, 意思不變。

例: Aaron hates asking his parents for money.
　= Aaron hates to ask his parents for money.
　(艾倫討厭向父母要錢。)

Mr. Hardy began working when he was sixteen.
　= Mr. Hardy began to work when he was sixteen.
　(哈迪生在十六歲時開始工作。)

7. 本文:

Actually, I want to meet some interesting guys, but I don't

know how **to**.

= Actually, I want to meet some interesting guys, but I don't know how to meet some interesting guys.
其實我想認識些有趣的男生, 但是我不知道該怎麼做。

8. 本文:
Why don't you try e-mail?　你何不試試電子郵件?

= Why not try e-mail?

9. **date** [det] vi. (與某人) 約會 & vt. 約 (某人), 和 (某人) 約會/交往 & n. 約會
go on a date with + 人　　和某人約會

例: My daughter is sixteen and she's already started dating.
(我女兒十六歲, 她已經開始約會了。)

Frank is dating a nurse.
(法蘭克正和一位護士小姐交往。)

Randy dreamed of going on a date with Demi Moore.
(藍迪夢想和黛咪・摩兒約會。)

10. **personal** [ˈpɝsənḷ] a. 親切的; 私人的

例: Please don't forget to take your personal belongings before you get off the train.
(在下火車前, 請別忘了帶走私人物品。)

＊ belongings [bəˈlɔŋɪŋz] n. 所有物 (恆用複數)

11. **introduce** [ˌɪntrəˈdjus] vt. 介紹
introduce A to B　　把 A 介紹給 B

例: It is Mary who introduced me to Jane.
(把我介紹給珍認識的人是瑪麗。)

12. **How about + 名詞/動名詞?**　　……怎麼樣/好嗎?

例: How about giving me a hand with my luggage?
(幫我提一下行李好嗎?)

請選出下列各句中正確的一項

1. The weather here is really bad. It's always _____ too hot _____ too cold.
   (A) neither, nor   (B) both, or
   (C) either, or   (D) not only, and

2. I _____ have the time _____ the money to go on a long vacation.
   (A) either, or   (B) neither, nor   (C) both, but   (D) only, but

3. _____ can she sing, _____ she can also dance.
   (A) Both, and   (B) Either, or
   (C) Neither, nor   (D) Not only, but

4. The increase in the price of rice was _____ the drought.
   (A) because of   (B) as a result of
   (C) owing to   (D) due to

解答:

> 1. (C)   2.(B)   3.(D)   4.(D)

L esson 45

Tough Guys Do Dance

硬漢也跳舞

Reading

閱　讀

Not only is Thai boxing violent, but it is also bloody. Yet it involves the arts of dance and music. It is both ugly and beautiful at the same time. That's why it's so exciting to watch.

Thai boxing was created by soldiers over five hundred years ago. The fighters use every part of their bodies, especially their feet, knees and elbows to strike their opponents. Their deadly style has earned them respect from other martial artists.

Surprisingly, the fights start off with a graceful dance. The dance is in honor of the boxers' teachers. There is even a small

band which plays along with the dance and during the fight. So, who says tough guys don't dance?

泰國拳不僅充滿暴力，而且還很血腥；然而它包含了舞蹈和音樂的藝術，並同時兼備了醜陋和美麗。那就是為何觀賞泰國拳會如此刺激的原因。

泰國拳是五百多年前由軍人創造的。拳擊手會使用全身上下每一個部位，特別是他們的腳、膝和肘來攻擊他們的對手。他們致命的打法為他們博得其他武術家的尊敬。

令人驚訝的是，格鬥以優雅的舞蹈揭開序幕。該舞是用來向拳擊手的師父致敬。甚至還有一支小型樂隊會在舞蹈和格鬥進行時伴奏。所以，誰說硬漢不跳舞？

Vocabulary & Idioms
單字 & 片語註解

1. **tough** [tʌf] a. 強硬的; 費力的

   例: Construction work is a tough job.
   (建築工作是種粗活。)

   * construction [kənˈstrʌkʃən] n. 建造, 建築

2. 標題:

   Tough Guys <u>Do</u> Dance　　硬漢也跳舞

   注意:

   助動詞 do、does、did 可作強調用法, 譯成『真的』、『的確』，即在肯定句中, 按主詞人稱及時態之不同, 在動詞前置 do、does 或 did, 然後動詞一律改為原形。

   例: I <u>did</u> try to get him to change his mind, but he wouldn't listen.
   (我真的試過要使他改變心意，但他就是不聽。)

3. **Thai boxing** [ˈtaɪ ˌbɑksɪŋ] n. 泰國拳

Thai [taɪ] a. 泰國 (人) 的

boxing [ˈbɑksɪŋ] n. 拳擊

4. **violent** [ˈvaɪələnt] a. 暴力的

例: Many people think some movies are too violent.
(許多人認為一些電影太過暴力。)

5. **bloody** [ˈblʌdɪ] a. 血腥的

例: Cock fighting is a very bloody sport.
(鬥雞是一種非常血腥的運動。)

6. **involve** [ɪnˈvɑlv] vt. 包括

be involved in...　　涉及……

例: Learning chess involves spending a lot of time and having patience.
(學下棋要花許多時間及耐心。)

They say John is involved in that scandal.
(據說約翰涉及那樁醜聞。)

7. **create** [krɪˈet] vt. 創造

例: Judo was created by the Japanese.
(柔道是日本人創的。)
＊ judo [ˈdʒudo] n. 柔道

8. **soldier** [ˈsoldʒɚ] n. 軍人 (尤指士兵)

9. **fighter** [ˈfaɪtɚ] n. 拳擊手; 格鬥者

例: The professional fighter died after he was knocked out.
(那名職業格鬥者被擊昏後就一命嗚呼了。)

10. **knee** [ni] n. 膝蓋

例: Little Johnny came home with bandages on both knees.
(小強尼回家時兩膝都包著繃帶。)

＊ bandage [ˈbændɪdʒ] n. 繃帶

11. **elbow** [ˈɛl͵bo] n. 手肘

12. **strike** [straɪk] vt. 擊; 打

　　動詞三態: strike、struck [strʌk]、struck。

　例: The teacher struck the student for not doing his homework.
　　(老師因為那個學生沒做家庭作業而打他。)

13. **opponent** [əˈponənt] n. 對手

　例: Jack isn't worried because his opponent is pretty weak.
　　(傑克並不擔心,因為他的對手很弱。)

14. **deadly** [ˈdɛdlɪ] a. 致命的

　例: A deadly disease is spreading in the city.
　　(一種致命的疾病正在該市蔓延。)

15. **style** [staɪl] n. 風格 (本文指『打法』)

16. **earn** + 人 + 事　　為某人贏得某事; 為某人帶來某事

　例: Bobby's naughtiness earned him a spanking.
　　(巴比的調皮搗蛋使他被打屁股。)

17. **respect** [rɪˈspɛkt] n. 尊敬, 敬意

　　hold + 人 + in (great) respect　　(非常) 尊敬某人

　　show respect to + 人　　對某人表示尊敬

　例: Everyone holds the social worker in great respect.
　　(人人都對那名社工人員表示崇高的敬意。)

　　No matter who you are, you should always show respect to your elders.
　　(不論你是誰,你隨時都應該尊敬長輩。)

18. **martial artist** [ˌmɑrʃəl ˈɑrtɪst] n. 武術家, 習武之人

　例: Bruce Lee was a martial artist of great skill.
　　(李小龍是一名功夫精湛的武術家。)

19. **surprisingly** [səˈpraɪzɪŋlɪ] adv. 令人驚訝地

例: Lucy was surprisingly rude to her boss.
(露西對她老闆的態度粗魯得令人吃驚。)

20. **start off** 開始/展開 (之後接不接受詞均可)

例: Let's start off the meal with an appetizer.
(我們先吃點開胃菜再吃飯吧。)

21. **graceful** [ˈgresfəl] a. 優雅的

例: Mary looks so graceful when she dances.
(瑪麗跳舞時姿態很優雅。)

22. **honor** [ˈɑnɚ] n. 敬意

in honor of... 向……表示敬意

例: We held a big banquet in honor of the VIPs.
(我們舉辦了一場盛大的宴會來款待貴賓。)

＊ banquet [ˈbæŋkwɪt] n. (正式的) 宴會
VIP [ˌviaɪˈpi] n. 貴賓, 大人物
= <u>v</u>ery <u>i</u>mportant <u>p</u>erson

23. **boxer** [ˈbɑksɚ] n. 拳擊手

24. **band** [bænd] n. 樂團, 樂隊

例: The band played till the early hours of the morning at the party.
(那個樂團在派對上演奏到凌晨。)

Grammar Notes
文法重點

本課複習對等連接詞"not only...but also..."連接對等的主要子句之用法, 並複習 why 作關係副詞的用法。

1. <u>Not only</u> <u>is</u> Thai boxing violent <u>but</u> it is <u>also</u> bloody.
   泰國拳不僅充滿暴力,而且還很血腥。

   not only...but also...　　不僅……而且……

= not only...but...

= not only...but...as well

   注意:

   not only...but also...為對等連接詞,可用以連接對等的單字、片語或子句;
   當其連接對等的主要子句時, not only 之後的主要子句要採倒裝句構; 且
   but also 在連接的主要子句中, also 要省略, 或置於句中, 而不可在 but also
   後直接接主要子句。倒裝原則如下:

   a. 句中有 be 動詞時, 主詞與 be 動詞要倒裝。

   > **例**: Not only <u>she is</u> pretty, <u>but also</u> she is clever. (✕)
   > → Not only <u>is she</u> pretty, <u>but</u> she is (<u>also</u>) clever. (○)
   > = Not only is she pretty, <u>but</u> she is clever <u>as well.</u>
   > (她不僅人長得漂亮,而且還很聰明。)

   b. 句中有助動詞時, 主詞與助動詞倒裝。

   > **例**: Not only <u>he can</u> speak English, <u>but also</u> he can speak French.
   > (✕)
   > → Not only <u>can he</u> speak English, <u>but</u> he can (<u>also</u>) speak French.
   > (○)
   > = Not only can he speak English, <u>but</u> he can speak French <u>as well.</u>
   > (他不僅會講英文,而且還會講法文。)

   c. 句中為一般動詞時, 則先在主詞前按動詞時態及主詞人稱之不同, 分置
   do、does 或 did, 其後動詞則一律改用原形。

   > **例**: Not only <u>I love her</u>, <u>but also</u> I want to marry her. (✕)
   > → Not only <u>do I love</u> her, <u>but</u> I (<u>also</u>) want to marry her. (○)
   > = Not only do I love her, <u>but</u> I want to marry her <u>as well.</u>
   > (我不僅愛她,而且還要娶她。)

2. **That's <u>why</u> it's so exciting to watch.**

= That's <u>the reason</u> it's so exciting to watch.

= That's <u>the reason</u> <u>why</u> it's so exciting to watch.

那就是為何觀賞泰國拳會如此刺激的原因。

上列句中的 why 是關係副詞, 其所引導的形容詞子句只用以修飾 the reason (理由), 但使用時, 我們可將 the reason 省略, 保留 why (如本句用法); 或將 why 省略, 而保留 the reason; 但亦可兩者均保留。

例: Peter goes swimming early in the morning every day. That's <u>why</u> he is so healthy.

= Peter goes swimming early in the morning every day. That's <u>the reason</u> he is so healthy.

= Peter goes swimming early in the morning every day. That's <u>the reason</u> <u>why</u> he is so healthy.

(彼得每天都會去晨泳; 那就是為何他這麼健康的原因。)

Substitution 代　換

1. **Not only is Thai boxing violent, but it is also bloody.**

   Not only do I like singing, but I also like dancing.

   Not only is Helen intelligent, but she is also pretty.

   泰國拳不僅充滿暴力, 而且還很血腥。

   我不只是喜歡唱歌, 我還喜歡跳舞。

   海倫不僅人很聰明, 而且還長得很漂亮。

2. **That's why it's so exciting to watch.**

   That's the reason why I'm not going to the party.

   That's the reason he's well liked.

   那就是為何觀賞泰國拳會如此刺激的原因。

   那就是為什麼我不去參加那場派對的原因。

   那就是他深受別人喜愛的原因。

Lesson 46
Anything for a Kiss
為了吻不惜一切

Dialogue
實用會話

Martin and Sally have just watched Thai boxing.

(M=Martin; S=Sally)

M: How did you like the fight, Sally?

S: I found it not only too violent but also very brutal.

M: You're right. It's amazing how the fighters can take not only the punching but all the kicking as well. I wouldn't be able to handle it.

S: Oh, don't be so modest, Martin.

M: No, really. I wouldn't fight one of those tough guys for all the money in the world.

S: Would you do it for a kiss?

M: That's a different story. Sure, I will. But you've got to pay in advance. (Martin tries to kiss Sally.)

S: No, please don't. I was only kidding.

馬丁和莎莉剛觀賞完泰國拳。

馬丁：妳覺得那場格鬥如何，莎莉？

莎莉：我發覺那種比賽不只是過分暴力，而且還非常殘忍。

馬丁：妳說的沒錯。那些拳擊手怎麼有辦法承受所有的拳打腳踢，真
是令人覺得不可思議。我可沒辦法挨上這麼幾下。

莎莉：哦，別那麼謙虛嘛，馬丁。

馬丁：不，是真的。就算是給我天底下的錢我也不會和這些硬漢中的
任何一個打。

莎莉：你會為了一個吻而那麼做嗎？

馬丁：那又另當別論了。當然，我會。但是妳要先付款。（馬丁試著
要親莎莉。）

莎莉：不，拜託不要。我只是在開玩笑。

Key Points
重點提示

1. **How do/does/did + 人 + like + 事？**　　　某人覺得某事如何？

= How do/does/did + 人 + feel about + 事？

= What do/does/did + 人 + think of + 事？

注意：

a. 本片語常用於詢問對方之看法, 例如: 和朋友一起去看電影後, 你可以問
對方：

How do you like this movie?
你覺得這部電影怎麼樣？

b. 無下列說法：

<u>How</u> do you <u>think of</u> this movie? (✕)
你如何來想這部電影？

而要說：

<u>What</u> do you <u>think of</u> this movie? (○)

= <u>How</u> do you <u>like</u> this movie?

= <u>How</u> do you <u>feel about</u> this movie?
你覺得這部電影怎樣？

2. 本文:

How did you like the fight, Sally?

= How did you feel about the fight, Sally?

= What did you think of the fight, Sally?
妳覺得這場格鬥怎樣, 莎莉？

3. **brutal** [ˈbrutḷ] a. 殘忍的, 不人道的

例: It was the most brutal murder I've ever seen.
(那是我見過最殘酷的謀殺案。)
＊ murder [ˈmɝdɚ] n. 謀殺案

4. **amazing** [əˈmezɪŋ] a. 令人訝異的
amazed [əˈmezd] a. (感到) 訝異的
be amazed at...　　對……感到訝異

例: John can eat an amazing amount of food.
(約翰的食量大得驚人。)

I was amazed at the teacher's lack of patience.
(那個老師如此缺乏耐性，令我十分驚訝。)

5. **punching** [ˈpʌntʃɪŋ] n. 拳打 (動名詞作名詞用, 不可數)
punch [pʌntʃ] vt. 用拳打 & n. 拳打

例: Tom punched his brother for stealing his girlfriend.
(湯姆因為弟弟搶了他女友而揮拳揍他。)

The old woman gave the burglar a punch in the face.
(那名老婦人迎面給了那個小偷一拳。)
＊ burglar [ˈbɝɡlɚ] n. 竊賊

6. **kicking** [ˈkɪkɪŋ] n. 踢 (動名詞作名詞用, 不可數)
kick [kɪk] vt. & n. 踢 (可數)

例: The horse kicked Barney in the backside.
(那匹馬踢了巴尼的臀部一腳。)

　　＊ backside ['bæk,saɪd] n. 臀部

One kick from a kung fu master could kill you.
(被功夫大師踢一腳可能會致命。)

　　＊ kung fu [,kʌn 'fu] n. 中國功夫

7. **handle** ['hændl̩] vt. 處理, 應付

例: The babysitter couldn't handle the kids.
(那個臨時褓姆應付不了那些小孩。)

　　＊ babysitter ['bebɪ,sɪtɚ] n. 臨時褓姆

8. **modest** ['mɑdɪst] a. 謙虛的

例: The modest man never talks about his accomplishments.
(那個謙虛的人從不談論他的成就。)

　　＊ accomplishment [ə'kɑmplɪʃmənt] n. 成就

9. **in advance**　　預先, 事先

= beforehand [bɪ'fɔr,hænd] adv.

例: Please tell me in advance if you're coming to visit me.
(如果你要來拜訪我請事先告訴我。)

10. 本文:

I was only kidding.　　我只是在開玩笑。

= I was only joking.

＊ kid [kɪd] vi. 開玩笑

例: A: Are you really getting married soon?
B: I was only kidding.
(甲：你真的快結婚了嗎？)
(乙：我只是在開玩笑。)

請選出下列各句中正確的一項

1. Jennifer enjoys not only jogging but _____ as well.
   (A) swim   (B) swims   (C) to swim   (D) swimming

2. Peter works too hard; that's _____ he's always sick.
   (A) why   (B) how   (C) when   (D) what

3. What did you _____ the concert?
   (A) like   (B) feel about   (C) think   (D) think about

4. Not only _____ well, but he also writes good songs.
   (A) he sings   (B) he does sing   (C) does he sing   (D) sings

5. The landlord wants you to pay the rent _____.
   (A) before   (B) before hand   (C) in advance   (D) advance

解答:

| 1. (D)   2. (A)   3. (D)   4. (C)   5. (C) |

Lesson 47
Fast-food Talk
速食趣談

Reading
閱　讀

Though it is generally accepted that junk food is not healthful, American fast-food restaurants are popping up all over the world. These restaurants are for people who are always in a rush. If they don't have time to sit down to a regular meal, they race over to the nearest McDonald's. There they can quickly satisfy their hunger.

Because Americans like things done immediately, they often order their food quickly at fast-food restaurants. They say,"A burger, fries and a coke!" Though it's not polite, it's

efficient. So when you are in the States, try to order this way.
After all, in America do as the Americans do.

雖然大家都普遍接受垃圾食物並無益於健康，但是美式速食餐館
卻如雨後春筍般在世界各地流行起來。這些餐館是針對總是在趕時間
的人而誕生。如果他們沒有時間坐下來好好吃頓飯，他們就會趕到最
近的麥當勞。在那兒，他們可以很快地填飽飢餓的肚子。

因為美國人做事喜歡快刀斬亂麻，他們在速食店裡點餐通常也很
迅速。他們會說：『一個漢堡、一份炸薯條和一杯可樂。』這種說法
雖然並不禮貌，卻很有效率。所以當你在美國的時候，試著用這種方
式點餐吧。畢竟，在美國就應該要跟著美國佬那樣做。

Vocabulary & Idioms
單字 & 片語註解

1. **fast-food** [ˌfæstˈfʊd] n. & a. 速食(的)

2. **generally** [ˈdʒɛnərəlɪ] adv. 普遍地, 廣泛地
   例: Generally speaking, women are more meticulous than men.
   (一般來說，女人比男人細心。)
   ＊ meticulous [məˈtɪkjələs] a. 過分細心的, 小心翼翼的

3. **accept** [əkˈsɛpt] vt. 接受
   例: I can't accept your expensive gift, I'm afraid.
   (恐怕我不能接受你那昂貴的禮物。)

4. **junk food** 垃圾食物
   junk [dʒʌŋk] n. 無用的廢物 (集合名詞, 不可數)
   例: Eating too much junk food isn't good for you.
   (吃太多垃圾食物對你不好。)

Let's get rid of all this junk in our room.
(咱們把房裡沒用的東西都清除掉吧。)

5. **healthful** [ˈhɛlθfəl] a. 有益健康的

healthy [ˈhɛlθɪ] a. 健康的

注意:

healthy 本意是『健康的』,但在現代美語中,常與 healthful 的用法相同,亦可表『有益健康的』。

例: Jogging is healthful exercise.
(慢跑是有益健康的運動。)

Grandma is old but healthy.
(祖母年紀大了但很健康。)

6. **fast-food restaurant**　速食餐館

restaurant [ˈrɛstrɑnt] n. 餐館

例: The food at fast-food restaurants isn't very healthful.
(速食餐館的食物對健康並沒有多大的益處。)

7. **pop up**　突然出現, 冒出來

pop [pɑp] vi. 彈(出), 跳(出)

例: Buildings are popping up all over the suburbs.
(高樓大廈在郊區各處如雨後春筍般地冒出來。)

8. **all over the world**　全世界

= around the world

= the world over

例: This TV program can be seen all over the world.
(這個電視節目全世界都看得到。)

9. **in a rush**　匆忙地

= in a hurry

= in haste (不可置於 be 動詞之後)

注意:

in a rush/a hurry/haste 均可作副詞用, 修飾動詞, 但前兩者亦可置於 be 動詞後作主詞補語, 而 in haste 則不可。因此本文中:

These restaurants are for people who are always <u>in a rush</u>.

= These restaurants are for people who are always <u>in a hurry</u>.

These restaurants are for people who are always <u>in haste</u>. (✕)

例: He finished his breakfast <u>in a rush</u> and went directly to the airport.

= He finished his breakfast <u>in a hurry</u>...

= He finished his breakfast <u>in haste</u>...

(他匆忙吃完早餐便直接到機場去了。)

10. **regular** [ˈrɛgjələ] a. 正常的, 一般的

例: The movie star doesn't live a regular life.
(那個電影明星過的不是一般人的生活。)

11. **meal** [mil] n. 餐

例: The poor man can only afford one meal a day.
(那個窮漢一天只能吃得起一餐。)

12. **race** [res] vi. 疾行, 跑 & vt. 與……賽跑 & n. 賽跑; 比賽

例: Let's race to the school.
(咱們用跑的去學校吧。)

I'll race you to the end of this street.
(我要和你賽跑到這條街的盡頭。)

The gray horse won the race.
(那場比賽由那隻灰馬獲勝。)

13. **the McDonald's** [məkˈdɑnəldz]n. 麥當勞 (美國最大的漢堡連鎖店)

* the McDonald's 之後省略了 Fast-Food Restaurant。

14. **satisfy** [ˈsætɪsˌfaɪ] vt. 使滿意, 使滿足

satisfied [ˈsætɪsˌfaɪd] a. 感到滿意的

satisfying [ˈsætɪsˌfaɪɪŋ] a. 使人有飽足感的

satisfactory [ˌsætɪsˈfæktərɪ] a. 令人滿意的

be satisfied with...　　對……感到滿意

例: I asked the question just to satisfy my curiosity.
(我問那個問題只是要滿足我的好奇心。)

　　＊ curiosity [ˌkjʊrɪˈɑsətɪ] n. 好奇心

The workers aren't satisfied with their pay.
(那些工人不滿意他們的薪水。)

We had a satisfying meal at the Italian restaurant.
(我們在那家義大利餐廳飽吃一頓。)

My son's schoolwork is quite satisfactory.
(我兒子的課業挺讓我滿意的。)

　　＊ schoolwork [ˈskuɫˌwɝk] n. 學業, 課業 (不可數)

15. **hunger** [ˈhʌŋgɚ] n. 飢餓 & vi. 渴望, 極想 (與介詞 for 並用)

hungry [ˈhʌŋgrɪ] a. 飢餓的

例: The beggar almost died of hunger.
(那個乞丐幾乎餓死。)

　　＊ beggar [ˈbɛgɚ] n. 乞丐

The prisoner <u>hungers for</u> freedom.
(那名囚犯渴望自由。)

The hungry boy ate six bowls of beef noodles.
(那個飢餓的男孩吃了六碗牛肉麵。)

16. **immediately** [ɪˈmidɪtlɪ] adv. 立刻, 馬上

例: Can you come over immediately? I need your help.
(你可不可以馬上過來? 我需要你的幫忙。)

17. **order** [ˈɔrdɚ] vt. 點 (菜)

例: The hosts ordered too much food for their guests.
(那些主人幫他們客人點的菜太多了。)

18. **burger** [ˈbɝgɚ] n. 漢堡

= hamburger [ˈhæmbɝgɚ]

19. **fries** [fraɪz] n. 炸薯條

= French fries [ˈfrɛntʃ ˌfraɪz]

20. **polite** [pəˈlaɪt] a. 有禮貌的

例: It never hurts to be polite.
(禮貌一點總是無妨。)

21. **efficient** [ɪˈfɪʃənt] a. 有效率的

例: We need efficient workers.
(我們需要有效率的員工。)

22. **after all**　畢竟; 終究

例: You can't ask John to do it. After, he is only ten.
(這工作你不能叫約翰去做。畢竟，他只有十歲。)

23. 本文:

..., in America do as the Americans do.
……, 在美國就應該跟著美國佬那樣做。

注意:

本句乃由諺語"When in Rome, do as the Romans do." (在羅馬時, 言行舉止要和羅馬人一樣。喻: 入境隨俗。)衍生而來。

Grammar Notes
文 法 重 點

本課旨在介紹如何避免雙重連接的錯誤句構。

Though it is generally accepted that junk food is not healthful, American fast-food restaurants are popping up all over the world.
雖然大家都普遍接受垃圾食物並無益於健康, 但是美式速食餐館卻如雨後春筍般在世界各地流行起來。

Because Americans like things done immediately, they often order their food quickly at fast-food restaurants.

因為美國人做事喜歡快刀斬亂麻, 所以他們在速食店裡點餐通常也很迅速。
Though it's not polite, it's efficient.
這種說法雖然並不禮貌, 卻很有效率。

請讀者注意下列要點:

1. **though** [ðo] (雖然) 亦可用 although [ɔlˋðo] 代替, 為副詞連接詞, 引導副詞子句, 修飾句中主要子句。我們因受中文『雖然……但是……』的影響, 而常將英文說成"Though (Although)...but..."的錯誤句構, 因為英文的文法中規定兩句之間的連接詞只能有一個, 而 though (although)與 but 均為連接詞, 如此一來, 形成錯誤的雙重連接句子結構。故我們若用 though (或 although)時, 則 but 應予省略; 若用 but 時, 則 though (或 although) 就應省略。

   例: Though he is rich, but he is not happy.　(✗)
   → 　Though he is rich, he is not happy. (○)
   = 　He is rich, but he is not happy.
   　　(雖然他很有錢, 但他並不快樂。)

   　　Although she was sick, but she still went to school. (✗)
   → 　Although she was sick, she still went to school. (○)
   = 　She was sick, but she still went to school.
   　　(雖然她病了, 但她仍然去上學。)

   → 　Even though it will probably rain tomorrow, but we will go fishing as scheduled. (✗)
   → 　Even though it will probably rain tomorrow, we will go fishing as scheduled. (○)
   　　(即使明天會下雨, 我們還是要按照計畫去釣魚。)

2. "Because...so..." (因為……所以……) 亦是錯誤的雙重連接句構, 因為 because 和 so 都是連接詞, 故用 because 時, 就不能再用 so; 而用 so 時, 則不可再用 because。

   例: Because he was once bitten by a dog, so he is now afraid of dogs. (✗)

→ <u>Because</u> he was once bitten by a dog, he is now afraid of dogs. (○)
= He was once bitten by a dog, <u>so</u> he is now afraid of dogs.
(因為他曾被狗咬過，所以他現在很怕狗。)

根據上述說明，可知本文三句亦可寫成：

It is generally accepted that junk food is not healthful, <u>but</u> American fast-food restaurants are popping up all over the world.

Americans like things done immediately, <u>so</u> they often order their food quickly at fast-food restaurants.

It's not polite, <u>but</u> it's efficient.

Substitution 代　換

1. **Though it is generally accepted that junk food is not healthful, American fast-food restaurants are popping up all over the world.**
   Carl is poor, but he's happy.
   Though he's rich, he is stingy.
   雖然大家都普遍接受垃圾食物並無益於健康，但是美式速食餐館卻如雨後春筍般在世界各地流行起來。
   卡爾很窮，可是他很快樂。
   雖然他很有錢，但他很吝嗇。

2. **Because Americans like things done immediately, they often order their food quickly at fast-food restaurants.**
   Tom is shy, so he seldom speaks.
   Because Tom's shy, he seldom speaks.
   因為美國人做事喜歡快刀斬亂麻，所以他們在速食店裡點餐通常也很迅速。
   湯姆很害羞，所以他很少開口講話。
   因為湯姆很害羞，他很少開口講話。

Lesson 48
Fast Food, Slow Service
急驚風遇上慢郎中

Dialogue
實用會話

Tess is a cashier at a fast-food restaurant. Michael is a customer in a hurry.

(T=Tess; M=Michael)

T: Good afternoon, sir. How are you today?

M: Save it, lady. Just get me a burger and fries.

T: Would you care for a drink or anything else?

M: Listen. Though I know you're trying to be nice, I don't have all day. If I want anything else, I'll mention it, OK?

T: Are you sure you don't want a dessert? A milkshake maybe?

M: No, just go and bring me my order, will you?

T: Wait a minute! You look familiar. You're Michael Jordan, aren't you? Tell me, how does it feel to be such a famous basketball player?

M: That's it. I've had enough. I'm going to a real fast-food restaurant.

黛絲是一家速食店的收銀員，麥可則是一位趕時間的顧客。

黛絲：午安，先生。您今天好嗎？

麥可：不必客套了，小姐。就給我一個漢堡和薯條吧。

黛絲：要不要來杯飲料或別的東西？

麥可：聽著，雖然我知道妳想要對我親切，但是我可沒那閒功夫。如果我還要別的東西，我會說的，好嗎？

黛絲：您確定不要來份點心嗎？來杯奶昔如何？

麥可：不要，只要把我點的東西拿來就行了，好嗎？

黛絲：等等！您看起來很面熟。您是麥可‧喬登，對不對？告訴我，當一個這麼有名的籃球員感覺如何？

麥可：夠了！我受夠了。我要去一家真正的速食店。

Key Points
重點提示

1. **cashier** [kæˈʃɪr] n. 櫃台收銀員

   例: The cashier handles money very carefully.
   (那名收銀員處理錢財都很謹慎。)

2. **customer** [ˈkʌstəmɚ] n. 顧客

   例: I don't believe that a customer is always right.
   (我認為顧客未必永遠都是對的。)

3. **Save it.** 　不必客套了/省省吧。

   save [sev] vt. 節省

   例: A: You're looking really pretty today, Sara.
   B: Save it.
   (甲：妳今天看起來真是太美了，莎拉。)
   (乙：省省吧。)

   It's wise to save money for a rainy day.
   (存錢以備不時之需是明智的作法。)

4. 本文:

Would you <u>care for</u> a drink or anything else?

= Would you <u>like</u> a drink or anything else?
要不要來杯飲料或別的東西？

5. **mention** [ˈmɛnʃən] vt. 提及, 說到

例: When you spoke to the boss, did he mention me?
(你和老闆談話時，他有沒有提到我？)

6. **dessert** [dɪˈzɝt] n. 餐後甜點

例: There are lots of desserts at the buffet.
(自助餐裡有許多飯後甜點。)
* buffet [bʌˈfe] n. 自助餐

Tom ordered an apple pie for dessert.
(湯姆點了一個蘋果派當點心。)

7. **milkshake** [ˈmɪlkˌʃek] n. 奶昔
注意:

milkshake 是一種牛奶加香料、冰淇淋等攪拌成泡沫狀的飲料。

8. **familiar** [fəˈmɪljɚ] a. 熟悉的

人 + be familiar with + 事物　　某人熟悉某事物

= 事物 + be familiar to + 人

例: I'm still not familiar with the roads around my new apartment.
(我對我家新公寓附近的路還是不熟。)

Is this name familiar to you?
(你對這個名字熟悉嗎？)

9. **Michael Jordan**　　麥可‧喬登 (曾為美國職籃(NBA) 芝加哥公牛隊
的當家後衛, 有『空中飛人』之稱, 為獲得最有價
值球員 (MVP) 次數最多的一位)

10. **How does it feel to + 原形動詞?**　　……感覺如何呢？

例: How does it feel to be elected class leader?
(當選班長的感覺如何?)

11. **I've had enough.** 我受夠了。

例: A: Why don't you try to make up with your ex-girlfriend?
B: I've had enough.
(甲:你為何不試著和前任女友重修舊好呢?)
(乙:我受夠了。)

請選出下列各句中正確的一項

1. The writer of this book isn't _____ me.
   (A) familiar to (B) familiar for (C) famous to (D) famous for

2. France is famous _____ its wines.
   (A) as (B) to (C) for (D) of

3. We canceled our trip _____ Dad got sick.
   (A) though (B) because (C) but (D) although

4. Although Jean is pretty, _____ .
   (A) she isn't very smart (B) so she isn't very smart
   (C) but she isn't very smart (D) and she isn't very smart

5. I'm in _____ to catch the train.
   (A) hurry (B) a hurry (C) haste (D) rush

解答:

| 1. (A) | 2. (C) | 3. (B) | 4. (A) | 5. (B) |

Lesson 49

Stop Snoring!

別打呼了！

Reading
閱　讀

Millions of families have trouble falling asleep. Do you know why? There's someone in the family who has a snoring problem. The problem can be quite serious. In some cases, couples have to sleep in separate bedrooms. And in others, kids can never study or even watch TV once Dad hits the sack.

So how can we avoid being a snoring nuisance? One way is to avoid eating a big meal before going to bed. Drinking alcohol near bedtime is something which also causes snoring. Changing the position in which the snorer sleeps also helps.

Another alternative is to wear ear plugs. But if all these ideas fail, you have only one choice: Wake the snorer up. Tell him it's his turn to watch you sleep.

數以百萬的家庭都有難以入睡的困擾。你知道原因何在嗎？因為家中有個人有打鼾的毛病。這問題可能相當嚴重。有些情形下夫妻必須分房睡。也有些情形是只要老爸一睡覺，孩子們可能就無法讀書或看電視。

所以要如何才能避免成為一個會打鼾的討厭傢伙呢？方法之一是避免在就寢前大吃一頓，接近上床時間喝酒也會引起打鼾。改變打鼾者的睡姿也會有所幫助，另一個選擇是戴上耳塞。但若這些方法都無效，你就只有一個選擇了：把打鼾者叫醒，告訴他輪到他看著你睡覺了。

Vocabulary & Idioms
單字 & 片語註解

1. **snore** [snɔr] vi. 打鼾

   snorer ['snɔrɚ] n. 打鼾者

   例: When Dad snores, even the neighbors can't sleep.
   (老爹打鼾的時候連鄰居都沒法兒睡。)

   It's awful to go camping with a snorer.
   (和會打呼的人去露營非常糟糕。)

2. **fall asleep** 　入睡

   例: If you can't fall asleep, try drinking a glass of milk before you go to bed.
   (如果你睡不著，可以在上床前喝一杯牛奶試試看。)

   ＊本片語中, fall 是不完全不及物動詞, 相當於 become (變成)之意, asleep [əˋslip] 則為形容詞, 表『睡著的』。

3. **separate** ['sɛpərɪt] a. 分開的, 個別的 & ['sɛpəˌret] vt. 分開, 區別

separate A from B　　隔開 A 與 B

例: It would be foolish to try to separate a dog from its bone.
(嘗試讓狗和牠的骨頭分開是不智之舉。)

4. **hit the sack**　　就寢, 睡覺

= go to bed

= go to sleep

= turn in

＊ sack [sæk] n. 原指『麻袋』, 美式俚語中則指『床』, hit the sack 則表 『睡覺』。

例: Everyone hits the sack at 10 p.m. at the school dormitory.
(學校宿舍的每一個人都在晚上十點就寢。)
　　＊ dormitory ['dɔrməˌtɔrɪ] n. 宿舍

5. **nuisance** ['njusəns] n. 討厭的人或事物

例: Traffic jams are a real nuisance.
(塞車真是討厭。)
　　＊ traffic jam ['træfɪk ˌdʒæm] n. 交通阻塞

6. **alcohol** ['ælkəˌhɔl] n. 酒精 (本文指酒)

例: In some countries, it's against the law to sell alcohol to people under the age of eighteen.
(在某些國家, 販賣酒類給十八歲以下的人是犯法的。)

7. **bedtime** ['bɛdˌtaɪm] n. 上床睡覺時間

例: Mom never lets me watch TV past my bedtime.
(超過我該睡覺的時間媽媽絕不讓我看電視。)

8. **position** [pəˈzɪʃən] n. 姿勢

例: Some people stand in strange positions when being photographed.
(有些人照相的時候站立的姿勢很奇怪。)
　　＊ photograph ['fotəˌgræf] vt. 照像, 攝影

9. **alternative** [ɔl'tɝ·nətɪv] n. 選擇

have no | alternative | but to + 原形動詞　　除了……外別無選擇
　　　　| choice

例: I have no alternative but to sue you.
(我非告你不可。)
　　＊ sue [su] vt. 控告

10. **ear plugs**　　耳塞 (人有兩個耳朵, 故用複數形)

plug [plʌg] n. 塞子

例: It's so noisy at the factory that the workers wear ear plugs when they are at work.
(那間工廠如此吵雜，因此工人們在工作的時候都戴上耳塞。)

11. **it's one's turn to + 原形動詞**　　輪到某人……

turn [tɝn] n. 輪流, 輪班

例: It's Dad's turn to do the dishes today.
(今天輪到老爸洗碗盤了。)

Grammar Notes
文法重點

本課介紹"millions of＋複數名詞" (數以百萬計的……) 和"have trouble＋動名詞" (做……有困難/麻煩) 的用法, 並介紹關係代名詞的種類及其用法。

1. **Millions of families <u>have trouble</u> falling asleep.**
數以百萬的家庭都有難以入睡的困擾。

a. millions of＋複數名詞　　　　　數以百萬計的……
hundreds of＋複數名詞　　　　　數以百計的……
thousands of＋複數名詞　　　　　數以千計的……
tens of thousands of＋複數名詞 (係從 ten thousand『一萬』變化而成)　　數以萬計的……

hundreds of thousands of + 複數名詞 (係從 one hundred thousand 『十萬』變化而成)

數以十萬計的⋯⋯

tens of millions of + 複數名詞 (係從 ten million『千萬』變化而成)

數以千萬計的⋯⋯

＊上列片語中的複數名詞前不可置定冠詞 the 或所有格 my, his, her...等。

例: Thousands of <u>the</u> fans were at the airport to welcome the soccer team. (✗)

→ Thousands of fans were at the airport to welcome the soccer team. (○)

(數以千計的球迷在機場歡迎該足球隊的蒞臨。)

This new sports car costs tens of thousands of US dollars.

(這部新跑車價值好幾萬美元。)

注意:

hundred, thousand, million 作形容詞時, 之前可置數字, 但 hundred, thousand, million 後不可加-s, 其後直接置名詞。

例: Two hundred<u>s</u> people applied for the job. (✗)

→ Two hundred people applied for the job. (○)

(有兩百人應徵那份工作。)

About six million Jews died in World War II.

(大約有六百萬名猶太人死於二次世界大戰中。)

b. have | trouble   + 動名詞   做/在⋯⋯(方面) 有困難/麻煩
      | difficulty
      | problem<u>s</u>
      | a hard time

類似用法:

have | a good time   + 動名詞   ⋯⋯(玩得) 很愉快
      | fun

注意:

在上述用法中, have trouble/difficulty/problems/a hard time/a good time/fun 之後理論上有一介詞 in, 故其後須接動名詞作其受詞, 而不可接不定詞 (to＋原形動詞), 但實際使用時, in 一律不可寫出, 而直接接動名詞。

例: Bob has trouble <u>to understand</u> his teacher's English. (✕)

→ Bob has trouble understanding his teacher's English. (○)
(鮑勃很難聽懂他老師的英文。)

Mr. Chen has problems <u>to make</u> ends meet. (✕)

→ Mr. Chen has problems making ends meet.(○)
(陳先生難以使收支平衡。)

I always have a good time <u>to visit</u> my old friends. (✕)

→ I always have a good time visiting my old friends. (○)
(我去看老朋友時總是很開心。)

2. **There's someone in the family <u>who</u> has a snoring problem.**
家中有個人有打鼾的毛病。

Drinking alcohol near bedtime is something <u>which</u> also causes snoring.
接近上床時間喝酒也會引起打鼾。

Changing the position <u>in which</u> the snorer sleeps also helps.
改變打鼾者的睡姿也會有所幫助。

上列句中的 who 及 which 所引導的子句稱為形容詞子句, 各修飾之前的名詞 someone、something 及 position。who 及 which 稱作關係代名詞。

注意:

關係代名詞具有連接詞的功能, 用以引導形容詞子句, 修飾之前的名詞。

關係代名詞共有 who、whom、which 三種, 茲分項說明如下:

a. 修飾人用 who 或 whom:

例: He is <u>the person who</u> can solve the problem.
　　　　　　　　　主格

(他是能夠解決這個問題的人。)

＊ who 引導的形容詞子句修飾其前的名詞 the person。

He is <u>a man</u> <u>whom</u> I enjoy working with.
　　　　　　　受格

(他是那種我喜歡與之共事的人。)

＊ whom 引導的形容詞子句修飾其前的名詞 a man。

  b. 修飾事物用 which:

例: No one will buy <u>a book</u> <u>which</u> is poorly written.
　　　　　　　　　　　　　　主格

(沒有人會買一本寫得很爛的書。)

＊ which 引導的形容詞子句修飾其前的名詞 a book。

I have found <u>the watch</u> <u>which</u> you lost yesterday.
　　　　　　　　　　　　受格

(我發現了你昨天丟掉的那隻手錶。)

＊ which 引導的形容詞子句修飾其前的名詞 the watch。

3. 使用關係代名詞時, 要注意下列要點:
  a. 關係代名詞前一定要有先行詞 (名詞)。
  b. 關係代名詞在其引導的形容詞子句中要作主詞或受詞。
  c. 否則關係代名詞前一定要有介詞, 而該介詞通常可移至句尾, 此時可省略關係代名詞。

＊ 由於 who 是主格, 故在形容詞子句中要作主詞, 而 whom 是受格, 故在形容詞子句中只能作受詞; which 在其引導的形容詞子句中則可作主詞或受詞。

例: Never trust people <u>who</u> break their promises easily.
　　　　　　　　　　　主詞

(絕不要信任輕易背信的人。)

He is a man <u>whom</u> you can <u>trust</u>.
　　　　　　　受詞

(他是你可以信任的那種人。)

He is a man <u>whom</u> I enjoy working. (✗)

＊在本例的形容詞子句"whom I enjoy working"中, 已有主詞 I, 而 working 乃不及物動詞變成的動名詞, 故 whom 無法作其受詞, 此時關係代名詞之前應置介詞。

→ He is a man <u>with whom</u> I enjoy working. (○)

= He is a man <u>(whom)</u> I enjoy working <u>with</u>.
(他是我喜歡與之共事的人。)

或: He is a man <u>for whom</u> I enjoy working. (○)

= He is a man <u>(whom)</u> I enjoy working <u>for</u>.
(他是我很樂意替他工作的人。)

He has a watch <u>which</u> was made in Switzerland.
　　　　　　　　主詞
(他有一只瑞士製的手錶。)

This is a problem <u>which</u> we should <u>notice</u>.
　　　　　　　　受詞
(這是個我們應該注意的問題。)

The apartment <u>which</u> I live is very small. (✕)

＊在本例的形容詞子句"which I live"中, 已有主詞 I, 而 live 是不及物動詞, 故 which 無法作其受詞, 此時 which 之前就應有介詞。

→ The apartment <u>in which</u> I live is very small. (○)

= The apartment <u>(which)</u> I live <u>in</u> is very small.
(我住的那間公寓很小。)

4. 關係代名詞的限定修飾與非限定修飾之別:

a. 限定修飾

普通名詞若不具特殊性, 而欲加強其特殊性時, 可用形容詞子句加以修飾, 但形容詞子句之前不得置逗點。翻譯時, 先譯形容詞子句 (譯成『……的』), 再譯被修飾的名詞。

例: I like <u>the student</u> <u>who studies hard</u>.
　　　　　　　　　　　限定修飾
(我喜歡那個用功的學生。)

I know <u>a college</u> <u>which is famous for its excellent facilities</u>.
　　　　　　　　　　　　　　　限定修飾
(我知道一所以其完善的設備而聞名的大學。)

b. 非限定修飾

專有名詞 (如: Peter、Bill、Taipei 等) 及獨一性名詞, 如: father (爸爸只有一個)、mother (媽媽只有一個), 之後若接關係代名詞引導的形容詞子句時, 該關係代名詞之前一定要置逗點, 此時該形容詞子句就稱為非限定修飾語。換言之, 專有名詞或獨一性名詞本身就具有特殊性, 不必再用形容詞子句加以限定。

例: I met <u>Nancy</u>, <u>who is an old friend of mine</u>.
　　　　　專有名詞　　　　非限定修飾
(我遇到南西,她是我的一位舊識。)

She has just come back from <u>New York</u>, <u>which is a very big city</u>
　　　　　　　　　　　　　　專有名詞　　　　非限定修飾
<u>in the States</u>.
(她剛從紐約回來,那是美國的一個大城市。)

That is <u>my only son</u>, <u>who is attending senior high school</u>.
　　　　獨一性名詞　　　　　　非限定修飾
(那是我的獨生子,他正在唸高中。)

c. 但若一般名詞前已有形容詞加以修飾而具有特殊性, 如: a good person (好人)、a great man (偉人) 等, 或該名詞本身就具有特殊性, 如: gentleman (紳士, 君子)、rascal (流氓)等, 則該名詞之後的形容詞子句可用非限定修飾 (即在關係代名詞前置逗點), 以減低該子句的重要性; 但亦可採限定修飾 (即關係代名詞前不置逗點), 以更增加被修飾的名詞之特殊性。

例: He is a good student<u>, who</u> studies hard.──非限定修飾
(他是個好學生,很用功。)

或: He is a good student <u>who</u> studies hard.──限定修飾
(他是個用功的好學生。)

He is a gentleman, who always keeps his promises.——非限定修飾

(他是個君子，總是信守承諾。)

或: He is a gentleman who always keeps his promises.——限定修飾

(他是個信守承諾的君子。)

5. that 亦可用來當作關係代名詞, 取代 who、whom 或 which, 但使用時有兩個條件:

a. that 之前不可有逗點, 換言之, that 僅出現在限定修飾的形容詞子句中。

b. that 之前亦不可有介詞。

例: I like Tom, that studies hard. (✕)

→ I like Tom, who studies hard. (○)

(我喜歡湯姆，他很用功。)

I like the girl who is standing over there.

= I like the girl that is standing over there.

(我喜歡站在那裡的那個女孩。)

He is a man whom we all respect.

= He is a man that we all respect.

(他是個我們全都尊敬的人。)

This is the car which he bought yesterday.

= This is the car that he bought yesterday.

(這就是他昨天買的那部車。)

He is the man with that I enjoy working. (✕)

→ He is the man with whom I enjoy working. (○)

(他是我樂於共事的人。)

6. which 亦可用來代替前面整個句子, 此時 which 之前一定要置逗點。

例: He is a hardworking student, which everyone knows.

(大家都知道，他是個用功的學生。)

7. 作受格的 whom 或 which (含 that) 在限定修飾的句構中可予以省略。

例: That is the man <u>whom (或 that)</u> I met yesterday.
= That is the man I met yesterday.
(那就是我昨天遇到的那個人。)

I like the movie <u>which (或 that)</u> we went to last night.
= I like the movie we went to last night.
(我喜歡我們昨晚去看的那部電影。)

8. 在限定修飾的形容詞子句中, 若子句句首介詞時, 之後的關係代名詞不可省略, 但介詞亦可移至句尾, 此時可省略該關係代名詞。

例: This is the apartment <u>in which</u> I live.
= This is the apartment <u>which</u> I live <u>in</u>.
= This is the apartment I live <u>in</u>.
(這就是我住的公寓。)

Tom is a nice man <u>with whom</u> I enjoy working.
= Tom is a nice man <u>whom</u> I enjoy working <u>with</u>.
= Tom is a nice man I enjoy working <u>with</u>.
(湯姆是個我喜歡共事的好人。)

Substitution
代　　換

1. **Millions of families have trouble falling asleep.**

Hundreds of cars were damaged as a result of the earthquake.

Tens of thousands of Madonna's fans were at the concert.

數以百萬的家庭都有難以入睡的困擾。

那場地震造成數百輛汽車損毀。

好幾萬的瑪丹娜歌迷出現在演唱會上。

2. **There's someone in the family who has a snoring problem.**

   This is the CD which I want.

   Sara is the girl that broke my heart.

   家中有個人有打鼾的毛病。

   這是我要的那張雷射唱片。

   莎拉就是那個使我心碎的女孩。

Lesson 50
Laser Cures Snoring
雷射可治打鼾

Dialogue
實用會話

A mother and son are talking.

(S=son; M=mother)

S: I can't stand Dad's snoring anymore, Mom. I didn't sleep a wink last night.

M: I understand. Neither did I. But what can we do?

S: I read in a magazine that there's some kind of laser which can cure snoring.

M: I read that, too. But it's pretty expensive. Besides, people who have tried it say it's painful and could cause voice change.

S: Oh, I didn't know that. I guess there's no hope then.

M: Well, I'll talk to Dad about it.

S: I hope he agrees to do it. Anyway, a voice change will do him a world of good. Have you heard him try to sing lately?

M: Come to think of it, you're right.

一對母子正在談話。

兒子：媽，我再也忍受不了老爸的鼾聲了。我昨晚整夜都沒合上眼。

媽媽：我了解。我也沒有。但是我們又能怎麼辦呢？

兒子：我在雜誌上看到有種雷射可以治療打鼾。

媽媽：我也看到了，但那挺貴的。況且嘗試過的人說那很痛苦而且可能會導致聲音改變。

兒子：哦，這個我倒不知道。我想大概沒指望了。

媽媽：說不定，我會和你老爸談談這件事。

兒子：我希望他會同意。況且改變聲音對他大有好處。妳最近聽過他唱歌嗎？

媽媽：這倒使找想起來了，你說的沒錯。

Key Points
重點提示

1. **laser** [ˈlezɚ] n. 雷射 (光)

= light amplification by stimulated emission of radiation

* amplification [ˌæmpləfəˈkeʃən] n. 擴大

   stimulated [ˈstɪmjəˌletɪd] a. 刺激的

   emission [ɪˈmɪʃən] n. 發射

   radiation [ˌredɪˈeʃən] n. 輻射

   例: The laser at the disco made Tom feel dizzy.
   (迪斯可舞廳的雷射燈光讓湯姆感到暈眩。)
      * dizzy [ˈdɪzɪ] a. 暈眩的, 眼花的

2. **cure** [kjur] vt. 治療, 使痊癒

   例: The herbalist cured the old man of rheumatism.
   (那個中醫治癒了那名老翁的風濕症。)
      * herbalist [ˈhɝbəlɪst] n. 草藥醫師, 中醫
        rheumatism [ˈruməˌtɪzm̩] n. 風濕症

3. **stand** [stænd] vt. 忍受, 忍耐 (= bear)

cannot stand + 名詞/動名詞　　無法忍受……

例: I cannot stand selfish people.
(我受不了自私的人。)

4. 本文:

I can't stand Dad's snoring <u>anymore/any longer</u>, Mom.

媽, 我再也忍受不了老爸的鼾聲了。

5. **not sleep a wink**　　沒合上眼, 一會兒也沒睡

wink [wɪŋk] n. 眨眼

例: My neighbors were so noisy that I didn't sleep a wink last night.
(我的鄰居吵得我昨晚沒辦法合上眼。)

6. **magazine** [ˌmæɡəˈzin] n. 雜誌

例: If you are learning English, you should read some English-teaching magazines.
(如果你在學英文，你應該看些英文教學雜誌。)

7. **painful** [ˈpenfəl] a. 痛苦的

例: My pet dog's death was a painful experience.
(愛犬的死對我來說是個痛苦的經驗。)

8. **voice change**　　聲音改變

voice [vɔɪs] n. 聲音

in a/an...voice　　用……聲音

例: The boss spoke to the secretary in a loud voice.
(老闆用大嗓門向祕書說話。)

9. **agree** [əˈɡri] vt. & vi. 同意

agree to + 原形動詞　　同意做……

agree with + 人　　同意某人 (的看法)

例: The bank agreed to lend us some money to buy a house.
(那家銀行同意借我們一點錢買房子。)

Although you sound convincing, I don't agree with you.

(雖然你說的頗具說服力，我還是不同意你的看法。)

＊ convincing [kən'vɪnsɪŋ] a. 令人信服的

10. **do + 人 + a world of good**　　對某人大有好處

例: Doing regular exercise will do you a world of good.
(規律運動對你有莫大的好處。)

11. 本文:

Come to think of it, you are right.

這倒使我想起來了, 你的話沒有錯。

Come to think of it,...　　我倒想起來了,⋯⋯

例: Come to think of it, the problem isn't so difficult to solve.
(我倒想起來了，這個問題不是那麼難解決。)

請選出下列各句中正確的一項

1. The family couldn't ＿＿＿＿ the noise in the city so they moved to the country.
(A) hear　　　(B) make　　　(C) stand　　　(D) have

2. Mr. Wang was so worried he couldn't ＿＿＿＿ a wink last night.
(A) take　　　(B) make　　　(C) do　　　(D) sleep

3. I had lots of fun ＿＿＿＿ with Mary this morning
(A) of chatting　(B) to chat　　　(C) chatting　　(D) on chatting

4. Do you have any trouble ＿＿＿＿ with that guy?
(A) communicate　　　　(B) communicating
(C) communicated　　　　(D) to communicate

解答:

1. (C)　　2. (D)　　3. (C)　　4. (B)

L esson 51
Thanksgiving
感恩節

Reading
閱　讀

Thanksgiving, which falls on the fourth Thursday of November, is one of the biggest American holidays. This holiday started in the early 1600's after settlers arrived in America. These people who came from Europe didn't know how to survive in the wild new country. Luckily, they met some friendly American Indians, who showed them how to hunt turkeys and grow corn. In the fall, after the harvest, the settlers had a great feast. They invited the Indians to thank them for their help.

Today the tradition continues. On Thanksgiving Day,

Americans invite their friends over for a turkey dinner and give thanks for what they have.

> 每年十一月第四個星期四的感恩節是美國最大的節日之一。這個節日是在十七世紀初期殖民者到達美國後開始的。這些來自歐洲的人不知道該如何在這個蠻荒的新國家生存。所幸的是，他們遇見一些友善的美國印第安人，這些印第安人教他們如何獵火雞和種植玉米。在秋收後，這些殖民者舉行了一場盛宴。他們邀請了那些印第安人以感謝他們的幫助。
>
> 如今這項傳統仍然持續著。在感恩節這天，美國人會邀請他們的朋友到家裡享用一頓火雞大餐並感謝他們所擁有的一切。

Vocabulary & Idioms
單字 & 片語註解

1. **Thanksgiving** [ˈθæŋksˌgɪvɪŋ] n. 感恩節

2. **fall** [fɔl] vi. 降臨 & n. 秋天 (= autumn [ˈɔtəm])

   fall on + 日期 (節日等) 降臨在某日/是在某日期

   例: Christmas falls on Wednesday this year.
   (今年的聖誕節是在星期三。)

3. **November** [noˈvɛmbɚ] n. 十一月 (月份名稱大寫)

4. **holiday** [ˈhɑləˌde] n. 節日, 假日

   例: Chinese New Year is my favorite holiday.
   (農曆新年是我最喜歡的節日。)

5. **settler** [ˈsɛtlɚ] n. 移民, 開墾者

   例: The English were the early settlers of America.
   (英國人是美國早期的移民者。)

6. **Europe** [ˈjʊrəp] n. 歐洲

7. **survive** [səˈvaɪv] vi. 生存; 生還 & vt. 比……活得久; 熬過

   survive + 人　　比某人活得久

   survive + 事物　　熬過……

   例: Three of the students died in the fire and one survived.
   (這些學生中有三人在大火中喪生，一人生還。)

   My grandma survived my grandpa by one year.
   (我奶奶比爺爺多活了一年。)

   Only half the passengers survived the shipwreck.
   (只有一半的乘客從那次船難生還。)

   ＊ shipwreck [ˈʃɪpˌrɛk] n. 船難

8. **luckily** [ˈlʌkɪlɪ] adv. 幸運地, 所幸

   例: Luckily, we fixed the roof before it started to rain.
   (所幸，我們在下雨之前就把屋頂修好了。)

9. **American Indian** [əˈmɛrɪkən ˌɪndɪən] n. 美國印第安人

10. **hunt** [hʌnt] vt. 狩獵, 獵取

    例: It's illegal to hunt tigers in India.
    (在印度狩獵老虎是違法的。)

11. **turkey** [ˈtɝkɪ] n. 火雞

12. **grow** [gro] vt. 種植 & vi. 長大成人

    動詞三態: grow、grew [gru]、grown [gron]。

    grow up　　長大

    例: Mom grows tomatoes in our garden.
    (老媽在我們花園種了蕃茄。)

    Jenny grew up to be a very beautiful young lady.
    (珍妮長大後亭亭玉立。)

13. **corn** [kɔrn] n. 玉米

14. **harvest** [ˈhɑrvɪst] n. 收成 & vt. 收割

    例: This year's rice harvest was affected by the typhoon.
    (今年稻米的收成受到了颱風的影響。)

    With the new machines, the farmers find it easier to harvest their crop.
    (有了新的機械,農人發覺收割農作物容易多了。)

15. **feast** [fist] n. 饗宴, 盛宴

    例: The couple had a feast on their wedding anniversary.
    (那對夫婦在他們結婚周年紀念日舉辦了一場宴會。)

    ＊ anniversary [ˌænəˈvɝsərɪ] n. 周年紀念日

16. **invite** [ɪnˈvaɪt] vt. 邀請

    invitation [ˌɪnvəˈteʃən] n. 邀請

    invite + 人 + over   邀請某人前來

    例: Let's invite my parents over this weekend.
    (咱們這個周末就邀請我的父母來吧。)

    At John's invitation, I sang a song.
    (在約翰的邀請下,我唱了一首歌。)

17. **tradition** [trəˈdɪʃən] n. 傳統

    例: It is a Chinese tradition to have a reunion dinner on Chinese New Year's Eve.
    (大年夜吃團圓飯是中國人的一項傳統。)

Grammar Notes
文法重點

本課介紹介詞與時間名詞的關係。

On Thanksgiving Day, Americans invite their friends over for a turkey dinner and give thanks for what they have.

在感恩節這天, 美國人會邀請他們的朋友到家裡享用一頓火雞晚餐並感謝他們所擁有的一切。

注意:

a. 表日期或星期幾時, 須使用介詞 on, 如: on Christmas Day (在聖誕節那天, 即十二月二十五日)、on January 1 (在一月一日)、on Sunday (在星期日)。

例: On Christmas Eve my parents give me a gift.
(我父母在聖誕夜時都會送我禮物。)

Ken is going to play golf on Sunday.
(肯恩星期日要去打高爾夫球。)

b. 表年、月、季節、上/下午及晚上時, 須使用介詞 in, 如: in 2003 (在二○○三年)、in July (在七月)、in summer (在夏天)、in <u>the</u> morning/afternoon/night (但: <u>at</u> night)。

例: I was born <u>in</u> 1950.
(我是一九五○年生的。)

Mr. Black sleeps <u>in</u> the morning and works <u>at</u> night (或 in the night).
(布雷克先生早上睡覺,而在晚上工作。)

c. 與日期或星期幾並用的早上、下午或晚上, 其介詞應以日期或星期幾為準, 故須用介詞 on, 如: on the afternoon of July 4 (在七月四日的下午)、on Monday morning (在星期一早上)。

例: The murder happened on the afternoon of June 10.
(那宗謀殺案是在六月十日下午發生的。)

Are you doing anything on Saturday afternoon?
(這個星期六下午你要做什麼嗎?)

d. 表時刻時, 則須用介詞 at, 如: at ten (o'clock)、at dawn (在黎明時, 約清晨六點)、at noon (在正午時, 約中午十二點)、at dusk (在黃昏時, 約傍晚六點)、at night (在晚上, 約八、九點以後)、at midnight (午夜十二點)。

例: I am going to meet my friend at three this afternoon.
(今天下午三點我要和我的朋友碰面。)

The cock crows at dawn every day.
(公雞每天都在黎明時啼叫。)

Substitution
代　　換

1. **Thanksgiving, which falls on the fourth Thursday of November, is one of the biggest American holidays.**
   The concert which is on Saturday will be a big success.
   The girl whom you like is my sister.
   感恩節是每年十一月第四個星期四, 也是美國最大的節日之一。
   那場在禮拜六的演唱會將會辦得非常成功。
   你喜歡的那個女孩是我的妹妹。

2. **On Thanksgiving Day, Americans invite their friends over for a turkey dinner and give thanks for what they have.**
   In the summer, I like to stay indoors because of the heat.
   At noon, the office workers have a lunch break.
   在感恩節這天, 美國人會邀請他們的朋友到家裡享用一頓火雞大餐並感謝他們所擁有的一切。
   在夏天, 因為酷熱的天氣我喜歡待在室內。
   中午是辦公室員工吃午飯休息的時間。

Lesson 52
A Thanksgiving Get-together
感恩節團聚

Dialogue
實用會話

Larry, who is from Taiwan, is studying in America. His classmate, Sue, who is American, is having a Thanksgiving Day party at her house.

(S=Sue; L=Larry)

S: Hi, Larry. Are you doing anything for Thanksgiving?

L: I don't have any plans.

S: Good. I'm having a get-together at my house. Would you like to come?

L: Sure, I'd love to. Should I bring anything?

S: No. There will be plenty of salad, ham, corn, potatoes, wine and, of course, turkey.

L: That sounds great. Do you want me to come by early to give you a hand?

S: That's not necessary. Just come over at around two in the afternoon.

賴瑞是台灣人，他現在在美國唸書。他的同學蘇是美國人，她將在她家裡舉辦一個感恩節派對。

　蘇：嗨，賴瑞。你感恩節要做什麼嗎？

賴瑞：我沒什麼打算。

　蘇：很好。我家裡要辦個聚會。你要來嗎？

賴瑞：當然，我非常樂意。我應該帶什麼東西嗎？

　蘇：不用了。到時候會有豐盛的沙拉、火腿、玉米、馬鈴薯、酒，
　　　當然還有火雞。

賴瑞：聽起來真棒。妳要我早一點來幫忙嗎？

　蘇：不需要。你大概下午兩點來就行了。

Key Points
重點提示

1. **get-together** [ˈɡɛttəˌɡɛðɚ] n. 聚會

　例: My former classmates and I had a get-together at my place yesterday evening.
　(我以前的同學和我昨天晚上在我家辦了個聚會。)

　　＊ former [ˈfɔrmɚ] a. 以前的, 從前的

2. **plenty of...** 　很多的……

　注意:

　plenty of 之後可接複數可數名詞或不可數名詞。

　例: I have plenty of English books in my study.
　(我的書房裡有很多英文書。)

　　＊ study [ˈstʌdɪ] n. 書房

　There's plenty of ice cream left; do you want some more?
　(冰淇淋還剩很多，你還要不要再來點？)

3. **salad** [ˈsæləd] n. 沙拉

　例: Westerners like to have a salad as an appetizer.

(西方人喜歡吃沙拉當開胃菜。)

　　＊ appetizer [ˈæpəˌtaɪzə] n. 開胃食物

4. **ham** [hæm] n. 火腿

5. **potato** [pəˈteto] n. 馬鈴薯

6. **of course**　　當然

例: A: Are you inviting your teacher to your party?
　　B: Of course not.
　　(甲：你要邀請你的老師參加派對嗎？)
　　(乙：當然不要。)

7. **come by**　　造訪, 看望

例: Please come by whenever you have time.
　　(有空就請你到我們家來玩。)

8. **give ＋ 人 ＋ a hand**　　助某人一臂之力, 幫忙某人

例: I'm moving tomorrow. Can you give me a hand?
　　(我明天要搬家。你能幫我忙嗎？)

 請選出下列各句中正確的一項

1. Michael Jackson, _____ is a famous singer, owns a castle.
　　(A) which　　　(B) who　　　　(C) that　　　　(D) whom

2. *War and Peace*, _____ I read several times, is my favorite novel.
　　(A) who　　　　(B) whom　　　(C) which　　　(D) that

3. Can you give me a _____ with this heavy luggage?
　　(A) help　　　　(B) hand　　　(C) break　　　(D) headache

4. Your suggestion _____ quite reasonable.
   (A) looks   (B) feels   (C) sounds   (D) smells

5. Can you come _____ on your way home? I have something
   important to tell you.
   (A) by   (B) off   (C) for   (D) with

解答:

   1. (B)   2. (C)   3. (B)   4. (C)   5. (A)

Lesson 53
Monkeying Around
猴子吃大餐

Reading
閱　　讀

　　Thai people believe that keeping monkeys happy brings good luck. So every year there's a day on which they have a special treat for monkeys called the Annual Monkey Feast. Hundreds of monkeys come from the mountains to "sit at" long buffet tables which are piled high with bananas, peanuts, watermelons and cabbage.

　　Monkeys will be monkeys. So they fool around and fights break out. But nobody seems to care. Neither do the monkeys. They just stare back at the crowds of people who turn out to

watch them. Then they continue to monkey around and have a good time.

> 　　泰國人相信讓猴子快樂會帶來好運。因此,他們每年都有一天會為猴子舉辦特別的宴饗,叫做『年度猴子盛宴』。好幾百隻猴子從山裡跑來『坐在』長長的自助餐桌前,桌上堆著高高的香蕉、花生、西瓜和包心菜。
> 　　猴子就是猴子,所以牠們會胡鬧和打架。但似乎沒有人在乎,猴子們也不在乎。牠們只是回瞪著跑出來看牠們的人群,然後繼續胡鬧,玩得不小樂乎。

Vocabulary & Idioms
單字 & 片語註解

1. **monkey around**　　胡鬧; 鬼混
= horse around
= fool around
= idle around
= goof around
* idle [ˈaɪdl̩] vi. 閒混
　 goof [guf] vi. 閒混
　例: The students monkeyed around before the teacher entered the classroom.
　　　(學生們在老師未到教室前嬉戲胡鬧。)

　　John goofs around too much, so he doesn't do well in his studies.
　　(約翰太混了,因此學業表現不佳。)

2. **treat** [trit] n. 款待; 樂事 & vt. 宴請, 款待
　 treat + 人 + to + 三餐　　請某人去吃……

例: Going to the amusement park is a real treat for the children.
(去遊樂場對孩子們來說是一大樂事。)

　　＊ amusement park [əˋmjuzmənt ˏpɑrk] n. 遊樂園

I treated my girlfriend to a candle-lit dinner on Valentine's Day.
(情人節那天我請女友享用一頓燭光晚餐。)

3. **annual** [ˋænjʋəl] a. 年度的

例: The accountant is busy preparing the annual accounts.
(會計忙著準備年度的帳目。)

　　＊ accountant [əˋkaʋntənt] n. 會計員

4. **buffet table**　　自助餐桌

buffet [bʌˋfe] n. 自助餐 (本文作形容詞)

例: I usually overeat at buffets.
(我吃自助餐時通常會吃得過多。)

　　＊ overeat [ˋovɚˋit] vi. 吃得過多

5. **pile** [paɪl] vt. 堆積

be piled with...　　堆積著⋯⋯

例: The boss's desk is piled with work.
(老闆桌上堆滿了工作。)

6. **banana** [bəˋnænə] n. 香蕉

7. **peanut** [ˋpinʌt] n. 花生

8. **watermelon** [ˋwɑtɚˏmɛlən] n. 西瓜

9. **cabbage** [ˋkæbɪdʒ] n. 包心菜, 甘藍菜

10. **break out**　　突然發生

break [brek] vi. 出現, 產生

動詞三態: break、broke [brok]、broken [ˋbrokən]。

例: War broke out between the two neighboring countries.
(那兩個鄰國之間爆發了戰爭。)

　　＊ neighboring [ˋnebərɪŋ] a. 毗鄰的, 鄰近的

11. **stare at...**　　注視……

stare [stɛr] vi. 瞪著, 凝視

例: Generally, it's considered rude to stare at people.
（通常，瞪著別人看是被認為很無禮的。）

12. **crowd** [kraʊd] n. 群眾

例: A crowd gathered to watch the street dancers.
（一群人聚集觀賞那些街頭舞者的表演。）

13. **turn out to + 原形動詞**　　出來/出現……

例: All his friends turned out to cheer for him at the tennis match.
（他所有的朋友都到場在那場網球賽為他加油。）

＊ cheer [tʃɪr] vi. (為某人) 加油, 打氣

14. **have a good time**　　玩得很愉快

have a good time + 動名詞　　從事……很愉快

注意:

理論上動名詞之前應有介詞 in, 但實際使用時只用『have a good time + 動名詞』。

例: I had a good time reading a novel on the weekend.
（我週末時看了本小說看得很愉快。）

Grammar Notes
文法重點

本課介紹簡應句的用法。

But nobody seems to care. Neither do the monkeys.
但似乎沒有人在乎, 猴子們也不在乎。

此處 neither 是副詞, 專用於否定的簡應句中, 簡應句有肯定簡應句與否定簡應句之分, 茲說明如下:

a. 肯定簡應句中用 so 或 too。使用 so 時, 其後須採倒裝句構, 且 so 為副詞, 故其前須置 and; 而 too 則置於句尾使用, 其前多置逗點。用法如下:

1) 句中有 be 動詞時:

例: He <u>is</u> a doctor, and so <u>is his father</u>.

= He <u>is</u> a doctor. So <u>is his father</u>.

= He <u>is</u> a doctor, and <u>his father is</u>, too.
(他是個醫生,他父親也是。)

2) 句中有助動詞時:

例: She <u>can</u> swim, and so <u>can I</u>.

= She <u>can</u> swim. So <u>can I</u>.

= She <u>can</u> swim, and <u>I can</u>, too.
(她會游泳,我也會。)

3) 句中只有一般動詞時, 在簡應句部分, 則須按主詞人稱及動詞的時態作變化, 借用助動詞 do、does 或 did:

例: He <u>failed</u> the exam, and so <u>did she</u>.

= He <u>failed</u> the exam. So <u>did she</u>.

= He <u>failed</u> the exam, and <u>she did</u>, too.
(他考試不及格,她也是。)

注意:

在對話中, 兩句指的是同一個人時, 不論句子是肯定句或否定句, 均用 so 引導, 且句子不倒裝, 此時 so 有『的確』的意味。

例: A: She is pretty.

B: <u>So she is</u>.
(甲:她很漂亮。)
(乙:她的確漂亮。)

A: You can't swim.

B: <u>So I can't</u>.
(甲:你不會游泳。)
(乙:我是不會。)

b. 否定簡應句中則用 neither、nor 或 either。使用 neither、nor 時, 其後須採倒裝句, 且因 neither 為副詞, 故其前須置 and, 而 nor 則為連接詞, 其前不必置 and; either 則置於句尾使用, 其前要有否定副詞 not, 再置逗點。用法如下:

1) 句中有 be 動詞時:

例: John <u>isn't</u> a student, and neither <u>am I</u>.

= John <u>isn't</u> a student. Neither <u>am I</u>.

= John <u>isn't</u> a student, nor <u>am I</u>.

= John <u>isn't</u> a student, and <u>I am</u> not, either.
(約翰不是學生, 我也不是。)

2) 句中有助動詞時:

例: Mary <u>can't</u> speak Japanese, and neither <u>can Sam</u>.

= Mary <u>can't</u> speak Japanese. Neither <u>can Sam</u>.

= Mary <u>can't</u> speak Japanese, nor <u>can Sam</u>.

= Mary <u>can't</u> speak Japanese, and <u>Sam can't</u>, either.
(瑪麗不會講日語, 山姆也不會。)

3) 句中只有一般動詞時, 在簡應句部分, 則須按主詞人稱及動詞的時態作變化, 借用助動詞 do、does 或 did:

例: Bill never <u>drinks</u>, and neither <u>does Peter</u>.

= Bill never <u>drinks</u>. Neither <u>does Peter</u>.

= Bill never <u>drinks</u>, nor <u>does Peter</u>.

= Bill never <u>drinks</u>, and <u>Peter does</u> not, either.
(比爾從不喝酒, 彼得也從不喝。)

Substitution

代　　換

1. **So every year there's a day <u>on which</u> they have a special treat for monkeys.**

   That's the old house <u>in which</u> I was born.

   He is the person <u>to whom</u> you should write.

   因此, 他們每年都有一天會為猴子舉辦特別的宴饗。

   那間老舊的房子就是我出生的地方。

   他是你應寫信去的人。

2. **But nobody seems to care. Neither do the monkeys.**

   Tracy sings well. So does her sister.

   My wife doesn't play mah-jong, nor do I.

   但似乎沒有人在乎, 猴子們也不在乎。

   翠西歌唱得很好, 她的妹妹也是。

   我太太不打麻將, 我也不打。

Lesson 54

Variety Is the Spice of Life
人生要多彩多姿

Dialogue
實用會話

Barney and Debbie are on vacation in Bangkok.

(B=Barney; D=Debbie)

D: So where are you taking me out to dinner tonight, Barney?

B: Let's go to Phuket. It has the most beautiful sunsets that you will ever see. That's also where you can get a wide range of exotic foods.

D: Sounds good. What have you got in mind?

B: I've been dying to try monkey brains again.

D: What? You've got to be kidding. No way!

B: Come on. Haven't you learned that variety is the spice of life?

D: You just said "again." Have you tried it before?

B: Sure, it's delicious.

D: No wonder! Sometimes you act like a monkey!

巴尼和黛比正在曼谷度假。

黛比：那麼今晚你要帶我到哪吃飯呢，巴尼？

巴尼：咱們去普吉島吧，在那兒妳會看到最美的日落，而且那兒有各種奇特的食物。

黛比：聽起來蠻不錯的。你想要吃什麼？

巴尼：我一直很渴望能再嚐嚐猴腦。

黛比：什麼？你一定是在開玩笑。門兒都沒有！

巴尼：別這樣嘛，妳難道不知道人生就是要多樣化才會有意思的嗎？

黛比：你剛才說『再』，你以前吃過嗎？

巴尼：當然，還挺好吃的。

黛比：難怪了！你的舉動有時候像隻猴子似的！

Key Points
重點提示

1. **variety** [vəˈraɪətɪ] n. 變化, 多樣性

   a variety of... 各式各樣的……

   例: Jennifer has a variety of old English coins in her collection.
   (珍妮佛收藏有各式各樣的英國錢幣。)

2. **spice** [spaɪs] n. 調味品; 香料

   spicy [ˈspaɪsɪ] a. 口味重的 (尤指辣的)

   例: Jenny's cooking needs more spice; it's too bland.
   (珍妮燒的菜需要再多加點調味料，味道都太淡了。)

   ＊ bland [blænd] a. (食物) 平淡無味的

   Indian food is usually very spicy.
   (印度菜通常口味很重。)

3. **Variety is the spice of life.** 人生多樣化才有意思。(諺語)

   例: Dave: Why are you dating so many different boys.?
   Anna: Variety is the spice of life.

(戴夫：妳為什麼和那麼多不同的男孩子約會？)
(安娜：人生要多樣化才有意思嘛。)

4. **be on vacation**　　度假

vacation [veˈkeʃən] n. 假期

例: When the boss is on vacation, the manager takes over.
(老闆休假時，工作由經理來接管。)

5. **sunset** [ˈsʌnˌsɛt] n. 日落, 黃昏

sunrise [ˈsʌnˌraɪz] n. 日出, 黎明

at sunset　　日落時

at sunrise　　日出時

例: Mary is always home at sunset.
(瑪麗黃昏的時候總是在家。)

6. **a wide range of + 名詞**　　形形色色/許多各種不同的……
= a wide variety of + 名詞

range [rendʒ] n. 範圍

例: There's a wide range of periodicals in the library.
(圖書館裡有各種不同的期刊。)
＊ periodical [ˌpɪrɪˈɑdɪkl̩] n. 定期刊物

7. **exotic** [ɪgˈzɑtɪk] a. 奇特的; 具有異國風味的

例: The exotic dancers got the audience excited.
(那些具異國情調的舞者讓觀眾很興奮。)

8. **What have you got in mind?**　　你 (心裡) 有何打算/計畫？

例: Paul: Are you free this weekend, Sara?
Sara: What have you got in mind?
(保羅：妳這個週末有空嗎，莎拉？)
(莎拉：你有什麼打算？)

9. **dying** [ˈdaɪɪŋ] a. 渴望的; 快死的

die [daɪ] vi. 死亡

be dying to + 原形動詞　　渴望/非常想要……
= be eager to + 原形動詞
= be longing to + 原形動詞
例: James is dying to get married and settle down.
　　(詹姆士渴望結婚安定下來。)
比較:
David is dying.　　大衛快死了。

10. 本文:
You've got to be kidding.　　你一定在開玩笑。
= You've <u>gotta</u> be kidding. (在口語中,講話速度很快時, got to 即變成 gotta [ˈɡɑtə])
= You must be kidding.

11. **No way!**　　門兒都沒有/不行!
例: A: Can you lend me your car?
　　B: No way!
　　(甲:車子借給我好嗎?)
　　(乙:門兒都沒有!)

12. **Come on.**　　好啦/別這樣嘛。
例:　Jeff: I don't want to visit your parents today.
　　Linda: Come on. Do it for me, OK?
　　(傑夫:我今天不想去拜訪妳的父母親。)
　　(琳達:別這樣嘛。替我行個好,好不好?)

13. **delicious** [dɪˈlɪʃəs] a. 美味的
例: The food in that restaurant is delicious but it's also very expensive.
　　(那家餐廳的菜很好吃可是也很貴。)

14. **No wonder!**　　難怪了!
No wonder + 主詞 + 動詞　　難怪……
注意:

no wonder 雖為名詞片語, 但卻可作副詞使用, 置於句首, 其後再接句子。

例: A: Rob can hardly make ends meet.

B: No wonder he's so frugal.

(甲: 羅伯幾乎是入不敷出。)

(乙: 難怪他那麼省吃儉用的。)

＊ frugal [ˈfruglꞮ] a. 節儉的, 儉省的

15. **act like + 名詞** 舉止像……

act [ækt] vi. 舉止, 行為表現; 演出

例: The hypocrite acts like a gentleman in front of others.

(那個偽君子在別人面前的舉止像個紳士。)

＊ hypocrite [ˈhɪpə͵krɪt] n. 偽君子

The problem with the actor is that he just can't act.

(那個演員最大的問題就是他不會演戲。)

請選出下列各句中正確的一項

1. Peter has a good time ＿＿＿＿ in the hills.

(A) bike   (B) biking

(C) to bike   (D) having biked

2. Fred has a wide ＿＿＿＿ of books in his study.

(A) range   (B) vacation   (C) luck   (D) piece

3. Mom: What have you got in ＿＿＿＿?

   Son: I'm thinking of getting a part-time job.

(A) thoughts   (B) spice   (C) mind   (D) buffet

4. Winnie was very sick. No ＿＿＿＿ she looked weary.

(A) way   (B) wonder   (C) kidding   (D) joking

5. John hasn't finished his homework yet. _____.
    (A) Neither have I   (B) So have I
    (C) I haven't, too   (D) I have, either

解答:

1. (B)	2. (A)	3. (C)	4. (B)	5. (A)

Lesson 55
Life after Death
死而復生

Reading
閱　讀

　　A 34-year-old married man who died recently had no children. When he died, his wife was not pregnant, either. But now that he's dead, he has a chance of becoming a father. How's that possible?

　　After a man dies, his sperm remains alive for some time. In this case, the woman asked doctors to remove the sperm from her husband's body and store it in a sperm bank. Now, she can have the baby that she has wanted for a long time. She says it's as if her husband would come back to life again when the child is born. If that is so, wouldn't that make her husband her son?

一位三十四歲的已婚男子最近死了，他沒有子女。他死的時候，太太也沒有懷孕。但如今他雖然死了，他卻有機會做爸爸。那怎麼可能呢？

當一個男人死了以後，他的精子仍可存活一段時間。在這種情形下，那位婦人要求醫生從她丈夫體內取出精子並將精子存在精子銀行。現在，她可以懷有她長久以來盼望的小孩。她說當孩子出生時，就好像她先生又活過來一樣。如果真是那樣的話，那她先生不就變成她兒子了嗎？

Vocabulary & Idioms
單字 & 片語註解

1. **recently** [ˈrisəntlɪ] adv. 最近 (地)

   例: I've been quite busy recently.
   (我最近相當忙。)

2. **pregnant** [ˈprɛgnənt] a. 懷孕的

   例: The gentleman let the pregnant woman have his seat on the bus.
   (那位紳士在公車上讓座給一名孕婦。)

3. **have a chance of** + 動名詞　　有……的機會

   例: James has a chance of becoming the next manager.
   (詹姆士有機會成為下一任經理。)

4. **sperm** [spɝm] n. 精子

   例: It only takes one sperm to make a woman pregnant.
   (只要一個精子就可以使女人懷孕。)

5. **alive** [əˈlaɪv] a. 活的, 在世的

   注意:

   alive 使用時通常置於 be 動詞或連綴動詞 (如 become、seem 等) 後作主詞補語, 或置於名詞後作後位修飾, 而不可置於名詞之前修飾。

例: I hope I won't be alive to witness a third world war.
(希望我在我有生之年不會見到第三次世界大戰。)

The police have to catch the spy alive.
(警方必須活捉那名間諜。)

6. **remove** [rɪ'muv] vt. 取出; 移開

例: Please remove your car from my parking space.
(請把你的車從我的停車位開走。)

7. **store** [stɔr] vt. 貯存

例: Mom stored the old furniture in the basement.
(老媽把舊家具存放在地下室。)

＊ basement ['besmənt] n. 地下室

8. **as if...** 彷彿/好像……

= **as though...**

注意:

as if、as though 均為副詞連接詞, 在其引導的副詞子句中, 動詞可用現在式 (表極大可能)、過去式 (表與現在事實相反)、過去完成式 (表與過去事實相反)等。

例: It looks as if she's going to cry.
(她看起來好像要哭了。)

Mrs. Smith treats me as if I <u>were</u> her child.
(史密斯太太對待我彷彿我是她的孩子一樣。)

She talked about Bruce as if they <u>had</u> <u>known</u> each other for a long time.
(她談論布魯斯的樣子好像他們已經彼此認識好久了。)

9. **come back to life again** 復活

例: If I could come back to life again after I die, I would want to be an artist.
(如果我死後能復生，我想要成為一名藝術家。)

＊ artist ['ɑrtɪst] n. 藝術家

10. 本文:

If that is so,... 若是那樣的話,……

= If that is the case,...

例: Alice: The stocks are going up every day.

Mary: If that is so, let's buy some.

(愛麗絲:股票每天都在上漲。)

(瑪　麗:那樣的話,我們去買進一些吧。)

＊ stock [stɑk] n. 股票

Grammar Notes

文法重點

本課介紹副詞連接詞 now that...(既然/現在……)的用法, 並複習 make 作不完全及物動詞的用法。

1. **But now that he's dead, he has a chance of becoming a father.**
   但如今他雖然死了,他卻有機會做爸爸。

   注意:

   a. now that是副詞連接詞, 譯成『既然』或『現在』, 引導副詞子句, 修飾主要子句, 且因受 now 的影響, 此副詞子句中之時態須為現在式或現在完成式。

   例: Now that Don <u>has</u> a job, he isn't so worried about money.
   (既然唐有了份工作,他就不再那麼擔心錢的問題了。)

   Now that Bill <u>has graduated</u>, he's looking for a job.
   (現在比爾已經畢業了,他正在找工作。)

   b. since亦可表『既然』, 但其後可接各種時態的子句, 而不受現在式或現在完成式之限制。

   例: Since the plane <u>was</u> delayed, we went to the airport bar for a drink.
   (既然飛機誤點,我們便到機場的酒吧去喝了一杯。)

Since we <u>don't</u> have much money, we can't afford to buy a house.
（既然我們沒什麼錢，我們便買不起房子。）

2. **If that is so, wouldn't that <u>make her husband her son</u>?**
如果真是那樣的話，那她先生不就變成她兒子了嗎？
上列句中的 make 是不完全及物動詞，加受詞 her husband 後，再接名詞 her son 作受詞補語。

注意：

a. make 作不完全及物動詞時，譯成『使……成為……』，加受詞後，可接名詞或形容詞作受詞補語。句型如下：

make＋受詞＋名詞/形容詞　　使……成為……

例： Marrying Prince Charles made Diana <u>a princess</u>.
（和查爾斯王子結婚使黛安娜成為王妃。）

We tried to make Father <u>happy</u> on his birthday.
（我們設法在爸爸生日那天讓他快樂。）

b. make 作不完全及物動詞時，加受詞後，亦可接原形動詞作受詞補語，此時的 make 稱使役動詞，譯為『使……』。句型如下：

make＋受詞＋原形動詞　　使……

例： Writing an English teaching book makes me <u>feel</u> good.
（撰寫英語教學書籍讓我感覺很好。）

Father makes me <u>do</u> my homework before I go to bed every day.
（每天我上床睡覺前爸爸都會叫我做家庭作業。）

注意：

雖然 make 加受詞之後可接原形動詞作補語，但由於 make 之後的受詞亦可直接接名詞或形容詞作補語，故不必造出下列的句子：

Marrying Prince Charles made Diana <u>be</u> a princess. （✕）

→ Marrying Prince Charles made Diana <u>a princess</u>. （○）

We tried to make Father <u>be</u> happy on his birthday. （✕）

→ We tried to make Father <u>happy</u> on his birthday. （○）

Substitution

代　換

1. **Now that he's dead, he has a chance of becoming a father.**
   Now that my son has a job, he supports himself.
   Since Jeff is not home, I'll pay him a visit some other time.
   如今他雖然死了, 他卻有機會做爸爸。
   我兒子既然有一份工作, 他可以自食其力了。
   既然傑夫不在家, 我改天再來拜訪。

2. **If that is so, wouldn't that make her husband her son?**
   Because of his diligence, the boss made Bill the new manager.
   What he said made her very angry.
   如果真是那樣的話, 那她先生不就變成她兒子了嗎？
   由於他的勤奮, 老闆讓比爾成為新任的經理。
   他的話令她非常生氣。

Lesson 56
Baby Trouble
生兒育女的煩惱

Dialogue
實用會話

Betty is talking to her husband Dan.

(B=Betty; D=Dan)

B: Don't you think it's time that we had a baby?

D: We're much better off without children. Think of all the trouble raising them.

B: But it's only natural that married couples have babies.

D: I don't want any brats who'll run around the house breaking things.

B: Then I'll have a baby by myself.

D: Don't be ridiculous. That's not possible.

B: Yes, it is. I can adopt or go to the sperm bank or...

D: Stop! Are you crazy? I forbid it.

B: Then, can we have a baby together?

D: OK. You win.

貝蒂正在和她的先生丹說話。

貝蒂：你不認為我們該生個小孩了嗎？

　丹：我們沒有小孩會過得比較好。想想養育小孩有多麻煩。

貝蒂：可是夫妻生小孩是很自然的事情。

　丹：我不想要有小鬼在屋裡亂跑弄壞東西。

貝蒂：那我就自己生一個。

　丹：別荒謬了，那是不可能的。

貝蒂：當然可能。我可以收養或者到精子銀行，或者……

　丹：不要再說了！妳瘋了嗎？我不准妳這麼做。

貝蒂：那麼，我們可以一起生個小孩嗎？

　丹：好吧，妳贏了。

Key Points
重點提示

1. **Don't you think it's time <u>that</u> we <u>had</u> a baby?**
   你不認為我們該生個小孩了嗎？

* it is (high/about) time + that 子句　該是……的時候了

  注意:

  "it is (high/about) time that..." 乃表示『該是……的時候了』，但卻還沒做，故為與現在事實相反的假設語氣，因此 that 子句中的動詞須用過去式。

  例: It is time that people <u>paid</u> more attention to the environment.
  （該是人們多加注意環境的時候了。）

  It's high time that we <u>changed</u> this old and unfair rule.
  （該是我們修改這條古老又不公平的規定的時候了。）

2. **be better off**　　境況較好, 日子過得比較好

* be better off 是 be well off 的比較級。

  例: Ben is better off running a grocery store.
  （班開了一家雜貨店日子過得好多了。）

3. **raise** [rez] vt. 養育; 舉起

例: It's not easy to raise children nowadays.
(現今養育小孩並不容易。)

If you have a question, raise your hand.
(有問題的人就請舉手。)

4. **natural** [ˈnætʃərəl] a. 自然的

it is natural + that 子句　……是很自然的事

例: It is natural that everyone wants to be rich.
(每個人都想有錢是很自然的事。)

5. **brat** [bræt] n. (貶義) 乳臭未乾的小子, (尤指沒有禮的) 小子

例: If you spoil your child, he'll turn out to be a brat.
(如果你寵你的小孩，到頭來他會變成沒有禮貌的小鬼。)

6. **ridiculous** [rɪˈdɪkjələs] a. 荒謬的

例: What a ridiculous suggestion Betty came up with!
(貝蒂提出的建議是多麼荒謬啊！)

7. **adopt** [əˈdɑpt] vi. & vt. 收養

例: Sandy couldn't have children, so she adopted a boy.
(珊蒂無法生育，因此她領養了一個男孩。)

8. **crazy** [ˈkræzɪ] a. 瘋狂的; 狂熱的

be crazy about...　對……瘋狂喜愛

例: John's crazy to think that Sue's in love with him.
(約翰瘋了才會認為蘇愛上了他。)

I'm crazy about Chinese food.
(我非常喜歡中國菜。)

9. **forbid** [fəˈbɪd] vt. 禁止

動詞三態: forbid、forbade [fɔrˈbed]、forbidden [fɔrˈbɪdn̩]。

forbid + 人 + to + 原形動詞　禁止某人……

= | bar | + 人 + from + 動名詞
| ban |
| prohibit |

例: That country forbids you to bring in more than one bottle of wine.
= That country prohibits you from bringing in more than one bottle of wine.
(該國禁止人們攜帶超過一瓶的酒入境。)

10. **win** [wɪn] vi. 贏, 獲勝 & vt. 贏得

動詞三態: win、won [wʌn]、won。

注意:

win 作及物動詞時, 不可接『人』作受詞; 表示『贏過/打敗某人』, 動詞須用 beat/defeat。

例: No one is expected to win all the time.
(誰都不能被期望永遠會贏。)

Who do you think will win the election?
(你認為誰會贏得這次選舉?)

Tim <u>won</u> the other boxer easily. (✗)
→ Tim <u>beat</u> the other boxer easily. (○)
(提姆輕易地就擊敗了另一個拳擊手。)

請選出下列各句中正確的一項

1. Tim looks as if he _____ just _____ into a truck.
   (A) is, runs   (B) have, run   (C) has, ran   (D) had, run

2. It is time that you _____ more maturely.
   (A) behave   (B) will behave
   (C) behaved   (D) had behaved

3. When I realized I had a chance _____ winning the game, I played harder.
   (A) of   (B) to   (C) for   (D) on

4. Dad _____ me to stay out later than midnight.
   (A) bars   (B) bans   (C) prohibits   (D) forbids

5. Mary _____ the speech contest for the second time.
   (A) won   (B) beat   (C) defeated   (D) adopted

解答:

| 1. (D)   2. (C)   3. (A)   4. (D)   5. (A) |

L esson 57

New Asian Generation
亞洲新生代

Reading
閱　讀

In the past, the children of Asia had very few choices. A son would usually follow in his father's footsteps and do the same kind of job as his father. But now, young people have higher education which opens doors to new kinds of jobs. TV exposes kids to new ideas from other countries.

So, the younger generation of Asians are doing things their parents never dreamed of. They're investing in stocks or dying their hair purple. Unfortunately, some are also getting into trouble with sex and drugs. Asian parents whose children are doing all this do have a reason to be worried.

　　在過去，生長在亞洲的小孩子沒有什麼選擇可言。做兒子的通常會繼承父親的衣缽並且做和他父親同樣的工作。但是現在，年輕人受到高等教育，這也為他們開啟了各種新工作的大門。電視使得孩子們接觸到來自其他國家的新觀念。

　　所以，亞洲年輕一代的人現在在做一些他們父母親做夢也沒想到的事情。他們投資股票或把頭髮染成紫色。不幸的是，有一些卻受到色情和毒品的戕害。亞洲籍的父母若其子女有這樣的表現，則的確有理由操心。

Vocabulary & Idioms
單字 & 片語註解

1. **Asian** [ˈeʒən] a. 亞洲 (人) 的 & n. 亞洲人

   Asia [ˈeʒə] n. 亞洲

   例: Ken looks Asian but in fact he's Spanish.
   (肯恩看起來像亞洲人，但是他其實是西班牙人。)

2. **generation** [ˌdʒɛnəˈreʃən] n. 代; 同時代的人

   generation gap　　代溝

   the younger generation　　年輕的一代

   the older generation　　年老的一輩

   例: The future of the world is in the hands of the younger generation.
   (世界未來的前途掌握在年輕一代的手中。)

3. **in the past**　　在過去

   注意:

   上述片語與過去式時態並用。

   例: In the past, life was much simpler.
   (在過去，生活純樸多了。)

4. **choice** [tʃɔɪs] n. 選擇

have no choice but to + 原形動詞　　　　除……之外別無選擇

例: The beggar has no choice but to sleep in the park.
(那名乞丐除了睡在公園裡外別無選擇。)

5. **footstep** [ˈfʊtˌstɛp] n. 腳步

follow in one's footsteps　　效法某人, 步某人的後塵

例: If you follow in your father's footsteps, we'll have two doctors in the family.
(如果你效法你父親，我們家裡就會有兩個醫生了。)

6. **higher education**　　高等教育 (指含大學以上的教育)

secondary education　　中等教育 (指國、高中)

elementary education　　初等/基本教育 (指國小)

secondary [ˈsɛkənˌdɛrɪ] a. (學校、教育) 中等的

elementary [ˌɛləˈmɛntərɪ] a. 初步的, 基本的

7. **open doors to...**　　開啟……之門, 為……提供機會

例: Learning a foreign language will open doors to more interesting jobs.
(學習外國語言能夠開啟更多有趣工作機會的大門。)

8. **expose** [ɪkˈspoz] vt. 使接觸到 (文化、知識等)

expose A to B　　使 A 接觸到 B

例: Traveling exposes you to different cultures.
(旅遊能讓你接觸到不同的文化。)

9. **invest** [ɪnˈvɛst] vi. & vt. 投資 (通常與介詞 in 並用)

invest in...　　投資於……

invest A in B　　將 A 投資在 B 中

例: Mr. Brown invested in real estate.
(布朗先生投資於房地產。)

＊ real estate [ˈriəl əˌstet] n. 房地產, 不動產

I wouldn't invest my money in gold if I were you.
(如果我是你的話，我不會把我的錢投資在黃金上。)

10. **stock** [stɑk] n. 股票

例: Our company's stocks are going up.
(我們公司的股票正在上漲。)

11. **dye** [daɪ] vt. 染色

＊ 本文中 dying [ˈdaɪɪŋ] 是動詞 dye 的現在分詞。

例: The strange basketball player dyed his hair green.
(那個怪異的籃球員把頭髮染成綠色。)

12. **purple** [ˈpɝpḷ] a. 紫色的 & n. 紫色

13. **unfortunately** [ʌnˈfɔrtʃənɪtlɪ] adv. 不幸地

例: Unfortunately, there's no one to take care of the sick old man.
(很不幸地，沒有人照顧那個生病的老先生。)

14. **drug** [drʌg] n. 毒品

take drugs　吸毒

例: It's hard to understand why so many adolescents take drugs.
(真難以理解為什麼有那麼多青少年嗑藥。)

＊ adolescent [ˌædəˈlɛsənt] n. 青少年

15. **worried** [ˈwɝɪd] a. (感到) 擔憂的

be worried about...　對……感到擔憂

例: Mr. Lee is worried about his weight.
(李先生對他的體重感到擔憂。)

16. 句型分析:

Asian parents <u>whose children are doing all this</u> <u>do have a reason to</u>
　　　(1)　　　　　　　　　(2)　　　　　　　　　　　(3)

<u>be worried.</u>

(1) 主詞

(2) 關係代名詞所有格 whose 引導的形容詞子句, 修飾 (1)。

(3) 述部; 其中助動詞 do 在此處為強調用法, 譯為『的確、真的』。

Grammar Notes

文法重點

本課介紹 in the past (在過去) 與過去式並用的用法, 以及 the same...as...(和……相同的……) 之用法, 並介紹關係代名詞所有格 whose 的用法。

1. **In the past, the children of Asia had very few choices.**
   在過去, 生長在亞洲的小孩子沒有什麼選擇可言。

   in the past (在過去) 為表『過去』的時間副詞, 故須與過去式的子句並用, 而不可用現在式。

   例: In the past, people were more sincere.
   (過去的人比較真誠。)

   注意:

   past 之後亦可接明確的時間名詞, 形成下列用法:

in	the	past	+ 數字 + 時間名詞	過去……(時間) 以來
for		last		
over				
during				
through				

   * 上述片語多與現在完成式或現在完成進行式並用。

   例: Our country has made great progress in the past ten years.
   (過去十年來我們國家進步了很多。)

   Doctors have been working over the last twenty years to find a cure for AIDS.
   (過去廿年來, 醫生們一直在努力尋找愛滋病的治療方法。)

2. **...and do <u>the same</u> kind of job <u>as</u> his father.**

= ...and do the same kind of job as his father <u>did.</u>

……並且做和他父親同樣的工作。

the same + 名詞 + as...　　和……相同的……

注意:

在上述用法中, the same 是形容詞, 表『相同的』; 而 as 則為準關係代名詞 (即既當連接詞亦做關係代名詞的詞類), 譯成『和』, 換言之, as 可視為關係代名詞, 在所引導的形容詞子句中做主詞、受詞或 be 動詞之後的主詞補語。且 as 即等於"as the + 前面的名詞 + 關係代名詞 (who、whom、which、that)"。

作主詞:

例: I have exactly the same car <u>as</u> was described in the magazine.

(我有一部車,跟雜誌裡描述的一模一樣。)

＊本句的 as = as the car that

作受詞:

例: I have the same book <u>as</u> you <u>do.</u>

(我有一本和你相同的書。)

＊本句的 as = as the book which, 之後的 do 是代動詞, 代替之前相同的動詞 have, 以避免重複。

be 動詞後的主詞補語: (通常省略 be 動詞)

例: He is not the same man <u>as</u> he used to <u>(be)</u>.

(他已非當年的吳下阿蒙。)

＊本句的 as = as the man that。

I have the same dictionary <u>as</u> this one <u>(is)</u>.

(我有一本和這本一樣的字典。)

＊本句的 as = as the dictionary that。

3. **Asian parents <u>whose</u> children are doing all this <u>do</u> have a reason to be worried.**

亞洲籍的父母若其子女有這樣的表現, 則的確有理由操心。

上列句中的 whose 是關係代名詞所有格, 其所引導的形容詞子句修飾其前的名詞 Asian parents。而句中的助動詞 do 則為強調用法, 譯成『的確』、『真地』、『確實』。

助動詞 do、does、did 作強調用法時, 即在肯定句的動詞前, 按主詞人稱及時態之不同置入 do、does 或 did, 再將動詞改為原形。

例: My son <u>does</u> work hard but he still doesn't do very well in school.
(我兒子真的很用功, 但他在學校的表現還是不太好。)

The ship <u>did</u> sink but nobody could find it.
(那艘船確實沈沒了, 但是沒有人能找得到。)

注意:

關係代名詞所有格 whose 的用法:

關係代名詞所有格 whose 係由人稱代名詞所有格 (his、her、their、my、your、our...) 變化而來, 和關係代名詞一樣, 引導形容詞子句, 修飾其前的先行詞 (名詞), 且不管先行詞是人或物, 關係代名詞所有格一律用 whose。

使用關係代名詞所有格時, 要注意下列三個要點:

a. whose 之前要有先行詞 (名詞);

b. whose 之後的名詞在 whose 引導的形容詞子句中要作主詞或受詞;

c. 否則 whose 之前要有介詞, 而該介詞亦可移至形容詞子句句尾。

例: I don't like Tom, <u>whose words</u> are seldom true.
                主詞
(我不喜歡湯姆, 他說的話很少是真的。)

I met Nancy, <u>whose parents</u> I <u>like</u> very much.
             受詞   及物動詞
(我遇見南西, 我很喜歡她的父母。)

I try to be friendly to Carl, <u>with whose sister</u> I would like to <u>make friends.</u>
(我試圖向卡爾示好, 我想和他妹妹做朋友。)

但由於 make friends with 是一完整的片語, 故最好將 with 置於句尾, 即:

I try to be friendly to Carl, whose sister I would like to
<u>make friends with</u>.

注意:

whose 代替物時, "whose＋名詞"亦可被"the＋名詞＋of＋which"取代。

例: This is a fancy sports car, <u>whose color</u> I like very much.
= This is a fancy sports car, <u>the color of which</u> I like very much.
(這是一輛拉風的跑車，我很喜歡它的顏色。)

Substitution

代　　換

1. **In the past, the children of Asia had very few choices.**
   In the past, the pace of life was much slower.
   In the past, fewer people got divorced.
   在過去, 生長在亞洲的小孩子沒有什麼選擇可言。
   在過去, 生活的步調慢多了。
   在過去, 離婚的人比較少。

2. **A son would usually do the same kind of job as his father.**
   I have exactly the same car as you do.
   This watch is the same price as that one.
   做兒子的通常會做和他父親同樣的工作。
   我有一輛車, 跟你的車完全相同。
   這支手錶的價格和那支相同。

L esson 58

Like Father, Like Son

有其父必有其子

Dialogue
實用會話

Tom, whose parents are conservative, is talking to Karen, whose parents are open-minded.

(T=Tom; K=Karen)

T: Boy, I'm really fed up with my dad.

K: Why? What's the problem?

T: My dad, whose upbringing was very strict, expects me to live by his old rules.

K: That's too bad. He must be crazy.

T: You know what? He even buys clothes for me, the styles of which belong to the fifties.

K: What a nut!

T: Hey, stop calling my dad names.

K: But I thought...

T: No matter what, he's still my dad.

K: Like father, like son!

湯姆的父母想法很保守，他正在跟凱倫說話，她的父母思想很開明。

湯姆：唉，我真的受夠我老爸了。

凱倫：為什麼？出了什麼問題？

湯姆：我那在嚴格管教之下長大的老爸指望我也按照他的老規矩生活。

凱倫：那太慘了。他一定是瘋了。

湯姆：妳知道嗎？他甚至還買五○年代樣式的衣服給我。

凱倫：好個瘋子！

湯姆：嘿，別辱罵我爹了。

凱倫：可是我以為……

湯姆：不管怎麼樣，他還是我的老爸。

凱倫：真是有其父必有其子！

Key Points

重點提示

1. **Like father, like son.** 有其父必有其子。(諺語)

    例: Husband: Our little Billy is really messy.
        Wife: Like father, like son.
    (丈夫：我們的小比利真是邋遢。)
    (妻子：有其父必有其子。)
    ＊ messy [ˈmɛsɪ] a. 髒亂的

2. **conservative** [kənˈsɝ·vətɪv] a. 保守的

    例: My conservative boyfriend will never wear such a colorful tie.
    (我保守的男友絕不會打這麼花的領帶。)

3. **open-minded** [ˌopənˈmaɪndɪd] a. 思想開明的; 心胸寬的

    例: To get along with others, you'll have to be open-minded.
    (和別人相處，你一定要心胸開闊。)

4. **be fed up with...** 厭煩/受夠了……

* fed [fɛd] 是 feed 的過去分詞。

feed [fid] vt. 餵

動詞三態: feed、fed、fed。

例: The taxi driver is fed up with all the traffic jams in the city.
(那個計程車司機受夠了市區大大小小的塞車。)

5. **upbringing** [ˈʌpˌbrɪŋɪŋ] n. 教養, 管教

例: Your behavior reflects your upbringing.
(你的行為舉止反應出你所受的教養。)

6. **strict** [strɪkt] a. 嚴格的

例: A strict teacher is not necessarily a good teacher.
(嚴格的老師不一定是好老師。)

7. **expect** [ɪkˈspɛkt] vt. 期望

expect + 人 + to + 原形動詞　　期望某人……

例: I didn't expect Sandy to be so picky about where we went for dinner.
(我沒料想到珊蒂會對我們晚餐的地點如此挑剔。)
　　* picky [ˈpɪkɪ] a. 挑剔的

8. **live by...**　　按照……(原則) 做人處事

live on...　　以……為生

例: Honesty is the word (which) I live by.
(誠實是我賴以做人處事的字。)

A man with a family can't live on such a small salary.
(有家的男人無法靠這點微薄的薪水維生。)

9. **rule** [rul] n. 規定

例: Is there an exception to this rule?
(這個規定有例外嗎?)

10. **clothes** [kloz] n. 衣服 (恆用複數)

cloth [klɔθ] n. 布 (不可數)

例: When women go shopping, they often buy clothes they don't really need.
(女人購物時，常會買一些她們不需要的衣服。)

This piece of cloth is for wiping the table.
(這塊布是用來擦桌子的。)

11. **style** [staɪl] n. 樣式; 格調
   例: This style of clothing isn't very attractive.
   (這種衣服的款式並不十分吸引人。)

   Ben may not have money but he has style.
   (班或許沒錢但是他有格調。)

12. **belong** [bəˈlɔŋ] vi. 屬於, 歸屬 (此字常與介詞 to 並用)
   例: This old watch belonged to my great grandfather.
   (這只舊錶以前是我曾祖父的。)

13. **...the styles of which belong to the fifties.**
   = ...whose styles belong to the nineteen fifties.
   ……這種樣式屬於五〇年代。

14. **What a nut!**　　好個瘋子！
   nut [nʌt] n. 瘋子; 精神錯亂的人
   例: A: William told his boss off and got fired.
   B: What a nut!
   (甲：威廉責罵他老闆而被炒魷魚了。)
   (乙：真是個神經病！)
   ＊ tell someone off　　痛罵某人

15. **call someone names**　　侮罵某人
   ＊ 此處 names 恆用複數, 表示罵人的各種綽號, 如『王八蛋』、『混蛋』、『豬』、『神經病』等。
   例: It's rude to call people names.
   (侮罵他人是粗魯的。)

16. **No matter what, he's still my dad.**

= Anyway, he's still my dad.

不管怎麼樣, 他還是我的老爸。

例: A: Are you still going to talk to your son even though he ran away from home?

B: No matter what, he's still my son.

(甲：即使你兒子逃家了，你還會和他說話嗎？)

(乙：不論如何，他還是我兒子。)

請選出下列各句中正確的一項

1. _____ the past few decades, pollution has been a serious problem all over the world.

(A) Of   (B) Over   (C) On   (D) Among

2. My sister wears the same size clothes _____ my mother.

(A) so   (B) that   (C) which   (D) as

3. The poor dog, _____ master left town, has become a stray dog.

(A) whose   (B) who   (C) that   (D) which

4. I hope you won't _____ in your uncle's footsteps and end up in jail.

(A) take   (B) go   (C) follow   (D) set

5. The students are fed up _____ doing homework day and night.

(A) to   (B) with   (C) of   (D) from

解答:

1. (B)	2. (D)	3. (A)	4. (C)	5. (B)

L esson 59

About Moral Values

道德價值觀

Reading
閱　　讀

More and more people are forgetting the saying, "Pride comes before a fall." I remember only a few years ago when things used to be so different. People used to be more modest and humble.

As I looked around at my schoolmates the other day, I realized how different things are. People are so much more pretentious nowadays. With their fancy clothes and stylish hairdos, they appear too materialistic, which is not to my liking. I know modernization is necessary for advancement. However, I hope we don't lose our traditional moral values along the way.

有愈來愈多的人忘記了『驕者必敗』這句俗話。我記得才幾年前情形完全不一樣。以前的人比較謙虛。

前幾天我看了看我的同學後，了解到現在事情是多麼不同。現在的人比以前浮華得多。他們花俏的穿著和時髦的髮型使他們顯得過於注重物質享受，這一點我很不喜歡。我知道要進步就必須要現代化。然而，我希望我們在這同時不要失去傳統的道德價值觀。

Vocabulary & Idioms
單字 & 片語註解

1. **moral** [ˈmɔrəl] a. 道德上的

   例: Abortion is a legal as well as a moral issue.
   (墮胎是項法律及道德上的問題。)
   * abortion [əˈbɔrʃən] n. 墮胎

2. **value** [ˈvæljʊ] n. 價值觀 (恆為複數); 價值 (不可數)

   be of no value　　毫無價值

= be valueless [ˈvæljʊlɪs]

   例: The youngsters' values are quite different from their parents'.
   (年輕人的價值觀和父母親的大不相同。)

   This old typewriter is of no value to us.
   (這台老舊的打字機對我們來說毫無價值。)

3. **pride** [praɪd] n. 驕傲

   proud [praʊd] a. 驕傲的; 自豪的

   take pride in...　　以……為榮

= be proud of...

   例: Rudy <u>takes pride in</u> being the top student in his class.
   = Rudy <u>is proud of</u> being the top student in his class.
   (魯迪名列班上第一，深感為榮。)

4. **Pride comes before a fall.**
驕傲來自跌倒之前。／驕者必敗。(諺語)

＊ fall [fɔl] n. 跌倒

5. **modest** [ˈmɑdɪst] a. 謙虛的
例: A modest man never boasts.
(謙虛的人絕不會誇耀。)

6. **humble** [ˈhʌmbḷ] a. 謙卑的(有卑下的意味)
例: Nobody knows Sue is rich because she is so humble.
(沒有人知道蘇很有錢，因為她是如此地謙卑。)

7. **schoolmate** [ˈskulˌmet] n. 同校同學

8. **realize** [ˈriəˌlaɪz] vt. 了解, 體會
例: The secretary didn't realize her mistake until it was pointed out to her.
(指給她看後，那位祕書才了解到自己的錯誤。)

9. **pretentious** [prɪˈtɛnʃəs] a. 虛飾的, 矯飾的
例: Pretentious people can't be trusted.
(虛浮不實的人不可靠。)

10. **nowadays** [ˈnauəˌdez] adv. 現今, 時下
例: Nowadays, people understand the importance of environmental protection.
(現今大家都了解環保的重要性。)

11. **fancy** [ˈfænsɪ] a. 奪目花俏的; 高級雅緻的
例: I seldom go to fancy restaurants because they're expensive.
(我不常去高級餐館，因為那裡太貴了。)

12. **stylish** [ˈstaɪlɪʃ] a. 時髦的, 入時的
例: Young people like to wear stylish clothes.
(年輕人喜歡穿著時髦的服飾。)

13. **hairdo** [ˈhɛrˌdu] n. 髮型

   例: Mom's new hairdo frightens me.
   (老媽的新髮型嚇了我一跳。)

14. **materialistic** [məˌtɪrɪəˈlɪstɪk] a. 注重物質享受的

   例: Materialistic people are never satisfied with what they have.
   (注重物質享受的人對他們所擁有的東西從不會滿足。)

15. **liking** [ˈlaɪkɪŋ] n. 喜好

   be to one's liking　　符合某人的喜好或期望

   例: Tim's style of writing isn't to my liking.
   (提姆的寫作風格不合我的口味。)

16. **modernization** [ˌmadənəˈzeʃən] n. 現代化

   modernize [ˈmadəˌnaɪz] vt. 使現代化

   例: To modernize our office, the boss bought the best computers.
   (為了使辦公室現代化，老闆買了最好的電腦。)

17. **advancement** [ədˈvænsmənt] n. 進步; 升遷

   advance [ədˈvæns] vt. 提升, 使進步 & vi. 前進

   例: There's little opportunity for advancement in this job.
   (這份工作鮮有機會升遷。)

   I went abroad to advance my education.
   (我出國進修。)

   As the enemy advanced, we fought back.
   (敵人向前推進時，我們便反擊。)

18. **traditional** [trəˈdɪʃənl] a. 傳統的

   例: Jack married a traditional Chinese girl.
   (傑克娶了一個傳統的中國女子。)

Grammar Notes
文法重點

本課介紹"主詞＋used to＋原形動詞"(過去常/曾經……)的用法,並複習關係代名詞 which 代替前面整個句子的用法。

1. **I remember only a few years ago when things <u>used to be</u> so different.**

   我記得才幾年前情形完全不一樣。

   People <u>used to be</u> more modest and humble.

   以前的人比較謙虛。

   以上兩句皆採用了下列句型:

   主詞＋used to＋原形動詞　　過去常/曾經……

   ＊ 這是一種表『過去的經驗』的句構, used 之後為不定詞的 to, 故之後接原形動詞。

   例: I used to <u>stay</u> up late studying when I was in senior high school.
   (我以前唸高中時常熬夜唸書。)

   There used to <u>be</u> a park in my neighborhood.
   (我家附近以前有座公園。)

   比較:

   主詞＋be used to＋名詞/動名詞　　習慣於……

   ＝ 主詞＋be accustomed to＋名詞/動名詞

   ＊ accustomed [əˈkʌstəmd] a. 習慣的

   ＊ 在上述用法中, used 是形容詞, 譯成『習慣的』或『適應的』, 其後的 to 則為介詞, 表『針對』之意, 故之後要接名詞或動名詞作受詞; 使用本句型時, 主詞通常是人或任何有思想的動物 (如狗貓之類)。

   例: Mr. Smith is used to his wife's nagging.
   (史密斯先生已經習慣了他太太的嘮叨。)

   ＊ nagging [ˈnægɪŋ] n. 嘮叨

The farmer is not used to <u>live</u> in the city. (✗)

→ The farmer is not used to <u>living</u> in the city. (○)

(那位農夫不習慣住在城市。)

2. **...they appear too materialistic, <u>which</u> is not to my liking.**

……他們顯得過於注重物質享受, 這一點我很不喜歡。

上列句中的 which 為關係代名詞, 代替其前整個句子"they appear too materialistic"的概念, which 在所引導的形容詞子句中作主詞。本句旨在告訴我們關係代名詞 which 除可代替物外, 亦可用以代替整個句子, 此時 which 之前一定要有逗點。

例: <u>Little Johnny failed the exam , which</u> made his father angry.

(小強尼考試不及格, 這使得他父親很生氣。)

Substitution

代　　換

1. **I remember only a few years ago when things used to be so different.**

There was a time when things used to be so cheap.

When Tom was a young boy, he used to bully girls.

我記得才幾年前情形完全不一樣。

曾經有過一段時期物價很便宜。

當湯姆還是小男孩時, 他總是欺負女孩子。

2. **They appear too materialistic, which is not to my liking.**

Lazy Sam was determined to study abroad, which was surprising.

Fat Freddy eats too much, which really isn't good for him.

他們顯得過於注重物質享受, 這一點我很不喜歡。

懶鬼山姆下定決心要出國深造, 這點真令人意外。

胖子弗來迪吃太多了, 這點真的對他沒有好處。

L esson 60
How to Attract Boys
如何吸引男孩子

Dialogue
實用會話

Jason is talking to Kate, a classmate he likes very much.

(J=Jason; K=Kate)

J: I don't understand why you dye your hair and wear all kinds
   of weird clothes, Kate.

K: I guess that's how I attract boys.

J: Yes, but the wrong kind of boys.

K: What do you mean?

J: The type of guys who go out with you wear earrings and have
   tattoos on their arms.

K: What kind of guys do you think I should go out with then?

J: Uh...somebody like me, for instance.

K: Oh, is that so?

J: The day will come when you know I'm right.

K: We'll see.

傑森正在和凱蒂說話，她是一位他非常喜歡的同學。

傑森：我不懂妳為什麼染髮又穿些怪異的衣服，凱蒂。

凱蒂：我想那就是我吸引男孩子的方法吧。

傑森：對，可是是那種不正經的男孩子。

凱蒂：你這話什麼意思？

傑森：那種會和妳交往的男孩子都戴耳環而且在手臂上有刺青。

凱蒂：那麼你認為我該和哪一種男孩子交往？

傑森：嗯……比方說，像我這樣的人。

凱蒂：哦，是這樣嗎？

傑森：總有一天妳會知道我說的話是對的。

凱蒂：咱們走著瞧吧。

Key Points
重點提示

1. **attract** [ətˈrækt] vt. 吸引
   例: This red miniskirt will surely attract boys' attention.
   (這條紅色的迷你裙一定會吸引男孩子的注意。)
   * miniskirt [ˈmɪnɪˌskɚt] n. 迷你裙

2. **weird** [wɪrd] a. 怪異的
   例: Ron came up with a weird way to solve the problem.
   (朗恩想出一個怪方法來解決那個問題。)

3. **earring** [ˈɪrˌrɪŋ] n. 耳環(多用複數)
   例: Mom has two pairs of pearl earrings.
   (老媽有兩副珍珠耳環。)

4. **tattoo** [tæˈtu] n. 刺青，紋身
   例: Many sailors and soldiers like to have tattoos on their arms.
   (許多水手和阿兵哥喜歡在手臂上刺青。)

5. **arm** [ɑrm] n. 手臂

6. **for instance** 舉例來說

= for example

instance [ˈɪnstəns] n. 實例, 例證

例: John is extravagant. For instance, he only shops at the most expensive clothing stores.
(約翰很奢侈。舉例來說，他只到最昂貴的服飾店購物。)

＊ extravagant [ɪkˈstrævəgənt] a. 奢侈的

7. 本文:

The day will come when you know I'm right.

= <u>The day</u> <u>when you know I'm right</u> <u>will come.</u>
　　(1)　　　　　　(2)　　　　　　(3)

妳會了解我的話是對的日子會到來。

→ 有朝一日妳會了解我所說的是對的。

(1) 主詞

(2) 關係副詞 when 引導的形容詞子句, 修飾 (1), 此處的 when 即等於 on which。

(3) 完全不及物動詞 come 的未來式

請選出下列各句中正確的一項

1. Living in the city all my life, I have become _____ to noise pollution.
   (A) accustomed   (B) customed
   (C) custom   (D) accustom

2. Mom _____ me a bedtime story every night.
   (A) used to reading   (B) uses to read
   (C) used to read   (D) uses to reading

3. My dad takes pride _____ being able to provide the family with a comfortable living.
   (A) of   (B) in   (C) on   (D) to

4. The way Sara cooks isn't _____ my liking.
   (A) at   (B) in   (C) for   (D) to

5. Brad eats a lot. _____, the last time I invited him to dinner, he ate ten bowls of rice.
   (A) For an instance   (B) For example
   (C) For instances   (D) For examples

解答:

> 1. (A)   2. (C)   3. (B)   4. (D)   5. (B)

L esson 61
Touring by Taxi
計程車逍遙遊

Reading
閱　　讀

One of the most convenient but expensive ways to get around a city in any country is by taxi. And in some cases, tipping is expected.

A taxi driver knows the city like the back of his hand. He can tell you whatever you want to know. At the same time he'll be your personal tour guide. He can take you wherever you want to go. So, however expensive the taxi ride may be, the advice you get from the driver will certainly be worth it.

在各國的城市內走動最便利的方式之一就是搭計程車。有時候你必須給司機小費。

計程車司機對他的城市瞭若指掌。你想要知道什麼他都可以告訴你。同時他也兼做你的私人導遊。不論你想去任何地方,他都會把你送到。所以,不論搭計程車多麼昂貴,你從司機那裡所得到的建議絕對是值得的。

Vocabulary & Idioms
單字 & 片語註解

1. **tour** [tʊr] vt. & vi. 遊覽; 觀光 & n. 觀光旅行 (與介詞 on 並用)

   例: My parents are touring in Australia.
   (我父母正在澳洲觀光。)

   Our company go on a tour to a different country every year.
   (我們公司每年都會到不同的國家旅遊。)

2. **by taxi**　　搭計程車

   注意:

   表示『搭乘交通工具』須用介詞 by, 其後直接加交通工具, 且該交通工具前不可置任何冠詞 (a、an、the), 如: by bus (搭公車)、by plane (搭飛機)、by train (搭火車)、by boat (搭船、坐船) 等, 而『步行』則用 "on foot"。

   例: It's too expensive to go there by taxi.
   (搭計程車去那裡太貴了。)

   We toured the city on foot for hours.
   (我們在該市徒步觀光好幾個小時。)

3. **convenient** [kən'vinjənt] a. 方便的, 便利的

   例: We found a convenient place to take a rest before continuing on our journey.
   (我們在繼續我們的旅行之前找到了一個方便歇腳的地方。)

4. **get around + 地方名詞**　　在某地四處走動

例: I get around town on my bicycle.
(我騎腳踏車在城裡走動。)

5. **tip** [tɪp] vi. & vt. 給小費 & n. 小費

tip + 人 + 錢 + for + 事物　　　因某事給某人 (錢) 小費

＊ 本文中的 tipping 為動名詞作主詞用。

例: The man tipped the bellboy US$10 for carrying his luggage to his room.
(那名男子給了那個幫他把行李抬到房間的行李員十塊美元小費。)

Usually, we leave the tip on the table.
(我們通常把小費留在桌上。)

6. **know + 事物 + like the back of one's hand**　　對某事物瞭若指掌

例: Tony grew up in the city and knows it like the back of his hand.
(東尼在該市長大,對那裡瞭若指掌。)

7. **at the same time**　　同時

例: Both the doorbell and the phone rang at the same time.
(門鈴和電話同時響起。)

8. **personal** [ˈpɝsənḷ] a. 私人的

例: Westerners avoid asking personal questions.
(西方人會避免問及私人的問題。)

9. **tour guide** [ˈtʊrˌgaɪd] n. 導遊

例: The tour guide entertained the tourists on the tour bus by telling jokes.
(導遊在遊覽車上講笑話逗觀光客開心。)

10. **He can take you wherever you want to go.**

= He can take you to any place where you want to go.
不論你想去任何地方, 他都會把你送到。

＊ wherever [hwɛrˈɛvɚ] adv. 不論何處

11. **advice** [əd′vaɪs] n. 忠告; 建議 (不可數)

　　advise [əd′vaɪz] vt. 忠告; 建議

　　give + 人 + a piece of advice + on + 事物

= advise + 人 + on + 事物

　　忠告某人某事; 就某事給某人建議

　　advise + 人 + to + 原形動詞　　　忠告/勸告某人……

例: As soon as I graduated, Dad gave me a piece of advice on how to do business.

　　(我一畢業，老爸就給了我一個如何做生意的忠告。)

　　I advised the old lady to put her money in a bank.

　　(我勸那位老太太把她的錢放到銀行。)

12. **worth** [wɝθ] prep. 值得

　　be worth + 名詞/動名詞　　　值得……

例: This old painting is worth a fortune.

　　(這幅舊畫價值不斐。)

　　What's worth doing is worth doing well.

　　(值得做的事就值得好好去做。)

注意:

本文第二段最後一句句尾"be worth it"是固定用法, 等於"be worthwhile" (是值得的)。

例: Learning English is <u>worth it</u>.

= Learning English is <u>worthwhile</u>.

　　(學英文是值得的。)

Grammar Notes
文法重點

本課介紹 whatever 及 however 的用法。

1. **He can tell you <u>whatever</u> you want to know.**

= He can tell you <u>anything that</u> you want to know.

你想要知道什麼他都可以告訴你。

上列句中的 whatever 是複合關係代名詞，即等於 anything that，譯成『所……的任何東西』，其所引導的名詞子句作句中 tell 的直接受詞。

注意:

所謂複合關係代名詞係由兩個詞類複合而成:

一方面含有先行詞 (如 anyone、the thing(s)、anything)，一方面又含有關係代名詞 (如 who、whom、which、that)。複合關係代名詞共有下列數個:

whoever	=	anybody who	(任何……的人)
whomever	=	anybody whom	(任何……的人)
what	=	the thing(s) that	(所……的東西)
whatever	=	anything that	(所……的任何東西)
whichever	=	any one that	(同一類的任何一個……, 表三者或三者以上)

a. whoever 的用法:

使用 whoever 作複合關係代名詞時，先視 whoever 為兩個字，即 anyone who; 由於 anyone 是代名詞，在主要子句中可作主詞或受詞，而 who 為主格的關係代名詞，故在所引導的形容詞子句中只能作主詞。

1) 作主詞

例: <u>Whoever</u> makes such a mistake should be punished.

= <u>Anyone</u> <u>who makes such a mistake</u> <u>should be punished</u>.
 　　主詞　　　　形容詞子句　　　　及物動詞的被動語態
 (任何犯此錯的人都應受罰。)

2) 作受詞:

例: I hate <u>whoever</u> tells lies.

= I <u>hate</u> <u>anyone</u> <u>who tells lies</u>.
 　及物動詞 受詞　形容詞子句
 (我痛恨任何說謊的人。)

千萬不可寫成:

I hate <u>whomever</u> tells lies. (✗)

理由:

因 whomever＝anyone whom, 而 whom 在其引導的形容詞子
句中只能作受詞, 不可能作主詞, 故 whom 之後不可能有動詞
tells。

b. whomever 的用法:

我們已知 whomever 等於 anyone whom, 因 whom 為受格的關係代
名詞, 故在所引導的形容詞子句中只能作受詞; 而且此處的 anyone 也
只能在主要子句中作受詞, 因此 whomever 絕不可作主詞。

例: <u>Whomever</u> you hate must be bad. (✗)

→ <u>Anyone</u> <u>whom you hate</u> <u>must be</u> <u>bad</u>. (○)
   主詞   形容詞子句   be 動詞 主詞補語
(你所討厭的人一定都是壞人。)

Give it to <u>whomever</u> you like.

＝ Give it <u>to anyone whom you like</u>.
         介詞 受詞 形容詞子句
(把它給任何你喜歡的人。)

c. what 的用法:

what 是最常見的複合關係代名詞, 即等於 the thing(s)that, 譯成『所
……的東西』, 使用時前面不可有先行詞(名詞), 且 what 所引導的名詞
子句在主要子句中可作主詞、受詞或 be 動詞後的主詞補語。

1) 作主詞:

例: <u>What he said</u> may be true.
     主詞
(他所說的可能是真的。)

2) 作受詞:

例: I <u>believe</u> <u>what he said</u>.
    及物動詞   受詞
(我相信他所說的話。)

I am interested <u>in</u> <u>what he said</u>.
　　　　　　 介詞　　受詞
(我對他所說的很感興趣。)

3) 在 be 動詞後作主詞補語:

例: This <u>is</u> <u>what happened yesterday</u>.
　　　 be 動詞　　　　 主詞補語
(這就是昨天所發生的事。)

注意:

因 what 等於 the thing(s) that, that 為關係代名詞, 在所引導的形容詞子句中作主詞或受詞, 因此 what 在所引導的名詞子句中也是作主詞或受詞。

例: <u>What is good for you</u> may not be good for others.
　　 主詞

= <u>The thing</u> <u>that is good for you</u> may not be good for others.
(對你有益的東西對別人未必有益。)

I can hardly believe <u>what I have just heard</u>.
　　　　　　　　　　　　 受詞

= I can hardly believe <u>the thing</u> <u>that I have just heard</u>.
(我幾乎無法相信我剛剛所聽到的話。)

d. whatever 的用法:

whatever 等於 anything that, 譯成『所……的任何東西』, 語氣比 what 要強; anything 在主要子句中可作主詞或受詞, 而 that 在所引導的形容詞子句中亦可作主詞或受詞。

1) 作主詞:

例: <u>Whatever he said</u> is true.

= <u>Anything</u> <u>that he said</u>　<u>is</u>　　<u>true</u>.
　　 主詞　　 形容詞子句　 be 動詞　 主詞補語
(他所說的任何話都是實話。)

2) 作受詞:

例: You may do <u>whatever</u> you like.

= You may <u>do</u> <u>anything</u> <u>that you like</u>.

       及物動詞　受詞　　形容詞子句

(你可以做任何你喜歡的事。)

He doesn't care about <u>whatever</u> may happen.

= He doesn't care <u>about</u> <u>anything</u> <u>that may happen</u>.

         介詞　　受詞　　　形容詞子句

(發生任何事他都不在乎。)

e. whichever 的用法:

whichever 與 whatever 的用法完全相同, 只不過 whichever 是指同一類的任何一項, 而 whatever 則指不同類的任何一項。如果同一類的東西是三者或三者以上時, whichever 等於 any one that; 若同一類的東西為兩者時, 則 whichever 等於 either that。

例: I have <u>a car, a house and an orchard</u> and you may have <u>whatever</u>

           不同類的東西

you like best.

(我有一輛車, 一棟房子和一座果園, 你可以挑一樣你最喜歡的。)

I have <u>three cars</u>, and you may have <u>whichever</u> you like.

      同一類的東西

= I have three cars, and you may have <u>any one that</u> you like.

(我有三輛車, 你可以挑一輛你喜歡的。)

There are <u>two books</u> here. You may take <u>whichever</u> you like.

      同一類的東西

= There are two books here. You may take <u>either that</u> you like.

(這裡有兩本書, 你可以拿其中一本你所喜歡的。)

2. So, <u>however</u> **expensive the taxi ride may be, the advice you get from the driver will certainly be worth it.**

= So, <u>no matter how</u> expensive the taxi ride may be, the advice you get from the driver will certainly be worth it.

所以, 不論搭計程車多麼昂貴, 你從司機那裡所得到的建議絕對是值得的。

上列句中的 however 是副詞連接詞, 表『不論/不管如何』, 即等於 no matter how。

注意:

凡表『不論/不管……』的副詞連接詞, 均可用 "no matter + 疑問詞" 來表示, 常見者有下列:

a. no matter how　　不論/不管如何

= however

　　how 是疑問副詞, 在其引導的副詞子句中, 除可修飾動詞外, 亦可修飾形容詞或副詞。

　　1) 修飾動詞:

例: No matter <u>how</u> you may <u>do</u> it, you should do it with care.

= <u>However</u> you may do it, you should do it with care.

(不管你怎麼辦這事, 都得小心。)

　　2) 修飾形容詞:

例: No matter <u>how</u> he is <u>competent</u>, I don't want to hire him. (✕)

理由: 應將形容詞 competent 移至 how 之後。

→ No matter <u>how competent</u> he is, I don't want to hire him. (○)

= <u>However competent</u> he is, I don't want to hire him.

(無論他多有能力, 我都不想雇用他。)

　　3) 修飾副詞:

例: No matter <u>how</u> he runs <u>fast</u>, he can't catch up with me. (✕)

理由: 應將副詞 fast 移至 how 之後。

→ No matter <u>how fast</u> he runs, he can't catch up with me. (○)

= <u>However fast</u> he runs, he can't catch up with me.

(無論他跑得多快, 都趕不上我。)

注意:

however 除可作副詞連接詞外, 尚可作連接性副詞 (有連接詞的意味, 但仍只是副詞, 而非連接詞), 譯成『然而』, 使用時, 常置於句首, 其後加逗點; 或置於兩子句中, 其前置分號, 其後加逗點; 亦可作插入語用, 置於

句中, 前後以逗點相隔。

例: She is pretty. <u>However</u>, I don't like her.
= She is pretty<u>; however,</u> I don't like her.
= She is pretty. I<u>, however,</u> don't like her.
(她長得很漂亮, 然而我卻不喜歡她。)

b. no matter what   不論什麼
= whatever

注意:

由於 what 是疑問代名詞, 故在所引導的副詞子句中, 要作主詞、受詞或在 be 動詞後作主詞補語。

1) 作主詞:

例: No matter <u>what</u> <u>happens</u>, you should stay with me.
= <u>Whatever</u> happens, you should stay with me.
(無論發生什麼事, 你都要和我在一起。)

2) 作受詞:

例: No matter <u>what</u> you may <u>do</u>, you should be careful.
= <u>Whatever</u> you may do, you should be careful.
(無論你做什麼事都得小心。)

3) 在 be 動詞後作主詞補語:

例: No matter <u>what</u> you <u>are</u>, you shouldn't do that.
= <u>Whatever</u> you are, you shouldn't do that.
(不管你是誰, 都不該做那種事。)

c. no matter who   不論誰
= whoever

注意:

由於 who 是疑問代名詞, 故在所引導的副詞子句中, 要作主詞, 或在 be 動詞後作主詞補語; 且因 who 是主格, 故不可作受詞。

1) 作主詞:

例: No matter <u>who</u> <u>does</u> it, he should be responsible for it.

= <u>Whoever</u> does it, he should be responsible for it.
(不管是誰做的,都得負起責任。)

2) 在 be 動詞後作主詞補語:

例: No matter <u>who</u> you <u>are</u>, you should obey the law.

= <u>Whoever</u> you are, you should obey the law.
(不管你是誰,都該守法。)

注意:

whatever 與 whoever 除可作副詞連接詞, 等於 no matter what、no matter who 外, 亦可作複合關係代名詞, 等於 anything that、anyone who。要注意的是, whatever 和 whoever 作副詞連接詞時, 所引導副詞子句與主要子句中間要有逗點相隔; 而作複合關係代名詞時, 則無逗點相隔。

比較:

1) 作副詞連接詞:

例: <u>Whatever</u> <u>he said</u> , it was a lie.

= <u>No matter what</u> he said, it was a lie.
(不論他說了什麼,那都是謊話。)

<u>Whoever</u> <u>made the mistake</u> , he should be punished.

= <u>No matter who</u> made the mistake, he should be punished.
(不論誰犯了這個錯,都應受處罰。)

2) 作複合關係代名詞:

例: <u>Whatever he said</u> <u>was</u> a lie.

= <u>Anything that</u> he said was a lie.
(他所說的話都是謊言。)

<u>Whoever makes the mistake</u> <u>should be</u> punished.

= <u>Anyone who</u> makes the mistake should be punished.
(任何人犯了錯都應受處罰。)

d. no matter whom   不論誰

= whomever

注意:

由於 whom 是受格的疑問代名詞, 故在所引導的副詞子句中只能作受詞。

例: No matter <u>whom</u> you <u>like</u>, it is none of my business.

= <u>Whomever</u> you like, it is none of my business.
(無論你喜歡誰，都與我無關。)

e. no matter which　　不論哪一個

= whichever

注意:

由於 which 是疑問代名詞, 故在所引導的副詞子句中要作主詞、受詞, 或在 be 動詞後作主詞補語。

1) 作主詞:

例: No matter <u>which</u> may be used, check it first.

= <u>Whichever</u> may be used, check it first.
(無論要用哪一個，先檢查一下再說。)

2) 作受詞:

例: No matter <u>which</u> you want to <u>buy</u>, you must make sure it is useful.

= <u>Whichever</u> you want to buy, you must make sure it is of useful.
(不管你要買哪一個，務必求實用。)

3) 在 be 動詞後作主詞補語:

例: No matter <u>which</u> it <u>is</u>, I don't like it.

= <u>Whichever</u> it is, I don't like it.
(無論是哪一個，我都不喜歡。)

f. no matter when　　不論何時

= whenever

注意:

由於 when 為疑問副詞, 故在所引導的副詞子句中只用以修飾動詞。

例: No matter <u>when</u> he <u>comes</u>, I will wait for him.
動詞

= <u>Whenever</u> he comes, I will wait for him.
(無論他何時來，我都會等他。)

g. no matter where　　不論何處

= wherever

注意:

由於where亦為疑問副詞,故在所引導的副詞子句中只用以修飾動詞。

例: No matter <u>where</u> he <u>lives</u>, I will find him.
動詞

= <u>Wherever</u> he lives, I will find him.
(無論他住在哪兒，我都會找到他。)

Substitution
代　　換

1. **He can tell you whatever you want to know.**

   Jack thinks he has no problem dating whomever he likes.

   There are several pens here. You can have whichever you like.

   你想要知道什麼他都可以告訴你。

   傑克認為他可以和任何他喜歡的人約會。

   這兒有幾支筆, 你可以拿任何一支你喜歡的。

2. **However expensive the taxi ride may be, the advice you get from the driver will certainly be worth it.**

   No matter how rich Sam is, he never forgets his friends.

   However frustrated Bill may be, he never loses his temper.

   不論搭計程車多麼昂貴, 你從司機那裡所得到的建議絕對是值得的。

   不論山姆多有錢, 他從不忘記他的朋友。

   不論比爾有多沮喪, 他從不發脾氣。

L esson 62
Keep the Change
不用找了

Dialogue
實用會話

Jimmy is at the Boston Airport. He hails a taxi. (T=taxi driver; J= Jimmy)

T: Where to, sir?

J: The Sheraton Hotel, please.

T: OK. Is this your first time in Boston?

J: Yes. What's a good place for sightseeing?

T: If you have a lot of time on your hands, you can walk the Freedom Trail.

J: I'm kind of strapped for time.

T: In that case, whatever else you do, you must check out the observatory on the 63rd floor of the John Hancock Building.

J: Isn't the building all glass?

T: That's right. You can't miss it. Here's your hotel. That'll be $17.50, please.

J: Here's $20.00. Keep the change.

吉米現在正在波士頓機場。他叫了一部計程車。

司機：去哪裡，先生？

吉米：麻煩到喜來登飯店。

司機：好的。您是第一次來波士頓嗎？

吉米：對。有什麼好地方值得觀光的嗎？

司機：如果您時間充裕的話，可以走一趟自由之路。

吉米：我的時間有點緊湊。

司機：那樣的話，不管您做什麼其他的事，一定要到約翰漢克大樓第
　　　六十三層的瞭望台看看。

吉米：不就是那棟全部玻璃帷幕的大樓嗎？

司機：沒錯，你一定會找到的。飯店到了，車資總共是十七元五角。

吉米：這是二十塊，不用找了。

Key Points

重點提示

1. **keep the change** (零錢) 不用找了

   change [tʃendʒ] n. 零錢 (不可數)

   例: The generous man told the taxi driver to keep the change.
   (那位慷慨的男子告訴計程車司機零錢不用找了。)

   I need some change to take a bus.
   (我需要一些零錢好搭公車。)

2. **hail** [hel] vt. 招呼, 呼叫 (車、船、人等)

   例: It's difficult to hail a cab when it's raining.
   (下雨時，很難叫到計程車。)

   ＊ cab [kæb] n. 計程車 (是 taxi 的口語說法)

3. 本文:

   Where to, sir? (美式口語用法) 　　去哪裡, 先生？

   = **Where do you want to go, sir?** (正式用法)

4. **sightseeing** [ˈsaɪtˌsiɪŋ] n. 觀光, 遊覽

go sightseeing　　去觀光

例: The honeymooners went sightseeing in the Alps.
(那對度蜜月的夫妻到阿爾卑斯山脈觀光。)

5. **have a lot of time on one's hands**　　某人時間充裕

例: Now that Dad has retired, he has a lot of time on his hands.
(現在老爸已經退休了，他有很多自己的時間。)

6. **Freedom Trail** [ˈfridəm ˌtrel] n. 自由之路 (波士頓市內一條富於獨立戰爭遺跡的路線)

7. **人 + be strapped for time**　　某人的時間很緊湊, 某人沒有時間

strap [stræp] vt. 以帶子捆紮

例: A: Can you help me with my homework?
B: Sorry. I'm strapped for time.
(甲：你能幫助我做家庭作業嗎？)
(乙：抱歉。我沒有時間。)

Eric strapped his little boy into a special car seat.
(艾瑞克把他的小男孩繫在一個特別的汽車座椅上。)

8. **check out + 事物**　　觀看某事物

= take a look at + 事物

例: Let's go check out the new pub.
(咱們到那家新酒吧去瞧瞧。)

9. **observatory** [əbˈzɝˌvəˌtɔrɪ] n. 瞭望台

例: Our teacher took us to the observatory to see how they forecast the weather.
(我們的老師帶我們到瞭望台去看他們如何預測天氣。)

10. **You can't miss it.**　　你不會找不到的/你不會錯過的。

＊ miss [mɪs] vt. 錯過

例: A: Can you tell me where the bank is?

B: Go straight ahead; turn right at the next traffic light and you'll see the bank next to the post office; you can't miss it.

(甲:你能告訴我銀行在哪裡嗎?)

(乙:從這裡一直往前走,到下一個紅綠燈右轉後你會看到銀行就在郵局隔壁,你不會找不到的。)

請選出下列各句中正確的一項

1. _____ he says, don't believe him.
   (A) Whatever   (B) Wherever   (C) Whoever   (D) Whenever

2. Rob's wife can find him _____ he goes.
   (A) whatever   (B) wherever   (C) whoever   (D) however

3. _____ told you the secret is going to be in big trouble.
   (A) No matter who   (B) No matter whom
   (C) Whoever   (D) Anyone

4. The man gave the waiter a thousand dollars and told him to _____ the change.
   (A) make   (B) take   (C) leave   (D) keep

5. _____ smart you think you are, there's bound to be someone smarter.
   (A) Whatever   (B) Wherever   (C) Whoever   (D) However

解答:

1. (A)	2. (B)	3. (C)	4. (D)	5. (D)

Lesson 63
The Dying Languages
凋零的語言

Reading
閱　讀

Today, more people than ever before are speaking to each other through satellite television, cellular telephones and computers. This means that people from different parts of the world need to be able to communicate in the same language. That language happens to be English.

Because of this, experts have predicted that more than half of the world's 6,000 languages may die out in the next century. Already almost all Californian Native American languages are in danger of extinction. They are being swallowed up by English

and other languages. It is a pity, but that is one of the prices of modernization.

現在透過衛星電視、行動電話和電腦來交談的人要比以往來得多。這表示來自世界不同角落的人必須能夠使用同一種語言來溝通。而那種語言正好是英語。

由於這個緣故,專家們預測世界上的六千種語言當中,可能會有一半以上於下個世紀相繼消失。幾乎所有加州當地的美洲土語已有消失之虞。它們正受到英語和其它語言的吞噬。這真是令人非常遺憾,但卻是現代化所要付出的代價之一。

Vocabulary & Idioms
單字 & 片語註解

1. **dying** [ˈdaɪɪŋ] a. 凋零的, 漸漸消失的

   例: Having concubines is a dying custom among the Chinese.
   (中國人擁有姨太太的習俗漸漸消失了。)
   * concubine [ˈkɑŋkjʊˌbaɪn] n. 妾, 姨太太

2. **satellite television**　　衛星電視

   satellite [ˈsætəˌlaɪt] n. 衛星 (於本文中作形容詞用)

   例: We can watch TV programs from around the world with satellite television.
   (透過衛星電視我們可以看到來自全世界的電視節目。)

3. **cellular telephone**　　行動電話

   cellular [ˈsɛljələ] a. 細胞的

   cell [sɛl] n. 細胞; 小密室

   注意:

   cellular telephone 之得名, 乃因它問世時功能並非很好, 而須把城市劃分

為許多區域設立中繼站轉接, 就彷彿蜂巢裡的小密室 (cell) 般, 故此名一直沿用至今。

例: Having a cellular telephone has become a status symbol.
(擁有行動電話已經變成一種身分表徵。)

　　＊ status symbol [ˈstætəs ˌsɪmbḷ] n. 社會地位的表徵

4. **communicate** [kəˈmjunəˌket] vi. 溝通; 聯絡

communicate in + 語言名稱　　用……語言溝通

communicate with + 人　　和某人溝通/聯絡

例: Larry can communicate in sign language with the deaf.
(賴瑞能用手語和聾胞溝通。)

I want to learn Spanish so that I may communicate with my parents-in-law.
(我想學西班牙語,那樣我就可以和我的岳父母溝通。)

5. **expert** [ˈɛkspɝt] n. 專家

6. **predict** [prɪˈdɪkt] vt. 預測

例: In fact, no one can predict the future.
(事實上,沒有人能預測未來。)

7. **die out**　　(語言、習俗等) 漸漸消失

例: Many good Chinese customs are dying out.
(中國許多很好的習俗正逐漸消失。)

8. **native** [ˈnetɪv] a. 當地的 & n. 本地人, 當地人

Native American languages　　美洲土語

例: Are you a native here, or just a visitor?
(你是這裡的本地人或只是個訪客呢?)

9. **be in danger of...**　　瀕臨……之險

例: Mr. Wang is in danger of being bankrupt.
(王先生瀕臨破產。)

10. **extinction** [ɪkˈstɪŋkʃən] n. 絕跡, 滅絕

    extinct [ɪkˈstɪŋkt] a. 絕種的, 滅絕的

    例: The dinosaur has been extinct for millions of years.
    (恐龍已絕跡數百萬年了。)

11. **swallow** [ˈswɑlo] vt. 吞 (嚥)

    swallow up...　　吞嚥掉……

    例: Some big fish will swallow up small fish.
    (有些大魚會吞嚥小魚。)

12. **modernization** [ˌmɑdə·nəˈzeʃən] n. 現代化

    例: Even country life is being affected by modernization.
    (甚至鄉村生活也受到現代化的影響。)

Grammar Notes

文法重點

本課介紹"比較級句構 + than ever before"的用法, 以及"happen to + 原形動詞" (碰巧/正好……) 的用法。

1. **Today, <u>more</u> people <u>than ever before</u> are speaking to each other through satellite television, cellular telephones and computers.**
   現在透過衛星電視、行動電話和電腦來交談的人要比以往來得多。

   注意:

   在比較級句構中, than 之後可接 ever、before 或 ever before, 表『比以往更……』之意。

   含比較級形容詞/ 副詞的子句 + than ever before

   = 含比較級形容詞/ 副詞的子句 + than ever/before

   比以往更……

例: It is more expensive than ever before to buy a house in Taipei.
(現在在台北買棟房子要比以前貴多了。)

Janet dances more beautifully than ever before.
(珍妮特現在舞跳得比以往好多了。)

2. **That language <u>happens to be</u> English.**

= <u>It happens that</u> that language <u>is</u> English.
那種語言正好是英語。

It happens＋that 子句 　　碰巧/正好……

注意:

在上列句構中, that 子句中的主詞可往前移位置於句首, 而因時態之不同,
有下列變化。

主詞＋happen(s) to＋原形動詞

主詞＋happen(s) to＋have＋過去分詞

a. 時態相同時, to 之後接原形動詞。

例: It <u>happens</u> that <u>he</u> <u>is</u> here.
　　　　　　　　　　　時態相同

= <u>He</u> <u>happens</u> <u>to be</u> here.
(他正好在這裡。)

It <u>happened</u> that <u>he</u> <u>had</u> some money.
　　　　　　　　　　　時態相同

= <u>He</u> <u>happened</u> <u>to have</u> some money.
(他剛好帶了錢。)

b. 時態不同時, to 之後接"have＋過去分詞"。

例: It <u>happens</u> that <u>he</u> <u>was</u> there.
　　　　　　　　　　　時態不同

= <u>He</u> <u>happens</u> <u>to have been</u> there.
(他當時剛好在那兒。)

It <u>happens</u> that <u>he</u> <u>knew</u> it then.

時態不同

→ <u>He</u> <u>happens</u> <u>to have known</u> it then.

(他碰巧當時知道這件事。)

Substitution

代　　換

1. **Today, more people than ever before are speaking to each other through satellite television, cellular telephones and computers.**

Winning the lottery made him richer than ever before.

This year, the country has spent more money than ever before on social welfare.

現在透過衛星電視、行動電話和電腦來交談的人要比以往來得多。

贏得那次彩券使他比以前有錢了。

該國今年花在社會福利上的錢要比以往多。

2. **That language happens to be English.**

We just happened to be out when you came to visit us.

I happen to have $500 with me.

那種語言正好是英語。

你來看我們時，我們正好外出。

我正好身上有五百元。

L esson 64

Speaking the Same Language
說同樣的語言

Dialogue
實用會話

Sally is talking with her friend, Don.

(S=Sally; D=Don)

S: Tell me, Don. How come you're from Spain but you can't speak Spanish very well?

D: It's not my mother tongue. My father is Spanish and my mother is American. We usually speak English at home.

S: Oh, I see.

D: Your Spanish is probably better than mine.

S: Yes, but you speak English more fluently than I.

D: How come? Aren't you American?

S: Yes, but my mother is Spanish.

D: Don't tell me...

S: That's right. We usually speak Spanish at home.

D: It doesn't matter as long as we can communicate.

S: That's true.

莎莉正在和她的朋友唐講話。

莎莉：告訴我，唐。為什麼你是個西班牙人但西班牙語卻說得不怎麼好？

　唐：那不是我的母語。我爸爸是西班牙人而我媽媽是美國人。我們在家通常都說英語。

莎莉：哦，我明白了。

　唐：妳的西班牙語可能比我的好。

莎莉：對啊，可是你英語說得比我流利。

　唐：怎麼會這樣呢？妳不是美國人嗎？

莎莉：對，可是我媽媽是西班牙人。

　唐：那該不會……

莎莉：沒錯。我們在家大都講西班牙語。

　唐：只要我們能溝通就無所謂啦。

莎莉：說的一點兒沒錯。

Key Points
重點提示

1. **mother tongue** [ˈmʌðɚ ˌtʌŋ] n. 母語

2. **fluently** [ˈfluəntlɪ] adv. 流利地

   fluent [ˈfluənt] a. 流利的

   例: Mr. White can speak Chinese fluently.
   （懷特先生能說流利的中文。）

   Are you fluent in Cantonese?
   （你廣東話流利嗎？）

3. **matter** [ˈmætɚ] vi. 是重要的

= be important

   例: It doesn't matter whether he comes or not.

   = It isn't important whether he comes or not.
   （他來不來都沒關係。）

4. **as long as...**　　　只要……

注意:

as long as 為副詞連接詞, 引導副詞子句, 修飾主要子句。

例: As long as you are willing to work, you will not go hungry.
　　(只要你願意工作就不會挨餓。)

請選出下列各句中正確的一項

1. The old building is ＿＿＿＿ of collapsing.
   (A) dangerous　(B) with danger　(C) in danger　(D) danger

2. People are more materialistic than ＿＿＿＿ before.
   (A) even　　　(B) ever　　　(C) used to　　(D) more

3. You can stay here ＿＿＿＿ you don't disturb me when I'm working.
   (A) as soon as　　　　　　(B) as long as
   (C) as far as　　　　　　 (D) as possible as

4. ＿＿＿＿ you came back from the party so early?
   (A) How often　(B) How fast　　(C) How old　　(D) How come

5. I know the truth because I happen to ＿＿＿＿ what they said.
   (A) have overheard　　　　(B) overheard
   (C) overhear　　　　　　 (D) have overhear

解答:

> 1. (C)　　2. (B)　　3. (B)　　4. (D)　　5. (A)

A Quick Note

A Quick Note

國家圖書館出版品預行編目資料

中級美語 / 賴世雄著 -- 初版.
　臺北市：常春藤有聲, 2004 [民 93]
　冊；　公分. -- (常春藤進修系列；E05)

ISBN　986-7638-19-0 (上冊：平裝)

1. 英國語言 -- 讀本

805. 18　　　　　　　　　　93000146

常春藤進修系列 E05
中級美語（上）

編　　著：賴世雄
編　　審：Carlos Souza・Carl Anthony
　　　　　張為麟・黃文玲・李橋・蔣宗君・張樹人
校　　對：常春藤中外編輯群
封面設計：羅容格・黃振倫・賴雅莉
插　　畫：張睿洋
電腦排版：朱瑪琍・劉濰崢・李宜芝
顧　　問：賴陳愉嫻
法律顧問：王存淦律師・蕭雄淋律師
發行日期：2005 年 9 月　初版/三刷

出 版 者：常春藤有聲出版有限公司
　　　　　台北市忠孝西路一段 33 號 5 樓
　　　　　行政院新聞局出版事業登記證
　　　　　局版臺業字第肆捌貳陸號

服務電話：(02) 2331-7600　　服務傳真：(02) 2381-0918
信　　箱：臺北郵政 8-18 號信箱
郵撥帳號：**19714777**　　常春藤有聲出版有限公司
定　　價：360 元

＊如有缺頁、裝訂錯誤或破損　請寄回本社更換

常春藤有聲出版有限公司
讀者回函卡

✍感謝您的填寫，您的建議將是公司重要的參考及修正指標！

我購買本書的書名是		編碼	
我購買本書的原因是	☐老師、同學推薦 ☐家人推薦 ☐學校購買 ☐書店閱讀後感到喜歡 ☐其他		
我購得本書的管道是	☐書攤 ☐業務人員推薦 ☐大型連鎖書店 ☐書店名稱＿＿＿＿＿＿＿＿ ☐其他		
我最滿意本書的三點依序是	☐內容 ☐編排方式 ☐雙色印刷 ☐試題演練 ☐解析清楚 ☐封面 ☐售價 ☐促銷活動豐富 ☐信任品牌 ☐廣告 ☐其他		
我最不滿意本書的三點依序是	☐內容 ☐編排方式 ☐雙色印刷 ☐試題演練 ☐解析不足 ☐封面 ☐售價 ☐促銷活動貧乏 ☐廣告 ☐其他		
我有一些其他想法與建議是			
我發現本書誤植的部份是	☐書籍第＿＿頁，第＿＿行，有錯誤的部份是		
	☐書籍第＿＿頁，第＿＿行，有錯誤的部份是		

✍我的基本資料

讀者姓名		生　　日		性別	☐男 ☐女
就讀學校		科系年級	科 年級 畢業		☐已畢 ☐在學
聯絡電話		E-mail			
聯絡地址					

請您填寫完後寄至：
台北市忠孝西路一段33號5樓　　**常春藤有聲出版有限公司**　　**出版部收**

填寫日期：西元＿＿＿＿＿年＿＿＿＿＿月＿＿＿＿＿日

A Quick Note